I0822397

THE DEEPER YOU SINK… THE DARKER IT GETS.

# The Situation Ship

A MURDER MYSTERY ROMANCE

# The Situation Ship

# The Situation Ship

## Kate Callaghan



Edited By: Emma O' Connell
Proofread By: Emma Craven
Cover By: Pru Schulyer



ISBN: 978-1-916684-19-5
ISBN: 978-1-916684-20-1

www.callaghanwriter.com

Readers! Please note: this is an adult romantic suspense with mature content and not suitable for those under 18. Trigger warnings not limited to: Death, violence, emotional and physical abuse, stalking, grief.

## The Deeper You Sink, The Darker It Gets.

Pop star Poppy Roe's glittering life of fame takes a sinister turn when she finds herself trapped in a nightmare aboard a luxurious cruise ship. As her every move is monitored by a sinister stalker, the ship becomes a hunting ground for a relentless predator. In a desperate bid for survival, Poppy turns to enigmatic detective Isaiah Rivers, also a passenger on the ill-fated voyage. Haunted by his own demons, he never expected to get caught up in a web of danger on the high seas. Determined to protect Poppy, he joins forces with her, seeking to unravel the twisted secrets that lurk beneath the ship's glamorous façade. Amid the horrifying murders, a thrilling romance blossoms, intertwining their fates in a dangerous dance of trust and vulnerability.

As danger lurks on every deck and passions ignite, Poppy and Isaiah must navigate a treacherous sea of suspicion and desire. Will they unmask the killer before the final note of their haunting melody? Prepare for a pulse-pounding tale of romance and suspense that will leave you breathless.

# Other Books By The Author

**Young Adult Dark Fantasy | A Hellish Fairytale Series**
Crowned A Traitor I
Where Traitors Fall II
When Traitors Rise III

Towerwood | Novella
Stepmother | Novella

**Village of Yule | Interconnected Stand-Alones**
The Naughty Or Nice Clause
Tis The Season For Secrets

**Village of FoxFord | Interconnected Stand-Alones**
Potions & Proposals
Don't Go Baking My Heart

**Romantic Suspense | Interconnected Stand-Alones**
Ms Perfectly Fine
Not Another Rockstar
The Situation Ship

If spice isn't for you, here's a list to help you skip through!

Chapter | 12

Chapter | 17

Chapter | 18

Chapter | 20

# Poppy & Isaiah's Playlist

Mastermind | Taylor Swift

Catch Me If You Can | The Cranberries

White Rabbit | Emilianna Torrini

Stay A Little Longer | ROSE

Who's Afraid Of Little Old Me | Taylor Swift

Dying On The Inside | Nessa Barrett

Mad Hatter | Melanie Martinez

Better Days | Dermot Kennedy

The Deeper You Sink, The Darker It Gets.

# The Situation Ship

KATE CALLAGHAN

*For those who've had to save themselves one too many times.*

# PROLOGUE
## A Message From Poppy

*If you're reading this, then I've died (hopefully of old age). I feel like it's only right that you should know my story, not what the tabloids spun about the last twenty-six years of my life. Below is my unfiltered and uncoerced confession for the events that occurred in 2024. Whether you believe it or not is up to you. After all, who would believe the confession of a murderer?*

'Murder' is such a harsh word. Is it really murder when my aunt, Martha Roe, took my life first? But this is a confession, not a justification for my actions.

On that fateful night, I waited for my aunt – the Hollywood legend Martha Roe – to complete her nightly routine, comprised of colourful pills washed down with a glass of vodka. Of course, she liked to pretty up her drinking by using a martini glass with an onion instead of an olive. She said 'one' helped her sleep – one being a bottle, between you and me – and went to bed.

Being a night owl, I started playing my favourite Beethoven piece on the grand piano. (Martha hated it when I played late. She said it gave her headaches.) I waited for her to appear at the top of the stairs with that pinched expression – a look I share, along with her cosmetically perfected nose and jawline. I was her mirror image, if forty years younger. I used to have a little bump on my nose that I got from my dad and a dimple in my chin like my mum. Both were long gone now.

But when Martha looked over the balcony at the top of the stairs to scold her darling niece for playing during her 'quiet time', I wasn't sitting on the stool in front of the Steinbeck. I'd used the back stairs that was only meant for the maid and kitchen staff to catch her at the top of the stairs.

Thirty minutes after her routine, she was more than a little unsteady, and when she heard me approaching, she tried to strike me for sneaking up on her. She missed and lost her balance; it could have been her low kitten-heeled slippers on the perfectly cream carpet, or the 'one' drink. Who's to say?

When I saw the terror in her eyes as she started to fall, I realised it was the first time that I'd seen her scared. She reached out for me to help her, but how many times had my pleas for help gone unheard? I repaid the favour. I let her fall.

It felt like she was falling forever, but then I heard the sickening relief of the thud as her body hit the marble floor of the foyer. I walked down the stairs, lingering an extra second or two on each step before I reached her.

As a pool of blood formed at the back of her head like a crown, she took her last breath, and it felt like I took my first.

Not wanting to linger, I dashed for the phone. I

howled, real tears pouring down my cheeks as I pleaded for help from the 999 operator. I wouldn't want to disappoint her with a bad performance – not after all the acting classes she'd paid for. I cradled my aunt's body to my chest, making sure to get just enough blood on me. I did the chest compressions as instructed (though the bent angle of her neck told me there was no coming back). I had to make sure the autopsy showed how desperately I'd tried to save her.

In the hospital, the moment the doctors confirmed she was gone, I sank to my knees and prayed for them not to give up. My aunt always said I'd never be an actress, but this performance would've earned me an Oscar. The officer at the hospital offered me a ride home, and I accepted, sitting numb in the car, not uttering a single word.

When the investigators were gone, I cleaned up the blood. I didn't want to traumatise the maid; my aunt had done that enough while she lived. I snapped the locks off the food cabinets in the kitchen, finally ending the diet she'd had me on for my latest tour. Also, I didn't want those calling to offer their condolences to notice. The house was clean and quiet, but I still feared that she would come out of her room and scold me for killing her. I considered burning the house down, but that seemed too dramatic. Selling it and all her possessions was a much better idea.

I said I wouldn't try to justify my actions, but you could argue that if she hadn't tried to strike me, she wouldn't have lost her balance and taken that fatal tumble. Did she fall? Did I push her? I can't quite recall. You can make your own deduction.

You might be asking yourself why I am writing this letter.

The problem with fame is that someone will write my story one day. They'll talk about the tragic loss of my aunt, how I couldn't bear to sing after her death, and how I started acting to pay homage to the Queen of Old Hollywood, who so selflessly raised me after my parents tragically lost their lives. This letter will set the record straight. Martha Roe was a monster, and since I killed her, she raised one too.

This letter will remain buried in the lockbox of an overpriced bank vault in Switzerland. I've left instructions for it to be delivered to a news outlet upon my death. My only comment on the above matter is that I won.

I'm free.

*Poppy Roe*

## Chapter 1
# Handcuffs on Holidays
### Isaiah

Isaiah wanted to strangle whoever had outed his little investigation into Poppy Roe to Captain Roberts. He suspected it was the blood technician he had asked to look at the blood spatter again at the latest murder scene. Not many liked having their work questioned.

He wouldn't have minded the lecture if he hadn't been so hungover. He didn't remember all of his friend Axel's bachelor party, but he'd undoubtedly remember this hangover. Even running his hands through his dark hair hurt.

"Three murders all connected to Ms Roe; I don't know how you can't see it," he said, cutting off his captain as she started to turn purple. He wasn't sure if she had breathed since he'd closed the door to her office.

Captain Roberts took a deep breath, confirming his suspicion. "Detective Rivers, you're wasting time and resources searching for a connection between cases that don't exist," she said, rubbing her forehead.

"A choreographer who worked with Ms Roe only weeks before she was found strangled in her studio," Isaiah began, sliding the first file onto her desk.

"Ms Devin had dozens of clients, and the place was ransacked. It was a B&E gone wrong, and there was no evidence that Ms Devin was a target," the captain said. "The case is still open and not your responsibility. You know the other officers don't like it when you butt in on their cases, and I'm sick of hearing about you sticking your nose in where it shouldn't be."

"I wouldn't stick my nose into any case if they stuck theirs in the right places," he said under his breath, earning himself a scowl. "The housekeeper ate so much her heart gave out at the Claren Hotel. That's not normal. She was found in Ms Roe's suite." He added the second file to the first.

"Ms Roe had checked out several hours earlier. No one saw them interacting with each other, and there was nothing suspicious on the cameras." Roberts leaned back in her chair, shrugging away his suspicions.

"What about her driver two weeks ago?" Isaiah asked, crossing his arms.

"Mr Fogerty was hired by Ms Roe's management agency from an independent chauffeur company. He drove her for three nights for her concert in Dublin. There is no evidence that she was connected to the car accident. Let me say that again – it was ruled an accident, not murder. He lost control of the vehicle due to his high blood alcohol level." She shoved the files back towards him, but in his gut, something wasn't right.

"Three murders following Ms Roe! Unless she's the grim reaper, this is too much of a coincidence," he argued.

"Enough, Isaiah. I think you need some time off. You just finished giving evidence for the Phoebe Fletcher case, and you're running on smoke. Starting to see things that aren't there."

"I don't need a break," he huffed, collecting his files.

Roberts' expression softened. "You're obsessing, and it's not healthy. I've seen too many detectives get lost in fixations. Take a break, or I'll suspend you for insubordination." He knew she meant it.

He scrubbed his stubble, trying not to say anything he would regret.

"You're the boss." He saluted, closing the door behind him.

"THE CAPTAIN WOULDN'T LISTEN about Ms Roe?" Isaiah's partner, Michael, swivelled in his chair to greet him.

Shaking his head, Isaiah dropped into his chair at the desk across from his friend. Other cases were building up, but he couldn't get Poppy Roe out of his head.

"Given her celebrity status, it's understandable that the captain doesn't want an investigation ending up in the media without solid evidence of a connection." Michael sighed.

"Status shouldn't matter; I just want to interview her. Her proximity to the victims shouldn't be ignored." Isaiah tapped his pen against the desk, trying to rid himself of pent-up frustration.

"They aren't your cases; you need to let it go," Michael warned, quietly so the other officers coming and going from the station couldn't hear them.

"I know, and I don't have much choice. Roberts will suspend me if I don't give it up," he grumbled, resigned to leaving a question mark over the whole thing.

"You can't help anyone if you're suspended. Once the funeral is over, Poppy will be out of the country, and you can move on to other cases," Michael said, drinking from his World's Best Dad mug.

"Funeral?" Isaiah asked, pulling at his navy tie. He'd been giving evidence in court early that morning, so it was mandatory.

"Martha Roe? Poppy's aunt? She was a big Hollywood actress back in the seventies. Took a tumble down the stairs and broke her neck. Tragic way to go – Poppy found her," Michael said, shuffling through the papers on his desk. "I have the report somewhere in this mess; I thought you'd already taken a look into it, considering your—"

"Obsession?"

"I was going to say curiosity," Michael said.

"You get a look at the scene?" Isaiah asked, wishing he had heard about this sooner. The other officers must have kept it under wraps to stop him from prying.

"No, it was a clear-cut case. Accidental death. Her tox report read like a medical encyclopaedia, and her injuries were consistent with a fall," Michael said, reading from the report.

"Four bodies in six months? The captain *has* to listen to me now."

"Martha Roe's case is already closed. Case and casket, for that matter. Ms Roe will be six feet under in a few hours. Roberts won't look kindly on you interrupting a funeral without cause."

"I'll stop by and pay my respects," Isaiah reasoned. "We did investigate, after all, so it would be good to have an officer there to show our respect. The funeral will be packed; what's one more person?"

Michael stared at him like he had lost his mind. "Gate-crashing a funeral? No wonder the captain's worried about your mental state."

"My mental state is fine, and I'm simply going to *talk* to

Ms Roe, off the record." Isaiah picked up his third cup of terribly diluted coffee, which was cold, thanks to the length of Roberts' scolding. Still, he'd take coffee any way he could. "I'm sure she'd appreciate a kind word from the department."

"I think you *want* the captain to suspend you. Is that it? You want to be fired?" Michael stood over him, thankfully still keeping his voice down.

"Roberts wanted me to take some time off, and as a member of the public, I see no reason that chatting with a public figure should break any rules." He prided himself on being discreet. With the captain's threats, he wouldn't mention Poppy's case again without concrete evidence.

"There'll be so many people and media at the funeral. With her security, you won't be able to get anywhere near her. If you cause a scene on *live TV*, you'll never hear the end of it," Michael exclaimed. Looking out for him, as always. "Why not wait until after the funeral? Her social media says she's going on some cruise – stepping away from the limelight to grieve for a while – so wait until things calm down."

"Away? Where's she going? Probably somewhere without extradition." Isaiah frowned up at his friend. It was a change, as he was the taller of the two, though that wasn't saying much since they were both over six feet. Michael was leaner, whereas Isaiah was stockier from his school rugby days.

"That's all you got from what I said?" Michael shook his head. "See for yourself." Grabbing his phone, he scrolled for a moment and then showed Isaiah Poppy Roe's social media page. She'd shared a photo outside a church.

*A legend can die but can never be forgotten. Please respect my need for space during this hard time. I'll be back once my heart has had time to heal.*

Despite it being posted only an hour ago, there were thousands of comments and likes.

Isaiah took the phone from Michael and flicked through his feed for a moment.

*Poppy Roe is rumoured to be setting sail with her long-term actor boyfriend following the death of Hollywood legend Martha Roe.*

He watched a few seconds of the live footage outside the church.

"The funeral starts at 11. I can make it," he decided, getting up and slapping his friend on the back. There was no way he would let Poppy slip away to God knew where when she was so close. "Thanks for the tip."

"I didn't show you this so you could confront her at her aunt's funeral! What exactly do you plan to do? Stroll up to her – *if* you get past her security and all the other grieving spectators – flash those beautiful brown eyes at her and expect her to answer your every question?!"

Isaiah grinned. "You could never say no to this face."

Michael rolled his eyes. "Keep pushing your luck, and the captain will wipe the smirk off that handsome face."

"Tell Roberts I'm taking that holiday she suggested. What I do on my time is my own business. If I happen to run into Ms Roe, it'll just be a happy coincidence," Isaiah reasoned, but Michael didn't look pleased.

"I want to state for the record that I think this is a terrible idea."

"You worry too much," Isaiah told him, putting on his jacket. Despite the summer settling in, it was still Ireland.

Michael was his oldest friend. They'd both made detective the same year after cracking a big case, but Michael loved the rule book. While Isaiah understood the need for the rules, he knew the law didn't account for the many shades of grey. He had seen too many innocent people locked up while guilty ones walked free to feel as confident as he once had in the justice system. His dad had been a detective, and his grandfather had served in the military. Serving was in his blood, but he cared more about protecting those who needed it than preserving a system.

"You don't worry enough," Michael said, returning to his desk. "I don't even know why you stick at this job. You can't follow the rules, and if you're not careful, you'll end up without a desk."

"I'll be fine. I'm not going to cause a scene."

"Don't call me if you get arrested for trespassing," Michael said, giving up.

"Fine, I'll call Francis instead. He's always had a soft spot for me, and he wouldn't let your partner rot in jail," Isaiah said, grabbing his files.

"Don't even think about dragging my husband into your nonsense," Michael called after him.

*A holiday is the perfect excuse to figure out what's going on without anyone breathing down my neck,* Isaiah thought as he stepped out into the drizzle and hurried to his car.

## Chapter 2
# Fired at The Funeral
### Poppy

In the back of the hearse, Poppy peered up at the blue sky trying to break through the dark clouds. Putting on her oversized sunglasses, she took a deep breath, preparing herself for the performance of her life – her aunt's funeral.

Although her aunt had preferred living in the States, Poppy had always cherished returning to Ireland, where she'd been born and raised until her aunt took custody of her at age eight. She had hoped that a quick burial in Ireland would limit the number of attendees. Still, hundreds had flown in to pay their respects. Given the scale of their combined fame, the media attention had been relentless despite her requests for privacy.

"We should get inside," her boyfriend, Joshua, said as he opened her door, playing the perfect gentleman for the cameras. She couldn't wait to officially break up; she was tired of their business relationship. They were friends, and while she cared for him, her aunt had encouraged the arrangement to keep other guys away. Joshua was happy to oblige, since it benefitted his career. But she was ready to go back to being friends.

Stepping out of the car in her aunt's black Chanel suit and pearls, Poppy let the cameras find her as the crowd's tears and cheers overwhelmed her senses. She reminded herself that she would be truly free in a few hours. Her perfect blonde hair was slicked into a low bun at the nape of her neck, and her large black sunglasses emphasised her bold red lips. Once she was sure they had got their shot, she started up the steps to the church and noticed an older woman being pushed and shoved by the door. Avid fans were grappling to get her attention, Poppy quickly caught the woman before she fell.

"Please don't push; my aunt would be grateful to all of you for wanting to attend, but please be mindful of each other," Poppy said softly. She wanted to scold the crowd, but with so many cameras around, now wasn't the time to lose her temper.

"Sorry to cause a fuss – I lost my balance," the elderly woman said as Poppy helped her through the doors and out of the rain.

"No fuss at all. I'm sorry you were almost trampled," Poppy replied.

Her security hovered at the door, watching the woman suspiciously as the coffin was removed and taken inside. Poppy noticed the ladybird brooch on the woman's black coat and realised she had seen it before.

"Sorry, but do we know each other?" she asked.

"No – I mean, sort of. I'm Emily Green, and thank you for your help." The flustered woman smiled at her. "I run the Ladybird House Orphanage. You were only with us briefly, when you were a little thing, before your aunt took custody of you. You probably don't remember your time with us; you were so young. Your aunt donated generously every year, and I wanted to come pay my respects."

That explained the brooch. Poppy not remembering her time at the orphanage wasn't surprising. It had been eighteen years since her parents had been killed in a car accident, and the memories had become a blur. What surprised her, however, was the knowledge that her aunt had donated to a children's charity for all those years. Was it for a tax exemption? Giving to children would have played in her favour in the media, so why make the donations anonymously? Aunt Martha never let a good deed go unpublished.

"I'm sure Aunt Martha would appreciate your coming. I'm sorry you had to wait out in the rain. My security will ensure you get home safely." Poppy reached into her small purse and pulled out a card. "Here's my email address in case you need anything. I can also stop by the orphanage and say hi to the kids?" She needed to get inside before the priest tracked her down.

"Really?" Emily beamed, putting the card in her coat pocket. "I'm sure the kids would love that."

"No need to thank me, and I'll make sure to keep up the donations."

"I didn't come for money, but your generosity is greatly appreciated, especially by the older kids." Emily beamed, tears of relief glistening in her eyes.

"Please don't mention it, and feel free to email me if there is anything else. I'll get back to you as soon as possible," Poppy said. She never shared her number – if she gave it to one person, suddenly everyone had it. Email was easier for situations like this.

"I will. Thank you, and I'm sorry again for your loss," Emily said, gently patting Poppy's arm.

"Are you not going to stay for the funeral?" Poppy asked.

"I really just came to see you and pay my respects. Now that we've talked, I have to get back to the children," Emily said apologetically.

"I'm glad we got to talk. Please allow Marty to take you home or wherever you need to go." Poppy waved over Marty, her aunt's longest-serving bodyguard, from her security team.

"Thank you, and I wish you every happiness in the future," Emily said as Poppy helped her navigate the slippery steps with her cane.

"Please grab my umbrella from the car and make sure Ms Green gets home," Poppy instructed Marty. She didn't want the elderly woman to struggle through the crowd or wait for a taxi in the rain.

"I'd be happy to escort you," Marty said brightly, offering Emily his arm.

"Such a gentleman." Emily smiled as she accepted his help, allowing him to lead her away from the gravel entrance. Poppy mouthed a thank you to Marty, who nodded in response. She watched as they left the grounds. In spite of her desire for a private funeral, discovering her aunt's single good deed made her feel there might have been some light in her late aunt's soul.

"Poppy?" Joshua called as he came over, running a hand through his highlighted hair, speckled with rain from greeting the fans outside. "Who was that? They want to get started."

"Just someone paying their respects," she said, following him down the packed pews to the front row. They'd never talked about her younger years; now wasn't the time to start.

In the first pew, Poppy stared at the casket, waiting for

Aunt Martha to pop out and tell everyone what Poppy had done that night. So far nobody seemed to even imagine that she'd had any involvement in her aunt's death, but Poppy would only truly be relieved when the casket was six feet under.

She kept her shades on for the service, a tissue clutched tightly in her hand to ensure she gave the right impression. Joshua awkwardly gripped her hand.

As the priest began the final prayer, Poppy heard a commotion outside but couldn't see anything. She was glad she had hired extra security. Martha would be so pleased to see how desperate people were to grieve for her. Poppy couldn't help but smile at the image of her aunt staring up at them, delighted by the crowds gathered in her memory.

"Ms Roe?" the priest whispered, reclaiming her attention. "If you'd like to join me at the front of the casket so the parishioners can offer their sympathies."

*Parishioners? I'm surprised half of those in attendance didn't burst into flames when they stepped into the church.* Poppy kept the thought to herself, offering the priest a small smile before following him up the small steps to stand with a few of her aunt's friends. The priest directed the queue of mourners eager to shake her hand or squeeze her a little too tightly. Poppy was relieved they had limited this part to only ten minutes. Luckily, she managed to muster up some tears, reminding herself to give her acting coach a big tip.

"Quite the turnout. If only Martha could see how beloved she is," her aunt's manager – and Poppy's by default – whispered in her ear. She shuddered in disgust. Since none of Martha's four ex-husbands had come to mourn her, Duggery Dayson was about as close as she got to having a life partner here.

"That's because they didn't know her. They loved the characters she played," Poppy whispered back, shaking hands with people who told her how sorry they were and how lucky she was to have been raised by such a beloved legend. It felt endless, no matter how many hands she shook or cheeks she kissed. Being a great actress didn't make her aunt a good person.

"Don't say such things. We're in a church," Duggery scolded her.

"And the church is all about being honest," Poppy countered, taking flowers from a young fan.

"Your aunt loved you and would want you to continue her legacy," Duggery pontificated. The smell of horrible cigars on his breath made her inch away from him.

"Loved me? It's a sin to lie in a church, and I have no plans to continue her legacy. You both forced me into this life, and now that she's dead, I will decide what happens next," she whispered as the priest thanked everyone for attending the service.

"We can talk about this later. Now isn't the time or place for one of your temper tantrums," Duggery snapped.

Poppy turned to face him and took his arms as though consoling him. He had been their manager since her aunt was a teenager, so she didn't know how he was still alive. She suspected he had made a pact with the devil to inflict as much misery as possible on turning people's dreams into nightmares in exchange for a long life.

"Don't worry, you won't have to worry about my temper tantrums any longer because you're fired," she whispered, giving him a final hug. Her hands shook as she dared to do what she'd desperately wanted to for as long as she could remember.

"You can't fire me!" Mr Duggery tightened his grip on her elbow. *This will be the last time he ever touches me.*

"Yes, I can. The lawyers are already breaking any legal ties between us. I wouldn't advise you to stop it, unless you want your dirty laundry aired publicly. You worked with my aunt for a long time, and there are too many skeletons to count."

"You ungrateful bitch," he hissed as the church started to empty around them.

"Unless you want to cause a scene, you will leave now. You will feign how overwhelmed you are, leave, and never show your face again." Poppy dabbed her eyes with a tissue.

"I've made you who you are. Your aunt would turn in her grave to see how you're treating me!" he whined, but she didn't buy his crocodile tears.

"You thought I didn't know about the pills you were feeding my aunt. How you made her dependent on you. How you wanted her to slip me the same pills, which she tried and failed. You controlled her for years and used her to get your claws into me. Leave, unless you want the police to take a closer look at her autopsy. I might suggest there might have been something wrong with her medication. Smile politely, fake tears, and never see me again," Poppy told him, finally daring to stand up to the weasel of a man she'd been terrified of for over a decade.

The priest interrupted at the perfect time. "Ms Roe, if you'd like to follow the casket out, we can start making our way to the cemetery."

"Thank you. I'll walk with you," Poppy said, wondering where Joshua had gone. He'd been beside her a minute ago. He was supposed to help shield her from everyone.

"Mr. Duggery will be joining you in the car?" the priest asked politely.

"Oh no, he won't be coming with us. He isn't feeling well and is leaving early," Poppy replied.

He gave her a confused look, and she nodded, biting

her lip as if to hold back a sob. She was actually trying to stifle laughter. The relief, joy, and elation swelling in her chest nearly made her break character. The two monsters in her closet were gone.

At the church doors, they watched as the casket was loaded. From the corner of Poppy's eye, she noticed her security team stepping forward to escort Mr Duggery to another car. To onlookers, it would only appear that she was giving her overwhelmed, grieving manager a private escort home. Knowing what was best for him, he didn't protest.

"Where's Dug going?" Joshua asked, putting out his cigarette. So that was where he had gone.

"I fired him."

"You what?" Joshua's eyes widened in shock.

"I don't need him anymore, and my aunt certainly doesn't," Poppy said bluntly, opening the car door. Joshua froze, staring at her as if she had lost her mind.

"Are you getting in?" she asked.

Joshua nodded. "Are you sure you should be making such big decisions right now? You're grieving," he said as he climbed in beside her.

"Exactly. Now that Martha's gone, I realise how important life is, and I think I need to make some changes." She removed her shades and placed them on her lap.

Joshua smiled nervously as their driver pulled out of the church courtyard. "Whatever you think is best," he said, taking her hand.

Poppy rested her head on his shoulder and stared out the window. Her aunt was dead, her manager was gone, and the gruelling tour she had devoted the last year of her life to was over.

## Chapter 3
# Hearses and Heartbreak
### Poppy

The skies cleared as the crowds dispersed, leaving Poppy alone at the grave. A rare lightness filled her heart. She twirled a vibrant poppy between her fingers, reminding herself to bring flowers to her parents' grave next week. Poppy had chosen this site for her aunt, who was buried here against her wishes. This burial felt like a final act of defiance against a woman who had always kept her from visiting her parents. A tear rolled down her cheek as she mourned the life that had been stolen the day her parents had passed away.

"Don't worry, I won't leave you alone too long," she murmured. "The press will expect me to stop by in the coming weeks, so at least I'll be able to see my parents and spend some time here with those who love me." She sniffled, dabbing her eyes.

"Excuse me?"

The soft voice startled her; she'd been so lost in thought she hadn't heard the woman's approach.

"You made me jump! Do you want me to fall in?" Poppy clutched her chest.

"Sorry, I didn't mean to frighten you. I wanted to wait until you were alone before we spoke." The woman looked around the same age as Poppy, though she was heavily tattooed and wore far more black eyeliner. Her gothic style suited the cemetery.

"Thank you for coming," Poppy said, quickly remembering to wear her mask. "How did you know my aunt?"

"I didn't. I came here to talk to you," the woman said bluntly.

Poppy glanced over her shoulder at her security team, waiting by her car on the main road. Joshua was with them in a cloud of smoke. She wasn't sure what she hated more – smoking or vaping.

"Me? I'm not giving interviews right now. Unless you want me to sign something?" This really wasn't the time or place.

"Oh, I'm not a journalist. I'd never be so disrespectful. I'm not really a fan of yours either," admitted the woman. "Sorry, no offence."

"None taken," Poppy said, slightly amused but wondering if she should be concerned. The woman didn't seem dangerous – just nervous.

"Today probably wasn't the best day for this," she babbled, "but it was the only way to see you. I know you have no reason to trust someone approaching you in a cemetery, but I had to tell you… I don't think Ms Roe's death was an accident."

Poppy's blood ran cold. She kept her face blank.

"And you are…?" she asked cautiously, wondering if this woman knew her aunt, or if this was some kind of hoax. She could be wearing a hidden camera.

"I'm Mina – Minerva, but everyone calls me Mina. I work at Heaven's Heart, the nightclub. I overheard some patrons in our VIP section talking about your aunt's death."

"Okay?" Poppy had been to that nightclub once or twice. It was very exclusive.

"Before it happened," Mina added, nervously picking at a button hanging off her coat.

Poppy took a breath. She knew her aunt had had enemies; it wouldn't be the first time a hater had plotted her death. She herself wasn't a stranger to hate mail or death threats.

"You have my attention; explain. But if you're from the press trying to spin a twisted story, I have a team of lawyers who will make mincemeat of you."

"No, no!" Mina waved her hands frantically. "I swear I'm not with the press. I'm a bar manager. I heard two men plotting to kill you and your aunt when I was delivering a bottle of champagne to the VIP area. No one pays attention to what they say around staff, especially not in Heaven's Heart. We're paid to be discreet, but then I saw the news about your aunt's death, and I panicked. I know coming here and blindsiding you isn't appropriate, but I didn't think going to the police was a good idea. My boss wouldn't like me mentioning the clients' business to the police."

Poppy shook her head. "I appreciate your concern for my safety, but you've wasted your time coming here. My aunt's death was an accident. I was there. As for the threats you heard, I can't count the number of threats we've received throughout our careers from strangers." The last thing she wanted was the police looking into her aunt's death.

"They weren't strangers! I saw you on TV when they mentioned her death. Two men were standing with you –

the same men I heard plotting." Mina fumbled for her phone.

Poppy's heart stopped. She knew instantly who the woman was talking about.

"I managed to record some of their conversations when they ordered another round of drinks." Mina stepped closer, holding up her phone.

Poppy leaned in to see Joshua and her now-fired manager talking closely. They had never been close, and they certainly weren't drinking buddies. If anything, Joshua despised Dug for being too involved in her life. He also resented him for never taking him on as a client when he had asked.

"It's hard to hear with the music," Mina said, handing Poppy a wireless earbud. "I tried to stay in the room as long as possible, but I missed parts of the conversation."

The sound was choppy, but she could hear enough.

"You don't always want to be in Poppy's shadow, do you?" Dug was saying. "Your relationship is a means to an end. I understand you're her friend – but is she yours? What has she done for you? She'll drop you one day, when the arrangement no longer suits her. What will you have to show for it? I was a fool for not taking you on as a client sooner. Forgive me for not seeing your talent. I'll take care of Martha; it won't take much. You know how much she loves her pills. And Poppy… well, what's another pop star going off the rails?"

Poppy pressed the earbud closer to hear better, waiting for Joshua to defend her, but the silence was deafening. Glancing at her aunt's casket, she couldn't help but wonder what Dug would say if he knew that she'd beat him to it.

"Poppy has been distant recently. Obsessed with the idea of acting. She's meant to be the singer, and *I'm* the actor – the perfect pair. But now I audition, and they ask if she'd be interested in being the leading lady," Joshua slurred, clearly drunk.

"Exactly. You've been so good to her over the years, and you don't want people to only think of you as Mr Poppy Roe. What about *your* dreams? How many producers and directors did you introduce her to? How many want her now instead of you? You've pretended to be her boyfriend as a favour to her, to help her, but what has she done for you?"

"But killing her seems too extreme."

"I understand your hesitation." Duggery clapped him on the shoulder. "But I know about the girl you've been seeing on the side. If it comes out that you cheated on the Princess of Pop, it'll be over for you. Even I wouldn't be able to save you from that scandal; her fans would skin you alive. In a few weeks, when you're on that cruise, just slip a few pills in her drink. It's not your fault if she accidentally goes overboard."

"I don't think—"

"Poppy will never be found, and you'll be in the clear to start afresh, without a shadow hanging over you, and with the woman you love on your arm. It's time for Joshua Clark to stand in the spotlight."

Joshua said something Poppy couldn't make out. But when they clinked their glasses, a pit formed in her stomach. He really wanted her dead because he was threatened by her success?

"Why come to me with this?" she asked when the video finished. "You could have brought this to them and blackmailed them. You could've made a fortune for yourself."

"To be honest, I've got my own problems to deal with. I don't need your death on my conscience," Mina said.

"I respect your honesty." Poppy took a moment to process, figuring she should keep Mina close to stop this information from getting out. "How would you like a job?" she asked calmly.

"A job?" Mina frowned. "I don't understand."

"I need a new assistant. I fired mine this morning, and I need someone I can trust. Not wanting me to die is a good foundation for trust."

"It's a great offer, but I like my work at the club," Mina said hesitantly.

"I'll triple your yearly salary, and you only have to work for me for three months. Three years' pay for three months of work – and then you can return to the club, if you wish, or stay on with me." Mina had mentioned troubles, and more often than not, that meant money.

Mina perked up. "I don't have any experience being a personal assistant."

"That's okay – there's only one thing I need your help with."

"Okay, but if you want to go to the police, I can't be a witness. My boss won't want me to get the club involved. I can give you the footage?"

"I don't want to go to the police."

"Then what do you need my help with?" Mina asked, putting her phone back in her pocket.

"That cruise they're talking about in the video is next week. That's when they plan on taking me out. So, I need you to help me kill my boyfriend," Poppy said flatly, watching Joshua walk down the hill towards them.

Mina gaped.

Poppy was only half serious. She wanted to see what Mina was made of. She wasn't going to kill him unless she had to, but she did need to know if he was still plotting her death – something that would be harder to pull off now that she'd let go of Dug. *Did Joshua try and talk me out of firing him because it would ruin their plan to kill me?*

"I can do that," Mina said.

Poppy smiled. She loved a girl's girl.

"You can do what?" Joshua asked, reaching them. "Pops, is everything alright?"

"Everything's fine." Swallowing her anger, Poppy took his hand. "This is my new assistant, Mina. I don't think you two have met. She couldn't attend the church service."

"What happened to Gabriella?"

Poppy eyed him. Dug had mentioned he was sleeping with someone else; she wondered if it was her ex-assistant. They had always been a tad too friendly, and Joshua wasn't the type to stray far enough to have to put in effort. Not that she cared; he could sleep with whoever he wanted, so long as he didn't try to kill her to be with them. It wasn't like they had feelings for each other.

She sighed. "Sadly, Gabs found a new position. Something about wanting a more challenging role? With all the funeral chaos, I didn't get to tell you."

"That's a pity. I don't know why she didn't tell me," Joshua said, frowning.

"Oh. I didn't realise you were close," Poppy said, enjoying watching him squirm.

He flushed and scratched his brow, his tell when he was nervous. "I wouldn't say we were close, but we got to know each other when we were on tour with you."

He was definitely sleeping with her.

"Not that it matters now." Joshua held out a hand to Mina. "Anyway, it's nice to meet you. I hope you look after our girl."

"Of course! I won't let anything happen to her," Mina replied, shaking his hand.

"We should get back to the hotel. The guests are waiting," Joshua said, glancing over his shoulder at the cars.

"You two go ahead. I just want to say one final goodbye," Poppy said, and they both nodded solemnly.

Standing at the grave's edge, she watched them walk up the hill before she dropped the poppy atop her aunt's casket.

"I always told you I'd come out on top." She smiled, turning her back on her aunt.

## Chapter 4
# Bodyguard on Board
### Isaiah

After a week at home poring over the case files, Isaiah was surprised that his captain hadn't reprimanded him for his fruitless attempt to gatecrash Martha Roe's funeral. It seemed Roberts assumed he had actually taken her advice and gone on holiday. However, his investigation was at a standstill until he could get in the same room as Poppy Roe. Once he made contact with the owner of Heaven's Heart nightclub, that would hopefully no longer be a problem.

"Sorry, sir, but this area is off-limits without an invitation," the bouncer said, prodding a finger into Isaiah's chest and preventing him from entering the VIP area on the second floor of Heaven's Heart nightclub.

He hadn't pushed his way through the crowd of sweaty bodies covered in too much aftershave and perfume to be turned away. "I'm not here for the bottle service; I want to see your boss, Mr Eckells," he said politely, stepping back. He knew that breaking the man's wrist would only get him kicked out, and he didn't want to deal with that on top of his hangover.

*I need to take it easy on the booze,* he thought; waking up with a hangover was beginning to become a habit. But his captain had told him to relax, and catching up on

Formula 1 with a few beers last night had felt like the perfect way to unwind after scrolling through Poppy Roe's social media accounts to make a timeline of her movements over the last few weeks, leading him to Heaven's Heart. Her latest post featured a bright pink suitcase and a caption that mentioned setting sail on the world's most exclusive cruise ship, the *Midas*. He would have to find another way onto that ship if he couldn't get into this VIP area. He needed to call in a favour from the owner.

"Mr Eckells doesn't see anyone while the club is open. I suggest you turn around and grab a drink at the bar," the bouncer instructed.

Isaiah took his badge out of his pocket and showed it just as a second, shorter bouncer joined them.

"That's not going to help you here," the first guy said. "Get going before the wrong person sees that pretty badge."

"Take it, show it to your boss, and if he wants me to leave, I'll happily walk away," Isaiah said, handing it over.

The shorter bouncer whispered something to his friend that Isaiah couldn't make out over the music.

"I'll be back. Make sure Mr Rivers doesn't go anywhere," the first guy said, taking his badge and heading down a dark hallway.

"You've a lot of nerve flashing that badge," the short bouncer said. "The boss isn't a fan of the cops. You should've left when we asked nicely."

"We'll see," Isaiah said with a smug smile.

His companion returned and lifted the rope for Isaiah to pass through.

"Mr. Eckells is in a meeting. Wait outside his office until

you're called," he said, clenching his jaw as if his words tasted sour.

Isaiah took a few steps, then turned back. "I think you forgot something," he said, holding his hand out.

The bouncer reluctantly handed him back his badge.

"Who the fuck was that?" he heard the shorter man ask behind him.

"He saved the boss's younger sister, so he gets a free pass."

"Shit, that guy? Was the boss pissed we didn't let him through? Should we apologise?"

"Shut it. I'm not apologizing to a cop," the taller bouncer said, clearly annoyed at being shown up.

Isaiah smiled, wishing he had witnessed Eckells scolding the bouncer. They must be new. Usually the bouncers at the back door knew to let him through.

Reaching Eckells' office, he frowned when he saw the door ajar. Eckells had a strict closed-door policy. The bouncer must have rushed out. Isaiah shouldn't be eavesdropping, but he figured it wasn't his fault if he overheard anything while he waited.

"I only need two weeks off to accompany her on the *Midas*," a woman was saying. "Technically, I'd still be working for you – it's your ship. Don't you want to have eyes onboard to ensure everything runs smoothly? You could even say I'm killing two birds with one stone."

Isaiah heard a chair creak.

"I warned you not to get involved with our clients. I'll hide the recording, which you never should have taken, because I don't want it used against you. Do you know what some of our clients would do if they knew you might film them? I think I value your life more than you do, with such behaviour."

"I don't record clients. This was the first and only time.

I can't just leave her to fend for herself, and it's not like you've never taken justice into your own hands. All I'm asking for is some time to help her, and if anything goes wrong, then that recording is all you need to know who's behind it."

"Mina, I understand that you have a big heart and want to help, but you don't want to get involved in a murder plot, no matter how justified. Neither do I, especially not aboard my ship," Levi Eckells replied shortly.

"We aren't going to murder anyone. Poppy just needs a bodyguard to make sure that if anyone wants to hurt her, they can't. I'm just an extra set of hands."

*A murder plot?* Isaiah's frown deepened. *What's Levi wrapped up in now?* Isaiah had known Levi since his rookie year, when the man was just a bouncer working for a rough crowd. Over the years, they had developed what could be considered a friendship. Levi had three rules in his line of work: he didn't get involved with drugs, women, or children. Instead, he spent most of his time dealing with those who did.

Isaiah stepped into the office, a dimly lit space with a large desk at the centre cluttered with papers and a few empty glasses. The room smelled faintly of cigar smoke, a testament to Levi's occasional indulgence.

"Not planning on murdering any of your rivals, are you?" Isaiah quipped.

"Speak of the devil. This is the man you need." Levi slapped the desk, getting up to greet his friend. "What's this about murder? You know me; I wouldn't hurt a fly."

"Not with your own hands," Isaiah agreed dryly.

He peered over Levi's shoulder at Mina. She wore a black shirt with the club's name on the breast pocket and a nametag that read *Bar Manager*.

"What has you darkening my door? My little birds tell

me that you've been benched. I thought you'd be sipping cocktails on some beach," Eckells said.

"So sorry – I didn't mean to interrupt your conversation, but I have some business to discuss with Mr Eckells," Isaiah said to Mina.

"No need to apologise. You're always welcome here. The doorman should've informed me when you arrived," Levi said sternly.

Last year, Isaiah had overheard a cop bragging about blackmailing Levi's younger sister with explicit photos to make her spy on her brother. Isaiah had made sure the cop ended up behind bars. Although the captain had backed him up, the rest of the station had been cold towards him ever since, accusing him of siding with a criminal. Still, it was nice to always have Levi's good will.

"My visit is rather impromptu – otherwise I would have called ahead," Isaiah said, noting that Levi didn't introduce Mina.

"The Great Detective Rivers taking time off? I'd have thought Hell would freeze over first. Since you have some time off, how about a handsomely paid bodyguard gig aboard the most luxurious cruise in the world?" Levi asked, sinking back in his chair. His smile highlighted the scar on the corner of his chin.

"Isn't he a cop?" Mina whispered to her boss, who appeared amused by the fear in her voice.

"Detective," Isaiah corrected, but Mina didn't seem relieved. She probably recognised him because the staff had pictures of all the local police officers to memorise. Levi ensured police officers received special attention and never paid for their drinks. He called it service, but Isaiah thought of it as babysitting.

"Mina, don't be so rude to our guest. He's a friend, so I overlook his profession. It does come in rather handy, now and then," Levi said with a wink, taking a cigar from a varnished box on his desk. "You wanted me to find you a bodyguard, and there's no one I trust more. Rivers is above board and will stop you from getting into trouble or, worse, causing any. I don't want my other guests disturbed. They pay for discretion and peace."

"What's the job?" Isaiah asked. This was perfect. He didn't even need to ask for a way to get on board.

"The *Midas* is sailing next week, and Mina is accompanying a VIP. My guest is looking for some security while on board." Levi chopped off the end of the cigar but didn't light it.

"Who's the guest?" Isaiah inquired.

"Poppy Roe," Mina said.

Isaiah let out a chuckle of disbelief. This was too good to be true.

"You're a fan?" Mina frowned suspiciously.

"I'm aware of some of the things she's done."

"I didn't expect pop to be your genre of choice," Levi commented, swivelling in his chair.

"I just go where the leads take me."

"All my guests can have one personal bodyguard, though it's only precautionary. I have the best security team on board, but some guests are twitchy. All your expenses will be covered, and looking after the princess of pop shouldn't be too much trouble." Levi was clearly unaware that the five-foot bombshell was a serial killer, or at least closely linked to one.

"I'm sure he doesn't want to spend his holidays helping us," Mina argued. "Surely someone from your security team could fill in. I've already asked around—"

Isaiah didn't need to be a detective to know she didn't want to get the law involved in whatever Ms Roe was planning.

"Very proactive of you, but sparing you is enough of a sacrifice, and Isaiah can be trusted. I'm sure he'll be able to assist Ms Roe with whatever she needs," Levi reassured her.

Given the way he looked at her, and how she was able to speak so freely without repercussions, Isaiah wondered if something was going on between them. Levi was roughly his age, in his late thirties, but he'd never settled down.

"Doesn't Ms Roe have her own team security she can bring?" Isaiah glanced at Mina, who suddenly found the carpet fascinating.

"Ms Roe is reorganising her staff, and she just needs someone short-term," she informed him.

*Hmm.* "Since I've nothing better to do, count me in. Sounds like easy money."

"Bring my woman back in one piece, or we'll have issues," Levi said.

Mina rolled her eyes. She looked closer to Poppy's age, maybe a year or two older. Despite the age gap, it was obvious Levi trusted and respected her to run his bar.

"I'm not your anything but bar manager," she snapped.

Isaiah raised his eyebrows at her tone. Very few dared to speak to Levi that way, if any. Even though he had topped Forbes' Forty Under 40 list of richest and most eligible bachelors, he clearly wanted the one woman who didn't want him back. Maybe it would humble him.

"For now." Levi winked, placing the cigar between his lips.

Mina blushed, but it was unclear if she was flattered or furious. Isaiah got the feeling he shouldn't be witnessing the exchange.

"If you two are done flirting, I'll be off," he said, not wanting to overstay his welcome. He'd got what he'd come for without having to cash in on his favour.

"You stay, I'll go. I'll email you the details, and don't be late to the dock," Mina ordered him before she stormed out of the room, shoulder-checking him on the way.

"Why do I get the feeling I've been set up?" Isaiah muttered.

"Don't worry, we're just pawns in their game." Levi sighed and tossed Isaiah a phone from his desk drawer. "It's a secure line. Call if you need anything. Keep Mina alive and my ship afloat, and we won't have any issues."

"I get the feeling that's going to be harder than it should be," Isaiah said, trying not to show how happy he was. Not only would he be on the same ship as Poppy Roe, but he'd have unfettered access to her.

"Have fun," Levi chuckled.

Isaiah hesitated before leaving, unwilling to pass up an opportunity to use his friend's connections.

"Something on your mind?" Levi asked.

"I need a favour," Isaiah admitted, his voice low and urgent. He had a feeling this wasn't going to be an easy ask, but he had no other choice.

"Take a seat." Levi extended a hand to the chair across from him. "What can I do? I had a feeling this wasn't a social visit."

"I need you to look into someone for me. I can't go through official channels and don't want anyone to know who I'm looking into," Isaiah said, sitting down.

Levi didn't even blink.

"Name?" He took out a notepad and a pen.

"Poppy Roe." Isaiah waited for the penny to drop.

Levi frowned. "Do you always do a background check on those you're meant to protect?"

"No, this isn't about the job." He didn't offer any more information, and Levi didn't ask.

"How much information are we talking about? Surface or deep-dive?" he asked, making notes.

"Deep-dive. The more information the better; no detail is too small."

"Any area or time in particular?"

"The last six months, but I'm looking for skeletons. Whatever you can get."

"Consider it done. I might not have the information you want by the time you leave, though, if you don't want to leave any rock unturned. I can send an encrypted file to the captain of the *Midas*, and they'll make sure you get it."

"Thank you. What do I owe you?" Isaiah felt like a weight had been lifted. He knew Levi would break the law, or at least dance around it, but if his colleagues wouldn't offer help, he had to seek it out elsewhere.

"Don't mention it. I'm happy to help."

Isaiah didn't want to owe him anything. "I can't let you do that."

Levi leaned his elbows on the desk. "Look after Mina. She means something to me, and I don't want her caught up in whatever Ms Roe is up to."

They exchanged a knowing look.

"I'll bring them both back in one piece."

Levi smiled. "Good. I'm glad you stopped by tonight. Seems like we're all getting what we want."

"Or, like you said, we're pawns in a much bigger game."

Levi chuckled and walked him to the door. "And doesn't that sound like fun?"

They said goodbye, but Isaiah wasn't so sure. Considering how easily everything was falling into place, he couldn't help but wonder if luck *was* on his side, or if this was just the start of a storm.

# Chapter 5
# Boarding Break Up
## Poppy

Sitting next to Joshua in the back of the car, Poppy cursed herself for having trusted him. Just sharing the same air as the man plotting to kill her infuriated her, and Mina's attempts to fill the silence with chatter about the ship's amenities only heightened her unease.

Days had passed since the funeral. She'd waited for Joshua to come clean and confess everything, but he'd kept away, claiming he was busy. The weight of his unspoken betrayal was becoming unbearable, casting a shadow of distrust over everything. Perhaps it was best for both of them that he had stayed away; otherwise, she might have been tempted to push him off the balcony of her new penthouse. Then again, two suspicious falls might be too much of a coincidence.

"When we first met, we agreed that I'd help you with your career, and you would be a buffer to stop my aunt from setting me up with men who could 'benefit' my aunt's career. Our relationship might be a lie, but I thought we were at least friends," Poppy said suddenly, unable to stand the silence a moment longer. She wanted to give him a chance, an inch, to come clean before it was too late.

"Of course we're friends. Where is this coming from?" he asked, fidgeting with his expensive watch. His stale breath and the dark circles under his eyes told her he had been out all night drinking. Maybe planning to kill his girlfriend had worn him out.

"Do you feel like I didn't hold up my end of the deal?" she asked, trying to make sense of his betrayal.

"Poppy, I'm too hungover to understand what you want to hear. Can we just enjoy our holiday, and when we return home, we can figure out our next move?" Joshua grumbled, his refusal to make eye contact a clear sign of his guilt.

Poppy gave up. As the *Midas* came into view at the end of the dock, flying the trident flag, a wave of relief and hope washed over her. The ship, a symbol of her escape from Joshua and her troubles, was a welcome sight. It was as if a heavy burden had been lifted from her shoulders and she could finally breathe.

"Who's that?" she asked Mina as she got out of the car, nodding towards a tall man with broad shoulders talking to a staff member with a clipboard at the end of the pier by the boarding area. He lifted his arm to adjust his collar, which was caught in his long navy jacket, and in doing so revealed the gun holstered at his hip. The weapon sent a shiver down Poppy's spine.

"As requested, your new bodyguard. Isaiah Rivers comes highly recommended by Mr Eckells. I should mention that he's also a detective on leave. I've spoken to him briefly, and I believe we can trust him to be discreet," Mina whispered. Joshua was overseeing the process of their bags being unloaded and brought to the ship.

"A detective? I thought you would hire a bouncer," Poppy protested. The thought of being under the watchful eye of a detective, especially one she didn't know, made her uneasy.

"Rivers showed up while I was making arrangements with Mr Eckells about the trip, and he offered Isaiah the job," Mina replied.

Poppy wished she hadn't let Marty retire after the funeral. He was the only one on the security team she trusted, but he'd wanted to spend more time with his family, and she couldn't deny his request. Isaiah was undoubtedly nicer to look at, but now wasn't the time to focus on his designer stubble and dark eyes.

"Where's Marty?" Joshua asked like an echo of her thoughts, staring at Isaiah like he had a disease.

Then again, it might be handy to have a detective around. She wondered if he had any cuffs on him.

"Marty retired; I told you that," she said, hoping a smile would ease his suspicion.

"So he is…?" Joshua winced as the sun got in his eyes.

"Our bodyguard for the trip. He's here to make sure we're safe," Poppy said, leading the way towards the boarding plank where Isaiah waited.

"How much protection do we need on a cruise ship?" Joshua argued, apparently frustrated by the change in plans.

"We've always brought security away with us. You've never complained before," Poppy pointed out sarcastically.

"That's different. We know Marty. We don't need to be protected by a stranger. I can look after us," Joshua said, loudly enough for Isaiah to turn from Mina and greet them.

"You must be Ms Roe." Poppy liked how Isaiah

directed his attention at her, ignoring Joshua's temper tantrum. "I arrived early to go over some details with the staff. I'm Isaiah Rivers, and I'll be your protective detail for the next two weeks."

"I'm afraid we've wasted your time. We won't need your services," Joshua put in before Poppy could reply, making a show of sizing up Isaiah. The two men were complete opposites; Joshua wore a Hawaiian shirt, socks, and sandals. In contrast, Isaiah wore a shirt and trousers with a belt, highlighting his toned body, all business.

Isaiah smiled, clearly not bothered by his attitude. "I'm sorry, sir, but I was hired by Mr Eckells, the owner of the *Midas*, to ensure Ms Roe's safety during her trip. Without his say, I won't be leaving her side. I'll merely be a shadow. You won't even notice that I'm here," he said coolly. Poppy silently thanked him for standing his ground. He wasn't easily swayed, which she respected.

"There's no point in arguing. Everyone has a bodyguard on the *Midas*. With so many important people on one ship, it's better to be safe than sorry," Mina interrupted, backing up Isaiah without hesitation. Poppy figured it was because they both worked for the same person. Still, she was curious about Isaiah's background. How had a detective ended up working for Levi Eckells? Was he corrupt, or did he like to moonlight as a bodyguard? She made a mental note to stop assuming the worst of people.

"Can I speak to my girlfriend alone for a minute?" Joshua snapped.

"Please don't take too long, sir. We're already running behind schedule. Captain Hamill doesn't like to be late, and we have the other guests to consider," the staff member with the clipboard said.

Ignoring her, Joshua started pulling Poppy to the side. When she didn't move, his fingers dug in harder. She gritted her teeth and resisted the urge to slap his hand away.

"Unless you want to lose that hand, remove it from Ms Roe."

Poppy wanted to tell Isaiah she could handle herself, but she was too amused by the stunned expression on Joshua's sweaty face at his command.

"Who do you think you are? You work for us," Joshua snapped.

"Mr Eckells assigned me to look after Ms Roe and Mina," Isaiah said plainly. "I'd like to ask you again to please remove your hand."

"Don't lecture me about what I can or can't do to my girlfriend!" Joshua glared at him, but Isaiah didn't back down.

Poppy wouldn't have put it past Joshua to take a swing at him, but instead he let her go. Isaiah looked at her as though to check if she was alright. She couldn't remember if anyone had ever stood in her corner before; it felt odd. Watching him return to Mina's side, she smiled softly in acknowledgment and followed Joshua as he stormed off.

"Your girlfriend?" she began. "Laying it on a bit thick, considering you've been screwing Gabriella."

He gaped. "How'd you—?"

"Don't look so frightened. It's not like we're a real couple. You can screw whoever you like. In fact, I was going to talk to you about ending this farce earlier. But, you disappeared after the funeral," Poppy said, giving him another chance to end it before anyone got hurt.

"I know we aren't a couple, but we shouldn't just decide this on a whim. I don't know what's got into you.

First, this new assistant—" Joshua glared at Mina, still within earshot. "No offence," he added nastily.

"None taken." Mina shrugged as Joshua pulled Poppy further away.

"And now a bodyguard we've never even met?" He huffed. "Maybe we shouldn't go. I thought this was a break for the two of us. I didn't think we'd have so much company. If you want to end this, we can, but I don't think we should rush into anything. As for Gabriella, she knows our situation, so you don't have to worry about her going to the press."

Poppy frowned. "I'm not worried about her going to the press. I'm just trying to give you back your freedom. I don't understand why you're so upset about a bodyguard and an assistant when this is how it's always been."

Joshua shook his head, but she refused to budge. There was no way he was getting her on the ship alone. No temper tantrum was going to change her plans.

"Sorry to interrupt, but are you going to be departing soon?" The *Midas* staff member in the navy suit smiled impatiently as their bags were boarded on the immaculate white ship.

"Just a minute," Joshua snapped, and the woman retreated. "I don't think I can do this. You've fired everyone who's been with you for years and moved out of your aunt's house, all in a matter of weeks. You're talking about acting and wanting to end things between us. I feel like I don't know you anymore."

Poppy hesitated. *If he doesn't board, then I don't have to worry about him killing me. And* I *don't have to worry about killing him.*

"If you get on that ship, we're done. I won't be there for you anymore," Joshua said, giving her the out she needed.

"If you don't, then we're done," she countered.

"Just like that? Am I nothing to you?! Fine, have it your way; I'm done being Mr Roe. You have fun with your new friends," he snapped, backing away from her.

Stung by the way he used Duggery's words, Poppy looked up and took a deep breath before responding, only to notice that a lot of the guests who had already boarded were watching from their balconies.

"Mr Roe?" She laughed. "You can't blame me because you feel inferior. You might not believe it, but you've benefitted from our arrangement as much as I have. You resent me for my success while all I have done is support you!"

"You're impossible to love," Joshua sighed, turning his back on her. He knew how much that would hurt her. It had been her aunt's favourite line whenever she stood her ground.

Poppy watched him go, grinding her teeth to stop herself from saying what she knew of his plans.

"Are you okay?" Mina asked, appearing at her side.

"Fine," she said sharply. "Frightening Joshua off with a detective is much easier than playing the doting girlfriend until he attempts to throw me overboard."

"For someone with murderous intentions, I expected more of a backbone," Mina sighed.

"He was just a puppet," Poppy said quietly.

"Ms Roe, if you'll be joining us, then I need you to board." The woman's patience had worn off. Poppy felt terrible for causing such a scene and delaying their departure.

"Yes, we're coming. I'm so sorry for the delay."

She looked over her shoulder as she boarded to see Joshua enter the car. Isaiah glanced at her, and Poppy realised he probably thought she was heartbroken about being dumped. If only he knew. Without Joshua, there was nothing to fear onboard, and the prospect of a holiday to reset was even more appealing.

Her ego faltered at being dumped in front of a crowd, but it was better than being killed.

## Chapter 6
# Whispers of the Sea
### Isaiah

Following Poppy on board, Isaiah found it hard to picture the petite five-foot-something killing anyone. Then again, looks could be deceiving. If beauty could lure a man to his death, then her deep blue eyes would sink him deep beneath the surface before he even realised he was drowning.

He admired her composure, considering that her boyfriend had brutally dumped her only minutes ago. No doubt a life spent in the limelight meant she had an excellent poker face.

"Welcome to the *Midas*. My name is Patrice, and I'll be your personal butler for your time onboard. If you would please follow me, I'll escort you to your suite," said the woman in a perfectly pressed navy uniform, smiling brightly. Isaiah appreciated how she ignored the scene she had just witnessed.

It was easy to be distracted by the ship's interior. He admired the dark wooden floors, marble beams connecting each level, and the faint scent of jasmine that greeted every guest who boarded. He could see why it was called the

*Midas*, with its golden chandeliers, wooden finishes, and plush carpets. The ship's opulence was overwhelming, making him wonder about the kind of people who could afford such luxury.

He deftly stepped aside to avoid a porter pushing a gold trolley filled with designer luggage. Following the porter was a woman decked out in an overwhelming amount of jewels, a tiny dog tucked under her arm. He noted that all the staff wore the same navy uniform with a gold trident embroidered on the breast pocket.

"Sir? If you'd please follow us," Patrice called. Isaiah frowned, realising he had missed what she said.

"Sorry, I was taking in all the extravagance," he replied, returning to reality.

"No apologies needed. The *Midas* tends to make most first-timers speechless," Patrice said, walking around a desk in the heart of the foyer, which was cluttered with guests. "Please take these smartwatches and always keep them on your person. They act as your room keys and track your purchases. You can book restaurants, spas, and everything you'll need while on board, since we don't allow money or phones."

"You want us to give up our phones?" Isaiah asked.

"Given the exclusivity of our clientele, we are required to guarantee absolute privacy and relaxation while on board. If you need to make a call, you can use the phone in your room or come to the front desk here, and we will accommodate any need you may have." Patrice outstretched her hand for their devices. All three of them hesitated. "Don't worry; they will be secured in your private safe and returned to you when we reach the end of our voyage at the Isle of Tranquillity."

"Two weeks of no doom-scrolling sounds good." Mina shrugged, exchanging her phone for the watch. Poppy and

Isaiah followed her lead, and he watched as their devices were secured in one of the many small safes behind the desk.

Patrice beamed. "I'll take you down to your suite." She guided them to a glass lift with gold doors, listing the ship's amenities as they went. Isaiah pretended not to notice Poppy sneaking glances at him as the lift descended to the third floor.

"Thank you for what you did out there," she said to him suddenly, while Mina chatted to Patrice. "Joshua has always had a flair for the dramatic. You helped de-escalate the situation before we became the laughing stock of the whole ship." She didn't say it as bitterly as he'd expected.

"No need to thank me; it's my job to help you however I can. Even if that wasn't the case, no man should ever put his hands on a woman."

"I'm sure you've seen plenty of that in your line of work, but I wasn't expecting it from my boyfriend," Poppy said, remaining by his side while the others walked ahead.

"More than I would like. In my experience, those closest to us inflict the most damage."

There was a flash of something in her expression: sorrow and guilt. She promptly concealed it with a small smile.

"Are we below sea level?" she called down the narrow hallway to Patrice.

"Yes, all our finest suites are below sea level – and thanks to our state-of-the-art lighting, you'll have a sea view," Patrice said.

The idea of sleeping underwater wasn't too comforting; Isaiah didn't want to wake up to find a Great White staring at him through the window. He also would have preferred something closer to the lift, but the access door to the emergency stairs opposite their rooms would do nicely if they needed to escape quickly from any danger on board.

"Mina and Isaiah, both of your rooms adjoin Ms Roe's suite, and your watches will give you access to all three rooms. It's protocol for those with security," Patrice said. "All you have to do is place your hand on the handle, and it should open." She demonstrated, and they followed her inside. "Mr Eckells has arranged the Empress suite for you – our best. The large floor-to-ceiling glass window allows for breathtaking views once we enter clear waters. Your bags have been placed in your allocated rooms." Patrice indicated the pile of Poppy's bags by a wardrobe. *I don't know why one person needs so much luggage for two weeks at sea.* Still, Isaiah was relieved the staff hadn't unpacked for them. He didn't want anyone to find the case files or gun in his suitcase.

He inspected his room, relieved to find it was closest to Poppy's and the emergency exit. It wouldn't be hard if he needed to get to her in a hurry.

"If you need any assistance, please ask for me when you dial the main desk. I'm here to cater to all your needs," Patrice said before leaving them.

"Thank you for your help; we'll let you know if we need anything," Poppy said, walking her to the door.

"This suite is insane. The bathroom is bigger than my apartment. Do you know the sink is real gold?" Mina exclaimed, sliding over the back of the cream couch and hugging a shell-shaped cushion to her chest.

"I'm not surprised. I don't think any expense has been spared," Poppy chuckled, picking up a bottle of chilled champagne from the dining table. "How about a glass to celebrate the start of our journey? And cheers to new friends," she added.

Mina handed her three champagne flutes from the bar

by the door to her room. Poppy popped the bottle of champagne between her thighs – clearly not her first time – and started to pour.

"I don't drink while I'm working," Isaiah said, placing his hand over the third glass as Mina swiped one and downed it in two gulps.

"Live a little. I doubt I'll even need your services this trip," Poppy said. "You can come and go as you please. There's no need to stick by me. I can even arrange a new room for you."

Isaiah narrowed his eyes. She was trying to get rid of him.

"I think I'm going to go unpack while you two talk." Mina looked between them, clearly not wanting to get involved.

"All guests must have a bodyguard; I'm afraid it's ship rules. You won't even notice me," Isaiah said, not giving her any wiggle room. Winning her trust was clearly going to be a challenge.

"I find that hard to believe. I suppose I could use you to block out the sun while I sunbathe," Poppy joked, standing up on her tiptoes and barely reaching his shoulders.

"If that's what you desire, I'll happily oblige."

"You aren't going to budge on this, are you?" she asked, looking him up and down.

"I get the feeling that neither are you." He resisted the urge to smirk as he stepped closer, forcing her to meet his gaze. "If we get to know each other, we might just get along."

"Careful what you wish for." Poppy downed the rest of her champagne and walked to her room.

Isaiah followed, nearly bumping into her when she stopped short in the doorway. They stared at the rose petals and heart-shaped bedspread on the bed.

"Clearly, they were expecting this to be a romantic getaway," Poppy said stoically.

He expected her to be upset, but her resilience was admirable. Like a marble statue – breathtaking, but emanating a coldness that might cause him to turn to stone if he touched her. He shook away the thought and reminded himself that he was here to find out if she had anything to do with the murders, not about her rocky love life.

"I can call someone to have it all removed?" he asked.

She frowned. "Why trouble someone?"

"Given your recent breakup, it makes sense that you'd be upset," he said, daring to poke to get some reaction from her.

"It's only a few rose petals – nothing to cry about." Poppy shook out the comforter, distorting the perfect heart shape. Then she disappeared into the bathroom, which could fit a family of four, and returned with a wireless hairdryer. Within seconds, the rose petals were blown away.

"Now it's just another bed," she said, tossing the hairdryer into a drawer under the wardrobe.

"Can I ask why you boarded after what happened at the dock?"

"Joshua and I had a mutually beneficial relationship, and now it's over." She shrugged. "You don't have to worry about me breaking down in tears. Besides, regardless of what Joshua decided, I wanted a holiday. Tickets for the *Midas* are rare, expensive, and non-refundable. I wasn't going to let them go to waste."

"But given all you've been through lately, wouldn't you rather be home in the States than surrounded by strangers here?"

She sighed. "Am I being interrogated? Or are you just really terrible at small talk?"

He pulled at his neck, not used to being called out. "Sorry, force of habit. You don't have to answer. I thought this might be easier if we got to know each other a little."

"Ireland is my home. I only lived in the States when my schedule called for it. As I'm sure you know, I don't have any family left. Being around strangers is normal for me. If I were completely alone with my thoughts, I wouldn't know what to do with myself," she said simply. "My turn. Why take this job? If you're a detective, I'd assume you have bad guys to catch."

"I've had some hard cases recently, and my captain thought it would be good if I took some time off," he admitted. Some honesty might take some of her walls down, but he didn't have to tell her everything.

"So you were ordered to take a holiday and instead you decided to work? We might have more in common than I thought. Neither of us knows how to relax."

He grinned. "Eckells mentioned this would be an easy gig, and boarding the *Midas* is a once-in-a-lifetime opportunity. Like you, I can't remember the last time I had a holiday myself; I'm not sure I even remember how."

"I don't think anyone has ever thought working for me is easy," she admitted.

"Mina seems to like you."

"She's new." Poppy chuckled, and it was the first time he'd seen her smile reach her eyes. He had a feeling she was being too hard on herself.

An awkward silence drifted over them, only breaking when the ship's horn sounded.

"Too late to back out now," she said as the *Midas* started to move. "Since we've got the pleasantries out of the way and you've refused to leave my service, could you give me some privacy? I want to change." She started unzipping the side of her dress.

Isaiah barely had time to turn around before it hit the floor. She was testing him, trying to make him uncomfortable – or checking to see if he would make an advance on her. He'd never cross the line. She was a suspect or, at the very least, a potential witness to multiple homicides.

"I'll leave you to it." He opened the door to the adjoining room. It was far larger than he needed, and the crisp white sheets looked all too inviting, even if the never-ending darkness of the ocean made his stomach tighten. Seasickness? He'd never been on a boat, so it hadn't occurred to him that he would get seasick.

To distract himself from the dark waters, Isaiah grabbed a small jewellery box from his bag on his bed. Holding his insurance policy, he knocked on Poppy's door.

"Come in, I'm decent," she called.

He found her wearing a white robe as she went through the exceptionally organised open suitcases on her bed. *Either she has a type-A personality, or she hires someone who does.*

"I have something for you," he said.

"What's that?" Poppy asked, eying the box like it might contain some lethal weapon.

"Since you would prefer I keep my distance, I'm here to offer you a deal." He opened the box, which contained a silver anchor charm.

"Pretty. Do you buy all your clients gifts?" He could have sworn he saw a smile flirt with the corner of her lips.

He couldn't resist. "Only the pretty ones."

Poppy rolled her eyes.

"It's for your charm bracelet. Mina told Eckells that you never take it off, so I had this made," he explained.

"Why do I get the feeling it's not just a charm?" Poppy looked at the dangling charms already on her wrist.

"This anchor will keep me apprised of your location at all times while we're on board," he explained, taking out the phone that Levi had given him. "Since they don't allow phones, this is the best I could do."

"You want to tag me like a dog?" she asked, staring at him through her long lashes.

"I'll only check it if there's an emergency. With this, I can give you all the freedom in the world while still ensuring your safety," he reasoned, glad he'd asked Levi for the tracker. Sailing into international waters with a potential killer was new for him, and he wanted to make sure he didn't lose track of her.

"If I say no?" Poppy crossed her arms over her chest.

"Then we'll be best friends by the time we arrive at the island off the coast of Greece in the next fortnight, because I'll never be further than fifteen feet from you."

With a grumble, Poppy offered him her wrist, and he tried to shake off a smile. She could take it off anytime – but why would she, if she had nothing to hide?

"Beautiful," he said, adding the charm. "You wouldn't even know it's there."

"I'll know," she said under her breath.

Isaiah's hand lingered on hers a little longer than necessary. He was surprised she didn't snatch it away. He was trying to earn her trust, but maybe for her it was another mind game.

"I'm unpacked and ready to relax. Am I interrupting?" Mina asked, lingering in the doorway.

"Not at all. I was just about to ask you if you could give me a hand. I think I've overpacked," Poppy said, fidgeting with her bracelet.

"I'll leave you to get unpacked and settled. Call if you

need me. I'm only a door away." Isaiah didn't want to crowd them. He knew they probably wouldn't talk freely with him there, but as soon as he left the room, he pricked up his ears.

"What happened with Joshua? Why did he leave at the dock? Doesn't this change everything?" Mina asked.

"Hush! He could be listening," Poppy whispered, not quietly enough. "Let's go into the hall."

Isaiah rushed to get his door on the latch to make out what they were saying without them hearing him open it.

"I guess Joshua backed out at the last minute, because he panicked when he saw a detective was going to protect me. Or his conscience kicked in, and he figured killing off his girlfriend was a terrible idea," Poppy was telling Mina.

So, Joshua was the one who'd intended to carry out the murder. It made sense that Isaiah's presence would panic him.

"What if this was part of the plan? What if he suspected you knew something and left so that you would let your guard down? What if he hired someone else to do his dirty work? At least a dozen people saw him drive away, giving him a great alibi," Mina countered, pacing back and forth. Isaiah was sure she would wear a hole in the hallway carpet.

"Relax. You're seriously overestimating their skills. Duggery couldn't pull off something that intricate. I bet Dug was planning to use Josh as his fall guy, which is why he involved him in his plans in the first place. But the lawyers called me last night and stripped Dug of anything related to me. Even if I die, he'll get nothing, making me worthless to him – dead or alive," Poppy said. "Given that, he could have decided to back out, and Josh didn't have the courage to go ahead alone. When he didn't come to my apartment last night, I wasn't sure if he'd even show up this morning. Isaiah's arrival was just the final nail in the coffin."

There was a pause, and for a moment he thought they had left. *I should call Michael and find out more about her manager*, he thought. If the man wanted to kill her, then he might be behind the other deaths connected to her.

"I have to admit, I'm relieved we don't have to be on guard anymore. Joshua gave me the creeps, and I could see how much he was sweating on the way over here. With him out of the picture, can we really relax?" Mina asked, sounding uncertain.

"I think you deserve a break. You helped me settle into my new apartment and find Isaiah, even if hiring a detective was questionable. If you hadn't shown me that video of them, I might already be dead. I appreciate all you've done for me when you could have walked away. Now we can relax without having to look over our shoulders."

"I hate to think that people who were meant to protect you, to care for you, wanted to kill you to further their career, and because they were jealous of your success," Mina said sadly. "I don't know Joshua, but maybe he would have backed out even if Isaiah hadn't come."

"I admire how you want to see the best in people, but I prayed every night until today that Joshua would confess or warn me about what Dug was planning, but he never did," Poppy said. Isaiah noted that she still didn't sound heartbroken.

"You're free of that coward now, but we should still err on the side of caution to be safe—"

Isaiah silently thanked Mina for her good sense.

"Don't worry, I'm not going to do anything crazy," Poppy replied, shaking her bracelet. "Plus, how much danger can I be in now that I'm tagged?"

"We can't be too careful. It's not like you thought *they*

were capable of murder, and look how that turned out," Mina said. "At least it's a cute accessory. Could you imagine if it had been some clunky ankle bracelet?"

"Don't mock ankle bracelets. They were once all the rage in Hollywood. But thanks for caring so much." Poppy laughed. "Let's put all thoughts of murder behind us, get a drink, and enjoy the sunset."

Isaiah digested all he had heard. Poppy wasn't planning on murdering her boyfriend, but on defending herself against those who plotted to kill her. Why wouldn't she go to the police and tell them what her manager and ex were planning? Isaiah moved to the other door so he didn't miss anything else they said, only to knock his shin on the desk. He coughed loudly to cover up a curse.

"Are you okay in there?" Poppy called, her voice filled with concern.

"All good. Just dropped something," Isaiah called, rubbing his shin to remove the sting.

"I didn't think detectives were allowed to be clumsy," Mina joked.

Isaiah smiled.

"I didn't think they were allowed to be so attractive either. How old is Isaiah anyway?" Poppy muttered, probably thinking he couldn't hear her. It was hard not to be flattered, considering she was used to being around celebrities and the surgically enhanced – he was just a regular guy.

"I don't know. He's younger than Eckells. So probably like mid-thirties," Mina whispered back.

"Take your time unpacking," Poppy called to him through the door. "We're heading to the pearl bar to watch the sunset – we'll be just fine!"

"What was that?" he asked, opening the door. He wouldn't let her run off without ensuring she had her bracelet on. Poppy was already out the door, but he caught Mina on the way out. "I didn't catch what Poppy said." Better to make sure they thought the suite was soundproof so he could keep listening in on their conversations.

"We're just off to the bar! For the sunset," Mina explained. "Do you want to join us?" She smiled supportively at Isaiah. "It could be a great opportunity for Poppy to warm up to you."

"I appreciate the thought, but my priority is keeping her safe, not warming her up." Their absence would give him a chance to look through her bags – perhaps uncover a journal, schedule or other clue that could connect Poppy's ex-manager to the troubling murders. "Still, a bit of charm might help. It's obvious she has difficulty trusting people." Mina nudged him pointedly.

Isaiah chuckled, a bit defensive. "Usually I don't have to convince those who hire me to let me protect them. You should go after her. If she doesn't want me to shadow her, then I want you to stay close."

"Got it! I won't let her out of my sight," Mina said with a playful salute before the door clicked shut behind her.

Isaiah took a deep breath and eyed Poppy's numerous suitcases, unsure where to begin and what he might discover.

# Chapter 7
# Muster Drill
### Isaiah

Blaring sirens woke Isaiah from sleep with a jump. He reached for the gun hidden under his pillow before he was fully conscious. Groaning, he listened to the announcement over the intercom, instructing everyone to gather at the muster point on B-Deck. He grabbed his phone from the nightstand. The tracker said she was in the suite, though not in which room.

"Poppy?" Isaiah banged on the adjoining door, but there was no reply. She had to be with Mina.

He grabbed his gun holster and wrapped it around his shoulders, cursing himself for falling asleep after an evening of searching through Poppy's belongings and finding nothing. He had tried to stay awake until they returned to the suite, but the seasickness had got the better of him, and he had drifted off.

"Why are you banging on the door? It's like 4am," Mina groaned, opening her door. She was wrapped in a bathrobe, her eye makeup smudged.

"Don't you hear the sirens?" he demanded, barely able to hear himself think, let alone sleep.

"I fell asleep listening to a podcast; what's wrong?" she grumbled.

"Is Poppy with you? We've got to get to the muster point."

"No, she must be in her room."

Wasting no time, Isaiah used his smartwatch to enter Poppy's room. Her empty room. He picked up her charm bracelet from her pillow; he was going to kill her.

"Where did you last see her?" he snapped, putting the bracelet in his pocket. The sirens only heightened his frustration, and Mina's semi-drunk state wasn't helping.

"Don't snap at me! I didn't know she left that thing here. We were at the bar like we said we would be. I started feeling sick, but she wanted to stay longer. Tequila and a rocking ship aren't a great combination, so I returned at around… midnight? I thought she'd be right behind me." Mina eyed the turtle-shaped clock on the bedside table.

"Four hours ago? Damn it. I shouldn't have given her so much space." Isaiah ran his hand roughly through his hair. Any trust he'd gained with Poppy wouldn't matter if she vanished on the first night. He left the suite and hurried down the hall, weaving through other guests as he headed in the opposite direction of the emergency lights.

"Where are you going?" Mina followed him in her bathrobe. The way she struggled to keep up told him she was still drunk.

"To the bar where you last saw her." He pounded the lift button, but the light flashed red in response. Had Poppy manipulated Mina into drinking so much to have some time alone? Given that someone had plotted to kill her less than twenty-four hours ago, the idea of her being alone and intoxicated on a ship made his stomach knot.

"Sir, you can't use the lifts during the drill. Please follow the emergency lights; all guests must go to their muster points," a man in a navy uniform said, blocking the lifts. He looked far too composed for so early in the morning.

"I need to find my client," Isaiah argued, looking at the door marked 'Stairs'.

"There's no need to panic about your client. This is a drill, and I'm sure they'll be waiting for you at the muster point on B-deck." Guessing his next step, the crew member blocked the door to the stairs with a forced smile.

"I just want to go to the bar and ensure she's alright. If it's just a drill, then where I go shouldn't matter."

"I'm sorry, sir, but there are several bars on board, and I can't let you check all of them during the drill." The man's false smile only added to Isaiah's irritation.

"What bar was it?" he asked, turning to Mina. She hesitated.

"I think it was opposite the theatre. The Pearl Bar?"

He understood how easy it was to get turned around on the ship. All the corridors looked the same, and with so many different amenities, it was hard to keep track of where everything was.

"The Pearl Bar, located in the Entertainment Lounge on A Deck, has already been cleared. All guests in that area have been escorted to the muster point. Please follow me, or I'll have to call security." The man's smile was tightening with every word.

"Isaiah, don't cause a scene," Mina urged. "They won't let you run all over the ship, and I'm sure Poppy will be with the other guests."

Taking a deep breath, he decided to trust Mina and followed her and the crew member to the deck. Poppy had better be there, or he would permanently weld the bracelet onto her wrist.

The exterior B-Deck was crowded with lined-up cranky guests shivering in the cold, who, in their bright orange life-jackets, looked as pleased to be there as he was. Once they reached their assigned row, his stomach sank when there was no sign of Poppy.

"I should've checked the bar; she isn't here," Isaiah said, his tone earning him a disgruntled look from the guest beside them.

"They won't keep us long – then we can look for her," Mina murmured quietly back.

"He said they cleared the bar, so if she wasn't there when the alarm sounded, she must have left before. Did she say where she might go?"

"No, but I was too busy trying to get back to my room without throwing up amongst the elite." Mina's teeth chattered as crew members talked them through the emergency protocols.

He scanned the crowd of shivering guests, hoping to catch a glimpse of her. "Once this is over, we'll have to split up. If you find Poppy first, bring her back to the suite. I'll meet you there," he instructed, wishing he had a way to contact her.

Once the drill was completed, a crew member addressed their row. "Thank you for your understanding and patience. I'm sure you all understand the importance of drills to ensure your safety and that of your companions. Feel free to explore the ship or return to your cabins."

"Return to our cabins? Maybe she heard the alarm and went back to the suite to look for us, but we missed each other," Isaiah mused.

"I'll cover A and B Deck; you take C and D," Mina

suggested. "I doubt she would go to any of the residential floors, so we can rule those out."

"Okay. I'll meet you back at Poppy's suite," Isaiah agreed, regretting that he hadn't sneaked away when he had the chance. The lifts would be crowded with guests trying to return to their rooms now. Thankfully, the map of the ship showed him a route through the glass stairways and gold-trimmed bridges, so he could move quickly without having to wait for lifts.

"Excuse me, but I'm looking for Ms Poppy Roe," Isaiah said to the spa receptionist dressed in a crisp white uniform and laying out magazines on the polished reception desk. Her name tag read 'Magda'.

He had already checked the cinema, the gyms, the theatre, and the virtual golf room. The only place left to look was the tranquillity spa. If he couldn't find her and Mina returned alone, he would have to summon her over the intercom, which he doubted she would appreciate.

"We were wondering when you would find us. We tried calling Ms Roe's suite, but we couldn't reach anyone due to the drill," Magda replied without looking up as she carried a tray full of sliced cucumber to a large water dispenser, adding it in. "Ms Roe is in the sea-salt pool room. We don't open for another hour, so you should take her back to her room before the other guests arrive."

"Why wasn't she sent to the muster point with the other guests?" Isaiah asked, curious as to why they had broken protocol for her.

"We felt Ms Roe was too inebriated to be out on the deck, and the night manager let her stay since she was quiet and kept to herself. Given her recent loss, we thought discretion and space were best," Magda whispered, even though no one else was around.

Isaiah noted how easily others talked about Poppy's private life. He couldn't imagine how it would feel for strangers to know his personal details.

"I'll get her back to her room. Thank you for looking out for her," he said, not wanting to waste time interrogating her further when she was trying to get set up for the day.

"Head through the relaxation room and take a left at the mud baths. You'll be able to see the pool through the glass doors. No shoes inside," she instructed, handing him a pair of white slippers.

"Thank you." He exchanged his shoes for them as Magda walked behind the desk for the tray of raspberries and lemon slices and filled another dispensary.

"No need to thank us. It's our job to make sure our clients feel safe and comfortable. I'll have your shoes brought back to your room," she said, scanning his smartwatch so the door to the spa opened for him.

Poppy sat in a white fluffy robe with her legs dangling in the water and a bottle of champagne beside her. Her humming echoed around the empty, tranquil pool area. A blackout ceiling with faux glimmering stars made it appear as though they were alone in the universe. The soft gurgle of the water and the gentle hum of the spa's jacuzzi created a serene atmosphere, a stark contrast to the chaos of the muster drill.

Given how people talked about her, this might be the only moment of true peace Poppy would get on board, so Isaiah allowed her to savour another moment. He listened to her soft, sad song, thinking how she didn't look like a major celebrity or a murderer. She just looked like a lonely young woman.

"I thought you were going to stay at the bar," he said calmly, crouching beside her. With her blonde hair fanned around her shoulders and face make-up-free, she looked strangely vulnerable; now wasn't the moment to lecture her about wandering off. Also, trying to reason with a drunk person was a waste of breath.

"I was at the bar. Then I fancied a swim, but they wouldn't let me. This was the compromise," she explained, looking at him with a hazy smile. Lifting the half-empty bottle of champagne, she kicked her feet in the water.

He was relieved they hadn't let her in the pool. He didn't think letting the princess of pop drown on his watch would be good for his career.

"Sleep off the booze, and you can go swimming," he suggested, carefully trying to take the champagne from her. She quickly cradled it to her chest. He didn't press, knowing that patience would be key to getting her back to the suite. "Can't I have a drink?"

"I thought you didn't drink while you were working? I hate champagne anyway, but it's all they had down here." She happily offered him the bottle. "I've never even been drunk before. I was only ever allowed a sip or two at award ceremonies."

"You've never been drunk? Ever?" Isaiah brought the bottle to his lips and pretended to sip – he just wanted to put her at ease, and she had drunk enough for the both of them. Given her short stature and apparent inexperience with alcohol, he didn't know how she was still conscious. He set the bottle between them, but she didn't reach for it again.

She hiccupped and shook her head. "Never. Aunt Martha had eyes everywhere, and she warned me about the importance of staying clear-headed and never losing control of myself." She wagged a finger at him. "But I can drink whatever I want, and eat what I want, and do whatever I want. Like, go swimming at two am. Do you know how embarrassing it is to be twenty-six years old and have no control over your life? Well, not anymore. Now it's my time." She kicked again, causing a big splash.

Have no control over her life? Her late aunt must have kept a firm grip on her. Isaiah felt a surge of protectiveness. He didn't think her sober self would like her confessing too much, so he settled for an easy question.

"If you could eat anything right now, what would you like?"

"Strawberries." She beamed. "I'd live on them if I could. Strawberry milkshakes, but I don't think Room Service will deliver to the spa."

He was sure guests could request anything on the *Midas*, no matter how ridiculous, and they'd oblige. A strawberry milkshake was simple enough.

"Why don't we head back to the suite, and we can see about getting you that milkshake? Mina's waiting for us, and she was worried when you weren't at the muster point."

"Why would Mina worry? We're completely safe now." Poppy sighed. "I've a hunky, chunky detective to keep me safe from all the big, bad wolves."

"Hunky chunky?"

"I thought detectives were meant to be coffee addicts who were too busy for the gym and all scruffy, grumpy, and sceptical?" She squeezed his bicep and smirked.

"That's the stereotype, I guess. Unfortunately, I do have a caffeine problem, and I often forget to shave when I'm engrossed in a case. But working out at home helps me think through ideas and cases and lifts my mood. I can be grumpy and sceptical, but you'd have to ask my desk partner. It probably depends on how much coffee I've had or which case I'm working on."

"All work and no fun – I know the feeling," Poppy sighed. "I bet you can't remember the last time you smiled."

"I do, actually. Just a moment ago, when you called me a hunky chunky detective."

"No! I didn't," she gasped. The alcohol was clearly affecting her short-term memory.

"I must have heard you wrong. But thank you for not reducing me to my looks."

"I'd never do that. I know how it feels to be judged solely by what I do and how I look. I found some peace here because I couldn't stand the whispers at that bar after Mina left," she said, pointing above them. "Whispers seem to follow me wherever I go. Right now, the topic of choice is my boarding breakup."

"He's an arsehole for leaving you like that, and you have every right to be upset," he replied.

"Upset?" She snorted. "More like disappointed that I got involved with Joshua in the first place. Besides, with my aunt gone, I no longer need him as a buffer..." She paused, clearly realizing she might be about to reveal too much.

"Buffer?" Isaiah prompted, and she rubbed her eyes.

"Ignore me. He's gone, and I've never felt better."

Isaiah might believe she was relieved he was gone, given that he'd heard about Joshua's plans to kill her. But that type of betrayal had to sting, even if their relationship had been some kind of arrangement.

"Can I help you up now? I don't fancy diving in after you," he said, changing the subject.

Poppy hesitated for a split second before offering him her hand, which he happily accepted.

"C'mon, let's get you to bed and that milkshake." He helped her stand so she didn't lose her balance.

"Thank you, but just so you know, I could've made it back to the room myself," she said. "I can handle myself."

"I don't doubt it. I'm only a helping hand," Isaiah said, suppressing his smirk. It wasn't her ability to take care of herself that he doubted, but more whether she could walk in a straight line.

"How about a piggyback? That way you can get to bed faster," he offered. If he let her walk back to her suite, it would take half the day, and he didn't have the patience to herd her to bed.

"I can't let you do that." She concealed a smile with her hands. "You're here to protect me, not babysit me. It wouldn't be appropriate," she added, though she looked tempted.

"Like you said, you're free to do whatever you want. Who has the right to judge?"

"Saving a damsel in distress, how chivalrous – but we have a problem," she mused. "You need to bend down."

He knelt on the tiles, and she squealed happily as she wrapped one leg around him, followed by the other.

"Comfortable, Princess?" he asked, standing up and gripping her thighs so she didn't fall.

"You could do with some softening." She massaged his shoulder muscles, and he shook his head. He hoped she would remember this when she sobered up – her mortification might make her more pliable. Sarcastic, sassy, sexy, and murderous? He was beginning to regret taking this job.

"Want to walk back to the room?" he threatened, but she shook her head and buried her face in his neck.

"Lead the way," she mumbled, resting her hands on his chest.

"CAN you press your hand to the door?" Isaiah asked a few minutes later, struggling to open the suite while holding her.

Poppy's soft breathing indicated she had drifted off on his shoulder. He glanced at her hands and realised she wasn't wearing her smartwatch. Twisting toward the door, careful not to drop her, he tried his hand on the handle, but a red X appeared, barring their entry. It had worked earlier.

He shook her gently, and she groaned. "What?"

"Where's your wristband?" he asked, hoping it was in one of the pockets on her robe.

"I had it when I came back to change into my bikini and my robe. Maybe I left it inside with my bracelet because I didn't want to lose it in the pool," she explained.

At least she hadn't left her bracelet on purpose so he couldn't track her. He really didn't want to go back to the spa or the bar to search for her watch.

"We can go through my room," he said, opening the door to his space and carefully setting Poppy down on her unsteady feet. Inside his room, he tried to open the adjoining door to hers, but it was locked from the inside.

"I don't remember locking it before we left," he remarked, wondering if Mina had secured it.

"Maybe Mina returned, and our smartwatches won't let us in if the room is occupied."

"Mina?" Isaiah called as Poppy sat on his bed, but there was no response. He walked down the hall and tried knocking on Mina's door, but again, there was silence. Maybe she had fallen asleep listening to something again and couldn't hear him. "She's probably still searching for you, or has passed out in your room."

Poppy yawned and lay back on his bed.

"I'll call Patrice to open the door," he began, but she shook her head.

"They'll take too long. Just let me stay here for a bit," she mumbled, snuggling into his pillow.

Isaiah rubbed his neck. He was tired, but he would clearly have to make do with the armchair until Mina returned.

Poppy leaned on her elbows as he pulled out the chair. "You don't have to sleep there; there's plenty of room for both of us on the bed." She stared up at him as though trying to read his mind.

"It wouldn't be professional," he said, and she rolled her eyes.

"It's not like you're a real bodyguard; no one is going to report you."

She knelt up on the bed so they were face to face, but almost lost her balance. Isaiah caught her waist to stop her from toppling over onto him.

"See, you can't seem to keep your hands off me," she teased, resting her hands on his shoulders. He still wasn't sure if she was flirting or testing him.

"I don't want you to fall off the bed," he told her as her fingers caressed the sides of his neck and she stared at his lips.

"Most men wouldn't think twice if I asked them to share a bed with me," Poppy said, staring at him like he was a puzzle to be solved.

He clenched his teeth as she stroked his chest. The realisation that he definitely would not be averse to this situation under different circumstances was alarming. "Then you clearly haven't been with decent men."

She pouted. "Unfortunately not. But you could change that." She inched closer, eyes half-closed, and he could almost taste the champagne on her lips. He needed to shut this down quickly.

Suddenly, Poppy's eyes snapped open and she sprang up from the bed. Before he could ask what was wrong, she shoved him aside and ran to the bathroom with a hand over her mouth, slamming the door shut. Isaiah let out a sigh of relief. Divine intervention.

"Let me know if you need anything," he called. "I'm right outside." He wasn't particularly comfortable with vomit, but he needed to make sure she was ok.

"This is so embarrassing. Please don't come in," Poppy pleaded through the door.

"I don't want you to pass out in there."

"You're such – a pain – in the ass," she replied between heaves.

"So is falling asleep on tile floors," he retorted.

He couldn't hear Poppy's response, but he guessed she was cursing him out.

"Do you need some water?" Isaiah asked gently.

After a short silence, the bathroom door cracked open slightly, revealing a manicured hand. "Please," she whispered.

"Here you go. Just take small sips," he said, handing her a chilled bottle from the minibar.

"You're so bossy," she mumbled, before closing the door again. Thankfully, she didn't lock it.

"Sure you don't need me to hold your hair back?" he asked, chuckling.

He didn't need to guess what she called him through the door.

"Well, I'm here if you need me," he sighed, settling back into the armchair by the door.

## Chapter 8
# Blood-Stained Tiles
### Poppy

Isaiah had been right about sleeping on the tiles, Poppy thought, stretching her neck and sore back. She opened the bathroom door slowly to find Isaiah asleep in the armchair by the desk. *He could have slept on the bed!* She wouldn't be the only one with a sore neck today.

The clock on the desk read 2:30pm; she couldn't believe she had slept so late into the afternoon. Tiptoeing across the room to avoid disturbing him, she tried to open the adjoining door, but it was still locked. She needed Mina's smartwatch to get in, since she didn't want to wake Isaiah and face a lecture.

After some not-so-subtle knocking, Mina opened the door. Her heavy eyes looked as hungover as Poppy felt.

"Oh, thank God. I was so worried about you," she exclaimed, wrapping her arms around Poppy. "Isaiah was freaked when you didn't return with me from the bar."

"I can see that," Poppy said, noticing the unmade bed in Mina's adjoining room.

"Don't look at me like that. I did look for you! When I returned, I figured Isaiah had found you because I couldn't get into either of your rooms. My smartwatch would only work on my own room door. Those shots of tequila did me in. I don't know if it's being at sea or what, but I've never been such a lightweight," Mina explained, still looking a little green.

"That's strange. We couldn't get into the suite either. Is the adjoining door on your side locked?" Poppy asked.

"I assumed you must have locked it when you got back."

"We should pay more attention to what doors we lock just in case," Poppy said thoughtfully. "It's not a big deal. I fell asleep in Isaiah's room after he found me in the spa."

"You slept with Isaiah?" Mina's hands covered her shocked smile.

"Not *with* Isaiah; I fell asleep in the bathroom. I've never been so sick. I'm never drinking champagne again." The words tasted bitter on her tongue. One thing was for sure: there was no risk of her becoming an alcoholic like her aunt.

"Isaiah could've offered you his bed if you were that sick," Mina remarked, clearly surprised by his ungentlemanly behaviour.

"Don't be hard on him. Poor guy slept in the armchair while I yacked my guts up all night," Poppy said. "I've never been so mortified in my life." She couldn't remember another time someone had stayed by her side all night to ensure she was alright.

"Aww, it's nice that he looked after you. Maybe we judged him too quickly." Mina walked to the suite's double doors.

To their relief, the door to Poppy's suite blinked green, allowing them to enter.

"The drill last night must have caused some glitches

with some of the doors; at least they're working now," Mina said.

"I should've come back with you – I can't believe I picked the night of a drill to wander off. I bet Isaiah is going to be keeping a closer eye on me now," Poppy said, wishing she hadn't left her bracelet behind. He must have been frightened when he couldn't find her. They weren't off to a great start.

The sight of her freshly made bed called to her, but the room service menu by her bed was even more tempting. "Are you hungry?" she asked Mina, who was lying on the couch.

"Starved," she grumbled.

"The brunch menu goes all day." Poppy beamed, picking up the room service menu. "Maybe I can make up for my disappearing act last night by ordering Isaiah breakfast. Do you think he's more of an Eggs Benedict or breakfast-sandwich-with-extra-bacon kind of guy?"

"Definitely a breakfast sandwich," Mina said, with a yawn.

"We'll get two of those, then." Poppy handed her the menu. "Order whatever you like; I'm going to take a quick shower before the food arrives."

"So, one of everything?" Mina joked.

"Make it two," Poppy laughed.

An odd metallic smell met her when she closed the bathroom door. Since the bathroom hadn't been used yet, she figured it might just be the cleaning products. As she washed her face at the sink, the smell grew stronger.

"What *is* that?" she muttered, dabbing her face dry with a fluffy towel. It wasn't the towels that were causing the odour. She examined the drain, wondering if something had been washed down and got clogged, but it didn't seem to be coming from there either. She decided that a shower would help wash away whatever might be lingering in the drains.

"Food should be here in thirty minutes," Mina called through the door.

"Thanks! Could you check if Isaiah is awake?" Poppy called back as her stomach grumbled. Thirty minutes was just enough time for her to scrub away the effects of her night out before diving into something delicious. She dreaded the thought that, after a night of drinking and throwing up, the smell could be coming from her. She pulled back the shower curtain.

*Blood. The smell is blood.*

Patrice, the woman who had greeted them only yesterday with warmth and a bright smile, stared up at Poppy accusingly with wide, blank eyes.

Poppy wanted to scream or call for Mina, but no sound came out; her vocal cords had knotted together painfully. She covered her nose and mouth to stop herself from gagging, breaking out into a cold sweat. All she could do was stare at the poor woman with a knife sticking out of her chest where her heart should be.

There was so much blood that she could barely make out Patrice's once perfectly pressed *Midas* uniform. The cream shell-shaped tiles were painted red, and the grout was varying shades of brown.

A scream shocked Poppy out of her frozen state. Mina had followed her inside.

"Don't look, don't look at her!" Poppy cried, trying to turn her away from the horrible sight.

"Is she—?" Mina stammered, covering her eyes even though she was already facing the wall.

"She's gone," Poppy choked.

Isaiah ran in with his gun drawn.

"Mina, go outside and call security. Then go out into

the hall and wait. Don't touch anything," he instructed. Mina didn't need to be told twice.

"Wh-what do I do?" Poppy stammered, trying not to look at Patrice.

"Just stand there. The scene has been disturbed enough, and you have blood on your feet," Isaiah said calmly. "I don't want you to trek bloody footprints around the room."

Poppy looked down. She hadn't even realised she'd stepped in a small pool of blood. "Oh God, I think I'm going to pass out."

"Just breathe and focus on me. What did you see when you first came in? Did anything look out of place or disturbed? No detail is too small."

Poppy took a deep breath and tried to focus her thoughts. "I don't think so. Mina helped me unpack my toiletries yesterday, and they're still in the same place by the sink where I left them before we went out," she said, trying not to think about the cold, thick slime beneath her feet. "The shower curtain was open when we left. Closed shower curtains always give me the creeps."

"You didn't see the blood before you opened the curtain?"

"No, I only realised what the smell was when I opened it..." She saw for the first time that blood was dripping from the end of the shower curtain. "Please get me out of here."

"I will, I promise, but I need to get this straight. When you opened the curtain it must have come out of the tub and dripped on the floor, but there was no blood on the floor for you to notice when you came in?"

Poppy nodded shakily. "I must have pulled the curtain out. I didn't realise it, and then I froze. I didn't snap out of it until Mina screamed."

"You're in shock. Freezing is a totally normal response," Isaiah said calmly.

"Our butler is dead in the bathtub. There is nothing normal about this!"

"Sorry – this is just a normal Tuesday for me," he answered, examining the bathtub. Her nausea increased the closer he got to the body. He was studying the knife when something sticking out of Patrice's pocket caught her eye.

"Wait, is there something in her pocket?" she said, swallowing her horror. "I think it's an old tape recorder."

Isaiah looked at her as if he was expecting her to have a panic attack, but she met his gaze levelly. She was used to pushing down the tough stuff.

"I'll be right back. Just close your eyes and breathe." Isaiah disappeared and returned a moment later wearing black latex gloves. She wouldn't ask why he had them, but maybe they were part of some bodyguard/detective start-up kit.

Carefully, he removed the object from Patrice's body.

"Why would she be carrying around a tape recorder?" Poppy asked, trying to get a better look.

He stood up and showed her the small device. "Have you seen this before?"

"No, it's definitely not mine."

"Hmm. She might have been using it to record guest conversations. Since they don't allow phones on board, it makes sense that she'd need some other device."

"Do you think she was planting it in the suite?" Poppy asked, worried about who might want to listen to her conversations. "Why was she even in our suite in the first place?"

"She might have come by when you weren't present for

the muster drill." Isaiah shrugged. "She discovered someone planting it and was murdered to conceal what she knew. Or she knew we wouldn't be in our rooms because of the drill, and she was going to plant the recording device herself."

"Or she just records guests to sell secrets or to protect herself from some self-entitled pricks. We shouldn't jump to conclusions that her murder is related to the recorder," Poppy reasoned.

"Why think it's unrelated?" Isaiah frowned.

"Because if someone killed her because she recorded something she shouldn't have, why didn't they take the recorder with them?" Poppy snapped.

"Good detective skills," Isaiah said, hitting the ejection button on the side of the recorder.

"Don't sound so surprised," she said, staring at the empty pocket.

"They didn't take the recorder because they took the tape instead," he said, returning the recorder to Patrice's pocket.

"I'm going to inform the captain and see if we can return to port as soon as possible." He took a picture of Poppy's feet, the shower curtain, and the pool of blood.

"Where did you get the phone?" she gasped.

"Mr Eckells gave it to me so I could reach him at all times. I'm sure he'll want to be apprised of what's happening on his ship," Isaiah said, looking up. "But this is our little secret. Not even Mina can know about the phone. Do you understand?"

Poppy nodded.

"Good. Sit on the lid of the toilet. Try not to touch anything."

He took pictures of the soles of her bloody feet before handing her a towel to clean them, then placing the towel in a disposable bag he found in a drawer. Once most of the blood was off, she felt a little better.

"Stay with Mina in the hall until I come out. Don't talk to anyone but me," he instructed her coolly. "Don't touch anything on the way out."

Poppy nodded and left him alone with the body without looking back.

"Was that really Patrice?" Mina was pacing when Poppy joined her in the hall.

"Yes," Poppy admitted. What was taking security so long?

"Do you think this has anything to do with the plan to kill you?" Mina fretted.

Poppy glanced up and down the hall to ensure no one was listening before pulling her into Mina's room.

"Shh! No, I don't think so." She shook her head, not wanting to believe it.

"You can't know that for sure. What if Patrice was mistaken for you? What if your ex and Duggery hired someone?" Mina said, rubbing her temples. "We couldn't get into your room last night! Oh God, what if she was being murdered right when we were just outside the door?"

"Take a deep breath. There's no way anyone would mistake us. She has dark hair and is far taller than me. You'd have to be blind and drunk to mix us up," Poppy pointed out.

"Okay, fair point. But what are the chances that your manager was planning to kill you, and now you have a dead woman in your bathtub?!"

"You need to calm down before security gets here. This might not have anything to do with me. Patrice had a recording device in her pocket, so I guess she recorded the wrong person saying the wrong thing, and someone followed her to our suite and shut her up."

"Right. I mean, if she was recording high-profile guests, she could've pissed off the wrong person," Mina said, nodding along, starting to level out.

"You didn't see or hear anything last night when you got back?" Poppy asked.

"No. I waited for you both to come back, but then I passed out watching TV. Even so, surely I would've heard someone being murdered, right?" Mina asked, pale and wide-eyed. "God, maybe I could have helped her if I hadn't had the TV on—"

"You can't blame yourself! You had a lot to drink. We also don't know when she was killed. We might have all been out when she came by. Isaiah and I were only next door; we would've heard a struggle or someone calling for help, so you can't put this on yourself," Poppy said, remembering how fast Isaiah had responded when Mina screamed in the bathroom. There was no way he would have ignored someone screaming for help in the middle of the night.

They both looked to the door when they heard voices in the hall.

"When security talks to us, say nothing about what my ex or manager were planning until we know more. Only answer the questions asked, and no more. We do what Isaiah says, and we'll be perfectly safe. It's why we hired him, right?" Poppy whispered quickly.

"Right." Mina nodded.

Poppy took a deep breath and opened the door just as the body was being carted away in a black body bag by men in black uniforms with *Security* written on the backs. They didn't even look up as they passed.

"Where are they taking her?" Poppy asked Isaiah.

"Every ship has a morgue. A lot of people die aboard ships. They'll keep her there until we dock," Isaiah said.

She shivered, not wanting to think about a morgue being only a few floors away. "Do they know why Patrice was here?"

"They checked her recent location when Mina called for help. They're assuming Patrice came by to check on us when you were marked absent during the drill. But they found your smartwatch on her, and they don't know why," Isaiah said. "She had been assigned to this floor for the past three years. There are no issues or marks on her record."

"Do you think she found my watch and was just trying to return it?" Poppy swallowed, fearing this might be her fault. *Mina might be right about the mistaken identity. Maybe someone saw her enter my room and thought it was me.*

"Maybe; we can't know for sure. Security wants to close off the suite, so grab your necessities, but don't go into the bathroom. We'll be moving to new rooms."

Poppy nodded as he gestured for her to go into the room. The smell of blood had taken over the whole suite.

She rubbed her wrist, trying to remember when she had taken off her smartwatch. Drinking had jumbled her memory, and her paranoia kept asking whether she had taken it off or if it had been swiped. Poppy knew she'd had it when she went to her room to change for the pool and said goodnight to Mina – not that she suspected Mina of killing Patrice. Then again, she had never suspected Joshua. Mina had said she was passed out in her room, but how could she confirm that?

Watched by a gruff security guard, she grabbed her large handbag from by the bed, which had all her daily essentials: a purse, makeup wipes, books, and an e-reader.

"Please leave the suitcases, Ms Roe," the guard said when she glanced at them.

"Are you just going to bark orders, or do you want to

introduce yourself?" She didn't like the thought of being without clothes or underwear, but it didn't seem right to cry over clothes when someone had just been murdered ten feet away.

"Head of *Midas* Security, Kenneth Colter, and this is my scene, so you'll do what I say."

"We'll follow your orders; no need for any hostility," Isaiah said soothingly.

"Sorry. It's not every day I pull a woman I've worked with for the past few years out of a bath filled with her blood," Kenneth said, pulling at his black cap.

"Bad day for all of us," Poppy said. "I'm sorry for your loss."

"Thank you, but we have a job to do, so please let's work together," Kenneth said.

"Has the captain been informed of what's happened?" Isaiah asked him as Poppy hovered by the door. She wasn't sure where she was going, but she just wanted to get out of there. She didn't know if they considered her a suspect.

"Yes, and Captain Hamill ordered us to secure the suite. The three of you will be moved to another area of the boat. You'll be brought to your new accommodation once we've asked you a few questions," the security guard said, eying them both like they were guilty.

"I've got everything," Poppy said quietly, not wanting to linger. Everything, except her suitcases. She wished she could bring her clothes, but nothing could leave the crime scene. She would just have to buy what she needed on board. She didn't look forward to seeing her credit card bill when she made it home – or at this rate, *if* she made it home.

Isaiah escorted her out, leaving the security guard to lock the suite. Mina was waiting for them in the hall with a suitcase and bags in her arms. She was allowed to keep her things, because technically her adjoining room wasn't part of the suite. Poppy noted the fear in her eyes and wished she had a better poker face. At least any onlookers shouldn't be able to catch a hint of Poppy's emotions if they looked at her. She had spent years crafting her mask, and it came to her naturally.

Without it, anyone could have seen how terrified she was. For weeks, Poppy had feared being suspected of murder, but she'd never expected it to be for the death of a stranger.

## Chapter 9
# 'She Slipped.'
### Poppy

"Wait here. Captain Hamill will call for you soon," Kenneth instructed before he entered the bridge.

Poppy, Mina and Isaiah obediently waited outside the glass door, through which they could see the crew hard at work on the bridge. As crucial as addressing the murder was, Poppy understood the captain still had a ship to run.

"Do you think we're under suspicion?" Mina whispered.

"No, the captain just wants to hear our statements and figure out how this could have happened," Poppy said, trying to calm her down.

"I suppose we'd have to be pretty stupid to kill someone in our own suite and then leave her in our bathtub with the murder weapon," Mina agreed.

*Let's hope that seems obvious to everyone,* Poppy thought, fidgeting with the tie on her robe, keeping the thought to herself so she wouldn't upset Mina again. She wished she could have put some clothes on before meeting the captain so she could feel less vulnerable.

Isaiah stopped pacing when the door opened.

"Ms Roe, I'm sorry to keep you all waiting. I wish we weren't meeting under these circumstances," said a woman in a crisp white shirt and lapels that signalled her authority, appearing through the door. Poppy accepted her outstretched hand. "I'm Captain Hamill – Octavia Hamill; my head of security was just getting me up to speed. Please follow me to my office."

They did as they were told; Poppy felt the eyes of the crew watching as they entered the bridge.

"This is my first mate, Davide Rossi," Captain Hamill said when they entered the small office. "He's going to be a witness to this conversation. It's part of the procedure – no need to worry. Please take a seat."

Poppy and Mina sat beside the captain's desk, while Isaiah stood behind them by the door. There was barely enough room for all of them.

"I need to hear from you in case we've missed anything. I'm sorry for the shock you've suffered. I can assure you that nothing like this has ever occurred on the *Midas*. Certainly not under my ten years' captaincy," Captain Hamill said, looking at her head of security, who would probably get a stern talking-to later. "I assure you that we're going to try and make this investigation as quick and painless as possible." The captain spoke as though they were talking about their luggage going missing and not the discovery of a dead body.

Despite the assurances, Poppy didn't like how the captain and first mate looked at them. She felt like they were about to be asked to walk the plank. She barely heard Mina and Isaiah introducing themselves over the blood rushing to her ears.

"We'll tell you everything we know, but I want to get

home. How long will it be before we get back to the port?" she asked, wanting to cut to the chase.

Captain Hamill looked at Davide as though Poppy wasn't speaking English. "I'm afraid that's impossible. We can't change our course and return to Dublin. There are protocols to follow," she said sternly.

"Someone's been killed. We can't just continue as though nothing has happened," Isaiah argued.

"Forgive my callousness, but turning back won't make a difference," Captain Hamill said.

"It will if a murderer is on board," Isaiah argued.

"If Patrice was killed, then my security team will catch them," Captain Hamill said with utter confidence. "However, turning back against the wind would only increase our time at sea. We'll only make port again for the day trip in Italy before continuing to Greece. Mr Eckells has been informed about the situation, and he has every faith that this situation can be resolved quietly and discreetly. Once we reach our destination, we will inform the authorities."

"If? What do you mean, *if* she was killed? She was stabbed in the chest. If you had seen what was done to her, you wouldn't be saying that!"

"I think you've been misinformed, Ms Roe. I was informed by the chief medical officer that Patrice was killed by blunt-force trauma to the back of her head. Regrettably, this could all be a tragic accident – a slip and fall."

"A slip and fall? I saw the knife!" Poppy exclaimed, noticing Mina's leg bouncing. Clearly, Poppy wasn't the only one feeling anxious, though her anxiety was quickly shifting to irritation.

"What happened was a tragedy. My security team will investigate, and I promise you that the safety of guests and staff is my top priority. But we can't rush to any conclusions that might cause a panic," Captain Hamill said calmly.

"In other words, you want us to shove what happened under the carpet so the other guests don't freak out?" Poppy demanded. "We're trapped with a potential killer on board and you want us to pretend it was an accident!"

Captain Hamill sighed.

"I'm sure the captain will perform a thorough investigation," Isaiah interrupted, resting a hand on Poppy's shoulder. She took the gesture as a hint to remain quiet. "What about preserving the evidence and the scene in the meantime?"

Poppy was surprised he didn't argue with the captain's plans, but maybe he would toe the line because this was what Mr Eckells wanted. Besides, he had about as much authority here as she did. His badge didn't do too much on international waters.

"Our medical staff will make sure that the body is preserved, and the Empress suite will be sealed off until an investigation can be carried out." Captain Hamill smiled at Isaiah.

"Have any other slips and falls occurred on the *Midas* since we left port?"

Poppy didn't know how they could ignore the knife sticking out of Patrice's chest. No one could look at the body and think it had been an accident. She didn't want to be part of a cover-up that would let a killer go free. *Though you were quite happy to cover up your own murder.* She shoved the thought down.

"No, Patrice's accident is a first. We all want to get to the bottom of this, but I'm sure you can understand how a murder could cause panic onboard. I've nearly two thousand souls aboard. A mass panic is a danger to my staff, the ship and our guests. As the captain of this vessel, I'm telling you that this was a slip and fall until we reach our final destination." Captain Hamill looked at the three of them sternly. "Do you understand me?"

They all nodded in agreement.

Captain Hamill took a deep breath, and the first mate returned to his duties as though this situation was no big deal. Poppy got the gut-wrenching feeling that 'accidents' were a standard protocol for any onboard incidents.

"I understand your position, but what if there's another… accident?" she asked. "Patrice's fall resulted in several knife wounds. I'm sure the medical officer would agree that even if she fell during the attack and hit the back of her head, with that amount of blood loss, you can't rule out exsanguination."

"Ms Roe, I appreciate your determination to investigate what happened to Patrice. She was one of my crew, and she will be dearly missed. However, if she was murdered, as you insist, then the three of you would be my key suspects. I would be forced to hold you in the brig until we docked at the end of our journey. I don't want to, but I'd have to – for the security of everyone on board."

The threat to lock them up didn't fall on deaf ears.

"That won't be necessary. We'll follow your orders," Isaiah assured her, and Mina nodded.

"Ms Roe?" Captain Hamill prompted, resting her elbows on the desk.

Frustration boiled under Poppy's skin, but Isaiah's hold on her shoulder warned her not to argue. His job was to protect her, and she understood that the captain was trying to protect everyone else on board.

"Sorry for being so rude. It must be the shock from the accident," she said, softening her tone.

"There's no need to apologise; I'm just relieved we're all on the same page. We've arranged new rooms for you on the third floor. The rooms are smaller, but closer to our security room," Captain Hamill informed them.

"Thank you. The rooms don't matter so long as we're safe and together," Poppy said, not going to complain about space when she had seen a dead body only a few hours ago. Also, she'd spent the last year on tour buses, so she would feel right at home. It was good to know she could get to Isaiah and Mina faster if something went wrong.

"Before you go and get settled, I need to confirm the whereabouts of all three of you last night to build a timeline of the incident," Captain Hamill said; clearly, she was more suspicious than she had let on. Would she investigate secretly, or would their statements be used against them later if the 'slip and fall' theory didn't hold?

"And to rule us out as suspects?" Isaiah added.

"Nothing like a few cocktails before slaughtering a maid and then calling security on ourselves." Poppy pressed her lips together; she hadn't meant for the comment to slip out.

"There's no need for that, Ms Roe. Please answer my questions so we can get through this as painlessly as possible," Captain Hamill said.

"You can check everything on our watches, the cameras—" Poppy reached for her wrist. "Right! My watch – I lost it in the bar last night. I was drinking, and I must have taken it off. Security said Patrice had it last night when she *fell*. You might be able to figure out her movements before the accident if you can trace it." She wanted to know if she had lost it or if it had been nicked so that Patrice could get into her room when she wasn't there.

"I'll call the security office. They should be able to tell us where it is and when it was last used." The captain picked up the phone on her desk and dialled. "I need a trace on a wristband. Empress suite. Poppy Roe."

There was a pause.

"When was the last time you remember having it?" Captain Hamill asked Poppy.

"I used it to buy drinks at the Pearl Bar at around eleven, but then I don't think I used it again," Poppy said.

"We can confirm you purchased a bottle of Cristal," the captain informed them.

"I went back to my room to change into my swimsuit at about midnight," Poppy said, "but I can't remember if the door was open. Or if I used my watch."

"You didn't. I just remembered I used mine to let you in to change, and I went to bed," Mina said, filling in the blanks. "But when I tried to get into your room later during the drill, it wouldn't let me."

The captain repeated the information on the phone.

"We can confirm that Mina's watch was used to open the door at midnight. There's no activity on Ms Roe's watch until about 3:30am." Captain Hamill finished. "It went offline roughly thirty minutes after entering the room."

"Poppy wasn't in her room at that time. When the alarm sounded, Mina and I checked her door, but she wasn't inside," Isaiah said.

Poppy jumped in, not liking being talked about as if she weren't there. "I went to the pool in the tranquillity spa for some peace. You can check; I'm sure they have cameras."

Another dramatic pause as the captain repeated her alibi.

"Our cameras have confirmed her whereabouts when she entered the spa," Captain Hamill said at last. "You were also marked absent on the muster drill."

Poppy's shoulders sagged, feeling vindicated. "The spa staff didn't want me to go, since I was drunk. They thought it was safer if I stayed with them."

"I found her just after four," Isaiah added, building the timeline.

"Are you saying there was a body in the bathtub when we went to check on her during the drill?" Mina went a warm shade of green.

"Most likely. The culprit could've been in there with her," Isaiah said.

"I think I'm going to be sick," Mina said, and Poppy leaned away just in case. She had already stepped in blood today. Being thrown up on was too much.

Captain Hamill handed Mina a bin from beneath her desk. "Where were you while they were at the spa?"

"Are you serious?" Mina gasped. "I was looking for Poppy! I checked the casino, theatre, and upper decks, and figured Isaiah would've found her. I was seasick and hungover, so I went back to bed."

"Did Patrice use her own wristband to enter the suite?" Isaiah asked after the captain had repeated Mina's alibi.

"We already checked. Fifteen minutes after Poppy's was used, Patrice's watch was used to enter the room. Then both watches were disconnected."

Isaiah sighed. "Then Patrice might have interrupted someone—wrong place, wrong time."

Poppy's blood ran cold. Was Mina right? Had someone been waiting for her to return and just killed the first person to come through the door?

"What was Patrice doing there at that time anyway?" she asked. "The alarms hadn't sounded yet, and if my watch was used to enter before she arrived, she wasn't stopping by to return it. She was in my suite *before* the drill, so she wasn't checking on me because I was absent."

"She shouldn't have been on duty, and there are no outgoing calls from your suite, so no one called her to come by," Captain Hamill agreed. She returned to the phone. "Mina's alibi is clear. We've confirmed you searched the top decks and returned to your room."

Mina slumped in her chair, clearly relieved.

"You're free to go, since none of you were involved in the accident. I hope you'll remember what we discussed and keep this matter to yourselves."

"You have our word," Isaiah said. Poppy and Mina followed his lead. As much as Poppy hated the cover-up, being locked up in ship jail with a killer on the loose didn't sound all that tempting. At least she could trust Mina and Isaiah. That only left a few thousand other people to worry about.

The first mate, Davide, entered the office with a tight grimace and rattled off something in Italian to the captain. He left Poppy, Isaiah, and Mina to observe awkwardly until another staff member with three new wristbands came in behind him.

"This is Elma Heinsberg. She'll be filling in for Patrice for the remainder of our voyage," Captain Hamill said as Elma greeted them with a warm smile.

"I look forward to working with you," Elma said with a flashy smile, clearly delighted with her promotion. Poppy guessed she wasn't aware of what had happened to her predecessor. "We hope you'll be satisfied with your new accommodation, and I'm sorry the Empress Suite wasn't to your liking." She handed them their new wristbands.

"Thank you, Elma. Could you give us a moment? We're just wrapping up," Captain Hamill said.

Elma left, quick to oblige.

"To err on the side of caution, I suggest you don't tell another guest where you're staying and don't wander about the ship alone. We don't want any more accidents," Captain Hamill told them as they put on their new wristbands.

"That's it? We carry on as normal?" Mina asked hesitantly, as if reading Poppy's mind.

"There's nothing for you to worry about. Other than Elma and me, no one knows where you're staying. We will also keep it out of our database. Your new suite has fortified doors and deadbolts; we usually reserve it for presidents. Given the situation, we're making an exception for you and your staff. All three rooms are connected, so should you need help, you're close to your security. There's a panic button behind each mirror and a direct line to the security desk and the bridge, but please only use those in case of an emergency."

"Thank you for making our safety a priority," Poppy said. Even though they were part of a cover-up, and she would have much preferred to return home, she felt a little more at ease with the extra precautions.

"No need to thank me. It's my job to keep my guests comfortable, and we haven't done a great job of that so far," Captain Hamill said. "Elma will see that the rest of your journey will go smoothly. Security has brought your belongings to your new suite. In a few hours, it'll be as though nothing happened."

Her tone wasn't reassuring; she was telling them to keep their noses out of ship business. Poppy wanted to shake her head. Time might pass, but she would never forget the smell, the sight of the knife piercing that poor woman's heart, or Mina's scream. She promised herself that if another body dropped, she wouldn't sit back and wait to be next like a fish in a barrel.

Isaiah thanked the captain for her help before Elma

escorted them off the bridge. Poppy fiddled with her new watch, vowing not to let it disappear again.

"I wish you'd asked her to update us on the investigation. How will you protect us if we're kept in the dark?" she asked Isaiah as the lift dropped them off on the dining level. She doubted a detective would be able to sit back and do nothing while a body ripened below.

"Because if I had insisted, we might have been confined to our rooms as suspects. We're key suspects and witnesses, so being allowed the freedom to move about freely is not to be taken for granted," Isaiah hissed. "She had every right to lock us up until we reached Greece."

"Why do you think she didn't?" Poppy asked as they crossed the glass bridge to the private lifts. Only staff had access to the administration floor. Elma used a key to activate the lift.

Isaiah shrugged. "Because our alibis checked out, and because of who you are. If you suddenly disappeared, the guests would whisper, and the captain doesn't want a panic."

Elma was prattling on with only Mina listening to her. "Your new suite is now on the top floor. Sadly, you don't have a below-the-sea view. Still, you have a balcony that offers exquisite views of the fireworks show and the sunset," she enthused.

Poppy nodded as though she'd been paying attention. "I'm sure we can find our own way, and we should really get something to eat. I know the captain wanted you to aid us with the remainder of the trip, but we really won't be needing such personal service," she said to the woman, wanting to talk with the others freely. She also didn't want another crew member to end up dead in her bathtub; dismissing her was for Elma's own benefit.

Elma's disheartened gaze quickly snapped back to the perfect smile. "Of course; your wish is my command. I won't keep you any longer." She hit the button for C Deck. "It's been a long day for all of you. Given that it's nearly four o'clock, you should be able to get a table without much of a wait. When you're ready to return to your suite, hit A1, and your wristwatch will lead you the rest of the way."

"Thank you," Mina said.

"It's my pleasure, and please call for me at any time," Elma said, getting out at the next level to let other guests on. Poppy eyed them, with their swimsuits and lazy smiles, envious of how they were unaware of the horror that had occurred only a few levels beneath them.

"Good thinking about the food; I'm starving," Isaiah said, cutting the tension in the lift.

"I just said that to get rid of her. How can you even think of food?" she asked.

"We haven't eaten since last night." Isaiah leaned in so the other guests couldn't hear. "We've all had a shock, and none of us are happy about the situation we are in now, so I suggest we get some food into ourselves and take a breather."

"I really just want to get to the room and sleep, but I suppose some food wouldn't hurt," Poppy said, crossing her arms.

One of them, a woman with long jet-black hair and perfectly tanned skin, was sneaking glances at Isaiah over her shoulder and giggling with her friend. Apparently a murderer wasn't the only thing Poppy had to worry about; she side-eyed Isaiah, who seemed oblivious or very good at pretending not to notice the ogling woman.

"The diner I ordered from this morning before—" Mina cut herself off. "Um, it serves an all-day breakfast buffet," she finished, her stomach rumbling.

The doors opened, and the smell of delicious baked goods greeted them.

"Never too late for breakfast." Isaiah smiled, letting Mina and Poppy off first. They strolled past all the international cuisines until Mina pointed out the diner. The smell of bacon and pancakes came in waves.

"It does smell good," Poppy said, reading the menu on the wooden stand outside the revolving gold door.

"Greasy food is the best cure for shock and your hangover," Isaiah said over her shoulder. She wanted to argue, but her growling stomach sided with him.

"We can't solve all the world's problems in a day, and we need to act normal if we don't want to end up locked up by Captain Hamill." Mina took her arm.

Giving in, Poppy followed them inside.

## Chapter 10
# Waves of Suspicion
### Poppy

After a hearty meal at the diner, they crashed early in their new suite, exhausted from the shock of the murder. Poppy didn't expect to sleep so well, but the adrenaline had worn off.

Mina woke her for breakfast, and she realised they had slept for over twelve hours. It was the reset they'd all clearly needed.

At their assigned table in the breakfast room, a waiter came by to take their order, but they decided to go for the all-you-can-eat breakfast buffet. The complimentary mimosa caught Poppy's eye, but the thought of champagne made her stomach flip, so she chose water instead.

"You need to eat something; it might help you feel better," she said as Mina happily accepted the extra glass in spite of her seasickness.

"Maybe if I drink, I won't notice the rocking as much," Mina replied, looking a little green.

"Let me make you a plate," Poppy offered. "Some carbs might give you some energy, if nothing else."

"I should be the one helping you," Mina said, starting

to rise. "It's my job."

"Forget about that. It's just breakfast." Poppy pulled down her pink cover-up, which had stuck to the back of her thighs because of the leather seats. She couldn't wait to get outside and enjoy some time in the sun. Even though they were in a new room, the bathroom was identical, so the less time she spent there, the better.

Isaiah was already exploring the endless options. Poppy lingered by the pancake and waffle station, piling some onto a plate for herself and Mina along with sweet and savoury sauces and a bowl of fruit.

"I've never seen a breakfast buffet with caviar and gold leaf-topped salmon parfaits before," Isaiah said from behind her, catching the plate before Poppy dropped it.

"Nice reflexes," she replied, taking it back from him. "I've never been so jumpy, and I didn't hear you coming." With her wedge flip-flops on the marble floor, everyone could hear her approach.

"Don't mention it, but you can thank me by explaining what aspic is. I know I don't want liver as my first meal of the day," Isaiah said with a smile. She could tell he was trying to lighten the mood.

"It's like jelly with meat inside; it's French," Poppy said, never having been a fan.

He shuddered. "I think I'll avoid that section."

His discomfort made her smile, but she couldn't let him see that she was warming to him.

"This should make you feel right at home," she said, picking up some extra crispy bacon with gold tongs. She dropped it on his plate, followed by a glazed doughnut.

"Ms Roe, I'm starting to feel that I've done something to offend you," Isaiah said, following close behind her. His cologne, with a light touch of cedar and sandalwood, smelled good.

"It's not that you've offended me, Mr Rivers. I hadn't known you for more than forty-eight hours, and a body has dropped. Forgive me for not trusting you implicitly." She didn't like it when he called her Ms Roe.

"I could say the same about you – or is it that you're embarrassed that I rebuffed your advances while you were drunk?"

She flushed, remembering her embarrassing attempt to kiss him before she'd run to the bathroom. "Don't think too highly of yourself. That was a test. I'm never wrong about people; I sense you want something from me. If it's not my body, you're here for some other purpose, and I'll find out what it is. No detective drops everything to board a ship as a bodyguard. Everyone wants something, and I know you aren't any different," she told him.

"If I continue to pass your tests, then I'm sure you'll start to trust me," Isaiah said, skipping the sushi section. Poppy made a mental note to come back at lunchtime. The octopus ice sculpture was a little off-putting first thing in the morning.

"If protecting me was your top priority, why not insist the captain turn the ship around? Why go along with the cover-up? You're a detective. Surely ignoring justice for the victim should be killing you."

Isaiah sighed, walking away. "This isn't the time or place to discuss this."

"This is the perfect time and place. It's not like we can go anywhere else for the next fortnight." She followed him. "If you don't tell me why you're so happy to overlook the murder, I might have to tell the captain that you can't be trusted. I could tell her that I woke up and you were gone. Then I can't give you an alibi for the other night, and you'll spend the rest of our voyage in the brig."

That got his attention. Isaiah glared at her. "You

wouldn't. You'd leave yourself and Mina unprotected to soothe your curiosity?"

"It's not curiosity; it's self-preservation."

He clenched his jaw, and she could hear him thinking it through.

"You don't want to try me!" She refused to be the first to break eye contact.

"Would you like a custom omelette?" a chef asked, interrupting them.

"No," they snapped in unison. The startled chef, along with the other guests in the queue, stared at them.

"Come with me!" Isaiah took her plate.

"Where are you going?" Poppy trailed after him. He put their plates down on a table filled with other guests, who stared at them in confusion. "Excuse us," said Poppy over her shoulder as he took her wrist and led her out of the breakfast room and into the kitchen.

There was no way they were supposed to be back here, but she wouldn't argue with him when he was on the verge of cracking. *I knew there had to be some secret motive beneath his calm exterior.*

"We need somewhere to talk privately," Isaiah barked at the busy kitchen, filled with wait staff and cooks.

"Take the fridge," the kitchen porter said, pointing away from the chaos of the cooks preparing a constant carousel of fresh food. Isaiah pulled her in that direction. Poppy was surprised they hadn't been told to leave, but this wasn't the type of ship to refuse a guest's request.

"What are we doing in here?" she asked, looking at all the vegetables surrounding them and shaking his hand from her wrist, not wanting a bruise. She caught a flash of guilt in his eyes as she rubbed the tender skin.

"You wanted us to have a frank and honest discussion.

No one can hear us here, and it's obvious we won't be able to enjoy our meal until you learn to be civil."

"I'm *being* civil," Poppy countered. "I want to know what you want and why you came on board. It's a simple request."

"I'm the only one with secrets, right? You aren't hiding anything?" He stepped closer to her, and she swallowed. He didn't know about her previous plans for boarding the *Midas*.

He shook his head, and his expression made her feel as though he was looking into her soul and reading her darkest thoughts.

"Were you shocked to find a body in the tub, or was it Patrice that surprised you? Were you expecting to find someone else?" he asked calmly.

Poppy suddenly wished she hadn't antagonised him. "I don't have to listen to this. You're just trying to deflect from your own motives." She pushed past him to the fridge door.

"My motives are solely a consequence of your own actions. I know what you were planning with Mina, and I took the job to see if you could really commit murder."

She stopped at the door, a cold sweat breaking out.

"If you don't know what I'm talking about, walk out."

She weighed her options: walk out and still be left in the dark about whether he was on her side, or confess and see what he would admit.

"It's not murder if it's self-defence, and Joshua never boarded the ship, so I had no way or reason to act against him." She let go of the door handle, fear creeping up her spine. "Did my manager hire you to protect Joshua? To carry out their plot if Joshua couldn't take care of me himself?" She doubted if anyone would hear her if she screamed. She backed away from him, only to hit a shelf full of produce. Carrots cascaded down around her. She was sure the chef would be pissed to have guests making a mess in their fridge.

Isaiah's eyes widened, and he held his hands up defensively. "No! You've been thinking I might've been hired to hurt you? Look, I was visiting Eckells at Heaven's Heart, the club Mina works at. I overheard her talking to her boss about your predicament with Joshua. Eckells hired me to ensure you and Mina are safe, and not cause trouble that'll blow back on the *Midas*."

Poppy let his words sink in. "You knew I was planning on killing my boyfriend, and instead of arresting me, you decided to come on board? Forgive me for thinking that those two things seem to contradict themselves."

"No body, no crime for me to investigate," Isaiah said. "Still, I wanted to know what could motivate the woman who seemingly has everything to kill, and I wanted to stop you before you did. Then I heard you and Mina talking about his plans to kill *you*, how he was working with your ex-manager."

Poppy's breathing levelled out as he confirmed he wasn't a threat. "But you said you wanted to stop me, not him. What if Joshua had come on board? Would you have protected him or me?" she asked, stepping closer, studying him.

"Would you have killed Joshua if he didn't try to harm you first?" Isaiah asked, closing the gap between them. She stared at his chest, and he tipped her chin up to face him.

"No, I'd never hurt anyone who didn't deserve it," she said firmly. "But given how you've spied on me, how do I really know you weren't hired to harm me? And you aren't just telling me all this so I let my guard down?"

"Because if I wanted to harm you, I could've easily drowned you in the spa pool. Or you might've fallen down any one of the dozens of staircases or fallen overboard—" He cut himself off with a shrug.

Poppy froze when he mentioned how her aunt had died. Had he looked into the case after taking the job?

"There are a million ways to ensure you'd never be found. But I assure you that I intend to keep you alive and safe," Isaiah finished.

"Telling me all the ways you could kill me is supposed to make me trust you? You could have killed Patrice to keep me closer."

"Telling you all the ways I could kill you should prove to you that I wouldn't have to kill anyone to get to you. Why keep you close and draw out the chase when I could just kill you and enjoy the rest of my holiday?" he said smugly.

"Fair point."

"I vowed to protect you, and I will." His sincerity cut through her suspicions.

Her breath puffed between them, visible in the cold air, and he pulled her close, keeping her warm. It seemed he meant what he said, even if it meant protecting her from the cold. Resting her hands on his chest, she didn't pull away.

"You're afraid – I can see it even as you try to hide it – but I swear you have nothing to fear from me," he said. "I agreed to go along with the captain's cover-up because being locked up in ship jail would trap us altogether, which wouldn't be ideal if there's someone out for your blood. We need to play along and let the captain believe we're following the rules, but we must keep our guard up. I don't think Patrice will be the last body to drop, because she wasn't the first."

"Wh-what are you talking about?" Poppy stammered, stepping out of his grasp.

"This isn't the first dead maid connected to you." Isaiah reached out to hold her hips, as if he didn't want her to escape.

Poppy frowned. "Another maid? I don't know what you're talking about."

"A housekeeper in the Claren hotel was killed. She was cleaning up your suite after you checked out, but she was found dead – ate so much that her heart gave out," Isaiah told her. "We believe she was force-fed."

Poppy felt the blood drain from her face. "She ate so much she died in my suite? Why didn't I hear anything about this?" she asked, feeling sick. "I'm sure my manager would've told me, or I'd have noticed the crime scene."

"You had checked out earlier that morning, and the hotel had no reason to inform you." Isaiah watched her reactions with narrowed eyes.

"The Claren Hotel? I'm trying to remember. I stayed in so many hotels during the tour…" Poppy's eyes widened, and her hands went to her mouth. "Oh God, I wasn't meant to check out until the following morning, but I decided not to stay the extra night before moving on to the next venue so I could get some sightseeing done in the next city. Do you mean… Am I the real target, but Patrice and the other maid were just in the wrong place at the wrong time? Why not come after me?"

"Maybe they saw the culprit's face, and the killer didn't want to leave any witnesses. Maybe the killer wanted to send a message that they could get to you, so they did to the housekeeper what they were planning to do to you. They aren't a professional, if they were they wouldn't have deviated from their target."

"Great, so not a professional hitman. That makes me feel much better," Poppy huffed.

"Since I've laid my cards on the table, can you start to trust me?" he asked, staring down at her.

He had given up more information than she'd expected. She wanted to know what else he knew, and keeping him at arm's length would help keep her alive.

"Can you trust *me*?" she asked softly.

"You weren't planning on killing anyone else on board?"

"Only if it's in self-defence," she teased.

"Then from now on, we agree to work together to make sure none of us gets hurt," he said.

"Deal."

"Good. For starters, I think you should stay in my room for the rest of the trip. I don't like how easily the killer could get into your suite," Isaiah said. "I don't want to give them another chance in case they have access to the ship's security."

"I can stay with Mina," Poppy suggested.

"Mina isn't the target, and the killer could hurt her to get to you. I promised Eckells nothing would happen to her, and I'd like to keep my head attached to my body."

Poppy wondered if Mina was in a relationship with her boss. Not that it was any of her business, but it was odd she hadn't mentioned it when they talked about Eckells before.

"Our rooms are connected anyway. It's not like it would be hard for you to get to me," she argued.

"We've already had issues with the doors being locked once. With the reinforced adjoining doors in the presidential suite, I'm not risking it," Isaiah said.

"Fine," she conceded, afraid he would cuff her to the bed if she refused when the time came.

"All this talk of murder doesn't seem to faze you all that much. You recover quickly for someone who's being hunted by a killer and has seen dead bodies," Isaiah said, eying her poker face.

"I've worked in the entertainment industry my whole life, and living with my aunt wasn't easy. It'll take more than a body and a killer to shock me," she countered. "Patrice wasn't even my first dead body."

Isaiah was silent.

"My aunt," she clarified. "I'm not some cold-hearted, self-absorbed bitch. She died, the maid and Patrice died, and that's tragic, but my getting upset won't do anything to change the facts. As much as I appreciate your care for my emotional and physical well-being, I'm not going to break—"

"Why did a waiter tell me that the rest of my dining party is in here?" Mina opened the door to the fridge, cutting Poppy off.

"We were having a private discussion, and it was rather loud out there," Poppy said with a forced smile.

"So you went to the fridge in the kitchen?" Mina asked, raising her eyebrows.

"We needed privacy," Isaiah explained, like it was the most normal thing in the world.

Mina didn't look like she believed them. "If you guys are going to hook up, could you at least do it where food isn't being stored or prepared? It's gross."

"We weren't doing anything like that," Poppy snapped, walking out. She glanced back at Isaiah, wondering if it was the cold or Mina's accusation that had made him so red. She enjoyed seeing him flush.

"Can we please enjoy our breakfast now, if you're both finished? Your plates were sent over from the table where you left them. It was embarrassing!"

A few staff members eyed Isaiah and Poppy as they left the kitchen, clearly having assumed the same as Mina. A fridge wouldn't have been her first choice, but she supposed being cold would be a good reason to keep him close.

"While you were gone, you got an invitation to the opening night of the opera in a couple of days! The captain's exclusive guest list only – and I thought the *Midas* couldn't get any more exclusive. I accepted for both of you, since you were busy flirting in the fridge." Mina wasn't letting them off easy.

Poppy hadn't realised they had been gone for so long; a lot of guests had already left the breakfast room. She nudged Mina as they reclaimed their seats. "We weren't flirting."

"I've never been to an opera, but I'm not sure it's for me. Why don't you take my invitation?" Isaiah said to Mina, but she shook her head.

"Invitations aren't transferable – says so here." She rolled her eyes. "You two better learn to play nice in front of the captain so she doesn't chuck us in the brig."

"You make a great point," Poppy said, looking at Isaiah. "We don't want her to think we have anything to hide by not attending."

"Since you insist, it's a date," Isaiah said, winking.

Poppy rolled her eyes as he played up to Mina's suspicions to wind her up. She doubted he would have let her attend alone anyway, and she thought it was kind of him to offer his ticket to Mina. They tucked into their food, and he filled her glass with plain orange juice as she ignored the mimosa.

She suspected she might have misjudged him. Maybe he really did have her best intentions at heart.

## Chapter 11
# Mani-Curious
### Isaiah

For the past couple of days, all three of them had played their roles perfectly, becoming the perfect guests. The security guards stationed at every corner had stopped paying them such close attention. Isaiah hoped the captain would tell the security to back off, since they had proved they could follow the rules.

The time had allowed him to learn more about his client. For one, Poppy wasn't good at bowling and didn't like losing. Her pout at the bowling alley last night as all her balls landed in the gutters had made it clear she was unfamiliar with defeat. But her determination to improve, to not let a game beat her, was inspiring. She and Mina had played until 3am, not giving up until Poppy finally scored her first strike. Their laughter had been contagious, making him forget why he was there in the first place.

They'd needed this dose of normality. Mina didn't seem as on edge, even deciding to go to the pool alone this afternoon. Until now, she'd clung to Poppy's side, making Isaiah wish Poppy had some of her self-preservation instincts.

He was currently sitting beside Poppy in the comfort of the nail boutique. She was reclining in a white leather lounge chair, her eyes closed in blissful relaxation. Isaiah, on the other hand, was bored and restless. The manicurist had left them in peace for a moment while their hands were moisturising in heated gloves.

"Don't you think you're putting on a bit too much of a show with this whole act?" he asked, scrunching his nose at the overpowering aroma of the salon. The potent mixture of floral fragrances and chemical scents lingered in the air, dulling his senses.

"If I spend any more time in the pool, I'll turn into a prune," Poppy said, wriggling her fingers in the gloves. "We've already been to the cinema twice and the bowling alley. I don't want to hang out inside bars or casinos because the other guests want to talk to me, and I'll lose my mind if we go back to the suite."

The manicurist reappeared.

"Have you picked a shade, Ms Roe?" she asked Poppy, removing the gloves from her hands.

"I think 'Summer Fling' is the perfect shade of red," she replied, matching the colour to her sundress.

"Excellent choice!" The manicurist smiled as she filed Poppy's nails.

Isaiah tried to settle into the lounge chair beside her, his hands submerged in a glass bowl filled with slices of lemon and cucumber. Despite the comfortable chair, his back was killing him from sleeping on the couch. He felt like a fish out of water in this environment. All the women in the surrounding chairs were staring at him like fresh meat.

"Are you comfortable, sir? Can I get you a coffee or herbal tea?" the manicurist asked him as he fidgeted.

"I'm fine, thank you," he responded, not wanting to be rude.

"Ignore him. He isn't used to such pampering," Poppy said, not even trying to hide her amusement.

"Don't get too comfortable. I might start thinking you're doing this to annoy me," Isaiah muttered, resigned to his fate.

"I'm simply making sure we're ready for the opera tomorrow. I thought you could use some relaxation. Next time, I'll send you for a massage instead."

"Nice try, but I wouldn't leave you for so long."

"Maybe a couple's one, then," she said, delighted. He'd noticed that flirting with him brought her the most amusement.

"Absolutely not. I'm on duty, and being naked face-down isn't exactly the best position to be in when faced with a threat."

"Do you ever not think about work?"

"No."

"Is your masculinity being threatened?" Poppy teased, side-eyeing him while the manicurist pretended not to listen.

"I'm very secure in my masculinity, thank you," he said, annoyed and amused, "but I don't want to have to reach for my gun with my hands covered in lotion."

Poppy's laughter caught him off guard. It was the best noise he'd heard since they'd got on board, though he wished it wasn't at his expense.

"You could've come here with Mina, and I could've waited outside," he pointed out.

"She wanted to go to the pool, and that's progress for her. Also, she found out a Formula One driver, Francis something, that she likes is on board, and I can't blame her for not wanting to pass up on that opportunity," Poppy said.

Isaiah snorted. He doubted Levi would be happy about Mina flirting with another man aboard his ship. Still, Isaiah wouldn't touch that situation with a twenty-foot pole. He was in charge of keeping her alive, not keeping her away from men.

"You look irritated. Is there something going on between you and Mina?" Poppy cut through Isaiah's thoughts, her tone carrying a hint of suspicion.

Isaiah shook his head. "Are you jealous?"

"No!" She snapped, not meeting his eye. "But it would explain why you were worried about her. Feel free to leave and go check on her."

"There's nothing between Mina and me. Eckells wanted me to look out for both of you; I told you that already," he stated firmly.

"Can I ask how you know Mina's boss? Are you a frequent visitor of the Heaven's Heart club?"

"The club scene isn't for me. I helped Eckells with a case, and we became friends." Isaiah didn't expand; Levi wouldn't like him talking about their past.

"So you helped him get out of trouble? Make something disappear?" Poppy asked.

He tried not to be offended by her assumption. "No, I'm not that type of detective. Someone he cared about deeply was attacked, and I helped him find out who." He kept his voice low; everyone on the ship worked for Levi. "I'm not on his payroll, if that's what you think. We both stay on our sides of the law."

"Isn't he paying you to help me?" She smiled.

"You're the exception, Princess."

"I feel so special."

"You ask a lot of questions. Are you still questioning

my trustworthiness?" he asked, noting that she flushed a little at the nickname, but didn't comment on it. She was known as the Princess of Pop, after all.

"Sue me for trying to get to know the man who's supposed to protect me," Poppy huffed.

"Poppy! Is that you?"

A woman in a pink head towel and white robe stood over them. Her ageing skin was covered in thick clay that Isaiah thought couldn't possibly be comfortable and was starting to crack as she smiled at Poppy.

The manicurist excused herself politely to let them talk. Isaiah stayed put. If Poppy wanted him to go, she would ask.

"Calliope, how lovely to see you. I didn't know you were a guest here." Poppy smiled at the woman, but Isaiah noticed it failed to reach her eyes. "Thank you for the white lilies you sent to the house. I was disappointed that you couldn't make the funeral."

"I don't blame you for keeping to yourself. It breaks my heart to think of all you've gone through recently." Calliope clutched her chest dramatically. "I hope you'll understand that I couldn't leave Monaco. We had spent weeks trying to get this chef on our yacht, and your aunt wouldn't have blamed me for embracing life. She always knew how to have a good time. We had a toast in her honour, and I saw the livestream; she would have loved seeing you in her Chanel. To think I even invited her to Monaco—but she refused because she wanted to be there for your last show!"

"I didn't know about that. She truly loves Monaco. If she'd been with you, she might still be alive," Poppy said, dipping her head low.

Isaiah didn't want the woman upsetting Poppy. He'd been so worried about how she was dealing with a potential killer that he'd forgotten about the grief she had so recently suffered. Still, it wasn't his place to intervene.

"Hush, don't think such things," Calliope said, resting a hand on Poppy's arm. "Martha was utterly devoted to you, and we can't change what happened; what happened was no one's fault. She has been in my prayers, as have you."

"Thank you. She would be comforted to know that," Poppy said. Her leg had started bouncing under the table; something about this woman had irritated her. However, anyone watching would never know from her tone or expression. Isaiah admired her masking skills.

"Martha and I were such kindred spirits back in the day. How many hours did we spend on sets together when we were only your age? I suppose our time has passed, and the industry belongs to the young. I can't help but feel she was taken from us too soon."

"My aunt would hate to hear you say so; she admired your talent. You should have seen how she reacted when you were nominated for an Academy Award last year. Her time may be over, but she would want you to embrace every opportunity," Poppy said, taking Calliope's hand before releasing it just as quickly.

Calliope's smile tightened at the mention of the award. Isaiah couldn't help but feel there was more to the story.

"I can only hope she's watching over us. I'm sure she would be proud to hear you'll soon be following in her footsteps. Some little birds have told me you'll be making your acting debut this year?"

"Just some small projects."

Calliope winked. "Right – best to keep your cards close to your chest. You never know when someone is listening. Especially on the *Midas*; the walls have ears."

"Oh, I have nothing to hide. It's just a small indie film

I've invested in – when there's more to say, I'll be happy to. Smaller projects are the right fit for me. I could never be able to live up to either of your talents," Poppy said, charm dripping from every word.

"Stop! You'll make me blush." Calliope swatted at Poppy playfully before turning her attention to Isaiah, as though she had only noticed his presence. "Forgive me for being so rude. Who is your dashing friend?" She offered him her hand. "The ladies and I were wondering who was keeping you company."

"This is Isaiah Rivers, my bodyguard," Poppy said politely.

"You bring your bodyguard to get manicures with you? I suppose you can never be too careful." Calliope smirked. "We thought you might've replaced Joshua with a real man. Your aunt never thought he was good enough for you, and you should have listened to your elders. We've been around long enough to know a scoundrel when we see one – and he caused such a scene at the dock before we departed. If I had been there, I would have given him a good slap. Don't let the humiliation get you down; hardly anyone is talking about it." Her condescension was thicker than the smell of acetone in the air.

"Better to end it than let it drag out. I'm sure they'll find something new to gossip about. How is your stepson, by the way? Or is he your fiancé now? I wanted to send you a congratulations card, but with the funeral, I was too busy," Poppy said.

Isaiah cleared his throat, trying to conceal his laughter.

Calliope's pinched smile threatened to undo her Botox. "Rory wasn't my stepson. He was my ex's stepson and already a grown man when we met, so it's not like he was any relation to me. You know how the tabloids can sensationalise."

"Wasn't Rory the man you introduced me to at GlaMORE magazine's Christmas party? He had just graduated?" Poppy asked, digging the woman's grave deeper.

The awkward silence that followed was almost unbearable.

"Rory is very passionate about his studies; he wants to pursue an MD. He'll make an excellent surgeon," Calliope said, trying to recover some ground.

"MD? Very impressive. You'll have great access to touch-ups in the future," Poppy said quietly. "Not that you need any."

"Anyway, enough about the men in our lives. You must join us for dinner tomorrow night – perhaps you can give your bodyguard a night off. I'd love to know more about your movie, and my niece, Sophia, wouldn't forgive me if I didn't ask you to have dinner with us. She is a huge fan and wants to get into the entertainment industry. Perhaps you could help her, like a mentor? She's a few years older than you – a little late to get started, but she has such natural talent."

Isaiah couldn't believe Calliope had the nerve to ask Poppy for favours after this conversation. He didn't know what type of world he'd walked into, but he didn't want to stay long.

"Being your niece, I don't doubt her talent for a moment," Poppy said, refusing to commit to anything.

"I'm sorry, but Ms Roe is busy tomorrow evening," Isaiah interrupted, giving Poppy an out. Her eyes widened at his quick intervention.

"Really? I'm sure we can add you to our dinner reservation. We're dining early so we can attend the captain's opera night. Even if you weren't invited, we'd still love to have you at dinner."

"Thank you; Isaiah and I were lucky enough to receive an invitation—"

"But unfortunately, I've already booked us a table at Sako before the opera," Isaiah lied. He'd overheard guests talking about the Michelin-starred sushi restaurant that had apparently booked up before the *Midas* even set sail.

"You were able to get a reservation at Sako? Poppy, I've clearly underestimated your bodyguard. I hope you enjoy your dinner and the opera – it's meant to be quite the show. No expense has been spared. I'm sure we'll find another night to dine together," Calliope drawled.

"I'm sure we will, but if we don't get a chance, I hope you enjoy the rest of your trip."

"When we return, I'll call Duggery, and he'll put something on the books." The woman obviously didn't want to let Poppy slip away.

"He's no longer my manager," Poppy said curtly.

"What a pity! Martha would be so distressed to think of you going it alone. Please don't hesitate to call if you need anything," Calliope said, feigning concern.

"I'll be sure to do that. I hope you enjoy the rest of your afternoon," Poppy said, signalling to the manicurist that they were ready to resume.

Thankfully, Calliope took the hint. "I've kept you long enough, and I should get back to my facialist. It was a pleasure to meet you, Isaiah. Look after her, or you'll have to answer to me." Calliope chuckled softly before leaving them to return to her friends.

"I'm sorry to keep you waiting. That was rude," Poppy said to the manicurist, who waved off the apology and returned to her work.

"A friend of your aunt's?" Isaiah asked, not wanting to pry but hoping that talking about it might lift her spirits. She seemed deflated after the encounter.

"Friend wouldn't be the term I'd use. Rival, archenemy, nemesis… They had a complicated relationship filled with jealousy and an odd sense of respect – or maybe understanding? I never truly understood it."

"She's an actress, so it's understandable there would be rivalry," Isaiah suggested.

"They acted together for years and even appeared in the same movies. I thought they were as close as sisters when I was growing up. My aunt wasn't big on relationships, but Calliope was constantly present. My aunt even slept with her husband so she could sue him for infidelity and take everything in her divorce – or so the rumour goes," Poppy said, as if it was a totally normal favour.

"A formidable pair," Isaiah remarked, wondering what had turned them against each other. "Did they grow apart?"

"I don't know if there was a specific moment or event, but the rumour has it that Calliope didn't want to live in my aunt's shadow anymore. She started taking on more leading roles and competing for the same parts. I'm sure part of her is genuinely sad about my aunt's passing. She knew her for far longer than I did. But I bet part of her feels relieved that my aunt is gone. I wouldn't want to compete against Martha. She was ruthless, and there was no such thing as second place – only first or last. I have to respect Calliope for giving her a run for her money. Over the past few years, Calliope has been thriving while my aunt spent most of her time managing my career as her legacy," Poppy explained.

"Isn't there competition in any field? From my experience, in law enforcement it's often about who solves the biggest cases, gets the most media attention, or climbs the ranks fastest."

"You make a good point. I think it all comes down to

wanting to make a name for yourself. Growing up in that environment, you get used to it," Poppy admitted as her manicurist left them, her hands under a glowing lamp.

"My line of work no longer seems so daunting." Isaiah preferred chasing down clues and criminals any day over the fickle world of fame.

"Did you see any of my aunt's movies?" Poppy asked suddenly.

It would have been difficult not to. "When my grandmother was in a nursing home, we watched her early films. I think your aunt was only in her teens. They brought her comfort as her memory faded," Isaiah told her.

"I'm glad your grandma found comfort in them. I loved the music, the costumes, and the glamour when I was young. Acting was the only thing my aunt truly loved, and I admired her passion. Is your grandmother still with us?" Poppy asked delicately.

"No, she passed away a couple of years ago." He hadn't thought about her in quite a while.

"I'm sorry," Poppy said softly, removing her hands from the lamp.

"Don't be. She lived a great life and wanted to be with my grandfather. He'd passed a decade earlier, and she wasn't the same without him. They were like two jigsaw pieces – neither complete without the other," Isaiah said, pushing down the grief he hadn't felt in years. He couldn't believe how easy it was for him to open up to Poppy. "You'd be excellent in an interrogation room."

"What makes you say that?"

"You can redirect a conversation to avoid talking about yourself with such ease."

"It's not one of my natural talents – it's years of PR training. I envy the love your grandparents had. My parents had something similar before they passed. I wish for that," Poppy said, her eyes lost in deep thought. Isaiah wanted to say something to comfort her, but she quickly straightened her back and snapped back to her charming self. "Want to know a Hollywood secret?"

"Do tell." Isaiah couldn't help but be intrigued by her stories.

"Did you see *The Silent Dancer*? It was my aunt's first film."

"The one about the red dress?" he asked, recalling it faintly. "I didn't realise it was her first. Impressive to be the lead in such a classic."

"So naive for a detective!" Poppy smirked. "My aunt poisoned the lead. Martha was meant to play the best friend, Betsy, but then the lead actress, May Darling, started missing shoots because she kept getting sick. My aunt was first in and last out of the studio. Always around to offer a helping hand when May was too ill to remember her lines or turn up on time. Impatient, and impressed with my aunt's dedication, the director gave her the leading role. It was Martha Roe's breakout."

"How'd Martha poison her?" Isaiah asked. "How did she not get caught?"

"Who would suspect a sixteen-year-old girl of poisoning a leading lady? May didn't die, but she did suffer with terrible stomach ulcers for years after."

"What did your aunt use?" Isaiah asked.

"She never told me, just made sure I understood the lesson." Poppy examined her bold red nails, flexing her fingers in delight.

"In what?"

"I told you. Never accept second place."

The way Poppy said it made his blood run cold. The light left her eyes for a split second.

"You're all done here!" The manicurist cut the tension, coming back to turn off the lamp.

Isaiah rubbed moisturiser into his hands while Poppy thanked the woman. He wondered how much of her aunt's lessons had rubbed off on her. Growing up in such a cold and calculating home was sure to have contorted her ideas on wrong and right, certainly regarding personal gain, but he had seen how Poppy treated the people around her. It took a strong heart to have been taught such lessons and walk a different path.

"What happened with the Academy Award?" he asked, suddenly remembering the odd turn in the earlier conversation. "Calliope looked like she swallowed a bee when you mentioned the nomination."

"Just me being petty. Martha had two awards for lead actress, defeating Calliope whenever they were nominated in the same category. Calliope had won two for supporting actress, but she didn't care about those. Calliope was always in my aunt's shadow – awards, movies, marriages, scandals – but her latest nomination was Calliope's chance to take her place as leading lady. Martha didn't even get a nomination; she was sick with jealousy."

"Did Calliope win?"

"No, my aunt blackmailed the selection committee. You would be amazed at how many secrets she collected over the years. If only she had used her powers for good," Poppy said sadly.

"Your aunt had a lot of enemies." Maybe it wasn't so odd for so many murders to have taken place around them, given Martha's reputation.

"Your point?" Poppy said.

"Are you sure her death was an accident?"

He was only half-joking, but a look of uncertainty

flashed in Poppy's eyes. She laughed, but this time it wasn't genuine.

"Trust me, none of her enemies would have had the balls to kill her. Karma just caught up with her. Don't feel too bad for Calliope, though."

"Why?"

"Who do you think took the role of Betsy in *The Silent Dancer* once it was free for the taking?" Poppy winked.

The mischievous glint in her eye as they walked out of the nail boutique made him nervous.

# Chapter 12
# Cabin & Closets
## Poppy

Poppy tried to avoid replaying this afternoon's conversation with Calliope as she soaked in the large tub in her bathroom. She hadn't thought she would be able to bring herself to get in a tub again after seeing Patrice's body, but it was her favourite place in the world and she'd desperately needed to relax, so she'd decided the best way to get over it would be to get under the water.

Instead of inducing a panic attack, the warm water had turned her muscles to mush while the lavender fragrance washed away her stress. She groaned when the phone on the bathroom wall rang; there was no way she was going to answer, in case it was Calliope trying to set up another dinner date. At least she didn't have to worry about running into her at the opera tomorrow night.

Thankfully, the phone stopped ringing quickly, allowing her to relax again.

"Can I come in?" Isaiah asked, tapping lightly on the door just as she closed her eyes.

"Come in," Poppy called, making sure she was covered by a blanket of bubbles.

As he entered, he focused his gaze on the marble tiles. She found his bashful concern for her privacy adorable.

"I got a call from the reception desk. I need to head down. Are you okay here for a while?"

"Poppy, do you have any moisturiser?" Mina walked into the bathroom, pausing when she saw Poppy in the tub and Isaiah by the sink. "I suppose I should be grateful this is a bathroom, not a fridge."

"Very funny," Isaiah replied. "But I'm glad you're here. I need you to keep an eye on Poppy while I step out."

"Keep an eye on me? I don't need a babysitter," Poppy protested.

"Don't put me in the middle of your foreplay," Mina joked, holding her hands up in mock surrender as she started to back out of the room. "I've got a dinner date tonight with a world champion. I need a nap and some moisturiser, because I think I'm starting to peel. I can't look like a burnt lobster on a date – it's gross. I don't have time to get caught up in whatever you two are doing."

Poppy winced in sympathy; Mina's freckled shoulders matched her own painted nails. She turned to Isaiah. "Why do they need you to go to reception?"

"Eckells sent me something that he wants me to review," Isaiah replied, shifting uncomfortably. His unease was palpable. Poppy wasn't sure if he was lying, or just feeling awkward about Mina's teasing. Or her diminishing bubbles.

"Did you speak to him? Is something wrong with the club?" Mina asked anxiously.

"I thought you didn't care about your boss?" Isaiah teased.

"Did you two spend more time in fridges while I soaked up too much sun?" was Mina's retort.

"No more fridges, but we did get our nails done." Poppy chuckled, proudly displaying her ruby-red manicure.

Mina looked at Isaiah and laughed. "Eckells would love to hear that his tough and terrible Detective Rivers had his nails done."

"Hey, a real man looks after himself," he said, rubbing his hands together. "And the salon wouldn't let me in unless I booked a treatment. Besides, I'm sure he'd be equally interested to know that you have a date with an F1 driver, one of his guests!"

Mina's smile faded. "You wouldn't."

"I would, so stay here with Poppy until I get back," Isaiah threatened.

"If you're so worried about me, maybe you could leave us with a gun?" Poppy suggested, trying to tease him.

"The thought of you with a gun frightens me more than any threat out there."

"It should," Poppy muttered.

"I think she's starting to like you," she heard Mina said as Isaiah closed the door behind them harder than necessary.

"If that's what liking me looks like…" Isaiah whistled. "I'd hate to be her enemy."

"You've no idea," Mina chuckled.

"I can hear the two of you!" Poppy called, stepping out of the tub and wrapping herself in a fluffy towel embroidered with gold tridents.

She found Mina in her room, still looking for moisturiser. Poppy told her where it was as she put on her denim shorts and crochet halter top.

"Where are you going?" Mina asked, frowning as she got the moisturiser out of the top drawer.

"I need you to stay in the bathroom and pretend to be me when he returns," Poppy told her, adjusting her outfit.

"I can't. I've got dinner plans," Mina insisted.

"Just move them back an hour," Poppy urged. "I won't be long, but this is my only chance to go out alone. I don't want to involve either of you in case I get caught." She didn't want them to end up in ship jail with her.

"At least tell me where you're going?" Mina asked, raising an eyebrow.

"I want to check out Patrice's room. I have a hunch about something, but there's no way Isaiah will let me wander into the staff quarters and risk upsetting the captain. I'll be in and out," Poppy promised.

Mina hesitated.

"Okay, I'll move my dinner date, but please hurry back," she said finally. "I don't want to face Isaiah's wrath."

"Here, take my smartwatch, so he'll think I haven't left the room," Poppy said, thrusting it into Mina's hands. "I'll knock to be let in."

"This is going too far. What if something happens and we need to find you?"

"Don't worry so much. I still have the anchor." Poppy waved her charm bracelet. "If I'm not back in the hour, you can send in the cavalry. I bribed a maid earlier while Isaiah went to get lunch. I know exactly where Patrice's room is, so it's not like I'm going to wander around aimlessly."

"Go before I change my mind," Mina sighed, rubbing moisturiser into the reddening tattoos on her arms.

"You can keep that," Poppy said, slipping on her

sandals. She grabbed one of Isaiah's baseball caps. A terrible disguise, but it was the best she could do.

Mina's eyes widened. "But it's so expensive. It's enough that you let me use some of it!"

"You can tell Isaiah that I bribed you." Poppy winked, closing the door behind her before Mina changed her mind.

AFTER A QUICK RIDE in the staff-only lift, Poppy found Patrice's cabin sealed with red tape. She sneaked under it, relieved to discover the door wasn't locked. Clearly, the captain was overly confident and believed no one would be bold enough to break into a dead woman's room.

Poppy didn't dare turn on a light, so she could only rely on the dim light coming through the porthole and under the door. As she rummaged through Patrice's clothes and belongings, searching drawer after drawer, she felt increasingly uneasy. It felt wrong going through a dead woman's belongings. The wardrobe was filled only with uniforms, and the mattress offered no clues. There were no suspicious photos, files, or scrawled notes in sight. Patrice's toothbrush still sat by the sink, and her unmade bed had pyjamas sticking out from under the pillow – indications that security hadn't touched her belongings, but simply sealed the room as they'd found it after her death.

Under the bed, Poppy discovered a small suitcase filled with Patrice's off-duty clothes. As she crouched on the floor, her head in her hands, she realized she had exhausted all the hiding spots in the cramped cabin. *I guess I was wrong.*

The sound of footsteps passing outside jolted her, a

reminder to speed up her search. She hurriedly pushed the suitcase back under the bed, only to find it resisting her efforts. When she reached under, she pulled out a lockbox – the kind used for petty cash – with the key still in it.

"Patrice was stealing from the guests," Poppy muttered to herself as she examined the contents. She found strands of pearls, a few watches, and a diamond pendant. "Is that what got her killed? Did she steal from the wrong person?" She placed the items back in the top tray; it wasn't like she could take them and ask the other guests which items belonged to them. Could Patrice have been in her room late at night looking for anything worth stealing?

She lifted off the top tray of the lockbox and gasped.

"Audiotapes?" she murmured, her voice echoing in the silent cabin, remembering the recorder they had found on Patrice's body.

She sifted through a dozen tapes, noting the different names and dates written on each case. Beneath the tapes, she found a little blue notebook. Flipping through it, she was shocked to see lists of names, dates, and amounts dating back years. *Patrice wasn't just stealing; she was blackmailing guests with their secrets.* The guests of the *Midas* wouldn't murder anyone over a few missing jewels, but secrets were a far more dangerous commodity.

Poppy searched for any tapes marked with the date of Patrice's murder to account for the one missing from the recorder when they'd found her. A case marked "Calliope Chase" stood out, but when she opened it, the case was empty. Was Calliope the one who'd taken the tape? Had she been Patrice's next target?

Scanning to the final entry in the notebook, Poppy found Calliope's name alongside the amount of fifty thousand dollars, with a question mark beside it. Patrice could have sold the tape to Calliope and then gone to Poppy's room to plant the recorder or search for anything worth stealing. This would explain why the tape recorder was empty, but if she had sold it to Calliope, wouldn't she have had the money on her? Poppy hadn't found any sign of money in Patrice's cabin.

A wave of urgency washed over her. The only way to find out for sure was to check Calliope's suite and see if she could locate the missing tape before it was disposed of – and before Isaiah found out about her leaving the suite. She tore the page out of the notebook and shoved it into her shorts pocket before returning the lockbox and suitcase to their original position.

Poppy traded one of the pearl necklaces from Patrice's treasure trove with the receptionist at the nail boutique in exchange for Calliope's suite number. Not that she needed much persuasion; it's always wise to be kind to those in the service industry. Fortunately, Calliope's suite was just one floor below. If Poppy got caught, she could easily say she was looking for Calliope to arrange that dinner.

She only turned on the small side crystal lamp on the dressing table to keep the room dark and avoid detection as she searched, the cream carpet muffling her footsteps. *I wish the suites were smaller so there weren't so many hiding places!* Having checked under the bed and found nothing, she got up, and her eyes fell on the jewellery box on the dresser. Where better to hide something valuable?

"Breaking into another guest's suite. Do you want the captain to arrest you? Are you tired of your freedom?" Isaiah demanded.

Dropping the jewellery box, Poppy looked up to find

him staring at her in the mirror. "Holy shit, you scared me to death!"

"I'm glad someone does," he snapped.

"How did you find me so fast?" So much for getting Mina to take her place. *I made her rearrange her date for nothing.*

"I got an alert when you left the suite. I told you after Patrice that I'd keep the tracker on. If I'm not within fifteen feet of you, I'll get an alert," he explained sternly. "I didn't think I'd have to use it, since we agreed not to keep secrets or run off."

"Speaking of secrets, where did you go earlier?" she challenged him.

"I told you, I had to go to the reception desk."

"What did Eckells want you to 'review'?" He obviously didn't want her to know, since he didn't send whatever it was to the room.

He huffed. "It was a call from Eckells. He wants to ensure I'm keeping Mina safe. He heard about the incident from the captain and wanted a personal update to ensure we followed the rules. I was going to tell you before I left, but then Mina came in, and her relationship with Eckells is... odd. I don't think she would appreciate him checking up on her."

She studied his expression for any hint of deception. "Okay, I believe you. So believe *me* when I tell you that I wasn't going to keep this a secret; if I found anything out, I was going to tell you – but in case I was caught, I wanted you to get out of it so you wouldn't get locked up with me."

"If I'm locked up with you, I can protect you!" Isaiah sighed. "How did you even get in here?"

"A maid was doing turn-down service when I arrived; I waited for her to leave and sneaked in before the door could close fully," Poppy said. "How'd you come in after me?"

"The door was caught on the latch, so it didn't close behind you either."

She was lucky he had come in after her, not someone else who'd noticed the door was left ajar. "Oops."

"What if the guest had returned? Whose suite is this?"

"Calliope's." She avoided eye contact, not wanting to see his reaction.

"And why are you risking getting us thrown into the brig?" Isaiah asked.

"Because of this." She showed him the small tape in her hand. "I found it in the top drawer of the jewellery box, shoved in the back."

"A tape?" He took it from her, and his eyes lit up as the penny dropped. "Patrice's tape recorder."

"Give the detective a prize."

"Cute, but how did you know it would be in here? Did she give something away earlier?"

"No, it wasn't what she said. It was what I found in Patrice's cabin."

His eyes widened. "You went down to the staff cabins?"

"Only for a few minutes, and I wasn't seen." Poppy put everything but the tape back into the jewellery box as she'd found it. She needed to know what was on it, and if whatever Patrice had learned was worth killing over. "But it was worth the risk, because I discovered Patrice was stealing from guests, recording their conversations, and blackmailing them. She kept a notebook of who, when and how much. Calliope's tape was the only one not in its case and the last entry in the notebook. We just need the tape recorder to play it, but you left it with Patrice's body."

"I'll find a way to get into the morgue," Isaiah said

without elaborating. The morgue was the last place she wanted to go, so she would entrust him with that task.

"Since I found a lead, are you still mad at me?" she asked, batting her eyelashes at him. His jaw clenched and his eyes narrowed, but the lecture didn't come. Not yet, anyway. "I know you said not to leave the room without you, but I'm still wearing the anchor charm, so I knew you'd be able to find me if anything went wrong—"

Before she could finish, Isaiah pulled her body against his.

"Stop talking," he snapped as she went rigid, motioning to the shadow beneath the door. Someone was outside the door.

A loud knock caused them to freeze.

"Ms Chase, I'm sorry to disturb you, but I left some cleaning products in the bathroom," the maid called out when they didn't answer.

Isaiah glared down at Poppy, and she shrugged. How was she supposed to know the maid would be so forgetful?

"We can't let her in," she whispered, only to hold her breath as the door handle started to move.

Isaiah surprised her by grabbing the back of her head and pulling her lips to his. He pressed her against the door, blocking the maid's entrance with their bodies. Poppy considered pushing him away, but heat coiled in her core. Rising onto her tiptoes to kiss him back, she could just about make out the shadow of the maid's feet outside the door.

"Is everything alright, Ms Chase?" she asked, concern audible in her voice.

"Yes, please come back later. I'm in the middle of something," Poppy managed to say as Isaiah's lips explored her neck, her chest, and any inch of skin exposed by her halter top.

"Let her hear you," he ordered, tugging at her hair. Poppy groaned.

"Should I call security? You don't sound like yourself," the maid fretted.

*Shit! I'm being nice to her, and that's not how Calliope treats staff.* "No, that's not necessary. Come back later, or I'll report you to your supervisor," Poppy threatened as Isaiah explored her body, finding that she didn't care who was outside the door as his hands clutched her waist. She smiled against his lips as he grabbed her ass, wondering what had happened to the beacon of self-control.

"I told you to let her hear you. Why don't you ever fucking listen?" he growled between kisses. His thigh settled between her legs, and when he moved his hips forward, she felt how hard he was against the side of her belly.

"I know," she panted. She couldn't stop smirking as she hooked her knee over his hip until his hardness was between her legs. "And I'm not even sorry."

Isaiah responded by pulling her hips closer and grinding against her until she cried out.

"Please don't stop!"

She forgot about the maid outside, too focused on his relentless lips. Ecstasy threaded through her limbs until she no longer cared about where they were and how much trouble they were in.

"We'll see about that." Isaiah bit down on her lip, and she whimpered. His pace made her legs tremble; she clung to his shoulders, forgetting about the show they were meant to be putting on for those outside. She held her breath as sparks of pleasure took over her body.

"Isaiah, please…" She tilted her hips forward, feeling him right where she needed him. Only a millimetre or two of fabric separated them. His groans told her he was as desperate for her as she was for him, making her all the more needy.

The banging resumed on the door. “Ms Chase, it’s security. Please open up.”

“Fuck it.” Isaiah moved them away from the door to the wall. The door clicked open, but he shielded Poppy with his body so that security couldn’t see who they were in the dark room. “Get the fuck out!” he barked, his lips breaking away from hers. “How dare you enter without permission?!”

“I’m so sorry. We thought something was wrong. Forgive the intrusion.” Security tripped over themselves as they hurried to close the door behind them.

Isaiah leaned over her, staring at the door, while she watched his chest rise and fall.

“They’re gone.” His voice was uncharacteristically gruff and breathy as he loosened his grip on Poppy’s thighs.

She opened her eyes, wanting more.

“We should get back to the room,” Isaiah said, with no care for what had just happened between them.

“Are you serious? That’s it?” Poppy felt like a bucket of cold water had been dumped over her. He couldn’t be so unaffected. He couldn’t be that good an actor. Not when she’d felt how much he wanted her.

He bent down, and she thought he would kiss her again. She closed her eyes, waiting, until she felt his breath brush her ear.

“Only good girls get to finish.” Isaiah smirked down at her.

Poppy ground her teeth and pushed him away. She hurried out of the suite, leaving him to follow. She didn’t say a single word to him and couldn’t bear to look at him.

Thankfully Mina had already left for her date; she wasn't in the mood to explain what they had been up to.

Poppy climbed into his bed in the suite and felt the mattress's side dip. She opened her eyes to see Isaiah leaning over her. He brushed a strand of hair from her cheek, and she hated how the slightest touch tightened her stomach.

"If you think about leaving again, I'm going to handcuff you to the bed," he warned.

He got up before she could come up with some sassy retort. She didn't doubt that he would chase her down again. She rolled over to watch him strip off his shirt.

"Are you going to sleep on the couch again?" Poppy asked as he tossed off the extra cushions and stretched out on it. There was no way that was comfortable for a guy his size.

"Anything else wouldn't be professional," he grumbled, taking the tape they had found from his pocket and placing it in the drawer by the bed.

"Are you kidding?" Poppy sat up. "Considering what happened between us, we're well past professional lines."

"What happened in Calliope's suite was a one-off – a necessary ploy to escape. I shouldn't have got carried away." His face was emotionless, but she knew he'd felt as much as she did. "It won't happen again."

"Don't do me any favours. That's the last thing I want." She picked up a pillow and tossed it at him. He caught it, and his smug smile made her want to strangle him. "I was just trying to make you more comfortable."

"Go to sleep, Poppy." Isaiah lay down.

Poppy rolled over, ignoring him. If that was how he wanted to play it, so be it.

## Chapter 13
# Dress the Part
### Poppy

"Are you going to keep giving me the silent treatment?" Isaiah asked, putting down his gold-coated chopsticks. The only thing they seemed to agree on was sushi for lunch.

"I'm not giving you the silent treatment; I just have nothing to say," Poppy replied as she got up from the table. She wished Mina was there to help break the tension, but she was with her F1 driver, and Poppy didn't want to interfere with her fun.

"If you're upset about what happened last night, I'm sorry. We promised the captain that we wouldn't get involved. If we'd been caught tampering with a murdered woman's belongings, it wouldn't have ended well for either of us." Isaiah stayed close behind her. She wished he'd stop wearing that damn cologne.

"I thought we agreed not to discuss it," Poppy said as they walked through the sea life tunnel, surrounded by exotic fish like they were in an aquarium.

"As much as you may not enjoy my company right now or being confined to your suite, you wouldn't have preferred being stuck in the brig for the remainder of the trip," he said, taking her arm and forcing her to stop walking. The last thing she wanted was for him to touch her; it made her skin tingle in a way that prevented her from staying angry. "We only have another week to endure, and after that, you never have to see me again."

Poppy felt like this would be the longest holiday of her life. Was this her karma for plotting to murder her boyfriend? She kept the thought to herself.

"That's fine with me, Mr. Rivers." She removed his hand from her arm and forced a smile before heading to the shopping pavilion, which was designed to look like a garden growing on the ship. The small waterfall cascading into a fountain made of shells in the centre of the boutiques and luxury shops felt like overkill, but she appreciated the vision. "If you don't mind, I have some shopping to do, so you can either come with me or wait outside the shop."

"Can't you call someone to come to the suite?" he asked, looking at the boutiques as if they were armed and dangerous.

"There are plenty of other people around. Nothing is going to happen. I might jump off the balcony if I have to stay in that suite for even one more moment." Poppy had never been one to feel claustrophobic, but the thought of being trapped in there was making her skin itch.

"Please don't. I'm contractually obligated to go after you," Isaiah said.

"That's all the more enticing." Poppy smiled, heading into a shop with beautiful gowns and tuxes – perfect for the opera tonight.

A sales assistant in a sharply tailored pink pantsuit greeted them from behind a glass counter filled with ties, bowties, brooches, cufflinks and hair pieces. "Welcome to

Beatrix's Boutique. What can I do for you? My name is Melina, and I'm here for whatever you need, from rack to couture."

"We need a tux, black tie, for the opera tonight," Poppy said. "I think silk peak lapels, silk stripe trousers, and maybe a bowtie with a wing-collared shirt."

"I thought you wanted to get something to wear," Isaiah whispered as she smiled at Melina.

Poppy shrugged. "Dressing you up will be so much more fun. I can pick up anything."

"As entertaining as being your Ken doll would be, I can dress myself. Just focus on yourself," he said, eyeing a plain dress shirt that was too casual for an opera.

"If only that were true," she said wryly, taking his hand and leading him to the tuxes. "We've focused on me enough over the past couple of days. It's your turn. The captain invited us personally, so we should at least look the part. We wouldn't want her to think we aren't grateful for her hospitality." She clapped her hands as they walked around the assortment of suits and dresses.

"Attending the opera? How thrilling! We're cutting it a bit close, since we won't have time for alterations, but I'm sure we can find you something perfect." Melina smiled, mirroring Poppy's excitement.

"We received an invitation at the last minute, so we're running a bit behind schedule," Poppy explained.

"With such a strong frame, finding him something will be easy. What were we thinking? Double-breasted or single-breasted jacket?" Melina asked as they surveyed Isaiah as if he was a mannequin.

"I think he can pull off the double-breasted, especially if we forego the waistcoat or cummerbund," Poppy said, like a pro.

"Black or navy? Or I have the perfect shades of

midnight or aubergine?" Melina suggested, going through a rack of various colours.

"I'm not wearing purple," Isaiah stated. The look in his eye told Poppy not to try him.

She smiled at him and went back to plotting with Melina. "I haven't picked my dress yet, so I think black is the safest."

"Shoes? Loafers or dress shoes?" Melina pointed to a wall rack of options.

"Absolutely no loafers," Isaiah interjected as she pulled out a few boxes. "Even if I'm attending as a guest, I need to be able to run in case of an emergency, and I don't want to have to worry about losing a shoe."

"Dress shoes it is. I love a decisive man." Melina winked. Poppy didn't like how her eyes lingered on Isaiah, but maybe she was sizing him up for the tux.

"Maybe a soft leather, not patent," Poppy added. She didn't want him to get blisters.

"Bowtie or necktie?" Melina asked.

"Bowtie."

"Neither."

They spoke in unison and glared at each other.

"I'll leave you to talk; I have an idea of size, so I'll go pull you out some options." Melina set off to put the clothing items into one of the changing rooms.

"C'mon, Mr Detective, get your butt in the changing room; the more you resist, the harder it's going to be." She smirked, taking his hand. "Don't look so tortured. Shopping is meant to be fun. I promise it isn't going to hurt." She opened the suede curtain and pushed him inside.

"Can I have some privacy?" he asked her in the mirror as he started to remove his t-shirt.

"I didn't expect you to be bashful," she teased.

Isaiah called her bluff and started to unbutton his trousers, so she closed the curtain.

"How are you getting on?" she asked a few minutes later, growing restless.

Isaiah stepped out in a black Armani tux with a simple dress shirt without the bowtie, fidgeting with his belt.

"You clean up well," Poppy commented. The jacket showed off his strong frame, as Melina had put it. She didn't know what else to say, but knew she was blushing and told herself to get a grip.

"It's a little tight." Isaiah tugged at the shirt collar and undid the two top buttons. She decided she wasn't going to force him to wear a tie.

"It's tailored, and you wear your shirts about two sizes too big. This is perfect," she said, fixing the button on the suit jacket.

"My goodness." Melina nudged Poppy as she reappeared to check on them. "Never let him dress himself in future."

Something was missing. "He needs cufflinks and a watch to complete the look."

"The tux is enough," Isaiah said, removing the jacket. "I have a watch – it was my father's, and it's not coming off."

"Vintage. I like it," Poppy said, glancing at it. The strap was very worn. "But how about a new strap?"

"Fine, but only the strap." Closing the curtain, Isaiah handed out the tux, and Melina took it to wrap it up.

"Have you had enough fun?" he asked, putting his holster back on.

"Nope. It's not like there's much else we can do, and this is the first time I've ever got to take someone shopping," she admitted. "You wanted me to stay close, so let me have my way."

"If this keeps you entertained and out of trouble, then have at it," he said, following her to the women's shoes. "I can wait while you pick out a dress."

Poppy picked up a pair of sparkly gold heels. "I already picked a satin cream cocktail dress while you were changing," she told him, adding the heels to the counter to be wrapped up with the rest.

He frowned. "That was quick. Don't you want to look around a bit longer?"

"It's not much fun for me." She'd just picked the first dress she'd seen in the window; she didn't find much joy in shopping for herself. Her aunt's voice had a way of worming its way into her head and picking her choices apart.

Noticing him looking at the jewellery through the glass counter, she changed the subject. "Shopping for your woman back home?"

She'd never thought to ask before. He wasn't wearing a wedding ring, but that didn't mean he wasn't attached. Still, even if last night's intimacy had just been an act, she doubted he would go so far if he had someone waiting. At least, she hoped not. After spending twenty-four hours a day together, it was hard to remember how little they knew about one another.

"No. Something for my niece," he explained. "It's her birthday soon."

"Your niece?" She didn't want to admit she felt relieved.

"Last time I spoke to my sister, she mentioned she wants to get her ears pierced."

"A pair of simple studs would be cute. Is there anything she likes? They have some little seashells."

"She's a big fan of yours, actually," he admitted. "She

loves any and all music; she wants to be a dancer or a singer."

"Really? She has good taste," Poppy said.

"She doesn't know you like I do," he said, but a small smile danced at the corner of his mouth.

"Ouch," Poppy whined, nudging him playfully. "Could I get her tickets for my next show? Or sign something for her?" She didn't like the wall he kept putting between them; it made her feel like a criminal being guarded instead of someone he was supposed to protect.

"I can't accept gifts from clients. It wouldn't be professional," he said gruffly as she leaned against him. Soon enough, his resolve would weaken; she wasn't the only one who had felt something between them last night, even if he wanted to deny it. His body couldn't lie.

"Not a gift, then. You can consider it a bonus." She turned her attention to the selection of studs. "I think the seashell earrings would be a good place to start," she added, her voice tinged with disappointment at his refusal.

"I probably won't make it home in time for her party. I don't need to worry about this right now." He scratched his head, visibly overwhelmed by the choices. It was sweet how much he cared about his young niece.

"Let me take care of it for you. Can you please gift-wrap the small seashell studs for us?" Poppy asked as Melina returned with their bags.

"Of course," Melina replied, pulling the earrings from beneath the counter.

"Also, we need a strap for a watch. Could you have it done by this evening?"

"I need to see the watch first," Melina said.

Poppy turned to Isaiah, who had clearly learned not to argue; he handed it over.

"Vintage Rolex, very nice. We can definitely have it

done. Do you have any colour or style preference?" Melina inquired.

"Classic, as close as possible to the original," Isaiah said reluctantly, clearly cautious about leaving the watch with her. "Just be careful with it."

"Would you like your purchases now, or when the watch is ready? We can have everything delivered to your suite this evening," Melina suggested.

"We'll take the bags ourselves." Poppy knew Isaiah wouldn't want her giving out their room number. "We'll collect the watch on our way to the opera later," she added. Seeing how much Isaiah cared about it, she doubted he would trust it to anyone else.

Later that night, Poppy heard the door to their suite click open while she tried to avoid burning herself again with her curling tongs. They had only about an hour to get ready before heading to the theatre, and she couldn't understand why she felt so nervous. Her hands trembled every time she thought about attending the opera. There was no reason to be frightened; Isaiah would be there with her, and no one would dare try to harm her in such a public setting. However, ever since she'd found the tape, she had been anxiously waiting for Calliope to discover that it was missing. Although the woman had no reason to suspect that Poppy was the culprit, she couldn't shake the knot in her stomach whenever she thought about it.

"I come bearing gifts," Mina announced, dancing across the suite before placing a tape recorder on the dressing table. Poppy finished clipping the rollers in her hair, then jumped up and wrapped her arms around Mina.

"How did you get this?" she asked, clutching the recorder.

"It's not Patrice's, so hopefully the tape will still play," Mina replied. "There was no way I could get into the morgue. But I ran into that Grammy-winning songwriter, LUV, who's married to the tech billionaire – that guy who invented Eagle Eye security. Anyway, he was using it to record himself with his guitar in the library, and I asked if I could borrow it."

"The ship has a library?" Poppy asked, intrigued, although she couldn't remember the last time she had read a book.

Mina nodded. "Eckells insisted on it when the ship was being built. He prefers books to people – even had a secret office made for himself." She paled. "Don't tell him I told you that."

"I won't," Poppy promised. After everything she'd heard about this man, she didn't know whether she wanted to meet him or hide from him.

"What secrets are you two keeping now?" Isaiah walked out of the bathroom, dripping water all over the carpet. Poppy swallowed as she watched droplets cascade down his chest, feeling a mixture of attraction and discomfort in his presence.

"You're making a puddle. You could have dried off before coming out," Mina scolded him.

"Poppy doesn't seem to mind." Isaiah winked, obviously noting that she was gawking at his bare chest.

Poppy didn't dignify his comment with a response. She simply picked up his clothes from the bed and tossed them at him. Isaiah caught them quickly, chuckling to himself as she blushed.

"What are you doing here? I thought you were off with

your driver?" he asked, dropping the clothes on the desk and turning his attention back to Mina.

"You really underestimate me, don't you?" Mina picked up the tape recorder and waved it at him. "A simple 'thank you, Mina; we are lucky to have you' would suffice. 'Thank you for getting the tape recorder so we can listen to the tape without having to go to a creepy morgue and search through a dead woman's belongings'."

Isaiah rolled his eyes, drying his hair roughly with a towel. "Thank you, Mina."

"You're welcome, Isaiah."

"If you two are finished, can we listen to the tape?" Poppy interjected. *These two bicker like siblings.*

She grabbed the small tape from the bedside table, thinking that hiding blackmail material next to a dusty bible seemed ironic. Inserting the tape into the recorder, she pressed the rewind button until it clicked.

For a moment, she hesitated, her thumb hovering over the play button.

"Do you want me to do it?" Isaiah asked.

Poppy wasn't sure why she felt so afraid – it was just a button – but she couldn't bring herself to press it. Instead, she handed the recorder to Isaiah, her mind racing with fear and uncertainty.

He set it down on the dresser between the three of them and pressed play.

All they heard at first was static. Poppy frowned, about to check if the tape had been inserted incorrectly, but suddenly Calliope's voice rang from the recorder.

"How dare you try to justify your mess? You can forget about the other half of your money. You fucked up, and I'm not paying for a messy job," she snapped. Poppy had never seen this side of her before.

The other voice was just a static whisper; she couldn't

make out who she was talking to. Could Calliope be using a phone or a radio?

"Don't take that tone with me. You said you would make it look like a simple overdose. No mess, no investigation – and most importantly, you were supposed to do it when Poppy wasn't home. You promised me no witnesses," Calliope barked. "You've had unfettered access, and you screwed it up."

Poppy's stomach flipped. *Calliope plotted to murder Martha?* It felt like the rug had been swept out from underneath her. The two had had a tense rivalry, but Poppy had never thought Calliope would hate Martha so much as to hurt her. *Witnesses? Is she trying to have me killed now because she thinks I'm investigating Martha's death?*

Whoever she was talking to had had unlimited access to Poppy's home. Was she talking to Dug? Poppy's eyebrows rose. Based on their conversation in the boutique, Calliope hadn't known that Dug had been fired since Martha's death, so his access was gone now. Still, she didn't understand why Duggery, after so many years of loyal service, would be willing to betray her aunt just to strangle some cash out of Calliope. He would've made more in the long run if her aunt had lived and Poppy remained under his thumb. The pieces didn't quite fit. Who the hell was she talking to? Were they on the ship, or had she smuggled on a phone? She'd hoped the tape would give her answers, but it was only adding to her questions.

"All you had to do was swap out her pills with the higher doses I gave you, and it should have knocked her out cold. There's no way she should have been able to get out of bed," Calliope continued.

Poppy felt a surge of shock and disbelief at the depth of the woman's hatred. She must have been really desperate for that Academy Award. Duggery had been in charge of securing her aunt's 'prescription', so he must have swapped out the pills for something more potent but underestimated the tolerance she had built up over the years.

"How can you tell me not to worry? Falling down the stairs? Breaking her neck? Poppy witnessed it. What if she insists on investigating the pills Martha was taking—?"

Calliope was cut off, and there was a moment of quiet before she spoke again.

"Calm down? Are you a fool or an idiot? You promised me that you would get rid of Poppy."

*That's why Dug persuaded Joshua to kill me.* Poppy was the only one in her aunt's life who could have thrown suspicion on her death. At least Joshua had had the sense to back out.

"Don't make the mistake of underestimating Poppy. She was raised by the devil in disguise, and you must take every precaution before proceeding. Don't contact me again if you know what's good for you," Calliope threatened, and the static returned.

The tape recorder clicked, cutting off the rest of the conversation. On the small tape, that was all there was room for.

Poppy took a moment to process what they'd discovered. Thinking back on the night of her aunt's death, she couldn't help but wonder if the pills would have killed Martha without the extra push. *Was she already a dead woman walking when she took the plunge?*

She saw Isaiah's lips moving, but she couldn't hear him. She rewound the tape to listen to it again, but he placed his hand over hers, snapping her out of the trance.

"Are you alright?" he asked.

Poppy nodded, swallowing the bile rising in her throat. Dug and Joshua were only pawns in a bigger game. Calliope was the puppeteer.

A plan formed in her mind. After the opera, she would find Calliope. She didn't want Mina or Isaiah around during their conversation in case she had to confess to things she didn't want them to know. There was no point in Calliope wasting resources trying to harm her. Poppy would keep the tape as insurance, and they could continue their voyage in peace. Mina and Isaiah would be safe.

However, once the voyage was over, Poppy would get justice for Patrice. Calliope was right; she had been raised by the devil. *And anyone who sins deserves to burn.*

## Chapter 14
# Captain's Opera
### Poppy

Poppy was utterly captivated by the grandeur of the theatre foyer. Her eyes were drawn to the magnificent chandelier, a sparkling masterpiece above the carousel bar. It was a marvel to her that such a space could exist on a ship. She could almost imagine herself in a Venetian opera house, as long as she didn't look out of the window. As she sipped her strawberry cocktail, her anticipation for the doors to open grew. Isaiah's unease, evident in his failed attempts to not fidget with his cufflinks, was a welcome distraction from her own nerves.

"Have you been to the opera before?" she asked him.

"No, but I went to Autumn Adler's concert last winter. She's—"

"The concert pianist! I met her at a charity auction a few years back. You must have good connections; her tickets go fast," Poppy said eagerly. "I'm so jealous you got to go to her show. I watched it online on my tour bus. Her music really pulls at the heartstrings."

"My partner helped her with a case and she gave him

some tickets, but sadly, his little boy was sick, so I got to go," Isaiah explained.

Poppy vaguely recalled hearing about Autumn being attacked during a show, but she'd been in the thick of her US stint and didn't know the details. *What a coincidence that my bodyguard's partner would—*

Her thoughts were interrupted when she spotted an old flame across the foyer raising his glass in her direction.

Poppy offered a small smile and quickly turned away, hoping he wouldn't interpret it as an invitation to join them. She couldn't bear the thought of engaging in a conversation with him.

"Someone you know?" Isaiah looked over her shoulder, fiddling with the new strap on his wrist.

"An ex, sort of," Poppy replied, helping him adjust the strap; it was a little stiff.

"Your ex is Scott Sanderson?"

"We weren't official. He worked on one of the music videos for my last album." He was the last guy she'd dated before Joshua. Her aunt had got rid of Scott by getting him a role in a movie shot halfway across the world, effortlessly ending whatever had been developing between them. Now Poppy knew Joshua had been hoping for the same treatment.

"And?" Isaiah prompted.

"Nothing." She shrugged. *What is with this ship? I feel like I'm being haunted.* "Why? Are you jealous?" she asked, watching Isaiah chug his beer.

"No," he huffed. "Why would I be?" But he stood a little closer, and the smell of his cologne made her think, *Sanderson who?*

She felt a surge of warmth towards Isaiah. His nonchalance about Scott's presence was comforting. It was as if he was telling her, 'I'm here. You're safe.' It was a feeling she hadn't experienced in a long time.

"Poppy Roe, looking gorgeous as ever." Scott's voice made her stiffen uncomfortably.

*I guess he didn't take the hint.*

"Scott, I thought you were still filming in Canada," she said as he leaned in to kiss her cheek. He rested his hand on her lower back, and she was about to move away when Isaiah interrupted.

"Please give Ms Roe some space," he said firmly, removing Scott's hand from Poppy's waist.

"Relax, big guy; we're old friends." Scott flashed a big smile and winked at Poppy. She couldn't believe she'd ever fallen for his charms.

"Friend or not, please keep your hands to yourself if you want to keep them. Understand?" Isaiah said, getting between them.

Scott backed up, and Poppy noticed the sway in his step. He'd clearly indulged a little too much at the open bar.

"Let's not get off on the wrong foot." Scott offered his hand to Isaiah. "I'm Scott. Scott Sanderson."

Isaiah's jaw clenched. "Isaiah Rivers, head of Ms. Roe's security."

Scott winced as Isaiah gripped his hand, and Poppy concealed her smile with the rim of her glass.

"It's a pleasure to meet you. I'm happy to see you're so protective of our girl." He smacked Isaiah's arm. Poppy noticed that his hand was slowly turning purple.

"It's my job to ensure her security, but Poppy's able to look out for herself," Isaiah responded, dropping his hand. Scott flexed it and turned to Poppy.

"I heard about what happened with Joshua. And to think I considered him a friend! He should never have treated you so callously." Scott sized Isaiah up, trying to stand a little taller. "I must admit I was relieved to hear you were single again." He stepped a little too close for her liking.

Poppy inched away. She could smell the whisky on his breath.

"Who told you she was single?" Isaiah pulled her towards him, his arm possessively wrapped around her waist. She could feel his heart pounding against her back. She didn't know whether to be annoyed by his possessiveness or turned on.

Scott's smile became strained. "My mistake – I was misinformed." He raised his hands in defeat. "Nice to see you again, Poppy."

"Nice to meet you; I hope your next film does better than the last," Isaiah said. Poppy's eyes widened. *Who knew he could be so petty?*

"It's a pleasure. I hope you both enjoy the rest of your trip." Scott gritted his teeth and returned to his friends without a second glance.

"Sorry," Isaiah said, releasing his grip once Scott was out of sight. "I didn't mean to overstep with your friend." He didn't sound particularly sorry at all.

"Please don't apologise. I didn't want him pawing at me."

"Instead, you had me pawing at you," Isaiah said wryly. "He just wasn't taking the hint to back off."

"I wasn't complaining," Poppy teased, running her hand down his chest.

Isaiah took her hand as it reached his heart. "You're going to be the death of me," he murmured, his gaze darkening and his grip on her tightening.

Poppy forgot they were in public for a moment, but the sound of clinking glasses demanded their attention.

Captain Roberts stood at the closed doors to the theatre, ready to address the guests.

"My honoured guests, thank you for joining me this evening. We pray to Poseidon for a safe trip and calm seas. As our special guests, you will be the first to watch tonight's performance. I hope this is a night you won't soon forget." She raised her glass, and the other guests cheered in response.

They took their seats in the red velvet chairs, though Poppy noted that the captain didn't – a staff member approached her, and she quickly slipped away. Poppy wondered if something had happened, but was distracted by the round of applause as the curtain rose.

The elaborate set, reminiscent of ancient Greek architecture with its large columns, lush drapery and rich colours, enveloped the audience, and the dancers in their flowing robes and embellished jewellery led the entrance of the singers. It was nice to be in the audience instead of on stage for once. When the singers' powerful voices echoed throughout the theatre, filling Poppy's chest with the very essence of human emotion, she closed her eyes and let the music and language penetrate her soul. She couldn't help but think how she would never be able to sing like that. The realisation of her own limitations and the beauty of the performance stirred a deep, bittersweet emotion within her.

As the antagonist and protagonist came to blows, the harmonies of the chorus and the booming orchestra added an overwhelming tension to the atmosphere. Poppy hadn't realised she was crying. She felt a surge of emotional vulnerability, a mix of fear and confusion, that she couldn't shake off. It was as though everything she had been keeping buried was starting to rise to the surface. Her heart began to hammer, and the thought of staying stuck in her seat for another hour made her skin crawl.

Isaiah was completely engrossed in the clash of good and evil, of love and loss, as the protagonist agonised over her fallen lover. She was about to lean over and tell him to breathe when, in the corner of her eye, she thought she saw Joshua.

*What the hell?*

She focused her eyes to try to make out the face of the man watching her from the shadow of the tiered balcony above them. It had to be a trick of the light, or the theme of the tragedy messing with her mind. Surely it couldn't be him.

She focused her attention back on the stage, but she couldn't shake the feeling that eyes were penetrating the back of her head. She snuck a glance over her shoulder, needing to be sure, but found the seat empty. A gleam of light from the theatre door opening and closing caught her eye.

Before she could think better of it, Poppy got out of her seat, desperately needing to know if Joshua was lurking on board or if her mind was playing tricks on her. If he was here, he could have been the one Calliope was talking to on the tape. Hopefully, the rest of the guests would be too enamoured with the performance to notice her hurrying up the aisle and out the doors to the foyer.

As Poppy rushed into the foyer, the bartender behind the bar looked up.

"Are you doing alright, Ms. Roe?" he inquired warmly,

setting aside the glass he was cleaning. "Can I get you something?"

Poppy hurried toward him, desperate for answers. "Did a man come out before me? He has highlighted blonde hair, about 5'11?" she asked, her heart racing.

The bartender shook his head. "I haven't seen anyone like that come through since the performance began. The ushers come and go, but no guests that I noticed. Are you alright? You look like you've seen a ghost."

"Are you certain?" she pressed. "I really thought I saw him."

"Honestly, I didn't see anyone fitting that description," he reassured her. "Would you like me to call someone?"

"No, I'm fine! Just a glass of water, please," Poppy said, settling into a chair and trying to regain her composure. She couldn't ask for help finding someone who had never boarded the ship.

"The opera can trigger some intense emotions. Take a few deep breaths," the bartender said, handing her the glass of water.

"Thank you – sorry for disturbing you. I just got a bit overwhelmed," she said, not liking to appear so vulnerable.

"Don't worry about it. I'll give you some space," he said thoughtfully, picking up a crate and disappearing behind a lush floral wall she hadn't noticed concealed a passageway.

It dawned on her that the *Midas* likely had many hidden routes to keep the staff's movements discreet. She couldn't imagine how many secret passages there were in the ship or how easy it would be to disappear if you knew your way. How easy it would be for someone to conceal their movements or disappear in an instant!

She shook away the paranoia. Joshua wasn't sneaking

around the ship's passageways. He wasn't some criminal mastermind.

With the quiet echo of the performance behind her, her senses started to level out again. She didn't know why imagining Joshua's face had triggered such a strong reaction. Maybe it was a combination of the opera's themes of betrayal and the music. Either way, she made no plans to return to her seat.

"What happened? One minute you were there, and the next you were gone. Are you feeling okay?" Isaiah asked, appearing and looking her over with worried eyes.

She wrapped her arms around him as he stood close, needing his steady presence. The steady beat of his heart settled her own.

"I thought I saw someone, and it unsettled me," Poppy admitted, releasing him. "My demons are chasing me." She tried to make light of her reaction, but she could see the concern in his eyes.

"Demons?" Isaiah took a seat beside her. "If there's something you need to get off your chest, then I'm here for you without judgement," he said, taking her hand in his own.

But there was a strange coolness in his tone, and she took back her hand. It sounded like he was looking for a confession, not to comfort her. Suddenly, she didn't feel so safe. Where had the switch in his attitude come from?

"Is there something you want to ask me?" she asked, leaning back on the barstool. "It sounds like there's something *you* want to get off your chest."

"I don't want to do this here," Isaiah said evasively.

"Do what?"

He looked guilty, shifting uncomfortably in his seat.

"You're starting to scare me," Poppy said, worrying

that she had made a mistake trusting him. He pulled an envelope out of his pocket. "What is this?"

"Open it," he said, glancing around to ensure no one else was listening.

She did as instructed. Background files on one, two, three individuals. It hit her. Isaiah wasn't here by chance; he was here to investigate her.

"Where did you get these?" she asked, looking at the payment transfers, photos, and crime scene photos for three people who had meant very little to her.

"Eckells faxed them over," Isaiah admitted. "I was investigating their deaths before we boarded, and I had him help me dig for details into the victims. I wanted to see if he could find anything my colleagues might have missed."

Poppy flipped through the pages. "That's why you went to reception the other night to pick this up." He'd been willing to leave her alone that night because he didn't want her to know about the investigation.

"All three of the victims worked for you and your aunt for long periods," Isaiah said, shoving the crime scene photos towards her. Gruesome crime scene photos.

"So? A lot of people worked for me and my aunt. Why are you showing me these?" Poppy snapped, turning over the images.

"But for three to end up dead in a matter of months is a big coincidence, don't you think? Very interesting," he said.

By 'interesting', she guessed he really meant 'suspicious'. Poppy clenched her teeth, feeling like a fool for trusting him. "This whole time, you've been trying to get me to trust you only because you think I'm some serial killer? Trying to get close to me in hopes of what? That I confess?"

"Your driver, your maid, and your choreographer. All were killed within months of each other – and then, in the fourth month, your aunt. Fifth, Patrice. People close to you end up dead." His voice was steely cold, and she knew she was talking to the detective and not her bodyguard.

"Is this why you accepted the bodyguard job? Because you're investigating me? You thought you could earn my trust and learn all my dirty little secrets?" Poppy demanded, her voice tinged with betrayal. "I don't even know why I'm surprised. I should have known you were after something; there's *always* something."

"Yes, I took the job because of the investigation. I have a duty of care to the victims. Whether or not you were involved remains to be seen, and there were two conclusions: you were involved in the murders, or someone is killing off those around you. I knew either you were a danger or were *in* danger," Isaiah said.

"So either I'm a killer, or someone is out to kill me? Quite the dilemma, not knowing if you need to protect me or others from me." He'd been after her from the start.

"It's my job to consider all possibilities, and it wasn't long before Patrice was killed – after you told me about your plans for Joshua."

Poppy seethed. "Joshua was only in a self-defence scenario. Patrice? I was with you when she was killed, so you can't throw either of those in my face! Why did you bring these with you today?"

"I didn't intend to, but considering your habit of going through people's belongings, I was being proactive."

"How could I go through your things while we're together?!"

"Mina. If she was willing to help you get rid of Joshua, then she'd have no problem helping you with something as trivial as searching my things," Isaiah said.

"Has anyone ever told you that you're paranoid?" She didn't admit to already having checked his belongings when he was in the shower.

"Yes, but I've always had good reason to be," Isaiah said. "If you had nothing to do with these three victims, then perhaps you can give me more insight into their lives."

"If I did, you wouldn't care so much about finding the killer," Poppy muttered. "If you know the truth about them, then you'd close the case."

"Sounds like there was no love lost between you."

"I can say I haven't lost sleep after hearing about their passing," Poppy admitted. "Does that make me a monster?"

"I don't think you're a monster," Isaiah said, "I just want the truth. I want to know why bodies keep dropping around you before more die."

"It's a good thing you don't think I'm a monster, because what would that make you, having kissed me? Having wanted me? You thought I was a suspect, yet you couldn't help but get close to me." Poppy leaned in. "Do you usually get so close to those you investigate?"

"I'm sorry—"

"For what? Accusing me of murder or kissing me?" she asked, getting off the bar stool to stand between his legs. "For telling me you'd protect me while secretly investigating me?"

Isaiah ran his hands through his hair. Clearly, this conversation wasn't going the way he hoped. Had he expected that after some flirting and heavy petting, she would roll over and reveal all her secrets, expose her demons? He was a fool.

"I don't know what happened between you and the victims, but I know that someone is after you. I don't know if these cases are connected to what's happening on board, but my gut is telling me you're hiding something. Tell me, before you or anyone else is hurt."

Poppy's heart sank. She hated herself for thinking he was on her side, that he was in her corner. Like everyone else, he had lied and concealed his true desires. She shoved him away as he tipped her chin to meet his gaze. He thought she was a monster, and he was right.

"The only thing I'm telling you is to go back to the suite. I don't want to look at you right now," she told him, trying not to let Isaiah see the tears in her eyes.

"Regardless of my investigation, it's my job to ensure you're safe. Even if you can't trust me and don't want to confide in me, it's my job to stop you from getting hurt," Isaiah said, but she couldn't trust his words. Was he only proclaiming to care about her safety to encourage her to reveal her secrets?

"I don't want to confide in you, because if I told you what you so desperately want to know, you wouldn't look at me the same way. Just leave me alone," she snapped, hating how hurt she sounded. How could a man she hardly knew hurt her far more than those she'd known for years?

"I'm not leaving you here, and you aren't going anywhere without me."

"What will you do if I try to leave? Arrest me? Oh, that's right – you can't. Don't worry about remaining professional or keeping me safe. I wouldn't want you to burden yourself with protecting a monster a moment longer."

"Poppy, I've never thought you were a monster—"

She cut him off. "Just a murderer."

He swallowed.

She backed away, desperate for some space. "You're fired."

Isaiah reached for her, but a cacophony of screams broke out behind them.

The theatre door was thrown open. Guests came rushing out, some crying while others looked ashen, just focusing on escape. The crowd separated Poppy and Isaiah. Her gut told her to run in the opposite direction of whatever had terrorised the audience. Still, the timing – thinking she saw Joshua, the captain being pulled away before the performance – she had to see with her own eyes.

"What happened?" she asked, stopping Scott as he tried to get past her.

"We thought it was part of the final act, but the actors started screaming. The blood – I think she's dead!" Scott shoved past her, turning a shade of green.

"Who's dead?" Poppy asked another guest, who ignored her.

She'd lost sight of Isaiah, but she didn't have time to think about him, not when there was another potential murder. There was only so much time before security arrived and sealed off the scene, and the captain covered up another murder. Poppy struggled through the crowd and climbed the stairs to the stage, already empty of actors.

A limp body sat on a throne wearing a porcelain mask. Poppy could see a trickle of blood still flowing from beneath the gold collar, coating the front of the cream toga identical to the ones the other dancers had been wearing. She lifted the collar, only to drop it quickly when blood spurted out. An artery had been pierced by something sharp. She left the collar where it was to try and slow the bleeding.

Steadying her nerves, she placed her hand on the woman's wrist to check for a pulse. It was there but faint.

Hoping to help the poor dancer breathe, Poppy pulled off her mask.

She gasped, dropping to her knees. Calliope sat on the throne, her eyes staring into Poppy's, searching, pleading for her help.

"It's okay, I've got you," Poppy panted, holding her hand. "Help! She's still alive!" she screamed, but with so much chaos, no one was paying attention.

Calliope squeezed her hand painfully, but she couldn't speak. The terror in her eyes told Poppy she wanted to say something, but her mouth wobbled and closed again.

"Save your energy. Help is coming! *Isaiah!*" Poppy yelled. With the amount of blood Calliope had lost, she wouldn't have long.

She expected Isaiah to appear by her side and pull her away for her safety, but there was no sign of him. He might have gone to get security to help everyone get out without being trampled.

"Where the hell is security?" Poppy muttered, feeling Calliope's pulse slow. Her grip on Poppy softened. "Calliope, just hold on. You're going to be okay."

But Calliope shook her head ever so slightly, and tears trickled down her cheeks. They both knew her fate was inevitable.

"You're not alone. I'm right here with you," Poppy said, offering her some peace at the end.

She barely got the last word out before the light left Calliope's eyes.

Poppy fell back on her feet, a surge of hot adrenaline flashing up her spine. Unable to take her eyes away, she didn't know if she was going to throw up or pass out. Her mind raced with endless questions.

She didn't even realise she was still holding Calliope's hand until she was shoved away by the sudden arrival of the medics. They didn't work on her long before calling it, and Poppy knew they were asking her questions, but all she could focus on was Calliope's drained expression.

The medics covered the body with a sheet, but it didn't quite cover her hand. Poppy went to adjust the sheet, only to notice something clenched in Calliope's freshly manicured fingers. Glancing around, Poppy freed the crumpled-up paper in her fist. Then, ignored by the medics, she went to the stairs at the edge of the stage to escape the mess and give the better-late-than-never security team space.

*Where the hell is Isaiah?* she asked herself, searching the theatre. Some curious guests lingered; others arrived to see what the commotion was about. *Vultures.*

Poppy hung her head. They'd lost the chance to find out more about Patrice's murder, but the tape had revealed Calliope wasn't working alone, which meant she wasn't the mastermind but another puppet. She waited for Isaiah, unable to decide whether she should read the crumpled note. Even if she felt betrayed by him, she needed to know what he thought about this latest development.

The hairs on her neck stood up suddenly. Poppy looked up.

As clear as day, Joshua stood by the door. The light streaming in from the foyer made him look ghostly, but it was him. He was no mirage or hallucination.

Poppy struggled to her feet, her legs still numb from the adrenaline rush. She started down the steps, ignoring the members of security she passed who urged her to stay. She had to get out of there before they detained her. She didn't want them to learn about the note, and she didn't want Joshua to escape.

## Chapter 15
# Deceit on Deck
### Poppy

"Hello?" Poppy called out as she went to the observation deck. "Joshua? I know you're out here!"

All she could hear was the water slapping against the ship's sides.

Utterly alone on the deck, she felt like she was losing her mind. She sat in a lounge chair and put her head between her legs to slow her pounding heart. The cool air helped settle her nerves as she took a moment to uncrumple and read the note for clues

To her confusion, *her* name was hastily scrawled on one side while the other simply read *You're welcome.* Poppy frowned. Was the note addressed to her, thanking her? Or was it a message from Calliope to the killer? She realised she might be the next target, and this note could be a thank-you to the killer in advance. Either way, she didn't want anything connecting her to Calliope's murder, so she ripped the note to shreds and tossed it over the railing.

Someone was either taunting her or trying to frame her. If the killer thought they were doing her a favour by eliminating Calliope, it meant they didn't understand why Poppy had gone after the three people in Isaiah's file. The killer wasn't someone who had been around long. Dug knew all Poppy and Martha's secrets; if he had been the one behind turning this luxury cruise into a nightmare, he would have known why Poppy had targeted the others and how Calliope didn't fit into Poppy's criteria, which made her doubt that Dug was the one pulling the strings. The possibilities made her head spin. She considered trying to track Isaiah down again, but she was still mad at him for flashing that file in her face while she was having a vulnerable moment.

Actually, she had expected him to come after her anyway, to scold her for running off and leaving him. Had he listened when she'd said he was fired? Was he letting her fend for herself? She couldn't be angry at him for listening to her, yet she was. All this was about more than what she did or didn't feel for him and how he saw her. They had to find the culprit, or bodies would continue to drop. At least he couldn't blame her for killing Calliope.

*It's not like you haven't killed before,* her conscience taunted her.

*That was different,* she argued with herself.

*Is it? Do you think Isaiah would think it's different? Murder is murder. He didn't call you a monster – you did. What would he think if he knew about what really happened to those in that special file of his? Do you think he'd come running to your rescue if he knew about the stairs and mopping up all that blood? How you enjoyed every second?*

"Stop it. They got what they deserved, and I'm not sorry." Poppy let out a steady breath, trying to focus on the moonlight reflecting on the still water instead of the harrowing images burnt into her mind. *Maybe the killer on board is connected to those people I killed?* If someone was trying to get back at her for her role in their deaths, why weren't they coming after her directly?

A sharp cry broke through her thoughts. Poppy rushed to look over the railing to the pool deck below. She couldn't see anyone, but heard the sound of rushed footsteps. Afraid someone else might be in trouble, she kicked off her heels and hurried down the steps, only to find the pool area empty.

Before she could return to the observation deck, a gargled cry came from behind. Poppy turned to find a man lying in a bubbling jacuzzi, its water crimson around him. She didn't even think about her safety before climbing in. It hit her: the white jacket she'd seen Joshua wearing earlier, the blond highlights…

"Joshua?" Poppy rasped, shaking him to try and wake him. His head was resting on the jacuzzi's side.

His eyes fluttered open. She turned off the bubbles as blood and water splashed everywhere.

"Poppy?" Joshua grabbed her wrist and pushed her away from him. "Get out of here. They might come back."

"What the fuck happened?" she gasped, trying to find his wound. "Did you kill Calliope?"

"No. I was meant to meet her on deck, but she never arrived." He gave up on trying to push her away as he lost more strength.

"She's dead," Poppy told him, placing her hand on his abdomen to stop the blood flowing freely in the warm water.

"Fuck. I should've known she would be next." He groaned as she applied more pressure.

"Who did this to you? Who killed Calliope?"

"I never should have let you board the ship. I'm so sorry," he panted, not listening to her. "I should've warned you!"

"Warned me about the plot to kill me?"

He nodded. He was growing paler by the second, and it wouldn't be long before he bled out if she didn't get help; he was already drifting in and out of consciousness.

"I was scared. I'm sorry." She could barely make out what he was saying. "I thought I could stop them, but I never should have left you. Forgive me, please." The words of a man who thought he was dying.

"You didn't leave me. You're here now," she said, trying to put him at ease. The more he struggled and wasted his energy, the faster he'd fade, and he was her only witness to who was doing this. She tried to call for help, but the place was deserted. Clearly, security had been diverted to the theatre. Where the hell was Isaiah when she needed him?

"Help me get you out of here. I can't lift you by myself, but we have to get you out of the water," Poppy urged, but Joshua shook his head.

"I can't feel my legs," he whined.

Poppy leaned him against her and realised he was wounded in his side and lower back. He'd been stabbed more than once. Her only option was to leave and get help; there was no way she was going to be able to get him out of the jacuzzi herself.

"I'm going to get help. Save your strength," she told him.

He grabbed her wrist as she got out of the jacuzzi. "Don't go! You can't trust anyone!"

"You need help! I'll be right back," she pleaded, freeing herself from his weak grasp. His eyelids were closing. With so much blood lost, she feared it would be too late to save him if she didn't go now, and she had already failed to help Calliope.

Soaking wet, Poppy slipped on the deck once or twice

before making it inside, where she ran into two security guards.

"Help me! A man has been stabbed, but I can't help him!" she pleaded.

They stared at her wide-eyed, and she realised how she must look. Her cream dress was now a shade of pale pink, and she smelt like iron and chlorine.

"Please calm down," one of them said. "Have you been drinking?"

"Are you kidding? A man is dying, and you're asking me if I've been drinking?!" Poppy demanded. The woman's bun must be so tight that it stopped her brain from working.

"You don't need to take that tone with us. We're trying to help," the other security officer said.

"There isn't time. Please come with me," Poppy begged. "He'll drown if he passes out. Please!"

She took off, forcing them to follow. They probably thought she was crazy, but they'd eat their words once they saw Joshua.

"He's over here. He can't feel his legs, so I can't lift him out myself. I think he's been stabbed in the gut or the back, maybe both. You need to call a doctor," she gabbled as they hurried around the pool.

"What are we supposed to be looking at?" the security guard with the tight bun asked as they reached the empty jacuzzi.

Poppy froze, staring at the clear water. Joshua was gone. There were no blood stains on the decking to show he'd made his way out. She rushed to the jacuzzi, placing her hand in the clear water. *This is impossible.*

"Miss? How much have you had to drink tonight?" the male guard asked.

"I'm not drunk! He was here, I swear. He was bleeding.

There was blood everywhere," she barked, but they were looking at her like she'd lost it.

"Who was here?" Tight Bun asked slowly, as if she were dealing with a child.

"Joshua, my ex. He couldn't have left himself. There was so much blood." Poppy paced, trying to work out how he could have disappeared so quickly with no trace. Had whoever had hurt him come back to clean up their mess?

The other security guard left her with Tight Bun to speak on his radio.

"Joshua was listed as your guest, Ms Roe, but he never boarded the ship," he said. "I've confirmed it with reception."

"I know he didn't board with me, but he got on somehow. He was working with Calliope, the woman killed in the theatre earlier this evening. She must have got him on board somehow," Poppy started, but it was apparent from their doubtful expression that they didn't believe her.

"Ms Roe, considering what you witnessed at the theatre, you might be in shock. Let's get you back to your suite. In the morning, things will feel much clearer." Tight Bun tried to ease her away from the jacuzzi.

She wouldn't be gaslit into believing her mind had made up Joshua's appearance and injuries. Her dress was still stained with his blood, proof she wasn't making it up or imagining things. "The cameras – check the fucking cameras! I'm not crazy. Someone must have taken him."

Tight Bun took her handcuffs off her belt, and Poppy took a step back.

"Ms Roe, if you don't calm down, we're going to have to detain you for your own safety and those on board. We'll check the cameras and clear this all up. Please come inside with us. You're soaking wet, and the wind is freezing out here. These are for your protection, as well as ours, until we get to the bottom of this."

Poppy wanted to resist, but she knew refusing the handcuffs would only make matters worse and she wanted to see what was on the cameras, so she offered her wrists willingly.

She let them take her into the bar lounge by the pool, where she stared at the jacuzzi as if she could make Joshua appear. What if he'd pulled himself out when she left because he was afraid? Adrenaline was a powerful drug. Still, she worried that her only lead was bleeding out somewhere. It didn't make sense. Even if he'd got himself out or someone had taken him, how could the water be so clear? How could he have just disappeared? There was no blood on the decking, only her wet footprints.

Tight Bun hovered over her while her partner radioed about the cameras. Poppy started to shiver, and Tight Bun covered her in a towel from one of the armchairs in the lounge.

Before Poppy could thank her, Isaiah appeared through the doors. His face was red, and he was breathless as though he had been running around.

"What's going on?" he demanded, crouching down in front of her as he examined her bloody dress. Where had he been? She guessed he had tracked her here, but she didn't know what had taken him so long.

"Are the cuffs really necessary?" Isaiah snapped at Tight Bun.

"Ms Roe believes she witnessed an attack on the pool deck, and she was upset. We wanted to make sure she didn't hurt herself." Tight Bun's condescending tone made Poppy want to lunge at her.

"I want to hear it from Poppy," Isaiah said. He crouched beside her, removed his jacket, and wrapped it around her shoulders. She hadn't even realised how badly she was still shaking.

"I saw Joshua when we were in the theatre. I followed him, but he had been stabbed. I found him in the jacuzzi," she explained. Isaiah listened without interrupting, much to her relief. "I went to get help, but when I came back, he was gone. These two idiots think I'm drunk and imagined the whole thing. He couldn't have just walked away! There was so much blood. Even if he did pull himself out of the water, he wouldn't have got far before passing out."

Tight Bun huffed. "Sir, we followed Ms Roe to the alleged scene, and there was no one on deck or sign of any such injury or incident. After what Ms Roe witnessed earlier in the evening, we believe she is in shock, and her mind played a terrible and frightening trick on her."

"I swear to you, I'm not losing my mind!" Poppy clutched Isaiah's hand, willing him to believe her. She looked at her hands, wishing they were stained with blood, but the water had washed it all away.

"I believe you," Isaiah said, helping her to her feet. The other security guard returned, and she looked up, hoping the camera footage would earn her an apology.

"Ms Roe, unfortunately, our cameras were updated at midnight, so we are missing about an hour of footage from the outer decks," he informed them. Poppy's stomach dropped.

"The cameras just happened to update right when and where a crime took place, but are now working fine?" she retorted. He obviously knew it was suspicious, but he didn't want to admit she might be right.

"I'm sorry, Ms. Roe, but it's a schedule loop to ensure we're running the tightest network to maintain your and everyone else's security. Can you give us any other evidence than your word? Did you actually see the man's wound, or was there a weapon?" Tight Bun asked.

"There was so much blood. I couldn't see exactly where he was hurt, and there wasn't any weapon I could see. I was more concerned about keeping him alive than gathering evidence!" She wished she hadn't left him. Then again, she hadn't expected to have to fight to be believed.

"I'm sorry, but with nothing to go on but your word, there isn't much we can do. You've witnessed a lot while on board, and shock can do strange things to the mind."

"Like make me see my ex bleeding out in a jacuzzi?" Poppy shot back.

"We want to see the captain," Isaiah said. His jaw was tight, and she knew he was as fed up as she was about their gaslighting. After what happened between them in the bar, she was surprised and relieved to know he had her back. That he believed her.

"I'm sorry, sir, but given what happened in the theatre earlier this evening, and that we have also received a storm warning, we don't need to add phantom stabbed guests to the captain's already stacked plate," Tight Bun said.

Poppy remembered that the captain had slipped away from the performance. That explained where she'd gone, but was it really a storm warning?

"So you aren't going to do anything? Just going to chalk this up to my imagination?" If they didn't believe her, she would discover the truth. Talking to them was a waste of time.

"We've no evidence of this guest even boarding the ship. The cameras sadly couldn't offer anything, so there is no reason for us to investigate further – no body, no crime." Tight Bun's partner dismissed them. "I suggest you and Ms Roe return to your suite for the night and get some rest. I'm sure things will feel clearer in the morning. Or, if you insist on pressing the issue, we can take you to the medical wing to be assessed."

*To be assessed?* Poppy opened her mouth to argue, but Isaiah held her close to his side. She glared at him, and he shook his head.

"Thank you for your help; it's been an exhausting evening, and some rest will help us relax," he said calmly. Poppy wished she was as good as him at bullshitting.

"Goodnight, then. We hope you enjoy the rest of your voyage," Tight Bun said pointedly.

"Fuck you too," Poppy hissed with a forced smile. She stormed out of the lounge and back into the cool night air to try and calm herself down. If she looked at their dismissive faces a second longer, she would end up locked up in the belly of the ship.

"You really are more vinegar than honey, aren't you," Isaiah said, following her to the observation deck, where she had left her shoes.

"It wouldn't have mattered if I lathered them in maple syrup and licked them clean – they weren't going to listen to me," Poppy said, heading to the lounger she'd been sitting on.

"Now, that's an image I'm not going to be able to get out of my head in a hurry. But I don't think you can lather maple syrup," Isaiah pointed out, following her.

"Can you stop being so logical for one minute? Where the hell were you when I needed you?" she shot back.

"I tried to reach you during the stampede, but one of the guests got trampled right in front of me. I had to help him out before he got crushed. After that, security wouldn't let me back in. When I tried to resist, they cuffed me and called First Mate Davide," Isaiah explained. "I didn't even know Calliope had died until he told me she was supposed to perform as a special guest during the final act. Her body had already been taken away, and Davide questioned me about what had happened. He took me to her dressing room as a second set of eyes and warned me the only way I was getting out of the cuffs to get to you was to help." He shook his head. "Calliope's dressing room was a mess. There was a bloody hairpin that we think was used to pierce her jugular. When Davide finally released me, you were already gone. I tracked your bracelet and found you in cuffs."

"Who would've thought a night at the opera would end with us both in handcuffs?" Poppy said, searching each row of loungers for her missing shoes.

"What happened after the theatre?" he asked, eager to hear her side of the story.

Poppy told him how she tried to help Calliope. She swallowed hard, trying to block out the memory of her fading eyes. "I followed Joshua outside, and found him in the jacuzzi. I think someone stabbed him."

"Joshua and Calliope were working together?"

"I think so, but from the recording, it sounded like she didn't know he was onboard."

"Maybe she heard he'd boarded the ship and thought he'd changed his mind about their plans, so she wanted to meet up," Isaiah reasoned.

"Pretending not to board certainly gives him a great alibi," Poppy said, "but it doesn't matter now if he's dead. I tried to ask him who was behind all this, but he wasn't making any sense."

"If we assume that Calliope and Joshua are dead, then whoever's behind the scheme to kill you is cleaning house. They clearly don't want to leave any traces."

"But shouldn't they do that *after* killing me?"

"Unless whoever is behind this wants you to know they're coming."

"That's a comforting thought," Poppy said sarcastically.

"Still don't think it could be your ex-manager?"

She shook her head. "I think he was just the middleman. He wanted money from Calliope and intended to use Joshua as a scapegoat. I believe someone hired Dug to put the pieces in place because there's no way he's smart enough to pull this off, and he wouldn't want to get his hands dirty."

"Is there anyone you can think of that connects to each person – not just those on the *Midas* but in the file I showed you?"

Her stomach sank as he brought up that damned file again. "Yes," she sighed.

"Who?" He placed his hands on her shoulders, looking directly into her eyes.

"Me."

"But you didn't kill Patrice, Calliope and Joshua."

"My head is throbbing, and I'm freezing. Can we please go back to the suite?"

Isaiah nodded and released her.

She checked under the last lounger and groaned, frustrated. "Where the hell are they?!"

"What's wrong?"

"My heels are gone! I took them off when I heard the scuffle so I wouldn't be slowed down, but I left them right by the loungers." She pointed to the empty floor.

"A body and a pair of shoes – a killer with a taste for designer heels," he quipped.

"What, *you're* doubting me now?" Poppy snapped, heading inside before she froze to death.

Once she'd had a hot shower and changed into dry clothes, she could think more clearly.

"I'm not doubting you," Isaiah assured her. "I just

think the security aboard the *Midas* is more interested in cleaning up messes than protecting those on board."

"You think they covered it up?" she asked as they got into the lift. "How? I couldn't have been gone more than five minutes."

"I think security saw what happened on the cameras and cleaned up while they kept you busy. They made sure not to leave a trace, including your shoes. They use Eagle Eye security – that software doesn't need updating like they said it does," Isaiah explained. "The captain might have been able to hide Patrice's death, but with Calliope's death being so public, there's no way they would want news of a second on the same evening."

"What about Joshua?! He needs help! Do you think they took him away to help him?" she gasped, unable to ignore the irony that she was trying to save the man she had plotted to kill just days ago.

"I don't know. If he was still alive when they got to him, he should be in the infirmary. Still, they won't let you anywhere near there," Isaiah said, buttoning up his jacket on her as her teeth began to chatter.

"At least the infirmary will be easier to get to than the morgue," Poppy said as the doors opened. "If he's alive, then he has the answers we need."

"Tonight we can't risk heading down there. We've already been in cuffs once this evening." Isaiah led her down the corridor. "Once things settle, I'll figure out a way to find out if he's in there."

"Okay," she agreed, lacking the strength to argue. The thought of Joshua being safe in the infirmary eased her worries. If the captain kept his presence a secret, the killer wouldn't know they had failed, and he would be safe.

*If* he was still alive. All the ifs were starting to make her head spin.

## Chapter 16
# Bitter Suite Confessions
### Poppy

Poppy took a moment to ensure Mina was secure in her room. Thankfully, she was fast asleep and curled around a pillow. Poppy didn't want to wake her and tell her what happened; one of them should have a nightmare-free sleep.

Isaiah was waiting for her in the sitting room.

"Mina's out cold," Poppy said, tossing his jacket onto the bed as he closed the door behind her.

"At least one of us is having a nice holiday," he joked as he opened the minibar and took out a small bottle of whisky.

"I thought you didn't drink on the job?"

"It's for you; it'll warm you up and help with the shock," Isaiah said, pouring the liquor into a crystal glass.

"Thank you," she said, taking a sip. Heat rushed down her throat into her chest.

She glanced at the door to Isaiah's room. Technically, she had fired him. It wasn't his job to protect her anymore, and she wasn't sure if he would still want her to stay with him. She didn't want to be alone; being with Isaiah distracted her from the sensation of blood on her skin.

Isaiah threw himself into the armchair. He looked as exhausted as she felt.

"I need a shower. I can still feel their blood on me." Poppy sighed, perching on the edge of a lounge chair.

"Take a shower," he told her.

"Can you stay here?" Poppy asked.

"You fired me. Are you sure you still want my protection?" Isaiah smiled softly.

"Please don't make me beg. It doesn't matter what happened in the bar, because we both need each other if we want to get off this ship alive. I need you to keep me safe, and you need me to solve this." She finished the whisky.

Isaiah nodded. "Your stuff is already in my room and bathroom, so there's no point in moving it out now." He stood up and led her into the bathroom, where he ran the shower, checking the temperature. About to leave, he paused in the doorway. "And you can fire me all you want. I promised to protect you, and I will. If you ever trust me enough to let me into that beautiful head of yours, I'm here. I'm sorry for how I approached things in the bar."

His apology made her heart swell. She wanted to tell him everything, even if the truth meant he wouldn't look at her the same way again.

"Can you stay up until I'm out of the shower?" she asked.

"Don't worry, I'm not going to sleep," he said, sitting down and reaching for the TV remote.

"Thank you," she said quickly, unable to make out his response as she shut the bathroom door.

With her ruined dress in the bin, Poppy rested her forehead against the cool tiles and let the hot water cascade down her back. Her mind was a battleground, torn between trust and fear. Could Isaiah be trusted? He had listened to and believed her when the others wouldn't. He had protected her even when she pushed him away, even when he suspected she was guilty of murder. But if she didn't come clean about what she'd done before boarding the *Midas*, she would be risking his and Mina's lives to save her own skin. Isaiah could only help so much knowing half the story. They would all be at risk if he was distracted by what he thought he knew about her and her past.

After scrubbing herself raw, Poppy finally felt clean, but the weight of her secrets remained heavy on her chest. She dried her hair roughly and twisted it in a claw clip to keep it out of her face. Staring at her bare face in the mirror, she prepared to expose her darkest secrets.

Isaiah lay on the couch as she emerged in his fluffy white robe. He stared at her, his silence echoing in the room.

Poppy noticed the envelope peeking out from his suit jacket and removed it. Sitting on the couch beside him, she tucked her legs beneath her and placed the envelope on the coffee table in front of them.

"What are you doing?" Isaiah asked as she pulled the photos from it and laid them out face up.

"We were interrupted at the bar earlier," she said, trying to keep her voice steady. She couldn't back out now. What she had done was clearly connected to the events unfolding on board. She couldn't risk the killer coming after Mina and Isaiah, so coming clean was the only way to move forward and figure out who was behind it all.

"When you said I wouldn't look at you the same way if I knew the truth…"

She pressed her finger to his lips, silencing him. If he spoke, she wasn't sure if she could go on.

"I need you to promise that you'll listen to everything I have to say without interrupting, and when I'm done, you'll still help me find the killer on board. Once they're caught and we reach the island, you can decide what to do with what I share with you," she said, removing her finger.

Isaiah's eyes narrowed, and Poppy held her breath as he hesitated.

"Please. I need your help, but I need you to work with me, not against me. If you meant what you said – that you don't believe I'm a monster – then I need you to hold on to that."

He finally nodded. "I'll help you, regardless of what you tell me."

Taking a deep breath, Poppy picked up the first photo.

"My first dance teacher, Augusta Devin," she told Isaiah. "A prolific dancer in her youth. My aunt hired her to train me – only the best of the best would do for Martha Roe's niece.

"Augusta trained me for years in every style, even though I was a terrible dancer. Like my dad, I had no rhythm and couldn't follow a count to save my life. Augusta demanded perfection, even if that meant training until my feet blistered, my muscles tore, and I suffered stress fractures. I trained as hard as possible and became what she wanted me to be – not out of love for dancing, but because I was terrified of her cane and my aunt's anger."

Poppy lifted the edge of the robe and revealed a long, thin scar by her ankle. "Augusta shattered my ankle with her cane when I was thirteen because I fell during a performance for her dance company. I was meant to be her star, but my light didn't shine bright enough for her. My aunt finally gave up on her dreams of making me a professional dancer and decided to switch me to singing lessons. I never had to see Augusta again.

"I had surgery, and they had to pin it. It still hurts when it's cold out, and when I dance now, I have to ice it before and after to stop it from swelling and aching. I had to get injections during my last tour because it started to give me trouble. One of my backup dancers had to have the same injections, and I found out Augusta had done the same to her. Apparently we're the lucky ones. Ms Devin had been ruining dancers' careers long before and after me."

She took another deep breath as Isaiah traced the scar with his fingers.

"I couldn't get what the dancer had told me out of my head. I didn't want her to hurt anyone else. I never dreamed of being a dancer, but I couldn't stomach how many dreams she'd shattered. I went to her studio and offered to buy out her studio if she would retire. She refused. I tried to let it go, but I thought she would give in if I offered her more money. The next time I went back to see her, I witnessed her beating a young girl with her cane. She wasn't going to stop. I thought she'd beaten me because I didn't have any natural talent, and she hated that my aunt forced me on her. But when I saw that sick, twisted grin as the girl cried, I knew she did it because she liked breaking our spirits.

"I waited for the girl to be picked up. When the studio closed, I used the same cane she used to torture us to make Augusta dance as hard and as long as she had made us. She was in her seventies, but her muscle memory was impressive. She danced until her heart gave out, and I knew she could never ruin another person. I didn't even need to use the cane, I think it was because she knew the pain it could inflict."

Poppy put the photo face down on the counter and moved on to the next. Thankfully, Isaiah didn't interrupt.

"Clarissa Keogh, head of housekeeping at the Claren Hotel. Also my former nanny and warden. When my aunt was out of town, Ms Keogh made sure the food stayed locked up and I kept up my dance training and studies. When I was eight or nine, my aunt went away to shoot a film, and it was the longest she'd ever stayed away. I won't bore you with the details, but when my aunt returned, she learnt that my tutor had called the police. I had been hospitalised for malnourishment because my dear, sweet nanny had 'misunderstood' my aunt's instructions and taken my diet too far. If my tutor hadn't called the police, I wouldn't be sitting here now.

"To avoid being suspected of involvement, my aunt pressed charges against her. I don't know what happened after that; I think my aunt made it go away because she didn't want it to get out that she was the one who'd instructed Clarissa to lock up the food in the first place. When I was released from the hospital and the police gave up on their investigation, it took one month before the locks returned to the cupboards.

"Mina asked me at breakfast the other day how I could eat so much. It's because I'm always afraid that I won't eat again. It's why I pack so many snacks – if I don't, my anxiety gets out of control. Anyway, I barely recognised her when I saw her at the Claren. She told me how proud she was of how far I'd come; she believed she'd played some part in my success. I invited her into my suite and ordered room service so we could eat together and catch up. Sadly, Clarissa choked, and when her face turned purple, I didn't do anything to help her."

Poppy put down the second photo and went to pick up the final picture of the crash scene.

"Poppy, stop. You don't have to go on." Isaiah rested his hand over hers.

The sorrow in his eyes made her want to give up, but she had already come this far. The more she shared, the lighter she felt.

"I'm almost finished, and you need to know the truth to see the connection," she told him, and he removed his hand from hers. She picked up the final image, a horrific car crash.

"Through all of this, I had one friend from school. Maisie. She didn't care who my aunt was and didn't mind that I was shy and introverted. I spent more time at her house than I did at mine when I could. Her family were kind to me and never made me go home or made me feel like I had overstayed my welcome. Maisie knew all my secrets and how I planned to move out when I got my inheritance from my parents when I turned eighteen. The year before that could happen, we snuck out to a party, and my aunt came home early from a trip; she called me back to the house to scold me, and Maisie insisted on coming with me to defend me. When we got to my house, my aunt was furious. She kicked Maisie out and insisted that Ed, the driver, drive her home." Poppy choked on the words she had never said aloud. "He – assaulted her."

She was silent for a moment.

"Maisie never spoke to me again – not that I blame her. I hated myself for putting her in that position. My aunt paid for her family's silence and fired Ed Fogerty. I lost my only friend and was pulled out of school. I didn't do my final exams, and my aunt sent me on my first tour to open for a band that same year because she wanted me out of the way and as far away from Maisie and her family as possible. When I got home from the tour, I was the 'Princess of Pop', and they had moved away. Ed was working for one of Joshua's friends by chance, and I heard Maisie wasn't the last girl he took advantage of. I hired him and made sure it would be his last drive." She didn't go into details. The memories of Maisie and what had been done to her were too painful to linger on. The one person Poppy had cared about, who'd welcomed her into her family, had had her life ruined because of their friendship.

She put down the final picture. She felt Isaiah watching her as she got up to take a pen from the desk. She wrote on the back of each photo: *Maid, Dancer, Driver.*

"The killer is mimicking the victims of my crimes," she said.

Isaiah swallowed.

"Patrice, our private butler; Calliope was a chorus dancer; and Joshua was a stunt driver before he was an actor. Now you know everything. You came on board because you saw what so many others couldn't." Poppy wished he would say something as he stared at her. "You've got your killer. You should be happy," she prompted.

Isaiah picked up the photos. She expected him to return them to the envelope. Instead, he ripped them up and tucked the pieces away.

"What are you doing?" Poppy asked anxiously, hoping they weren't part of an official investigation. She didn't want him to get in trouble because he felt sorry for her.

"I don't know. It's not what I expected. You're not who I thought you'd be," Isaiah said, his voice trembling with the weight of his realisation, running his hands through his hair. "I'm sorry for everything they did to you. I can't even begin to process what you've told me, but I know I can't judge you for what you did."

"Can't judge me? You should want to lock me up and throw away the key," Poppy exclaimed, gripping his shirt and forcing him to look at her. She'd expected him to be livid. She'd expected him to say he'd known it all along, and have her locked up in the brig until they reached the island. Instead, he was just looking at her like he wanted to wrap her in his arms and not let her go.

"They hurt you and others. I wish you'd had someone to help you, to stand up for and protect you, so you didn't feel like this was your only option," he said, taking Poppy's hands in his. She released her hold on his shirt.

"I don't want your pity. I didn't tell you what they did because I wanted you to feel sorry for me," she said. Isaiah was looking at her like she was the victim, not the monster he had suspected she was. "I killed those people, and I'm not sorry for what I did. They deserved what they got."

His expression didn't waver. She didn't know why she was angry about his lack of reaction. Her chest grew tighter, and she wasn't sure if she wanted to scream or cry.

"Don't you think I'm a monster? A killer? I saw the way you looked at me at the bar when you showed me the photos – but now that you've heard my sob stories, you're looking at me like I'm some wounded puppy. Don't you think I should be punished for my actions?" How could he be so willing to look the other way?

"I think you're punishing yourself enough for the both of us," Isaiah said gently.

"I'm not punishing myself. I'm not sorry!" she argued, angrily wiping tears from her eyes.

"You've said that, but I think you're lying." Isaiah brushed the tears from her cheeks. "You want me to think you killed them in cold blood and that you don't feel anything. But you did this because you felt too much. Being faced with those who traumatised you and learning they were still hurting others – the heart and mind can only be pushed so far before something snaps." He sat closer, his hands resting on her hips so she couldn't turn away from him. She'd thought confessing would push him away, not bring him closer.

"I wanted revenge. I wanted to make them suffer. I wanted to go to sleep and know they could never hurt another person," she admitted. "I did it for the starved kid, my broken body." More tears fell. A knot in her throat tried to stop her from expelling her grief, but she forced herself to go on. "For Maisie. I hired a private investigator to find her, and I sent her Ed's death notice with an anonymous note; I wanted her to know justice had been served, even if it came ten years too late."

For a moment, they locked eyes in a tense silence. Poppy tried to tell him to let her go but couldn't find the words. Months of blocked, untamed emotion poured out of her in wretched sobs. He held her close, not saying a word. She couldn't stand his tenderness.

"I'm sorry for all the pain you've suffered; I wish I could've been there to protect you, to help you, but I've got you now."

His words barely registered before his lips claimed hers in a fierce and unrelenting kiss. All her anger and confusion melted away into an aching need for him.

Isaiah broke the kiss, his chest heaving, his breath coming in heavy gasps. Poppy clung to him, and he pulled her onto his lap. She couldn't remember a time when someone had held her like this.

"I hate what they made me. I wanted to be better than them. I never wanted to be like them, but I couldn't let them get away with what they had done. I could have gone to the police, told the press and ruined them, but I wanted the satisfaction of knowing they were rotting in Hell." She leaned away from him.

"And that's exactly where they deserve to be. No matter what that brain of yours tells you, you aren't like them. You're incredibly intelligent, kind, and passionate. I've seen how you treat those around you and put others before yourself. You've got a good heart. I've met monsters, and you couldn't be further from them."

"You're only defending me because you have feelings for me – because you've got to know me. Before you boarded this ship, you thought I was just like any other criminal that crossed your path," Poppy said, hiding her face in her hands, but he didn't loosen his grip on her.

"Regardless of my feelings for you, I'm not and would never be disgusted by you. Do you *want* me to think you're a monster?" he asked. "Did you kill Patrice? Calliope? Or attack Joshua?"

"No! I'd never have harmed them. I told you, I would only have protected myself against Joshua. I tried to save him tonight. I tried to get them help. I didn't want them to die!"

"Do you think *I'm* a monster?" Isaiah asked.

"Why would I?" She frowned, drying her tears as she focused on his expression. She'd never seen him look scared before.

"Since we're confessing, then I should even the playing field. Eckells and I are friends and… colleagues; I'm unsure how to define our situation. Eckells is on one side of the fence, and I'm on the other. When an unforgivable case comes my way and the culprit escapes from my side of the fence, I ensure that Eckells doesn't let them get away – and vice versa. He has informants all over the city and works with me unofficially. When one side can't ensure justice, the other takes action."

Poppy let that sink in. This was how he'd got the bodyguard job so easily; his relationship with Eckells was far more close-knit than she'd expected. At least they used their power for good instead of self-gain.

"I see why his staff is so good at cover-ups," she said, thinking they had enough skeletons together to fill quite a few rugs and wardrobes. "When did you and he start working together?"

"I got a tip out of the blue one day from him when he was a bouncer at the club he now owns. He'd overheard talk of a private party with underage girls. He managed to get the address, and I went undercover to bust it. Except when I got there, I discovered the girls weren't just underage; they were – young, and the party wasn't so much a party but a small group of sick men. I reacted."

"When you say reacted…?"

"The men were never found, and the children were sent to good homes." He let out a breath. "No one else on this earth knows about this. Eckells cleaned up the scene and took care of the children who were victimised. We've had a mutual understanding ever since."

"Why tell me this?" she whispered.

"Because we need to start trusting each other, and if someone is on board targeting you, then we have to work together to make sure that you make it off this ship." He took her hand. "So I'll ask you again. Do you think I'm a monster?"

"No, I don't think you're a monster. We did wrong for the right reasons. We can't be the monsters, can we?" She shook her head, resting her forehead against his chest. Exhaustion started pouring through her veins.

Isaiah picked her up and carried her over to the bed.

"We might not be saints, but I don't think we're the bad guys," he said, tucking her into bed.

"How about we settle for something in between?" Poppy asked as he lay beside her.

"I can live with that," Isaiah agreed, cradling her body against his as he brushed her hair.

"Me too." Poppy turned to face him, covering them

both in the blanket. Isaiah rested his forehead against her and kissed her tenderly.

"Get some sleep," he said as she brushed her lips against his. "Tomorrow, we have a real monster to catch."

"Thank you," she sighed, staring into his dark eyes. She couldn't remember the last time, if ever, she'd felt so light, so free.

"For what?" he asked softly.

"For being here with me. For not using my past against me," she said, yawning.

"I only wish I had found you sooner," he told her.

Poppy snuggled into his chest. Listening to his steady heartbeat, she fell asleep in his arms.

## Chapter 17
# Stormy Alliances
### Isaiah

"Poppy? Can you come in here?" Isaiah called out as he heard the door open. Poppy had been having breakfast with Mina, catching her up on the events from the previous night. He'd wanted to give them some space to talk, so he'd been on a morning run, leaving them safely in the suite.

"Are you changing your mind about last night?" she asked tentatively, peering around the bathroom door. "Because there's no takebacks on letting me get away with murder."

She was still in her pyjamas, pink shorts with red hearts and a matching top. After their long conversations last night, Isaiah had crashed into a deep sleep, so she must have got up at some point to change. He had never slept so soundly when he was supposed to be on alert, especially with someone else in his bed.

"No takebacks necessary. I need help with the after-sun lotion. I think I managed to get sunburned," he said, struggling to reach his back.

His run had also been to assess whether the captain

had increased security on the outer decks. Despite the crew's insistence that nothing had happened on the lounge deck, they had ordered everyone to keep away from the jacuzzi area where Poppy had found Joshua.

"My hands are at your service." She smirked, hopping onto the bathroom counter to reach his shoulders and neck.

"Since when are you so eager to help? Are you up to something? You're not normally this compliant," he noted, raising an eyebrow as she didn't make fun of his burn or make him beg for assistance.

She rolled her eyes. "So paranoid! Turn around, please," Poppy ordered.

He didn't move. She bit her lip, and he couldn't stop thinking about how her lips had tasted the night before… and how much he wanted to see those pretty shorts on the floor.

"Are you going to give it to me?" she asked, staring at him.

"What?" Isaiah asked blankly.

"The lotion?" Poppy took the bottle from him and squeezed some onto her hands.

"I'm sorry. I thought you wanted me to *give* it to you." Isaiah winked, resting his hands on either side of her thighs. Her eyes lingered on him, as if she were documenting every scar and freckle he had.

"Naughty, but priorities first. We don't want the burn to get worse." Poppy rubbed the lotion between her hands and turned him around so his back faced her. "Why does it look so irritated?"

"I accidentally used your toner on it first. It stung like hell, so I think I'll stay away from your stuff for my safety," Isaiah rambled, trying to distract himself from how good it felt to have her hands on his sensitive skin.

"You could've read which products were which," she teased, clearly enjoying his mistake.

"I did, and I discovered that your tiny pot of eye cream costs more than I make in a week." He picked up the small jar from the counter and pointed out the price still printed on the bottom.

"It works miracles for dark circles. Half of these products were sent to me; companies send stuff in the hopes that I'll post about it. Ironically, the more money I make, the less I have to pay for things. I donate most of the products to shelters and charities instead of letting them go to waste." She snatched the jar from him and put it back by the sink. "Now turn around so I can do your chest."

Isaiah did as instructed, standing between her legs so she wouldn't have to stretch. He loved the smell of her fruity shampoo.

"You're all good. I don't think it'll blister."

"Thank you for the help," he said, brushing her hair over her shoulder. "How can I repay your kindness?" His eyes lingered on her lips.

"There are a few things that spring to mind," Poppy said, staring at him with her bright, mischievous eyes.

"Do tell?" Isaiah said, with his face so close to hers he could count the fair freckles on the bridge of her nose.

She rested her hands on the sides of his neck. "I thought you didn't want to cross professional boundaries?"

"You fired me, remember?" He pulled her sharply against him. Poppy shrieked in surprise and wrapped her legs around him like he'd hoped she would.

"Don't worry; I won't let you fall," he whispered, brushing her ear and making her tremble. His lips trailed along her ear and neck, teasing her sensitive skin. She cupped his face and brought her lips to his, taking control, but he slipped his hands under the hem of her top and she shuddered. Her kisses grew more passionate.

"Wait, wait," he panted. "Do you want me to stop? To slow down?" He ran his hands through her hair as they locked eyes.

"No, I want this." Poppy shook her head. He tried to keep a level head as her hands ran over his muscles.

"Say that again," he said, pressing his lips against hers, giving her a taste of what was to come before pulling away.

"Don't stop. Ever."

The words were music to his ears. He lifted her off the bathroom counter.

"Sorry! I dug my nails into your sunburn," she said as he groaned.

"Don't be sorry; it would take a lot more than that to hurt me," he promised, loving how her body folded to his as he carried her out into the bedroom.

Sitting down on the bed, he let her straddle his lap and bit back his groans as she nipped and sucked on his neck, rolling her hips and sending shockwaves of pleasure through him. He held her hips tightly so she couldn't finish him before they even got started. She groaned in frustration. His grip loosened on her waist, and she tangled her hands in his hair, crushing his lips to hers.

"Are you in a rush?" he asked, smiling as she pulled his shorts off. Poppy couldn't seem to get him naked fast enough.

"Yes, because I have to meet Mina – so if you don't want her interrupting us, I suggest less talking and more action. Unless you want to press pause until later?"

She chuckled as Isaiah flipped her onto her back and pinned her hands to prevent her from stripping him.

"Absolutely not," he said, tossing aside his shorts while she slipped off her PJs. He inhaled sharply, taking in the sight of her all flushed for him. He wanted to take his time and savour every moment, but he'd take everything she was willing to give. It didn't matter how much time they had. All that mattered was her.

She moved to the edge of the bed, rising to her knees and placing her hands on his chest. "Enjoying the view? Or are you going to do something about it," she teased.

"Don't test me, Princess," he growled.

"Or what?" She bit his lip as she kissed him, and he gripped her thighs and tossed her back on the bed. He loved how confident she was.

She squirmed and arched her back as he kissed every inch of her body, begging for more. She pulled down his boxers and wrapped her fist around him, making his eyes roll back in his head, but if she was going to tease, he was going to make her beg. He smiled wickedly as he sank between her knees and kissed the dips in her hips, sliding her underwear down her thighs. Tremors of pleasure took over her body as he tasted how ready she was for him; he held her thighs tight to stop her from trying to hide from him. Her hands slid up over the back of his neck and into his hair, gripping tight as she panted.

He didn't let up until Poppy arched her back and cried out in sheer ecstasy. His heart pounded as he trailed his lips over her stomach, savouring every quiver as she came down until her lips found his, seeking, demanding more. He was more than happy to oblige.

"I can't take much more, Poppy," he groaned as she wrapped her legs around his waist. "Are you sure?"

"I've never wanted anything more," she rasped, brushing her lips against his.

Isaiah reached into the bedside table and removed the complimentary condoms. Ripping open the packet, he nearly lost control as she helped him ease it over him. A feral groan escaped him as he filled every inch of her. She rolled her hips, taking all of him. Teeth clashed, tongues twisted, and her hands gripped his hair, his shoulders, her nails dragging so ferociously down his back that he was sure he'd have marks tomorrow. She moaned and sighed against his lips, and with every thrust, he felt her tightening around him. He was so damn close. He wanted to drag it out forever, but neither could wait that long. He thrust wildly as she dug her nails into his hips, begging for more.

Her body took all he had to give, ruining him. Arms around each other, they rode wave after wave of ecstasy. Every muscle in his body tightened, and tremors overtook him until he had nothing left to give but a low groan into her neck. They melted into each other in a collection of satisfied, heavy breaths; he didn't want the moment to end. Lying by his side, tucked under his arm, she stared at him with satisfied eyes.

"Next time, you won't be able to escape me so quickly," he said, rolling onto his side as she caught her breath. "I don't care if it's God himself waiting on you."

"I'm counting on it," she said before he kissed her long and hard, wanting her to remember the taste of him for the rest of the day.

Isaiah showered while Poppy slipped on her purple one-piece swimsuit. Unable to stop himself, he tried to get her to join him but she tiptoed out of reach and away from the spray of the water.

"Nice try, but Mina's waiting for me to go to the pool. I'm late enough, thanks to you, and I don't want her to think I've forgotten about her. She was freaked out enough hearing about what happened with Joshua last night," Poppy said, tying a matching sarong around those hips he would never get enough of.

"I'll join you; give me a minute," he said, not wanting to leave them unprotected.

"Are you kidding? You should stay out of the sun. We'll be fine in the crowd." Poppy chuckled. "I don't want to stay indoors all day, and you're already a nice shade of red. How about we compromise? Mina and I will lounge for a bit, and then I'll meet you later in the shade. I promised Mina a holiday, and so far it's been murder and mayhem. I think she needs some girl time, and so do I. I can't gossip about the hunky man in my bed if he's right beside me."

"Fine, but only because they've increased security on the outer decks, and you aren't to go anywhere alone," he instructed.

A loud bang on the adjoining door made Poppy jump.

"Are you finished screwing each other's brains out? We're burning daylight, and you promised me cocktails and sun," Mina shouted through the door.

Isaiah enjoyed how Poppy flushed at being overheard. They hadn't exactly been quiet, and he'd forgotten about Mina being so close.

He gave in reluctantly to her plan. After all they had discussed last night, he trusted her and knew she could handle herself.

"Got your bracelet?" he asked as Poppy lingered at the bathroom door.

She waved it at him. "Don't worry; I've no desire to wander off."

"Okay, I'll see you later."

She saluted him. "Yes, sir, and don't forget to reapply the lotion when you get out."

"That's your job." He winked, and she rolled her eyes.

When he'd heard them leave, he turned off the shower and got dressed. With Mina and Poppy out enjoying themselves, he didn't want to waste any time.

Isaiah followed the STAFF ONLY signs to the galley, nearly running into two waiters smoking outside the canteen's open door. He paused at the next door to listen in on their conversation. There was no better place to catch up on gossip than the smoking area.

"Sorry I couldn't help you at the bar last night. I had to help security get a guy out of a jacuzzi," one of them said, his husky voice sounding like he smoked multiple packs daily.

"Was he drunk?" his female companion asked.

"No, someone had stabbed him. We got him to the infirmary, but it took three of us to clean up the mess before anyone else found out," said the first waiter. "With what happened in the theatre, we were ordered to clean it up and ensure no guests learnt about another killing."

"Maybe we shouldn't be talking about this. I need this job, and all these deaths are giving me the creeps. The less I know, the better."

"How can you not be curious?" asked Husky. "I heard the guy was Poppy Roe's ex. He didn't even board the ship, and then suddenly, he's found clinging to life, and she's the only witness? It doesn't add up. Also, I heard Patrice was found in Poppy's suite. It's why they closed off the Empress suite."

Isaiah hated how they gossiped as if Poppy wasn't a real person, as if these people hadn't tragically lost their lives.

"Patrice's death was an accident. You can't connect those events. As for Joshua, I bet Poppy wanted to keep his presence on board a secret," the woman said.

"Well, the admin staff got an earful this morning.

Poppy should have followed the rules. All privately listed guests still have to sign a log in case an emergency arises. Our guests might want to keep their guests' secret, but if they die, we're the ones in trouble," the woman said.

*A private guest!* Was that how the killer was moving around unchecked? Whose guest could they be?

"C'mon. Her suite, her boyfriend, and she was at the theatre when Calliope dropped. Don't you think that's odd?" Husky asked quietly. Isaiah clenched his fist, resisting the urge to throw him overboard.

"I think you need to stop watching so many conspiracy theory shows. What if Poppy sneaked Joshua on board to kill him for breaking up with her in public? Or Joshua sneaked on board to have an affair with Calliope, and Poppy killed them both? That would make for one hell of a movie." The woman laughed.

"Make fun of me all you want, but I'm keeping my distance from her and her friends. That bodyguard looks like he knows how to make a body disappear, and her friend apparently works for Mr Eckells," Husky said.

"If this is Mr Eckells' business, then we should keep our heads down and our mouths shut," the woman said.

"Fine, I'll keep my nose out of it, but at least Poppy's ex will live to sell the story. We took him to the infirmary, so I'm sure we'll hear through the grapevine what happened," Husky mused.

Isaiah heard the door close. Guessing their break was over, he slipped away before they discovered he had been eavesdropping. At least he'd confirmed two things: Joshua was alive and in the infirmary.

He followed the signs to the infirmary one floor down, only to find Davide, the first mate, waiting for him. He didn't look surprised. In fact, he looked a little relieved.

"You couldn't leave it alone," he said, blocking Isaiah's path.

"Would you believe me if I told you I got lost?"

"I would believe you're lying," Davide said, hands in his pockets. Two security guards were lurking behind him.

*Damn.* Isaiah had been hoping to speak to Joshua.

"He isn't in there," Davide said, reading his mind. "So I suggest you go find Poppy and keep her out of trouble."

"Don't bullshit me. Where else would you keep an injured man? Let me talk to Joshua. Just to confirm that he's alive, so Poppy can stop worrying. If I can talk to him, we can figure out who the killer is and put all this chaos to rest."

"I'm afraid that won't be possible," Davide said, staring down at his perfectly polished black shoes.

"Do I need to remind you that I'm here under orders from Mr Eckells? He wants me to solve this case before a larger scandal is created. You already have three bodies on your hands. Do you want more, or will you let me help?" Isaiah demanded.

"It's not about what I want," Davide said, finally opening the door to the infirmary to reveal six empty beds. "I'm afraid Joshua succumbed to his injuries. We wanted to keep his survival hidden in case the killer tried to finish the job. Unfortunately, we weren't equipped to handle the extent of the internal bleeding he suffered, and sadly he passed away in the early morning."

Isaiah narrowed his eyes. "If you're telling me the truth, then there's no harm in showing me to the morgue. If I'm going to believe you, then I need to see the body and talk with the doctor. Then, and only then, will I get back to Poppy."

To his surprise, Davide said, "Follow me," and led the way to the stairs.

"You've certainly changed your tune. I thought you'd be under orders to throw me overboard for trying to investigate," Isaiah remarked.

"The captain called Mr Eckells last night after the two incidents, and he assured us you could be an asset. Trying to keep you from getting involved would be pointless. So, Captain Hamill has instructed me to assist you – within reason," Davide explained, not sounding too pleased about it. "I suppose I can see why Mr Eckells likes you. You don't back down from a fight. The morgue is this way."

Isaiah noticed that the security guards stayed close behind him as he followed the first mate to the infirmary one floor down. At the end of the sterile white corridor, Davide knocked on the steel door, and a man in a white coat opened up. The smell of bleach and other chemicals was overwhelming.

"I'm under orders not to let anyone inside," the doctor said, eyeing Isaiah suspiciously.

"I wouldn't be here if I wasn't under orders. You can call the captain if you want to confirm, but you'll only be wasting our time," Davide informed him.

The doctor hesitated before allowing them to enter the morgue, leaving the two security guards guarding the door.

"This is Dr Rancliff. He's our medical examiner," Davide said.

"Isaiah Rivers." Isaiah offered his hand, but the doctor seemed unhappy about his presence and ignored the gesture. He walked over to the steel bed, where a body lay covered by a sheet. Isaiah couldn't tell if it was Calliope or Joshua.

"Mr. Rivers is here to see Joshua's body. Please tell him everything he wants to know, and then we'll leave," Davide said, leaning against the counter.

"Are you sure? This is against procedure," Dr Rancliff

said, moving closer to the covered body. Isaiah didn't like being talked about as if he weren't there, but he needed the information, so he bit his tongue.

"Isaiah can be trusted, and Captain Hamill has given me strict instructions to provide him with any information he requires."

Still looking unconvinced, Dr Rancliff lifted the sheet covering Joshua's body, confirming that the first mate had been telling the truth. Isaiah rubbed his forehead, dreading telling Poppy that Joshua was dead.

The medical examiner took a deep breath. "The victim was stabbed numerous times. One puncture hit the lung, causing it to fill with fluid, and another struck his lower abdomen and heart. There was no saving him, despite our best efforts. We believe the assailant isn't skilled with a blade or literate in anatomy."

"Why do you think they weren't skilled with the weapon?" The killer wasn't doing too badly, given Joshua was their third victim.

"The killer kept stabbing, unsure of where to strike. There was also some hesitation in the blow to the shoulder. From the angle of the stab wound, the killer is shorter than Joshua, which could be another reason for the excessive wounds."

"That's something we know, then. What about his clothes? Was there anything in his pockets?" Isaiah asked, hoping for a phone or something that could indicate who Joshua had been dealing with or, as Poppy had said, who he'd been working against.

"No, there was nothing in his pockets," the doctor said, pointing to a tray on the counter behind him where Joshua's belongings were placed. "He was wearing trousers, a shirt, and a belt. There was no phone or jewellery."

"To have so little on him, he must have been staying somewhere on board, but we haven't figured out where yet. We're trying to track his movements, but it'll take time," Davide put in.

Isaiah leaned down to get a better look at the wound on Joshua's abdomen, noticing that the skin around it was torn. "Calliope was stabbed in the neck with a thin metal hairpin we found in her dressing room. We assume the killer used whatever was on hand, indicating that it wasn't planned, but this was clearly done with a knife that had a serrated edge, which explains the heavy bleeding," he said. "What about the knife used on Patrice?"

"It was the same – a serrated knife. You've got a good eye," Dr Rancliff said. "But it would be difficult for a guest to bring such a weapon on board."

Isaiah didn't understand why the killer wouldn't use their weapon of choice on all three victims. Something about Calliope's murder had been more frantic and spontaneous.

"Not for a bodyguard or a member of security," he pointed out. "I've got my sidearm and a switchblade that I was allowed to carry on board."

"Are you suggesting it's a member of our security team? I can assure you that everyone on staff has been working with us for half a decade without incident," Davide said, puffing out his chest, offended at the insinuation.

"I'm not pointing fingers at your crew. The weapon could have been used by a bodyguard or stolen from a bodyguard or a member of your staff, and that's if the killer didn't have it with them when they boarded. I'm only talking out loud. There's no need to get defensive."

Davide sighed. "Sorry, I'm just protective of my staff.

Many have families to support, and I don't want anyone falsely accused."

"I've no intention of pointing fingers at anyone without clear evidence," Isaiah assured him. "I'm just used to bouncing ideas off my partner."

"Glad we cleared that up. Bounce all you need," Davide said, his defensive tone softening.

"Were there any defensive wounds on Joshua or skin under the fingernails?" Isaiah asked, noticing there were no bruises or scratches on the body.

"I swabbed his skin and took samples from under his nails for any trace evidence that the water didn't wash away. I'm keeping any and all evidence contained until we can send it for testing when we dock," Dr Rancliff replied, pointing to a medical-grade fridge. "Based on the lack of defensive wounds and the shallow stab wound to the shoulder, I believe he was attacked from behind and caught off-guard. He didn't have time to defend himself before being struck again in the abdomen."

"Were there any other injuries noted around the time of death?" Isaiah enquired, hoping for additional clues.

"There's a bump on the back of his head. When he was stabbed in the abdomen, he might have fallen backwards and hit his head on the edge of the jacuzzi. The water in his lungs – we aren't sure if the killer attempted to drown him before fleeing when they heard Ms Roe approaching, or if he swallowed the water upon losing consciousness before we could rescue him," Dr Rancliff explained, setting a chart with the injuries marked out on the table.

"Having jacuzzis built into the floor no longer seems like a good idea," Isaiah quipped, contemplating how easy it would have been to drown Joshua once he was already down. *The killer didn't need to be particularly strong.*

"Not when someone tries to use them as a murder weapon," Davide agreed. "We've closed them off for now."

"What about Calliope? Did she have any defensive wounds?" Isaiah asked.

"Calliope put up a fight. I'm surprised she could even muster the strength to make it to the stage. She had scratches on her arms and neck. She didn't go down easy, and there was a bloody smudge on her back that didn't match her injuries. The killer might have grabbed her and transferred some of their blood onto her. There were also some hair fibres between her fingers, which might be from the killer. Again, I've taken samples, and I'll send them out once we dock," Dr Rancliff said.

*Finally, some good news.* Blood and hair samples felt like hitting the jackpot.

"What colour was the hair?" Isaiah asked. "Long, short?"

"Dark," Dr Rancliff said, reading off a list. "Long."

Isaiah concealed his relief. Poppy couldn't have done it.

"With the blood and hair, we should be able to put a name and face to this monster," Davide said. "There's a nasty storm approaching, and we'll use it as an excuse to dock longer in Amalfi, where we can send all the samples to the local lab for testing. We've already called ahead for them to be picked up."

"The storm is a great excuse to stop the guests panicking. When will we dock? Do the other guests know?" Isaiah asked, liking that the captain already had a plan to get the evidence tested.

"No, we're waiting until this evening to make the announcement, since the sea will be a little rough and it'll help sell the urgency. We should dock in the early morning. The storm will pass over us and the Amalfi Coast while we search the ship, get the evidence tested, and then we can continue to Greece without alarming the guests," Davide said. "We also don't want the killer to know what we're up to."

"Good idea," Isaiah said, trying not to reveal how excited he was to have his feet on solid ground.

"What if the killer gets off and doesn't get back on again?" Dr Rancliff asked. "Not that I want a killer to stay onboard."

"I believe their target is Poppy. Each of the victims has been connected to her. I think the killer is playing a game of cat and mouse, and the ship is the perfect playground. Even if disembarking in Amalfi saves them from getting caught for the murders they've already committed, they won't be able to give up their game when they're so close," Isaiah said. *Maybe I should get Poppy off the ship and run.* But he knew deep in his gut that would only cause the killer to chase them.

"How is Ms Roe?" Davide asked, sounding guilty. "She was quite distraught last night, and we were sorry to have to put her through additional emotional turmoil. Once we dock, we'll be able to give her real answers."

"I'm not going to speak for her. Your priority is the ship, and mine is Poppy. Now that we're working together, we can protect both," Isaiah said, not wanting to make him feel better about how they had gaslit a traumatised woman.

"Fair enough," Davide said, not pressing further.

"Is there anything else you can tell us?" Isaiah asked the doctor.

"This is all the information I have for now," Dr Rancliff said, covering up Joshua's body and sliding it back into the wall.

"Now you know what we know. How do you wish to proceed?" Davide asked.

Isaiah wanted to get back to Poppy, but he also didn't want to waste the opportunity, since the first mate was feeling so compliant. "I want to see the security footage. Don't bother trying to lie about updates or glitches, because I know you use Eagle Eye software. I want to see whatever you refused to show Poppy last night."

Davide hesitated, but then shrugged. "You'll need to come with me to the surveillance room on the engineering level."

Isaiah thanked the doctor for his time, and they left.

## Chapter 18
# Captain's Confrontation
### Isaiah

To his astonishment, Poppy was in the surveillance room with Captain Hamill.

"What are you doing here?!" Isaiah demanded.

Davide immediately went to the captain's side, while the security guards who had escorted them waited outside.

"How nice of you both to join us. Ms Roe is here with me because she was found searching the lounge deck, despite the area being cordoned off to guests," Captain Hamill informed him while Poppy stared at the floor.

"Sorry for causing trouble, but I lost a charm from my charm bracelet last night, and I wanted to look for it," she told them, holding up her wrist to show the captain, who didn't look amused. "I found it and was about to leave the area when your charming head of security, Colter, decided to drag me here."

"I have enough to deal with without guests going where they shouldn't," Colter said, looking away from the surveillance screens as Poppy mentioned him. Isaiah glared at him, hoping for his sake that when Poppy said 'dragged', it wasn't meant in the literal sense.

"Are you alright? Did he put his hands on you?" he asked her. The thought of anyone touching her made him grind his teeth.

"I'm fine. He didn't touch me," Poppy assured him, waving her hands frantically like she was afraid Isaiah would lose his temper.

"Ms Roe wouldn't have been dragged anywhere if she had followed the rules and not crossed the caution tape," Captain Hamill said impatiently, dismissing Colter from the surveillance room.

"I waited to ask a security guard to see if they would look for the charm for me, but there was no one around. I figured since your security team told me I'd made up last night's incident, there should be no reason why I couldn't look around the jacuzzis," Poppy said. "And it only took me a moment to find it."

"Lost charm or not, you crossed into an alleged crime scene without any care for the evidence you disrupted." Captain Hamill's eyes narrowed as she ran out of patience. "Despite your promises not to get involved in ship business, you can't seem to leave crime scenes alone, and your bodyguard was caught trying to sneak into the infirmary."

Poppy stared at Isaiah in surprise. He hadn't shared his plans to search for Joshua with her because she would have insisted on joining him; he'd hoped she would get time to relax with Mina and recover after witnessing what had happened to Calliope and Joshua. Judging by her scowl, he'd made the wrong decision and would likely face her wrath later. On the other hand, she hadn't informed him of her plans to search the lounge deck, so he could argue that they were even.

"You'll assist in the investigation from now on," the

captain was saying. "Eckells claims it would be beneficial if we all worked together due to your connection to the victims. All the evidence we've gathered from the murders of Calliope and Joshua will be sent to a lab in Amalfi on the coast of Italy once we dock, and the local police have agreed to rush it, so we should get answers before we reach our final destination."

Isaiah flinched as Poppy paled.

"Joshua's dead?" she gasped, looking at Isaiah for answers. He hated that this was how she'd found out.

Captain Hamill shuffled uncomfortably. "I'm sorry, Ms Roe. I assumed you already knew."

"When? Joshua was alive when I left to get help. Why would I assume he was dead?" Poppy argued. The hurt in her voice cut Isaiah; he took her hand to calm her down. Thankfully, she didn't pull away. Isaiah caught Davide glancing between them, clearly noting that something more than a professional relationship had developed between them, but now wasn't the time to discuss their romantic situation.

"I'm sorry, Ms Roe, but we did everything possible to help him. There was too much damage done," Captain Hamill said, clearly sorry for putting her foot in it.

"If your crew had spent less time convincing me that I was crazy and listened to me, he might still be alive!" Poppy snapped, gripping Isaiah's hand tighter.

"I can assure you there was no delay in getting him help. My crew merely detained you so we could work to help him. We didn't have the equipment we needed."

"You said something about docking? Are we cutting the trip short?" Poppy asked.

Captain Hamill explained the situation with the labs and the plan for the storm.

"Why don't we just remain in Italy? Why risk continuing the trip?" Poppy asked.

"If you wish to remain in Italy, that's up to you. We will arrange suitable accommodation for you, and you will remain informed of the investigation."

"I don't see why you would *want* us to come back. If the killer is after me and we disembark, then your precious ship is safe. You'll be able to cover up Calliope and Joshua's death with a nice and tidy slip-and-fall, like Patrice," Poppy snarled.

The captain stood a little straighter, as though trying to contain her reaction. Everyone in the room knew Poppy was right; the killer would surely follow if they left the ship. Even if Davide wanted to help them trap the killer on board, it didn't mean the captain did.

"It did cross my mind to kick you both off when we docked, since my priority is the safety of my ship. However, you're our guests, and it is up to you whether you wish to stay or leave. If you stay, so will the killer, and I want them to pay for what they've done aboard my ship," Captain Hamill said. "This person killed a member of my crew and two of my guests – guests I promised to keep safe. Regardless of what you believe or what you decide, these crimes won't be swept under anything. If you decide to stay behind, so will the killer, but you'll have the protection of the local police and, hopefully, a name and a face when the results come in. All that matters now is making it to port and getting the evidence to the lab. Everything else is another day's problem."

"You really want to work with us now?" Poppy asked suspiciously.

"What? You suddenly don't want our help?" Davide asked, as though she was the unreasonable one.

"You can't blame her for struggling to trust your

motives. You did try to gaslight her into believing she didn't find her friend clinging to life only last night." Isaiah didn't bother to hide his irritation.

"We were already dealing with one crisis. We needed to avoid a panic. We're sorry for the hurt we've caused you, and we'll do everything possible to bring this person to justice. Still, we need your help." Davide was much more amiable than the captain. Both Poppy and Captain Hamill had one thing in common: pride. Davide looked to Isaiah for help. They needed to come together, even if there was still blood in the water.

"A good show of faith would be to show us last night's surveillance," Isaiah said, trying to put them all on an even playing field. Poppy nodded in agreement.

"Fair enough. I'll bring up the footage just before Poppy appears on the lounge deck." Davide scrolled through the video until the screen focused on Poppy's arrival on the observation deck. Joshua and the culprit had only been a short flight of stairs below.

"I heard a scuffle, or what I think was Joshua being pushed into the jacuzzi, so maybe scroll back to catch them arriving," Poppy said as they stood behind Davide, watching the screens on the wall.

"There! Stop," Isaiah said. He frowned; Joshua was clearly in focus, but a second figure was hazy. "I thought Eagle Eye software didn't appear grainy like this." He squinted at the pair.

"I think Joshua is with a woman? They look like they're arguing, but why is the camera focusing on him, not her?" Poppy asked.

"We weren't lying last night when we said something corrupted the footage. We think she must be wearing something that's messing with the software." Davide sighed. "Eagle Eye warned us about the weakness in their system. The AI system has trouble reading a certain shade of green, but only those who run the system and purchase it know the fault. The software can still assess the person it's targeting – height, weight and body temperature – so we can only assume it's a woman."

"We can also assume she knows about the ship's surveillance to take such precautions. We've had security watching these monitors twenty-four hours a day; as soon as the footage started to lose focus, we sent a team to investigate," Captain Hamill added.

Isaiah guessed that was how they had cleaned up the scene so fast. They'd been lying in wait until Poppy went to get help.

"It could have been a woman wearing a green dress, then? Can't we scan the rest of the footage looking for a blurry figure?" Isaiah asked. "Dark hairs were found on Calliope. She got a handful of the killer's hair in the struggle."

"We tried to follow her movements, but just watch," Captain Hamill said, motioning for Davide to continue the playback.

Silently, the group watched Joshua frantically pacing by the grainy figure. Isaiah wished there was audio. He felt Poppy clutch his hand tighter as Joshua turned to walk away. The grainy figure followed, clouding the image, and seconds later, Joshua was down by the jacuzzi.

Isaiah glanced at the other monitor as Poppy arrived on the observation deck. The grainy figure rolled the injured and bleeding Joshua into the jacuzzi and, as expected, tried to hold his head under the water before Poppy came running. Isaiah held his breath, watching the killer waiting under the short stairs as Poppy tried to help Joshua. If Poppy had turned around, she would have come face-to-face with the murderer. Instead, she'd struggled to keep Joshua's head above water and hadn't noticed the killer sneak out of their hiding spot and back inside the door.

"Can't we follow her into the hall?" Poppy asked, watching security arrive on the scene and get the now unmoving Joshua out of the jacuzzi. "I want my shoes back, by the way," she added, side-eyeing Davide.

"They'll be returned to your suite." Davide nodded, not putting up a fight. "I wish following the killer into the hall was as easy." He swiped to another viewpoint, but no one was in the hall.

"She can't have disappeared," Isaiah said, wanting to look at the corridor in person to see if there were any blind spots.

"I've scanned every second of footage from every angle, and there's no blurry figure anywhere to be found – nor is there any other woman with dark hair even in the area," Davide explained, as though the culprit was a ghost.

"Did you check the area in person?" Isaiah asked. "Last night, they might have been so busy trying to cover up the scene that they missed something important."

"Why do you think we had the area marked off? We checked anywhere and everywhere a guest could get to."

"Okay, if we can't track her, we focus on Joshua. Have you figured out when Joshua boarded the ship? If he was with anyone? Can we go back that far into the footage?" Poppy interrupted. "Joshua isn't—" She hesitated. "*Wasn't* some ninja with a special set of skills. How did he get past the security you're so proud of?"

The Captain exchanged a nervous look with her first mate.

"I get the feeling we aren't going to like the answer," Isaiah muttered as the tension in the air thickened.

"We discovered Joshua boarded the ship with the help of one of our crew members. Joshua told the crew member that he wanted his presence kept quiet, since he had a surprise for Ms Roe. Since he did have a ticket, we had no reason to suspect that he was a danger to Ms Roe, so we made an exception. An exception that we deeply regret," Captain Hamill explained. "However, Davide traced Joshua's movements from the theatre to his room. Security found nothing suspicious."

"Who was the member of staff? Can we talk to them? They might be the fucking killer!" Isaiah exclaimed, hoping they had this person locked up for interrogation.

"We know they aren't the killer," Davide said, rubbing his brow.

"How? Who is it?" Poppy barked.

"Patrice," Captain Hamill said quickly, like ripping off a bandage.

It felt like all the air had been sucked out of the room.

"We found out when we went through Patrice's log. She left you at the Empress Suite and subsequently scanned Joshua's ticket at the general entrance, not the VIP one you came in, before we left port. Since it was filed under our private guest list, it took us a while to find it."

Isaiah glanced at Poppy, afraid she was about to lunge at them for not telling them sooner. At least he was close enough to hold her back before she pounced on their new allies – not that he would blame her. This was all a lot to absorb.

Poppy let go of his hand as she started to pace. "Let me get this straight: Patrice, the first victim, was blackmailing Calliope, the second victim, who was mad at Joshua for not going through with the plan to kill me and let Joshua, the third victim, on board secretly." To Isaiah's surprise, she began to laugh. They gave her a moment to compose herself.

"Patrice was blackmailing guests?" Captain Hamill said when she was calmer.

Isaiah took the lead while Poppy took a seat. "Poppy discovered Patrice was recording guests and keeping the tapes for blackmail. We found a tape with Calliope talking about a plot to kill Poppy, but we didn't know who she was talking to. Patrice was blackmailing her, and we think Calliope killed her."

"Have you got the tape?" Captain Hamill asked.

"I'll hand it over once we're done here," Isaiah said, worried about Poppy as she rested her head in her hands.

"There are about half a dozen other tapes in her cabin you'll want to destroy before your other guests find out about them," she interjected.

"You were in her cabin?" Captain Hamill fumed.

"I think we should focus on the fact that our three suspects are dead," Isaiah said. "Now you know about Patrice's connection to Calliope, and we know their connection to Joshua; we're even."

"I don't think Calliope killed Patrice," Davide said suddenly.

"Why not?" Poppy asked.

"Because the same type of knife that was used on Patrice was also used on Joshua, and Calliope was already dead when Joshua was killed."

"The killer could have stolen the knife from Calliope's changing room," Poppy argued, but Isaiah wanted to hear Davide's reasoning. A fresh set of eyes never hurt.

"Then why didn't the killer use the knife on Calliope? It would've been much more effective than the metal hair-pin. The killer went to see Calliope before meeting with Joshua and didn't have their weapon of choice on them.

They were working together, or Calliope figured out something she shouldn't have and confronted the killer, or they disagreed on how to proceed with their plans. Either way, the killer didn't have the knife until she met with Joshua. I don't think she expected to end up fighting with Calliope," Davide said, adding another fork in the road. "I think the key to this is Calliope. If her death wasn't planned, then the killer probably messed up or wasn't as careful."

"So we focus on Calliope. Is there anything else that needs to be shared?" Captain Hamill asked, looking around the room. "Now's the time."

No one spoke up.

"Then I suggest we get back to our duties. Davide, I want you to take another sweep of Calliope's dressing room and the theatre footage. I want every female guest who attended the opera or was even on that level accounted for," the captain ordered, before turning her attention to Poppy and Isaiah. "Here is the number to the bridge. It's a direct line to me from your suite. If anything happens, or you wish to share any other information, you can speak to me exclusively. Please inform our security before any more snooping. We're all on the same team, and I don't want two more deaths on my conscience."

Isaiah hesitated, unsure of whether she could be trusted. The *Midas's* security was meant to be one of the best teams in the world. Yet, through either stupidity or complacency, so much had slipped through the cracks. Still, since they had limited allies, they couldn't be picky.

"While security is going back over the videos with Davide, what are we supposed to do?" Poppy asked, holding her chin high. Isaiah admired her steel. He couldn't imagine how hard it must be for her to keep it together.

"You two will act like any other guests. Once we dock

in Amalfi in the morning, all guests will disembark the ship, but not without a smartwatch, private or not; all guests will be kept track of from now on. While you enjoy your day trip, we will search the ship from top to bottom. The evidence we collected will also be sent to the lab, and hopefully, when we dock in Greece, we will have a name to put to our killer." Captain Hamill sounded confident, but Isaiah couldn't help but notice her hand shaking by her side. Running a ship was no easy feat, but running one with a killer on board had to be eating away at her. "There's a private dinner tonight for those who knew Calliope, and I think you should both attend. If the killer is part of her group or someone who knew her, then they might be tempted to show themselves."

"Nothing says grief like a tasting menu. I wish I could stay in the tub," Poppy said under her breath.

"It seems we have a gameplay we can all agree on," Isaiah said, looking to Poppy. She nodded, but he could see she was already lost in thought. He wasn't sure if she was even paying attention.

"And we all agree that if anything happens in the meantime, we let each other know?" Captain Hamill said, and everyone nodded again.

"If the killer's tracking our movements, we don't want them to think we're working together," Poppy said, reminding herself to update Mina when they were together again. She could enjoy a few more hours of sun to herself before they dropped another murder bomb on her. "I'm not sure about tonight, but maybe it would be useful. Calliope boarded with her niece. Despite having known Calliope for most of my life, I've never met her. Getting to know her tonight might give us some insight into who she has been close to recently."

"Her name is Sophia Monroe, and she was devastated

when we broke the news about her aunt. She was in her suite when Calliope was killed – seasick. She asked that we arrange the dinner to honour her memory and stop others from gossiping about how she died," Captain Hamill informed her. "Since you were seen helping Calliope, the other guests are also talking about your involvement…"

"And you also want them to stop talking about it? Poppy attending will put an end to their curiosity," Isaiah put in.

"Yes," Captain Hamill admitted.

"Fine, we'll be there," Poppy said, heading for the door. "We should go, or Mina will wonder where we are."

Isaiah followed her.

"Are you not going to lecture me about my snooping?" she asked once they were alone in the hallway, but he shook his head.

"Why would I? It's good that everything is out in the open now. We can work together," he said, walking by her side.

"I keep replaying what happened with Joshua. I wish I'd asked who hurt him sooner. The killer could have attacked me but didn't. Why?"

"You can't blame yourself. You were in shock. I saw his injury report – it wouldn't have changed anything," Isaiah reassured her. "As for the killer, maybe they didn't have time or didn't expect you, but I'm grateful they didn't. The thought of losing you—" He couldn't finish the sentence.

"Of course, it would be terrible for your reputation to lose a client," she said sarcastically.

"That's not it," he confessed, taking her arm so she was forced to stop and look at him. "It's because I care about you far more than I should, and the thought of losing you, of someone hurting you, puts a knife in my heart."

"Sorry, that wasn't fair. I hate that you're caught up in

this, whether it's your job or not. That you and Mina are in danger because of me worries me most. I should've known better than to start caring about anyone. You shouldn't have taken this job."

He hated to see the fear in her eyes. Unable to resist, his eyes drifted to her lips, and he took her face in his hands and brushed his lips against hers, wanting to remove all traces of fear and hurt. Her lips moulded to his as she fisted his shirt, pulling him closer until they were pressed against the wall beside the lift.

"I'm sorry. Someone could see us," he said, sliding his palm down her throat to her shoulders to keep her still.

"Who cares!" Poppy lunged at him without a care in the world.

He would take anything she was eager to give. He held her firm against him, using his body to conceal her. He wanted to be gentle, but her demanding kisses set a wildfire in him. He nipped at her lower lip, and she moaned softly as he reminded her who was in charge.

"I can't lose you," Isaiah said, his grip tightening on her hair as her eyes met his.

"You won't," she panted, resting her hands on his chest. He was sure she could feel his heart hammering.

"Seeing the killer so close to you earlier, I thought my heart was going to stop." He couldn't bear to think of what could have happened. He almost wanted to thank the killer for not taking Poppy's life at that moment.

"Don't worry so much. The killer was enjoying watching me suffer too much to hurt me," Poppy quipped.

"Don't joke," Isaiah said, running his thumb along her smiling lips. He wanted to taste her again, but the ping of the lift doors opening sadly ruined the moment.

The group of guests stared at them as they separated. With Poppy's rosy cheeks, it wasn't hard for them to guess what they'd interrupted. Isaiah and Poppy joined them, forced apart and to remain silent until they reached their suite, where Poppy started running a bath as soon as she entered.

"You know what I can't get out of my head?" She started undressing, then smirked before he averted his gaze.

"That kiss?" he asked, lingering in her doorway. When he looked up, she was wearing a robe, and he could think again.

"That too, but why didn't Joshua board with us and explain what was happening?" The sweet scent of oranges filled the space as she poured a fruity bubbling lotion into the bath.

"He got in over his head. Maybe he wanted to stop the killer without exposing his role in the plan. Private guests have more discretion; he was trying to keep his movements secret. Once the killer found out he was on board and working against them, he became a target." Isaiah regretted that he had been so distracted by his suspicion of Poppy, he hadn't noticed who lurked in the shadows. He wished Joshua had been honest with her. Poppy might not have boarded if she'd known the full extent of the danger, but voicing blame now was pointless.

"Why didn't he just come with us? Why did he think he could handle it alone? I have no clue who the woman in the footage could even be. I would've said Calliope, but she was already dead," Poppy said, pinning her hair up as the bathroom filled with steam. "Even though he got tangled up in this mess, he was my friend once, and it's awful knowing he died filled with regret."

"It's okay to mourn for your friend, even if he went down the wrong path. We'll find out who he was working with or against," Isaiah promised, though she didn't seem reassured.

She took a deep breath, and he sensed there was more she wanted to get off her chest. Slipping off her robe, she sat on the ledge of the tub with her back to him as it filled. He studied the tiles, trying not to be distracted by her bare curves.

"I'm sorry he's dead, but I'm also relieved I'm not imagining injured people in jacuzzis. Even if we're working together, it's troubling to know that security is more skilled at covering up than solving crimes. My brain feels like it's about to snap with all the possibilities," she said, shaking her head.

"I recommend therapy when you get home."

Poppy chuckled. "My aunt hated therapists. She preferred pushing through with a martini, pills and bitter smiles. The first two I'll happily pass on, but I'm afraid I might have inherited the last." She glanced at him over her shoulder. It took all his willpower not to scoop her up in his arms and take her to bed.

"I don't think your smile could ever be bitter," he said, causing her to roll her eyes. He wanted to change the topic, not wanting her to think about her aunt. She had enough on her plate. "Can I ask you something?"

"Anything – I think we're past secrets," Poppy said, slipping into the steamy bubbles.

"Why are you so drawn to water? You take more baths than anyone I know, and you went to the spa when you were stressed during our first night on board."

Poppy rested her chin on her forearms as the bubbles swelled around her. "Whenever I was away from home for work, or even at home with my aunt, the bathroom was always where I was left alone. Until you."

He smirked.

"Can we be silent and enjoy the peace for five

minutes?" she asked. "Just five more minutes of pretending that no one is trying to kill me?"

"Five minutes sounds good."

Poppy rested her head on the edge of the tub. "And during those five minutes, you can undress and get in this tub with me, because it's far too big for one person," she teased, leaning over the edge and spilling water on the floor as she kissed him.

"Your wish is my command." He stripped off his clothes and climbed in behind her so he could hold her in his arms.

After endless caresses beneath the bubbles, neither could take much more teasing. Isaiah carried her out of the bathroom, her legs wrapped around his waist and she nipped at his neck, making him harder. Each step to the bedroom was a laboured effort; it took all his strength not to lay her out on the bathroom tiles and take her.

On the bed, her eyes burned with need as she propped herself up on her elbows to watch him. He placed a soft kiss on the inside of her thigh. She gasped when he shoved her legs apart and kissed up her thighs before devouring her. Her groans matched his own as his tongue explored her needy core. Feeling her legs tremble against his shoulders and her breathless moans was intoxicating. He loved driving her to the edge, only to pull away before she had a chance to explode.

"Isaiah, don't stop," she pleaded, gripping his hair, driving him on. His name on her lips was something he could listen to for the rest of his life. Her back arched off the bed as she told him she was close, lost in the sensation of his tongue on her. It didn't matter who she was; in spite of all her fame and fortune, nothing was going to steal this moment from them. *She's all mine.*

He didn't stop until her moans turned into cries of

release. With a satisfied grin, he pressed a gentle kiss against her inner thigh.

"If only I'd known this was how to make you smile, I'd have had you on your knees sooner." She chuckled softly, her cheeks flushed as she stared up at him. "You have the best smile." She ran her fingers along his spine, sending shivers down his body. Her lips pressed against him. He shuddered as she eagerly tasted her arousal on his tongue before he eased down her body. His lips trailed from one breast to the other, nipping just enough so she would feel him tomorrow, then returned to hers as he caressed between her thighs and she writhed against him. Poppy's hands drifted from his hips, and a groan escaped him as her delicate touch caressed him.

"I need you," she rasped in his ear beneath him as he teased her.

"Such sweet words. Now look at me. Don't close your eyes or I'll stop," he ordered, pulling her up from the bed so she was straddling him. Her hooded gaze met his as she rocked her hips against his. The desire in her gaze ruled him.

"Take what you want, Princess," he ordered, and his lips silenced her moans as she eased herself onto his hard length, taking every inch until his eyes rolled back in his head. With her chest against his, he wondered if she could feel his heart hammering.

"You're what I want," she gasped. "What I need."

His eyes snapped open, and her mischievous smile nearly undid him.

"Is that an order?" He thrust forward, and she bit his shoulder to silence herself. "Fuck, Poppy," he growled, fisting her hair to stop her before she ruined him for life.

"I'm the boss, after all," she said, rolling her hips.

He tried to hold her still, trying to draw out the

moment, but wrapped up in her body, he couldn't stop himself from making her his.

"Then I should make sure my client is satisfied with my performance." He laid her down, pinning her hands above her head so she was at his mercy. She arched her back off the bed as his thrusts came faster and faster; he released her hands as he felt her tightening around him, and she dug her nails down his back as she came undone, clinging to him. Her writhing sent him over the edge, and he buried his head in her shoulder as he cried out her name. Sweat clung to their bodies as they held each other, trying to catch their breath.

Once he could remember his name, he pressed his lips to hers, and she unwrapped herself from him.

"I don't think I can move," she panted as he rolled away from her carefully.

"Good, because you aren't to leave this room." He winked, discarding the condom in the bin. The sheets were pulled from the bed, and he smiled to himself as he watched her wrap herself up in them. "What are you doing?" he asked as she turned on the bathroom light.

"I'm not going to walk around naked, and we have Sophia's dinner to get to!" She blushed, closing the bathroom door.

He hadn't expected her to be self-conscious, but he wanted her to be comfortable. When she came back, showered and dressed in a short red dress, she stood by his side of the bed.

"Can you zip up my dress the rest of the way?" she asked. She smelt like that delicious shampoo, and it made him hard again. He didn't think he'd ever get enough of her.

"I think I like you all wrapped up," he said, brushing her hair over her shoulder. He kissed between her shoulders and felt her shiver. He loved how her body responded to his touch.

"Oh yeah?" She frowned a little as he kissed her shoulder and then her neck. She tilted her head, giving him better access. He didn't need to be told twice.

"Because then I get to unwrap you." His lips brushed her ear as he tugged down the zipper and brushed the tiny straps from her shoulders.

She gasped as he pulled her down onto the bed. They were going to be very late to dinner.

## Chapter 19
# Secret at Supper
### Poppy

"Thank you all so much for attending. It would mean a great deal to my dear aunt that you all came tonight, despite the foul weather, to honour her memory," said Sophia, Calliope's niece, as they waited for dessert to be served. Despite her grief, Sophia's deep auburn hair was coiled to perfection, and even with her tears, her makeup didn't dare budge.

Poppy and Isaiah stood with about two dozen other guests at a long table, raising their glasses in Calliope's memory. The storm had kept everyone else away, leaving them alone in the Silver Dining Room, a welcome break from the gold – though the room felt like an odd choice, given the rough seas. The glass shards dangling from the chandelier above made Poppy uneasy, as if they might crash down at any moment. After a twelve-course tasting menu wrapped up with a mint sorbet, she didn't want to even look at another plate of food. She had expected more griping from the other guests about the prolonged docking in Amalfi, but by the third course, they had given up on the topic.

Isaiah nudged Poppy with his elbow, silently asking if she was alright. She smiled softly and shifted her focus back to Sophia, who was at the head of the table. With her bright round eyes and red hair, there wasn't much family resemblance. Why hadn't Calliope ever brought her to events or award ceremonies if they were so close? Perhaps, unlike Poppy's aunt, Calliope had wanted to spare her niece from a public life. *Not everyone chooses to exploit those they're supposed to love and protect.*

"Though Calliope was taken from us so cruelly and before her time, I think passing on stage would've brought her some peace," Sophia continued. "Poppy, is there anything you'd like to say? We've just met, but since our aunts were such great friends. I'm sure you could share a few words with us."

Everyone turned to look at Poppy, awaiting her response as Sophia sat down.

"Sorry, I wasn't expecting to say something," Poppy said, trying not to fidget with the edge of the pale blue tablecloth.

"I hate to put you on the spot, but since you were with her in those last moments when I couldn't be—" Sophia dabbed her eyes with her napkin.

Backed into a corner, Poppy couldn't say no. Her niece might not look much like her aunt, but getting what she wanted was apparently a shared trait. Poppy didn't see any tears, but she wouldn't call out a grieving woman in front of her friends.

"Please, Sophia. You didn't know what would happen, and she wouldn't want you to have such regrets. I only knew Calliope as part of a pair. My late aunt, Martha, had a sisterhood with Calliope long before I was born. They loved to laugh and gossip, argued constantly, and were often rivals in their careers. They greatly loved and admired each other. I'm sure they're enjoying a bottle of red together wherever they are now," Poppy said, raising her glass. "To friendship and sisterhood."

There were quick cheers as Poppy downed the glass of champagne to wash away the bitter taste from her tongue.

"I hope we can have such a friendship. Our aunts would want us to look after each other," Sophia said, smiling at Poppy. Her tears were long gone.

Poppy smiled, knowing she had been manipulated, and took her seat.

"Are you okay? That must have been difficult," Isaiah said quietly, resting a reassuring hand on her thigh beneath the table.

"You were right. We should've stayed in bed and watched the waves." She placed her hand over his, grateful to have him by her side.

"Something to look forward to." Isaiah brought her hand to his lips, not caring who was watching as he kept his words low. "I haven't had much luck. I asked about a woman in a green dress, but everyone's had too much to drink and can barely remember what was served for the first course, let alone what a woman wore yesterday. Did you manage to get any leads from your end of the table?"

"Nothing. All they can remember is the chaos following Calliope's grand entrance on stage," Poppy whispered, trying to mask her disappointment with a smile so everyone else at the table would think they were merely flirting.

"Should we call it a night?" Isaiah asked, but Poppy's reply was interrupted by the guests across from them, who had spent the entirety of the dinner ignoring them.

"Forgive us for not introducing ourselves sooner. I'm Douglas Mengur, and this is my wife, Naomi. I didn't realise you were the niece of Martha Roe. Poppy, isn't it?"

"No need to apologise. We arrived late, so there wasn't much time before the food arrived." Poppy's voice betrayed her discomfort. She was aware of the dismissive attitude the Mengurs had towards them. They clearly viewed Isaiah as a nobody, when he was worth far more than the wealthy man married to his fourth wife who'd made his fortune through questionable property development.

"My daughter is a huge fan. We went to your concerts in Milan and Paris," Naomi said kindly. "You really have a great voice. I'm sure your aunt was very proud of you."

Poppy forced a smile, *pretending not to know who I am, and still attending my concert? That's a new level of pompousness.*

"I'm sure she would appreciate some VIP tickets now that we're better acquainted." Douglas winked at her, causing Poppy to wish she could peel her skin off. Naomi smiled, but her mortification was evident, impossible to conceal.

A slice of passionfruit cheesecake was placed in front of them for dessert, but Poppy couldn't take another bite of food.

"I'm so glad you enjoyed the concerts. I'd be happy to invite you to a future show. Unfortunately, I don't plan on performing again anytime soon. Still, when I do, I'll let you know," Poppy said, eager to ease Naomi's discomfort.

"That's very kind of you! Please don't go to any trouble," Naomi said, resting her hand over her husband's. "He's had a little too much to drink, so please ignore him."

Douglas snatched his hand away, and Naomi flinched.

"This must be your fiancé?" he asked, changing the subject while his wife withdrew into herself.

"Isaiah is my head of security," Poppy said, playfully brushing her heeled foot up Isaiah's calf, enjoying how it made him squirm.

"I didn't think staff were allowed to join us. I'm sure they'd prefer the time off," Douglas said smugly. Poppy felt Isaiah's hand tighten on her thigh, silently telling her he was okay.

"I agree with Naomi, Douglas. You've had too much to drink," a retired movie director, Samantha, interrupted, breaking the tension. "It's a pleasure to have you both with us. Ignore him, and tell us how you got into the security field? I'm sure you have plenty of riveting stories to share."

"I'm afraid I don't have many stories to share. I'm a detective, so most of the time, I'm investigating other people's worst deeds and dirty laundry," Isaiah said, trying to brush them off.

"A detective?" Naomi asked, sitting a little taller. "How did you end up protecting Poppy? If you don't mind me asking?"

"I'm afraid that's a rather short story. Isaiah and I have a mutual friend, and he had some time off, so I hired him for the trip," Poppy said, unsure of how they'd become the ones being questioned.

"You must have one case you've solved that you wouldn't mind sharing with us," Sophia interjected from the head of the table.

"I don't think he can talk about cases. I wouldn't want him to get in trouble," Poppy said, giving him an escape.

"There's one case that comes to mind, and it's long closed, so there's no harm in sharing," he said, prompting a murmur around the table as everyone settled in.

"You don't have to if it could get you in trouble," Poppy whispered, despite being eager to learn more about his work.

"Don't worry." Isaiah winked at her. "A few years ago, my partner and I investigated a suspicious death. A man had allegedly died in his sleep. The officers called my partner and me to the scene because of his age, health, and his wife's odd behaviour. The coroner found no signs of foul play, but it was curious why a seemingly healthy man would die suddenly."

"But if there was nothing suspicious," Naomi interrupted, "why keep investigating?"

"We planned to close the case after the coroner's report, but when we returned to inform the wife, we noticed she was cleaning her husband's disorganized office. She apologized for the mess, explaining that he didn't like her entering his office. It struck us as odd that she was so quickly disposing of his belongings after his death, not to mention the large amount of stamps and envelopes she was tossing out. Her behaviour was concerning, but we recognized that everyone grieves differently and decided to close the case. Weeks later, the deceased man's girlfriend came to the station, insisting we reopen the investigation. She believed the wife had discovered their affair and killed him. While affairs can be a clear motive, there was no evidence of harm, but she provided letters they'd exchanged to show he was in good health—"

"Letters? Who sends those nowadays?" Douglas interrupted, prompting Poppy to kick him.

"Sorry, just a cramp," she said, smiling nervously.

"Don't keep us in suspense," Sophia urged before Douglas could scold her.

"The victim wrote letters to set up meetings, as his wife often checked his phone and email," Isaiah continued.

"Sounds like the wife followed him to one of their meet-ups and killed him," the director, Samantha, mused.

"If she did, how did he return to his bed?" the lead opera singer interjected. "A dead body is heavy."

Everyone at the table turned to look at her as the last

comment raised the alarm. The opera singer shrugged. "What? I watch a lot of crime TV."

"Sadly, you're mistaken. The neighbours confirmed that neither left the house the night he died," Isaiah said, successfully drawing everyone's attention back to him.

"The wife clearly found out about the affair and killed him," Douglas scoffed.

"But how?" Isaiah asked.

No one had any ideas.

"How do you seal an envelope?" Isaiah asked Poppy.

Poppy frowned. "Lick it?"

"Precisely. The wife painted the envelope seals with a substance I won't name. I don't want to give any spouses at the table any ideas." This earned him a few laughs, some more nervous than others. Poppy certainly wouldn't blame Naomi for wanting to poison her husband.

"She poisoned him?" Naomi gasped. "Surely that would have taken—"

"Months," Isaiah finished for her. "Revenge and patience can be best friends in the right circumstances. She bought the substance from her plastic surgeon, who was practising with an expired license, so we had no way of knowing about him or the drugs he was illegally selling. Since the doses were so small and consumed over a long period, his symptoms would have been minor until it finally stopped his heart."

"How did you catch her?" Sophia asked, and the table leaned in. Everyone was so desperate for an answer that Poppy would have heard a pin drop.

"When we first went to the house, we took some discarded bin bags from the skip. My partner's idea – I can't take credit for his forward thinking. We tested the envelopes the girlfriend had given us and those in the house for the same compounds, and sure enough, we had our murder weapon."

"Serves him right," Samantha huffed. "I don't blame her. Cheated on for years, and she had the patience and brains to develop such a scheme. I wish she hadn't been caught."

"It's my job to investigate. What happens after that is up to the judge and jury," Isaiah said, as the guests stared at him in admiration.

"Thank you for entertaining us. It's thrilling to discover how the pieces come together." Sophia clapped her hands gleefully.

Poppy noticed his forced smile as the table erupted into applause. She hadn't needed to hear the story to know he was a great investigator. If he wasn't, he wouldn't be sitting beside her now.

The guests started to ask more questions – could he tell them about another case? How long had the woman got? How had he felt about it?

Poppy didn't want to know the answers. He had protected her, a confessed killer, and she couldn't help but wonder if he would one day regret putting aside the truth to protect her and grow to resent his feelings for her. With the dessert plates being taken away, she decided it was time to make a break for it.

"Thank you so much for having us, but I'm starting to feel a little seasick. If you wouldn't mind excusing us," she announced, placing a hand over her stomach to emphasize her point.

"Thank you," Isaiah whispered, pulling out her chair. She should have known he would suspect her sudden illness.

"Yes, please go and get some air. We've kept you long enough, and thank you for coming," Sophia said, walking down the table. "I really hope we can talk again soon. Our aunts would want us to look after each other now that they are gone."

Poppy was surprised when Sophia wrapped her arms around her and squeezed tightly. She froze before returning the gesture to avoid seeming rude.

"Thank you again for having us," she said, unsure what else to say. "I'm sure we'll cross paths again," was the best she could come up with.

"I'll make sure of it! Now, be off with you," Sophia said, shooing them out of the dining room.

They said a quick goodbye to the table, but the guests had already moved on to other topics.

"If you didn't feign being sick, I was going to. Every minute at that table felt like an hour," Isaiah asked, pulling her close to his side with a mischievous grin. Poppy had never been so happy to skip dessert.

"Smarter than you look. I had to get you out of there before they made you get up on the table and dance," Poppy replied, kissing his cheek. "You handled their nonsense like a champ, and I definitely owe you one. Add one slice of cheesecake to my debt." It felt like a weight lifted from her shoulders as they escaped the party.

"Don't worry, I've got my dessert right here." He ran his hand over her waist, sending shivers up her spine as they walked past a few other half-empty dining rooms and restaurants.

"You're insatiable." Poppy rolled her eyes – not that she minded being his dessert. In fact, she was looking forward to an after-dinner treat.

"Only when it comes to you," he said, kissing her hair.

"Stop that. We need to focus."

"You're right! I'm all business." Isaiah removed his hands from her and stepped to the side for emphasis. "Since we didn't discover anything new from our fellow dinner guests, I have an idea," he said, directing them toward the rainforest bar, the only one that seemed to be crowded.

"It had better not involve food. I think those twelve courses will keep me stuffed for the rest of the trip," Poppy said, placing a hand on her food baby.

"Don't worry, this doesn't involve food. Did you notice the mirrored walls in the glass room? The waiters were using those secret passages, and I was thinking that if we can follow the passages to the lounge deck where we last saw the killer disappear, we might be able to find something and salvage this night." He offered her his hand.

"It couldn't hurt to try," she said, happily taking his hand as he led her inside.

The sounds of monkeys chattering and chirping birds, combined with the heavy foliage and rocking of the ship, overwhelmed her senses. The storm was ramping up as the night wore on, and the décor made it feel like they were trapped inside a swaying rainforest. She struggled not to laugh as Isaiah tried to walk in a straight line. The place was packed, so they went unnoticed. That was precisely what they wanted to get into the staff area, but they had to linger a little so they wouldn't get caught.

"Forgive me for my lack of grace," he said, gripping her hand tighter and looking as adorable as Bambi on ice. "How are you doing this in heels?"

"Years of dancing. I think you just want to hold me closer," she teased.

"That's a bonus." He winked, bracing himself against

a table filled with guests downing their umbrella-filled cocktails. He apologised for interrupting them, but they were too drunk to care.

"Just focus on one of the trees. Any fixed point will help you with your balance," Poppy said, putting her arm around him before he ended up on the floor.

"Right, fixed point."

Poppy watched as Isaiah spotted and followed a waiter carrying a tray.

"Hopefully, he'll lead us to a passage opening," he murmured as they walked towards the bar. Unfortunately, the waiter started taking drink orders behind the bar instead of leading them to the hidden entrance. "Keep your eyes on the other waiters. Those clearing tables will have to discard the glasses, so it shouldn't take too long."

They didn't have to order drinks; the bartender placed two fruity cocktails in front of them as they stood at the bar waiting.

"We might as well enjoy ourselves while we wait," Poppy mused, smelling the strong scent of banana from her cocktail.

"Oh God," Isaiah said, taking a long draw from a sparkly straw. She wished she had a camera to get a shot of his face. His lips puckered, and he shivered. "That's deceptively strong."

"Since we've some time to kill, was that story you told at dinner true?" Poppy asked, taking a sip of her own drink. He wasn't lying about the strong taste of liquor; from the bright yellow colour she had been expecting something sweet, not bitter.

"No." He smiled to himself.

"Are you kidding?" Poppy shoved him playfully, tipping him off balance again. She grabbed his jacket to stop him from falling over.

"I'd never talk about official cases over dinner. I just wanted that guy across from us to shut up," he admitted.

"How did you come up with it so quickly?" she asked, her voice barely above a whisper, as they watched the waiters around the room.

"Some old crime show episode. Not a bad episode, but licking all those envelopes? Could you imagine the paper cuts?"

He grimaced, but Poppy was distracted by a waiter disappearing through the side of a tree between the lagoon and the stage. A secret passage, just like the one the killer must have slipped into. Poppy wished security had thought to put some cameras in the passages. Clearly hers wasn't the only situation they wanted to hide.

## Chapter 20
# Close Encounters
### Poppy

A sudden crash from the fake lagoon drew the staff's attention away from the bar. Drunk guests and a storm weren't a good combination. Poppy grabbed Isaiah's arm and headed for the tree. Sure enough, the thick trunk was an illusion; staff could walk straight through it into a long, narrow corridor. They tiptoed past the kitchen. Once clear of any staff, the sound of the faux Amazon disappeared behind them.

"How are we supposed to know which door to check or what to look for?" Poppy asked, making a note of all the different access doors. It was a maze of short and long staircases and long straight stretches followed by quick twists and turns.

"We'll know it when we find it. We already wasted the evening at dinner, so we might get lucky searching the corridors until we reach the lounge deck. The captain only ordered Davide to search the immediate area, so widening the search can only play in our favour," Isaiah said, following her. Thankfully, the corridor was so narrow they could use the walls for balance.

"Speaking of good stories, talking about your aunt and Calliope can't have been easy. I'm sorry you were put on the spot like that."

She was glad he couldn't see her face in the dimly lit space. "It wasn't the first time, and I doubt it'll be the last time." She was tired of spinning pretty lies.

"Is it because you grew up watching them that you wanted to get into acting?" Isaiah asked, as they walked up a short staircase.

"Maybe. I've always wanted to act. To focus on indie movies and support female directors and writers. There are so many stories that don't get to be told, so I want to invest in as many projects as I can. To finance that goal, I'm working on a remake of one of my aunt's Broadway shows; they offered me such a ridiculous check that I couldn't refuse. With what they're paying me, I was able to fund four smaller projects. I've been rehearsing for months in secret. Singing, dancing, and acting all wrapped up in one. It'll be a good way to break into acting without shocking everyone. Getting the lead role was one of the happiest days of my life. For the first time, I'm working on things I wanted to do without outside influence or pressure," she told him. She'd been afraid to admit to everything that was going right in life in case it all fell apart. Then again, given that a murderer was after her and those around her, her karma was fairly balanced.

"I'm sure those you're helping appreciate you helping them realise their dreams. Did you get to celebrate?"

"No, I didn't dare to tell anyone. Then the studio made the casting announcement a week after my aunt died. They thought it would be good publicity, since she played the role on stage," Poppy said. She hadn't agreed to their PR release, but she'd understood it had to come out at some point.

"Did you want to tell her?" Isaiah asked. "She put you through hell. I'm sure the thought of you taking her place would have driven her crazy."

"I considered it, but I didn't want her to ruin it for me. She would have tried to make me give up the role or contacted the casting director," Poppy said, frustrated that such a happy moment was tainted by her aunt's threats.

"When all this is over, we're going to celebrate!" Isaiah said enthusiastically. "You should be able to sing, shout, and scream about everything you've achieved. No one is going to threaten or hurt you anymore."

"I could've celebrated, but I was afraid of her finding out that I dared to step out of line. The moment Martha adopted me, my life was hers. You might think 'poor little pop star with millions of fans, fame and fortune', but I was her prisoner. My every move was controlled: what I wore, what I ate, and my medication. She put me in therapy for my parents' death only to bribe the therapist into recording the session so she could make sure I wasn't talking badly about her. Everything I earned up to eighteen funded her lifestyle. All my masters, she owned. I couldn't breathe without permission. My victories were hers, but my failures were solely mine. I wanted this movie, this victory, to be mine for as long as possible. I wanted to make sure that I got my ducks in a row before she found out." Poppy paused, feeling like she had said too much. "It must be the detective in you, because I can't shut up around you."

She glanced over her shoulder when he remained silent. She hoped she hadn't scared him off with her trauma dumping.

"What's wrong?" she asked, looking at the staircases that led to the spa and the tranquillity room one floor below. "Did you see something?" She studied the corridor, but there was nothing to notice, and his gaze was fixed solely on her.

"I can't help but wonder why your parents left you with her. Surely they must have known she wasn't the child-raising type?"

Isaiah was asking questions she didn't have any answers to. Poppy thought about the woman who had come by the funeral from the orphanage she couldn't remember.

"I don't think my parents had any will. I was in an orphanage for a few months before my aunt came and got me, or so I've been told. I don't remember much from that time. Martha was my mum's sister, but they'd never been close since my mum was much younger. We only visited Martha at Christmas, so I doubt they wanted her to be my guardian. But there was no one else willing." Poppy had spent most of her life wishing someone else had come for her. "But I don't blame my parents. They were the best people in the world, and it's not their fault that they died."

"I'm sorry you had to live in such a home. Even if your aunt wasn't, your parents are proud of you. Your strength and courage have helped you survive, and you still treat others with love and kindness. You have no idea how much I admire you. Not many would have the strength to continue to stand up and fight for themselves," Isaiah said, with so much heart it nearly broke her.

"You really are a terrible detective." Poppy turned to face him and wrapped her arms around his neck. She'd never thought he would talk about or feel for her like he did. Her soul had been chipped away at, her heart forever corrupted by what she had done, but he made her feel whole. She felt a surge of affection for him, a feeling she had tried to minimise and suppress.

"How so?" Isaiah chuckled as he returned the embrace.

"How can you think of me so highly, knowing what I've done? I'm afraid you'll resent your feelings for me one day."

"We all have our secrets, a past, but there's nothing you could do that would make me resent how I feel about you," Isaiah said, and the certainty in his words made her weak in the knees.

"What are you two doing here?" a maid carrying a rubbish bag barked at them, her voice cutting through the silence like a knife.

Poppy looked at Isaiah. "I'm sorry, we got lost. We were in the forest bar—"

"And you walked inside the tree? Did you think you were Alice going down the rabbit hole? You wouldn't be the first guests to do that. Follow me, and I'll take you back to the main deck."

"Thank you. We had too many fruity cocktails and got turned around..." Poppy fell silent when she watched the woman pop open a chute hidden in the wall and send the rubbish down.

"What? You've never seen a rubbish chute before? It takes everything down to the incinerator," the maid explained, closing it back up. The dark walls concealed its presence. Like the passages, you had to know what you were looking for to spot them.

"The ship has so many secrets. It's hard not to be mystified," Poppy observed. *The killer could have discarded the weapon and the dress in the chute.* If they could find the chute in the passageway the killer had used, they might be able to find something – blood, prints, maybe even the weapon or what she had used to mess with the cameras. Isaiah and Poppy locked eyes, telling her he had the same thoughts.

"A rubbish chute mystifies you? If only all guests were so easily impressed," the maid said, turning her back on them. Poppy ignored the woman's sneer. With guests like Douglas Mengur on board, she couldn't imagine what the maid had to put up with.

Silently, the woman led them out of the staff passageway to the B-Deck. They waited a few minutes before sneaking back in and following the arrows to the lounge deck. The closer they got to it, the slower they approached. About to make the final turn, Isaiah motioned for Poppy to step aside. She let him go first. He drew his gun and checked the corners to make sure no one was lying in wait.

"It's clear," he said quietly, putting his gun away.

"Find the rubbish chute," Poppy said, quickly running her hands over the walls. Neither dared to speak; anticipation thickened the air around them. Poppy sighed in relief when she felt the square crease in the wall and popped the chute open.

"Everything goes to the incinerator. Even if the killer tossed the weapon or her clothes, it should be long gone," Isaiah reasoned.

"Don't jinx us," Poppy snapped, desperate for a new lead. She looked at the chute, but couldn't bring herself to check. The fear of disappointment froze her solid.

"Want me to check?" Isaiah asked softly. Poppy nodded and held her breath as he looked inside.

She waited for him to say something, but he shook his head and stepped aside. She inspected the steel chute next, but it was empty.

Just as she was about to give up hope, something caught her eye in the corner. A glimmer; a shimmer of hope. She reached further into the back until her fingertips touched the sharp steel edge where the chute dropped off, and she felt something snagged in the corner, rough and heavy. She didn't know what was caught, but she pulled it up anyway.

In the dim light, a heavy green fabric shimmered. It was the dress the killer had used to trick the cameras. Relief flooded over Poppy, a wave of emotion she couldn't contain as she held the dress, confirming it was real.

"You found the dress," Isaiah said in disbelief.

Poppy felt the blood drain from her face as she noticed the plunging neckline and the mesh sleeves. The dress was familiar – too familiar. She read the designer label and checked the hem for the alterations she knew would be there. Isaiah was talking to her, but all she could think was how this was impossible. It couldn't be *her* dress, yet it was in Poppy's hands.

"I know whose this is," she stammered, her voice barely above a whisper. She handed him the dress as if it would burn her if she held onto it any longer.

"Whose?" he asked, taking it. A puzzled frown distorted his features as she found the courage to speak.

"Martha Roe's."

"COULD Martha have given the dress to someone?" Isaiah asked, filling the silence in the lift.

"No way. Martha wore that dress when she won her first Academy Award. She never let anyone borrow her things, especially not something so valuable or precious," Poppy said. She'd never have been allowed to enter Martha's wardrobe. "It must have been stolen, either from the house before she died or from the storage unit I rented after." She had put her aunt's things in storage when she'd put the house on the market. However,

Martha had dozens of evening dresses, so keeping track of all of them would have been impossible. She'd packed up in such a hurry, she never would have noticed one was missing.

The lift binged, but the doors failed to open when they stepped forward. Isaiah hit the button for their floor again, but the doors didn't open.

Poppy panicked. "Please don't tell me we're stuck." The small screen started blinking between 1 and 2. *We aren't stuck*, she thought repeatedly, hoping the gold doors would open.

"It's okay. It's probably just a glitch because of the storm," Isaiah said, hitting the alarm. The high-pitched ringing didn't help with her nerves.

"That doesn't make me feel any better," Poppy said, taking his arm as the lights flickered. "Oh God, please don't let the lights go out."

Isaiah turned to face her. "I'm right here. Nothing's going to happen to us."

She rested her forehead against his chest and tried to slow her breathing.

"I'm not usually claustrophobic," she said, envying his calmness.

"You don't have to justify yourself. I'm scared, too," Isaiah said, stroking her hair.

She started to forget where she was as he kissed the top of her head. Wanting to distract herself, she began kissing his neck and jaw until he claimed her lips.

"Poppy." He said it like it was a warning or a question, but she didn't let up.

"What? Can you think of a better way to distract ourselves from being trapped?" She smiled against his lips as he pressed his body against hers.

"You're a bad influence on me," he whispered, so close

his nose brushed hers. He dropped the green dress on the floor, unable to keep his hands off her.

"You're only realising this now?" she rasped as he backed her up against the wall and pinned her hands above her head.

Poppy shrieked as the lights flickered again. The thrill of his hands on her body and the fear of plunging to their death clashed within her.

"Focus on me, and only me. When your senses are overwhelmed, it's easier to distract them than silence them," Isaiah said, his fingertips pushing the hem of her short red dress up her thighs.

"Yes, sir." He tasted like champagne and mint sorbet. She forgot where they were again, only for the lamps to flicker. She clung to him as the alarm repeated and her heart rate quickened.

"Just focus on me, Princess," he growled, tightening his hold on her.

Poppy gasped as he trailed his lips along her neck and shoulders. Her tiny red straps gave him all the access he needed to drive her crazy. It was easy to forget about the suspects and clues around him; getting lost in his touch was her new favourite hobby. Isaiah reached under her dress as his hot breath caressed her breasts, pushed up thanks to her corset. She flushed when she felt him slide her lacy red underwear down her thighs.

"You promised me dessert," he whispered, a mischievous glint in his eye.

Poppy thought he was going to take her then and there, but he surprised her by sinking to his knees. His eyes locked on hers until he pressed his lips to the inside of her thighs, forcing her to widen her stance.

"Happy to oblige," she giggled. Her eyelids fluttered closed as she savoured each kiss and gentle caress. He slipped a hand behind her knee, and she felt a moment of shyness as she placed her leg over his shoulder, giving him the access he needed to devour her.

All hesitation disappeared as his tongue circled and twisted, and each turn sent her closer to the edge. Poppy clutched his hair, his shoulders, anything to try and steady herself as waves of pleasure rocked her body. The alarm and flashing lights went unnoticed; all she could think about was his relentless hunger and the sound of her racing heart. Her limbs trembled as he controlled her pleasure. Her hips bucked forward, demanding more from him, but he held them firmly, making sure to take his time and draw out every moment of pleasure until she shattered into a million pieces, fearing that the only person who could put her back together again was him.

Poppy slumped against the wall, unable to speak as she came down. Like a gentleman, Isaiah kept her steady as he adjusted her dress and stood up.

"Satisfied?" she asked, trying to catch her breath. She noticed he put her underwear in his pocket instead of giving them back.

"For now," Isaiah panted, kissing her cheek. "Are you —?"

He couldn't finish his question as she slid her hands down his chest.

"What do you think?" she teased, reaching for his belt.

Scooping her up in his arms, he cradled her trembling body against his. Instinctively, her legs coiled around his waist, and a deep groan echoed from deep in his chest. She didn't need to be told how desperate he was for her; she could feel him straining against his trousers.

She was about to free him when the doors binged open. Poppy wanted to scream, and Isaiah rested his forehead against her and let out a tortured laugh. The ship was mocking and tormenting them from every possible angle. She now had another reason to hate fucking lifts.

"Maybe we could ride a few more floors? We might get stuck again," she suggested, no longer caring about the lift – not when she wanted him so desperately.

"Your words are music to my ears." He kissed her gently, and her body took that as a yes. However, Isaiah eased her down until her feet touched the floor again. "But we can't risk getting stuck again."

"You're right. We should get back to our suite." Poppy swallowed her desire and forced herself to be sensible, even if her body screamed at her. He straightened the straps on her shoulders while she redid his belt.

"To be continued." Isaiah kissed her forehead. He picked up the dress she had forgotten about before following her out of the lift.

When Poppy noticed the emergency lighting in the hall, she knew they had made the right decision to leave the lift; the whole ship was obviously having power trouble. She stayed close to Isaiah, who kept her a step behind him, clearly on edge. With the lights out and everyone distracted by the storm, it felt like the perfect time for the killer to strike. He handed her the dress while his other hand remained on his weapon.

A light shone from an open door as someone came into the corridor, and Poppy reassured Isaiah before he drew his gun.

"It's okay. That's just Mina's room." Isaiah relaxed slightly. "Mina?" Poppy called, but the figure walked in the opposite direction.

Terror washed over her. Was that the killer leaving their suite? She wanted to chase after them, but Isaiah stopped her. As they reached the open door, Poppy held her breath, terrified of what they might find.

Her heart skipped a beat when she saw Mina standing by the bed, safe and sound.

"You scared me!" Mina said, pulling off her headphones. Poppy rushed over and embraced her tightly. Isaiah slipped out of the room, giving them some space.

"We saw someone leaving your room and thought the killer got to you!" she exclaimed as adrenaline flooded her body.

"Poppy, the only one who might kill me is you," Mina joked, her laughter filling the room. "You're squeezing me to death!"

Her humour was a welcome relief in the tense situation, bringing a smile to Poppy's face. "Sorry!" She let go and checked for injuries, noticing that Mina's eyes were red and puffy. She had been crying. "What's happened?"

Mina explained that the person they had seen leaving her room was Francis, her F1*friend,* whom she had kicked out – because his girlfriend would be boarding with him when they docked tomorrow.

"What a dick! You deserve so much better, and so does his girlfriend," Poppy snapped, surprised he'd had the balls to come to her room and casually tell her about his girlfriend boarding as though it was no big deal.

Mina looked exhausted. "I don't even want to think about him a second longer."

"This has been a holiday from hell. I'll make it up to you. Tomorrow in Amalfi, we'll go shopping, eat, and have ice cream," Poppy promised.

"You don't have to. I might just relax at the beach, clear my head of murder and men," Mina said with a long sigh.

"Or you could leave this cruise and go home. I can book your ticket, and you'd be safe in 24 hours," Poppy offered, wanting to give her an out.

Mina took her hand. "We started this together, and we'll finish it together. No one will scare me away." Her words were a comforting reassurance of their unbreakable bond despite having known each other for so little time.

"Do you have a love bite on your neck?" Mina asked, leaning in close.

Poppy's hand flew to her neck, and they burst into laughter. "We got stuck in a lift."

"Got stuck or stuck in?" Mina teased.

"Oh God, don't put it like that!" Poppy hit her with a pillow.

"I'm heartbroken, so you must tell me everything," Mina insisted.

They settled on Mina's bed for a debrief and dismantled the minibar. The best way to cure heartbreak was definitely a sleepover with chocolate, tiny bottles of alcohol, and endless movies on the *Midas* streaming platform.

## Chapter 21
# On Shaky Ground
### Poppy

With the sun on her face and solid ground beneath her feet, Poppy would never take land for granted again.

The scenery of the Amalfi coast had proved to be so captivatingly beautiful that Poppy regretted how little time they would spend here. The freedom to go anywhere, without the fear of someone lurking in the dark corners, made her feel safe again, and when she walked out of the goldfish bowl and through the busy market, it made her never want to set foot on the *Midas* again.

When they'd got off the ship she'd been given back her purse and phone, but she didn't dare turn it on. She wasn't ready for what might be waiting for her. Still, she had found some cash in her purse that she was happy to spend. Retail therapy had become her new favourite form of therapy, along with taking baths with Isaiah. If it hadn't been for the murderer targeting her and those close to her, she would be thoroughly delighted with her life. She had a very attractive bodyguard who turned a blind eye to her violent past, a best friend willing to commit murder alongside her, and no one dictating who she should be, what she should do, or where she should go.

"We are going to run out of hands," Isaiah said as she paid an older woman at a stall for a crochet dress for Mina and some bangles. Isaiah had got up extra early to talk with Captain Hamill and ensure the evidence was picked up and sent off properly before disembarking for the day.

"Nothing says 'I'm sorry for taking you on a murder cruise' like handmade clothing," Poppy said as Isaiah took the bag from her and added it to the small pile. She didn't get to go to many markets back home, so she wanted to support as many of the small businesses as possible.

"How about we go inside and get some coffee or something cold? I'm starting to melt," he said, and she was undoubtedly tempted. It was coming up to lunchtime, and they'd been on their feet since leaving the ship at ten a.m.

"We could go in there," Poppy said, pointing at a boutique with pink shutters.

Red velvet curtains and a mannequin wearing a red lacy nightdress decorated the window.

"Not a chance," Isaiah said, shaking his head bashfully.

"Mr Rivers, I dare say you're blushing," Poppy teased, heading towards the door. "You could help me pick something out."

He tipped her chin up. "I'm not going in there. And I prefer to be surprised. You go ahead and have fun – I'll go get us something to cool down."

"Wasn't it your rule that we don't go anywhere alone?" Poppy said, trying to tempt him.

"It wouldn't be the first rule we've broken on this trip," Isaiah said. "I won't be long, and I'll be waiting out here when you're ready." He kissed the side of her head and waited for her to head inside before heading to the cafe down the street.

It was hard not to get wrapped up in the pretty, unique sets inside the boutique. She loved pretty underwear – not just to show it to someone, but because it always made her feel powerful. Poppy decided to take the nightdress in the window and the blue, pink and red sets, since she wouldn't get to come back anytime soon. She wished Mina had come shopping with her, but the poor girl deserved a day at the beach.

She expected to find Isaiah waiting outside, but there was no sign of him in the quiet street.

"Isaiah?" She peered around the shop corner, but the benches were empty. He wouldn't have gone far; he might have got caught up in a queue or sat in the shade under the awning because she'd taken longer than expected.

A shiver crept up her spine when she started down the cobbled alley to return to the market. Poppy glanced over her shoulder, hoping to see Isaiah, but no one was there. She took a deep breath. Days on board the *Midas* had made her paranoid.

She was only halfway to the café when the faint footsteps started to echo behind her. She started walking a little faster, hoping to return to the busy market and find Isaiah.

Emerging from the alley, she headed straight for the café with a sense of urgency, only to be abruptly halted as she collided with an easel and the woman with striking lilac hair sitting beside it.

"Shit, that stings," Poppy exclaimed, rubbing her scraped knees. Her heart sank as she saw the mess she had made of the woman's paints and easel. "I'm terribly sorry; I didn't mean to bump into you. Can I help?"

When the woman with the lilac bob and tattooed sleeve didn't respond immediately, frantically cleaning up her paints with paper towels. She gently tapped her on the shoulder, and the woman removed some earbuds. Poppy heard music blasting.

"I'm really sorry about this," Poppy repeated, reaching for a few paper towels from the nearby chair to assist in the cleanup and hoping she hadn't ruined the piece the artist was working on. It was astonishing how a small amount of paint could spread so far.

"Sorry, I had my headphones on full blast, and I didn't want to let the paint set on the stones," the woman said, pouring water from her bottle over the cobbles to wash away the remaining stain. Poppy stood the easel back up, and the woman placed her canvas on the stand.

"I'm so sorry. I smudged your landscape," Poppy exclaimed, admiring the market scene. The only difference from reality was that the people had been turned into caricatures. Poppy was sure she recognised the style, but she couldn't place the artist. "Please let me compensate you."

"Please, don't worry about it! I was just having some fun. Using oil paints is always a gamble," the woman reassured her, handing Poppy the bags she had dropped. Poppy moved her purchases to one bag to use the other as a makeshift bin for the paint-covered paper towels.

"Especially when you're mowed down by a stranger on the street," she said, embarrassed that her fear had caused her to hurt another person. With everything back in place and the incident erased except for the smudge, she could focus on the artist properly. The lilac hair, the nose piercing, the art on the canvas she'd knocked to the floor – she pieced it together.

"Phoebe! Phoebe Fletcher," she exclaimed.

Phoebe laughed. "I don't think they heard you the next street over."

"Sorry!" Poppy clamped her hands over her mouth. "I recognised your work, and then it hit me. I'm—"

"I didn't know painting the cobblestones was on the agenda."

Both women looked up to see Isaiah and a striking man carrying a tray of coffee. Poppy let out a sigh when she saw they were iced; the heat had started to make her skin prickle.

"You could have helped us instead of watching," Phoebe said, flicking some paint from her hands onto the man, who wore a white T-shirt and had a spider tattoo on the side of his head.

"I only went to get coffee. How'd you manage to cause trouble in less than five minutes?" Isaiah asked, taking the makeshift bin and throwing it out. Poppy noticed how the man checked on Phoebe, and she smiled at him reassuringly. Definitely a couple.

"You were supposed to wait for me outside the boutique. This time, you were the one who wandered off," Poppy argued, to the amusement of the other couple.

"I didn't wander off," Isaiah said, "I ran into Axel when I was in the queue outside the café. I didn't think you'd be so quick. But I see you've already met Phoebe."

"Axel?"

"I think we've met." Axel offered her his hand. "Last year's music video awards?"

Instantly, Poppy recalled that terrible night. She'd lost in her category, and the cameras had caught her aunt giving her a good scolding. She couldn't believe she hadn't placed Axel instantly; not many people had giant spider tattoos on the side of their head, or such exquisite cheekbones.

"Right! Brothers of Anarchy. You won…" Poppy couldn't remember what, but she knew they'd won. It had been an emotional speech, because they'd lost their lead singer in an accident earlier that same year.

"Phoebe and Axel, this is Poppy."

"Poppy Roe!" Phoebe said. "Sorry I didn't recognise you, and I've covered us in paint. What a great first impression. Isaiah mentioned taking some time off, but we didn't realise he'd snatched up such a gem."

Poppy loved her spirit instantly.

"We wouldn't be covered in paint if I hadn't run into you," she pointed out. "And I think I snatched *him* up. A mutual friend recommended him, and since he was already taking a holiday, I hired him to be my bodyguard for mine." She suspected he didn't want people to know about his secret investigation into her.

Isaiah locked eyes with her, and a silent *thank you* told her she had made the right decision.

"Don't worry, she's always covered in paint," Axel teased.

Phoebe looked like she wanted to argue, only to look down at her paint-covered overalls. "He has a point."

"Are you staying close by? We've got a villa that we're renovating, and you're more than welcome to stay with us," Phoebe said enthusiastically. "The place is a bit messy, but I'd love to have you."

"That's so kind of you, but we're only making a pit stop. We have to be back on the *Midas* by midnight," Poppy said, though she would've much preferred to stay.

Phoebe's eyes widened. "The *Midas*? I'm jealous; I've heard the gallery on board is out of this world."

*She wouldn't be jealous if she knew about the ship's current death toll.*

"If you want to go, I can book it next year," Axel said, like it was nothing. Poppy and Isaiah exchanged a look. They couldn't exactly recommend it, considering the murderous voyage they'd had so far.

"Don't you dare; I get so seasick! But it would be

incredible to have my work featured there," Phoebe said, her eyes brightening.

"I'm sad to say I haven't been to the gallery," Poppy admitted, "but Isaiah knows the owner. I'm sure he would be excited to see your work."

"No, no, I'm just dreaming out loud. Isaiah has already done so much for us," Phoebe said admiringly. Poppy wanted to know their story; clearly, he was a very dear friend to them.

"Lunch?" Axel asked, changing the subject. Poppy guessed he didn't want his friend to feel put on the spot. "Our favourite restaurant is only around the corner."

"We aren't taking no for an answer, and I want to hear everything about your trip," Phoebe added, looking between them as she packed her supplies.

"Lunch sounds great. I'm starving," Poppy said, giving in to her infectious friendship.

"Lead the way," Isaiah told Axel, who helped Phoebe carry her supplies. Poppy noticed the artist was wearing a thin supportive sleeve on her wrist and instinctively picked up her light stool. Phoebe smiled at her in acknowledgement and grabbed her toolbox, filled with small paint pots and brushes. It was only a short walk through a narrow alley to get to the little corner restaurant.

As the greeter welcomed Phoebe and Axel with a warm embrace, it was clear they were regulars. The greeter kindly offered to stow Phoebe's art supplies before leading them to a table beneath a blossoming tree that Poppy couldn't identify. The shade of the tree and the surrounding blooming flowers created a cosy, private corner for them.

"Are you dating?" Phoebe asked abruptly, once the waiter had dropped off a jug of water topped with various fruits.

Poppy choked on her water, taken off guard.

"Sorry, was that rude? He pulled out the chair for you and ensured you got the seat in the shade. Isaiah is a sucker for acts of service."

Isaiah glared at Phoebe, but Poppy noticed she obviously didn't care.

"Are you sure you aren't the detective?" he growled.

Phoebe rolled her eyes. "What? You're usually all business, and I want to know more about how the gorgeous and talented Princess of Pop managed to tame the great Detective Rivers. For that, I commend you." Phoebe winked at her.

Poppy didn't know what to say. She didn't want Isaiah to feel uncomfortable, but she enjoyed them digging him out. It was nice to see a different side of him.

"You benefited from my workaholic tendencies," Isaiah scolded Phoebe as he filled Poppy's glass in an automatic gesture. Axel laughed as Isaiah evidently realised he had just reinforced Phoebe's earlier point. Poppy concealed her amusement behind her menu, and he squeezed her thigh beneath the table.

"How do you know each other?" Poppy asked, trying to get the topic off them and their bodyguard-turned-lover situationship.

The table fell into an uncomfortable silence, and Poppy immediately regretted her attempt to change the subject.

"It's a long story," Isaiah said, respecting their privacy. Poppy suddenly remembered something about a dead fiancé and a murder investigation. She recalled the news articles and the public scrutiny they had faced. It had been a difficult time for them, and she could see the pain in their eyes as they remembered it.

"Sorry, I shouldn't have asked." Poppy decided to focus on her menu. "The linguine sounds tasty!"

"Don't be sorry. It's not like all the details aren't already out in the world. Isaiah and Axel are just protective of me." Phoebe smiled sadly. "Isaiah helped us with a case. It's not the best mealtime story, but he ensured the person trying to hurt us was put away for a long time."

Axel picked a fallen petal from Phoebe's hair, and Poppy could see the worry in his eyes, but they both looked at Isaiah with genuine respect.

She reached for his hand under the table and held it on her lap. Having him by her side helped her breathe a little easier. If he'd kept them safe, then there was hope for her.

"I'm glad he was able to help you, and I'm sorry about what you had to go through," she told them.

"You mentioned you were renovating the villa? I thought you were supposed to work on another album?" Isaiah asked Axel, who had rested a protective arm around the back of Phoebe's chair.

"August and Nick are working on the production, so I had some time. We thought we'd use it to renovate and sell the villa to put more funds in the arts centre back home," Axel said.

"Phoebe opened an arts centre for those in the arts with disabilities," Isaiah explained to Poppy.

"That's incredible!"

"Our current plan is to buy the two buildings next to my art studio so we can expand. I can also put in a second floor and lifts to make sure it's accessible for everyone," Phoebe said, her excitement infectious. "We started with a small group, and I hate having to turn anyone away because we lack space and resources, so with the extra investment, we can give more people a place to come and express themselves freely." She blushed. "Forgive me, I'm rambling. It's a passion project, and I didn't expect so much interest."

"No, please don't apologise. I love what you're doing," Poppy said, wanting to know more.

"I convinced her to get away from the villa and her phone. She's so busy looking after everyone else that she forgets to come up for air," Axel said, and Phoebe nudged him.

"You came up for air, and then I knocked you down," Poppy said, glancing at the brace on Phoebe's wrist. She hoped she hadn't hurt her. It looked like the one her song-writers used for carpal tunnel, although it matched the pink bikini under Phoebe's paint-covered overalls.

"Please don't apologise. Clearly, we were destined to run into each other." Phoebe beamed. "I know you aren't staying long, but if you're interested, we're holding an auction tonight to help raise funds for the centre; the event is casino-themed. All winnings go towards research for underfunded diseases and disorders, and the auction will help those who are chronically ill and disabled and want to get involved in the arts. It starts at 8 and takes place at a boutique hotel on the beachfront, so you can return to the ship well before midnight."

Poppy glanced at Isaiah. He shrugged, leaving it up to her.

"We would love to. Thank you so much. Would you mind if I brought a friend, Mina, with us? She's travelling with me, and I'm sure she would love to come," Poppy said, wanting to support her. It also meant they could delay getting back on board a while longer.

"Of course! The more the merrier," Phoebe said. "It's black tie, so dress to kill."

Isaiah smirked, and Poppy glared at him.

"Did I miss something?" Phoebe asked, looking to Axel, who looked just as confused.

"Nothing – he's just excited to wear the tux I got him again," Poppy teased, and Isaiah's smirk disappeared.

"I'd love to help you with the centre when we get home. I can make donations, or I can stop by and help. I have some time now that I've finished touring before I have to start filming," Poppy said, eager to do some good.

"You aren't going back to the States?" Isaiah asked her.

Poppy realised they had never spoken about what would happen after the *Midas*; they had been too focused on surviving.

"No, Ireland's my home. I'll go to and from for work, but I want to stay in Ireland," she said firmly. Her relationship with him had nothing to do with her decision. It had been her plan all along to come home.

Isaiah looked relieved, and she realised he must have been wondering about their future. She felt guilty for not considering his feelings or thoughts about it.

"We'd love to have you involved in whatever form suits you best," Phoebe exclaimed, breaking the tension.

Poppy's heart leapt in her chest as a sudden camera flash caught her off guard, a stark reminder of the current state of her raw nerves. She was used to being in the spotlight, but this sent her pulse racing.

"Sorry, they tend to pop up now and then when they know we're here," Phoebe said, and Axel looked over his shoulder to wave away the pap.

"It's fine," Poppy said, her voice steady but her panic growing. "I need to wash my hands before the food arrives." She hurried off, determined to regain her composure, before anyone noticed.

Poppy braced herself against the copper sink in the bathroom and took some deep breaths. It wasn't the paparazzi that bothered her or having her picture taken, but the unexpected intrusion. Her body was so on edge after recent events that something as trivial as a flash had made her spiral. She wished it hadn't happened in front of Phoebe and Axel. She didn't want Isaiah's friends to think she was a drama queen.

The ornate tiles in the bathroom started to blur, and she flexed her hands to try to stop the shakes.

"Poppy?" Phoebe knocked lightly on the door. "Are you alright? It's me."

Her soft voice drew Poppy's attention away from the tightening sensation in her chest. She opened the door, feeling as red as the tomatoes in the bruschetta she had ordered.

"I had a similar reaction to paparazzi a while back, so I understand how overwhelming it can be. Run your wrists under the cold water. It'll help calm you down," Phoebe suggested, her tone warm and non-judgmental.

"Thank you," Poppy said, doing so. "I don't know where it came from. I haven't had an anxiety attack in public in a long time. I think I'm just overwhelmed at the minute."

"That's totally understandable, and nothing to feel bad about. I hope you don't mind my invading your space. Isaiah might have mentioned that you've recently been struggling with unwanted attention. I wanted to check you were alright," Phoebe said kindly.

Poppy admired her for being so open with a perfect stranger, and then remembered that Phoebe was the Phoebe Fletcher who'd been accused of causing the death of her boyfriend after a fight while he was driving. Poppy recalled her ex-assistant telling her how merciless the press had been, practically driving the poor woman underground.

"I should be used to people taking my picture. I saw the flash, and it was like the world went white. I couldn't sit there a second longer," Poppy confessed, her vulnerability laid bare.

"Sorry, the guy wanted Axel's autograph. Since we've become regulars, it's been happening more often. This used to be our secret spot, but for the most part, we're left alone."

"Nothing for you to apologise for. I don't know how much Isaiah told you, but it's been more than a little unwanted attention," Poppy said, looking at her in the mirror.

"I guessed as much when I saw Isaiah carrying his gun when he sat down. You're in safe hands with him. You couldn't have picked anyone better to protect you," Phoebe assured her.

"It's been hard to trust someone new, and we didn't exactly see eye to eye in the beginning, but he won me over. We've only known each other a matter of days, but I trust him, and I know he has the best intentions," Poppy admitted, breathing a little easier. Phoebe was one of those people who made it easy to spill your secrets if you weren't keeping guard.

"Are you sure nothing more is going on than just best intentions? I saw how he looked at you; it could even make *me* blush. He looked about ready to attack the waiter for even asking for your order." Phoebe chuckled, lightening the mood.

Poppy shook her head, focusing on the water coming from the tap. "He's suspicious of anyone who gets close to me. Let's just say the last few people who've come my way haven't lived long enough to discuss it."

Phoebe took a minute to digest what she was saying, and Poppy hoped she hadn't said too much. She didn't want to put her burdens on her, but having her listen was helping ease her anxiety attack. The walls had stopped closing in, and her hands weren't shaking as noticeably.

"I don't know what situation you're in exactly. You probably can't tell me everything, considering we've just met. But if I could give you one piece of advice – getting through this will be much easier if you do it together. When I was going through my own hell, I thought keeping Axel at a distance, keeping all those I cared about away from me, would help keep them safe. In the end, the people we love want to protect us just as much as we want to protect them, and sometimes keeping them at a distance only puts them in more danger."

Poppy took in every word. It was as though Phoebe had read her thoughts.

"I'm afraid to care about him because I don't want someone to hurt him to hurt me. He wasn't supposed to be here, and I wasn't supposed to be feeling the things I am, and this isn't the time to be feeling anything for anyone," she rambled.

"I can't give you much advice about what to do with feelings you should or shouldn't have. I fell in love with my brother's best friend and ex-fiancée's bandmate, all while being hunted down by their crazy ex-manager. The timing is never perfect or even halfway decent. I like to believe Axel was my silver lining in a dark cloud. Isaiah might just be yours," Phoebe said, handing Phoebe a towel.

"What if caring about him gets him killed?" Poppy asked bluntly.

Phoebe took a moment to process that.

"Isaiah risks his life for strangers every day." She shrugged. "It's his job to protect people. You're worth protecting, and none of what's happening is your fault. It took me a long time to realise that," Phoebe said, giving her a hug she hadn't known she needed.

Phoebe pulled away and rested her hands on Poppy's shoulders. "Okay, this is when Axel would tell me to mind my business or practice what I preach. So I will tell you that the food is at the table, but take all the time you need to catch your breath. We aren't going anywhere."

Poppy had never been so happy to run into someone in her life. She would have thanked God for putting Phoebe in her path if she believed in him.

"What you said really means a lot. You've helped me more than you know," she said. Phoebe's eyes were as glassy as her own. Poppy gave her an out before they both became blubbering messes. "I'll be out in a second. I just want to fix my mascara."

"I know I said take your time, but with those two out there, I wouldn't be too long, or your food might not be there when you get back," Phoebe warned, heading for the door. Poppy chuckled.

Steady on her feet again, she walked through the restaurant and noticed Isaiah was out in the smoking area on the phone. She thought about returning to the table – after all, they had agreed to trust each other – but she couldn't stop her feet. Hidden from him by the terrace, she heard him curse.

"Can you see my face in them?" he asked, his irritation palpable. "I should've known there would be photographers at the dock. Thank you for keeping it from the captain. I don't think I'd have a job to return to if Roberts knew where I was."

There was a pause, and Poppy wished he was on loudspeaker so she could hear the other side of the conversation. She hadn't considered that he might be fired for helping her.

"Don't worry about looking into Joshua. He's dead – killed. Along with Calliope Chase, the movie star, and a crew member, Patrice," Isaiah explained bluntly. There was a pause. "No, Poppy isn't the killer. I was wrong about her. You haven't seen it in the news because the ship is covering it up until we can get solid answers. No one wants a panic."

Hearing Isaiah defend her made her heart ache. He had been right about her. If he had been going to rat her out, this would have been as good a time as any. He could easily have had the police waiting for her when they docked.

"We can't come home. It wouldn't change anything. The best way to lure out the killer is to wait it out. Poppy is clearly their endgame, and they won't be able to resist striking sooner or later." It seemed whoever was on the other end didn't want them getting back on board.

"No, I haven't got too attached." Another long silence and an even longer sigh. "I'm not going to get myself killed."

Poppy rolled her eyes, but she didn't blame him for not telling the person about their close relationship; then he would be receiving a different type of lecture.

"All the evidence we have gathered is being tested by a local station here. The reports will be forwarded to your email – I want to ensure you have all the information in case anything goes wrong. Just make sure Roberts doesn't find out. I've got to get back. Yes, Mom, I love you too," Isaiah said sarcastically before hanging up. He ran his hands through his hair and took a moment to steady himself.

Poppy hurried away before he caught her eavesdropping. She pretended to bump into him as he returned to the table.

"Who were you talking to?" she asked, looking at the phone in his hand.

"My partner back home. Michael worries if I don't check in, and the last thing we need is him sending out a manhunt for a missing detective," Isaiah said.

Poppy nodded, but noticed the conversation had unsettled him.

"We should get back to the table," he said. "And then if you want to go out tonight, we should head back to the ship to get changed."

"Do you not want to go back?" Poppy asked, wondering if his answer would tally with what he'd said on the phone to his partner.

"I want to solve this, but I don't want you to be in danger. Putting you back on that ship is like serving you up on a platter." He rubbed his brow.

"Even if we stay here, go to the beach, eat ice cream and lounge around in the sun, we can't be sure whoever is doing this won't just follow us. Hell, they could be in this restaurant right now staring at us. I want to be safe, and I love that you want me to be safe, but we both know that won't happen until the person doing this is dead or in prison," Poppy said, finding courage in Phoebe's words.

"Then we keep going. We attend the event tonight and return to the ship as planned," Isaiah said. She felt the whisper of his hand on her lower back, and the remaining pangs of her anxiety attack slipped away.

Back at the table, they moved to lighter topics. Poppy particularly enjoyed Axel's story about how Phoebe destroyed a guy's car with a crowbar and a tub of paint. Phoebe hadn't run, and neither would she.

# Chapter 22
# Casino Conspiracy
## Poppy

"I'm in desperate need of a drink," Phoebe said, joining Poppy on the porch as she sat on one of the deck chairs looking out at the beach.

The cool night air caused goosebumps to prickle her skin. Still, she needed a break from the hustle and bustle of the successful casino night inside the double doors behind her. Seeing so many who desired to help others filled her with a great sense of hope. For so long, all she had seen was the greed and selfishness of those around her, and tonight had healed a small crack in her armour.

"Ask, and you shall receive." Poppy handed her the untouched glass of sangria she had brought for Isaiah before Axel had taken him off to the poker table. Phoebe took a big gulp and sat down beside her. They both took off their heels and put their feet in the sand.

"I'm so glad I found you out here. I've been running around like a headless chicken, and my heels are pinching like crazy. At least the auction went without a hitch, and we reached our goal," Phoebe sighed. "Thank you so much for inviting some of the guests from the *Midas*. It's been a great help with funding. Some have even spoken to me about wanting to help fund special projects or pay for courses for those who want to further their art careers!" The words came out in a flurry of overwhelming enthusiasm.

"They had big pockets and nowhere else to be. Gambling, drinks and charity – I don't think they could have found a better distraction," Poppy said.

"Thank you. You've no idea how much this night means to me, and I can't wait to tell the group at home. We haven't even estimated what the tables have taken in yet. Still, Axel said we should have enough to purchase one of the buildings by the end of the night, and selling the villa should cover the others and the renovations!" Poppy could tell Phoebe was trying to control her excitement.

"You deserve every cent and more. What you're creating will make many feel included and seen. I'd be happy to fund an art therapy program if you're open to the idea," Poppy said cautiously.

"I love that idea! Hopefully, when we have more space, we can start offering programs with professionals. I'd certainly love to be part of a therapy art group," Phoebe said, staring up at the stars.

"I'm not an artist, but having struggled with depression for years, having a space to share with others who are suffering to create, if and when we want, sounds like the perfect escape," Poppy said, happy that she liked the idea. "Hopefully, my bid will help make it become a reality."

Phoebe's eyes widened.

"You didn't!" she exclaimed as Poppy revealed the pink slip from the auction.

"I had to purchase a painting! The city being reclaimed by the forest took my breath away."

"You didn't have to, but I'm glad you were drawn to

it. That's from my new collection, slightly different from my usual work. By the way, I fixed up the one we smudged today, and since we made it together, I'm going to send it to you," Phoebe said, clearly not taking no for an answer.

"Are you kidding? Two for the price of one – an even better deal," Poppy said, excited to decorate her new penthouse with artwork she loved.

Mina hadn't arrived at the event yet. She'd returned to the suite late from the beach and said she would join them later. That had been nearly two hours ago. Poppy wondered if she didn't want to come because she didn't want to run into Francis, but she shouldn't miss out on the fun because some idiot had treated her poorly.

"I hope everyone's having a good time. Maybe we should have asked for more lighting on the beach?" Phoebe fretted as they stood on the porch leading to the beach. The moon reflected off the ocean and all the small boats.

"Everything, from the theme to the food to the thought you put into every auction item, is perfect. You couldn't have done any more," Poppy said, looking over her shoulder to the guests gathered around the roulette and poker tables, laughing, cursing or cheering. "Reaching your goal is a testament to how much everyone is enjoying themselves."

Phoebe followed her gaze, taking in the night's success. "I've been organising tonight for months and wanted it to be perfect. Everything feels like it's going too well."

"Don't question it, and let yourselves celebrate. Tomorrow might bring new challenges and questions, but tonight's a triumph. You deserve to revel in it."

To her annoyance, she noticed Francis, Mina's F1 Driver, walking towards them with a leggy blonde. She'd guessed he might make an appearance.

"You're right, I know you're right. I need to stop being so paranoid," Phoebe said, finishing her drink.

"Nice to see you again, Poppy," Francis said as the others caught up. Phoebe immediately got to her feet and embraced the woman warmly. Poppy should have forced a smile for Phoebe's sake, but she couldn't bring herself to be polite as they were joined by the pair.

"I wish I could say the same," she muttered, wishing the latest world champion would take a long walk off the short pier.

"Sorry, I missed that?" Francis said, stepping closer. The smell of his expensive cologne verged on sickeningly sweet, and his khaki trousers and pink polo were a little low-effort for the black tie event.

"I said, what's your friend's name?" Poppy faked a smile, but he didn't look convinced.

It didn't matter, because the woman with him startled her by getting between them and kissing her cheeks. She was certainly friendly, and of course she couldn't be held responsible for her boyfriend's actions.

"Poppy! I've been dying to meet you. Phoebe was telling me about you while we were getting ready, and I was so excited you could come tonight," she said, returning to Francis's side.

"Melissa is the event planner. She helped me put all this together," Phoebe explained.

"I was merely your hands and eyes. I can't take too much credit," Melissa said. "I hope you don't mind that I dragged him along. Francis wasn't meant to make a stop here, but since he was part of the auction, I wanted him to see all you've achieved tonight."

"You're more than welcome, Francis," Phoebe said. "Your donation was the highest bid in the auction, so you've made many artists very happy this evening."

"If there had been some concert tickets, I would have snapped them up instantly. I promised Phoebe that I wouldn't fangirl. I will try to contain myself," Melissa said eagerly, "but I must tell you I was at your last concert! I loved the vintage set-up, and cried so much when you said you wouldn't release any music in the foreseeable future. Your last two albums got me through my last breakup. That's all I'll say before Francis drags me away."

"I'm happy that they helped," Poppy said, trying not to be won over by her, but struggling. She didn't want to ruin Phoebe's perfect image of the couple, especially not when Melissa was innocent and Francis had made the mistake.

"I'm going to get a drink. Anyone want another?" Phoebe asked. Francis shook his head, and Poppy motioned to her full glass.

"I'll come with you before I say anything more to embarrass myself," Melissa said, taking Phoebe's arm as they returned inside, leaving Poppy with Francis.

"Did you bid on anything?" Francis said politely. "I donated a helmet."

"They're gone. You don't have to make small talk. I'm not going to tell Melissa about Mina and risk causing a scene on Phoebe's big night, but it doesn't mean that I have to talk to you or be civil."

"What are you talking about?" Francis backed away from her like she was some raving lunatic.

"If you want to play it like that, then that's up to you, but we both know that you treated my friend like shit. You used her for your little holiday, and then last night you dumped her so that when your girlfriend came onboard, you'd be in the clear," Poppy snapped. "I saw you coming out of Mina's room. You don't have to lie."

"What? There's been a misunderstanding. I don't know what Mina told you or who you saw coming out of her room, but I wasn't in her room last night. She ended things with me at breakfast yesterday when I asked her to go for dinner. She told me she was sick," Francis told her. "If anything, I'm the one who got dumped."

"But… you're here with Melissa? Your girlfriend."

"Gross! He's my brother," Melissa said, joining them with a couple of desserts on a plate.

Poppy stood dumbfounded. Why had Mina lied? It didn't make sense.

"I want to apologise for the misunderstanding," she said, humiliated.

Melissa smiled stiffly. *I guess she's not that much of a fan anymore.* If only she could frighten off the killer so easily. She felt like a fool for not seeing the resemblance – the fair hair and deep brown eyes. Anger had blinded her. Poppy wanted to sink into the sand and disappear.

Thankfully, Isaiah wrapped an arm around her, distracting everyone.

"Please keep me away from the poker table; I think I owe Axel my soul at this point," he announced. Poppy could have married him right then and there for sparing her. He held a hand out to Francis. "Isaiah Rivers – big fan, your last race was incredible. The recovery you made when you got delayed in the pits will go down in history."

"Don't inflate his ego too much, or his head won't fit in his helmet," Melissa said, nudging her brother.

"Ignore her. It was a hard race, but we eventually turned it around." Francis's scowl disappeared as Isaiah distracted him with stats and compliments while Poppy put her shoes back on.

"I look forward to seeing what you do next," Isaiah concluded.

"I'll try my best not to disappoint," Francis said, grinning.

"Do you mind if I steal Poppy away? I need her luck."

"We wouldn't want to keep your lucky charm from you," Francis agreed, and Poppy didn't doubt he would be happy to see her go inside.

"What happened? Looked like you were arguing," Isaiah said as they passed the craps table.

Poppy filled him in on Mina's lie.

"Who was the woman with him, then?" Isaiah asked, evidently making the same mistake she had.

"His sister."

"Oof. Accusing him of dating his sister and being a cheater – I'm glad I interrupted that conversation," he said, and she swatted his chest. "Why would Mina lie?"

"I don't know, and I wish she was here so I could ask her," Poppy said, looking around the room in case Mina had arrived. Maybe she hadn't wanted to come because she was afraid of being caught out in a lie. Or had she used the break-up as an excuse to be left alone? Her mind swam with dozens of questions, and she couldn't help but feel her trust in Mina waning.

"She still isn't here?" Isaiah asked. "She called me about an hour ago and said she was on her way. I assumed she was with you or around here somewhere."

"She might've been trying to find us," Isaiah said, but Poppy could tell from his creased brow that he was worried.

"Over an hour ago? Why didn't you tell me?"

"I figured she would've found you."

A tense silence fell between them. She feared they thought the same thing. Either Mina was involved with the killings, or she was in trouble. Neither option was comforting.

"She called me from the suite, so it's the best place to start. I'm going to go back to the ship and see if I can find her," Isaiah decided, walking Poppy towards the poker table where Axel was playing. "I need you safe in a crowd. I don't want to think the worst, but I want you here if Mina's involved and not working alone. Axel, Poppy is going to be your good luck charm. Please keep an eye on her. She has a tendency to wander off."

"I know the type," Axel said, focused on his cards. Phoebe, on the opposite side, glared at him.

"Don't worry, we've got her," she said.

Poppy didn't want to involve them, but there was safety in numbers. The ship was docked only down the pier, so Isaiah could walk there and back in minutes.

"I'll stay, but be careful." Her gut told her Mina wasn't involved, and she worried she might be in danger. She had to have a good reason for lying.

"If I'm not back in thirty minutes, call the captain and alert security," Isaiah said, obviously surprised she wasn't arguing. When he kissed her, she knew she had done a terrible job of hiding the concern on her face. "Mina'll be fine. We'll have time to ask her questions when I find her. Don't leave with anyone, even if they say I sent them. Stay here unless I come to get you."

"Be safe." Poppy hated watching him go alone. At least security was still on the ship, and she was sure he would alert them when he boarded.

"Can we deal you in, Ms Roe?" a politician with terrible posture and an even worse poker face said as she joined the table. "It's for a good cause."

"Then you'll feel better when you lose." Poppy smiled, glancing over her shoulder to see the doors close behind Isaiah.

"You can take my place; I'm going to get dessert," Phoebe said, folding her hand. With the next hand dealt,

Poppy checked her watch as what promised to be the longest thirty minutes of her life began to tick down.

When Phoebe returned, Poppy was sure she would tell her that Isaiah was back with Mina and that everything was okay. Instead, she handed her an envelope with her name on it.

"A fan wanted me to give you this. She was too nervous to come over and talk to you herself," Phoebe explained, sitting opposite Axel. Poppy opened it.

*Engineering level, 11pm. Come alone if you want to end this.*

*Or the next time you see Isaiah, it'll be in a pool of his own blood.*

A fan hadn't given Phoebe the envelope. The killer had.

A knot formed in her stomach when she thought of how the killer had stood next to Phoebe – could have hurt her in the crowd and disappeared. This was a warning, a message to say they could get close to anyone anytime.

"What did she look like? What was she wearing?" she asked, trying to conceal the panic in her voice.

"Brown hair, and wearing a waiter's uniform. I think she didn't want to be seen interacting with the guests," Phoebe said.

"Can you see her now?" Poppy asked, searching the crowd. Phoebe stood again to help.

"I don't see her. Everything okay? Did they write something nasty?" Phoebe asked as she was dealt back into the game.

"Fine. Just a nice note." Poppy forced herself to keep her voice steady. She didn't want to alarm Phoebe or Axel, and she didn't think either would react well to the truth.

"I'm out of this game, but keep my seat. I'm just going to the bathroom."

"Do you want me to come with you?" Phoebe asked, as Axel eyed her suspiciously.

"I'll be fine," Poppy lied, clutching the envelope. "Don't worry, I'll be right back to take your money."

The dealer distracted the players, giving her time to slip away. She walked through the guests to the bathroom to ensure Phoebe hadn't followed her before leaving the event room and heading out of the hotel's main lobby.

# Chapter 23
# Lost at Sea
## Isaiah

Isaiah walked through the ship, unsettled by the silence. He'd called the suite, hoping Mina would pick up, but there was no response. He'd already contacted the captain and asked her to send security to the room, but they hadn't arrived yet.

"Mina?" He knocked on her door, which swung open without any resistance.

Drawing his gun from its holster, he cautiously opened the door, scanning the room. The lights were on, and Mina's open purse was on the bed. She hadn't left.

He meticulously searched every corner before holstering his gun again. Was this a distraction to let the killer get to Poppy? Just as he was about to leave, he noticed a piece of fabric sticking out from the wardrobe. He approached it slowly and pulled on the handle, but he didn't have a chance to react before someone lunged at him.

Isaiah collapsed under the dead weight and rolled the body onto the carpet. Blood stained his shirt and hands, and he looked down at Mina, forcing himself to focus and remain calm despite her shocking injuries. It looked like she'd been stabbed in the side. Checking her pulse, he couldn't feel anything. He started CPR.

"Don't do this, Mina! Come back to us," he begged, pressing on her chest in a desperate attempt to keep her heart pumping. His arms ached, and he started sweating profusely. It began to feel hopeless.

Then Mina inhaled sharply, before coughing up a splatter of blood on his shirt.

"You're okay. Breathe slowly," Isaiah said, applying pressure to the wound in her side.

She looked up at him, panicked, and clawed at his hands.

"I know it hurts, but I've got to stop the bleeding. Try to stay still. You're safe. Just try not to move," Isaiah instructed.

She let out a strangled cry in response. The terror in her eyes shook him to his core.

"What happened? Who did this?" he asked, but before Mina could respond, she passed out. He needed to get her to the hospital quickly. Otherwise, she wouldn't last the hour.

The door swung open and Isaiah drew his gun, fearing the killer had returned to finish the job.

"It's me! What the hell happened?" Captain Hamill said, raising her hands to show she wasn't armed.

"Mina's been stabbed. I had to restart her heart, and she just passed out. She's losing too much blood," Isaiah explained, lowering his gun as two members of the security team joined them.

"Call the police and an ambulance. We need to get her to a hospital."

Captain Hamill's team sprang into action, returning moments later with a stretcher.

"We can get her off the ship to the dock and meet the ambulance to save time," Captain Hamill said, maintaining pressure on Mina's wound as they carefully placed her on the stretcher.

"Get her to the dock, and I'll follow closely behind," Isaiah said, eager to see if the killer had left any traces or clues. He searched his own room and then Poppy's, discovering a cracked bathroom mirror with hair caught in the broken fragments, a sign of the desperate struggle between Mina and her attacker. Mina was a fighter; he'd expected nothing less. Blood smears on the floor suggested that she had been dragged away or had tried to crawl to safety.

More chilling, the phrase "I know what you did" was written in Mina's blood across the mirror. Isaiah took a picture of it and then wiped away the evidence. He didn't want the police to discover what the killer had left for Poppy – it would only lead to questions being asked in the wrong direction. There was nothing else in the suite to note, and he wanted to ensure that Mina was being cared for.

When he reached the dock, sirens had already drawn a crowd from down the beach. He focused on Mina as she was loaded into the ambulance. She seemed unconscious, her face concealed by an oxygen mask. The captain was already talking to the police, who were in the process of blocking off the pier to keep onlookers at a distance.

The paramedics spoke to him in Italian, which he didn't understand.

"Is she allergic to any medications? Is there any condition we need to be aware of?" one of them asked in English.

"I don't know, but please, just keep her alive!" Isaiah was desperate to prevent another loss and to protect Poppy from losing her friend.

"We'll do our best," the paramedic said, making no promises. Not that Isaiah could blame him. "She'll need surgery. We will keep her under observation. Captain Hamill mentioned that she is in danger of further attacks, so we'll ensure there is security outside her door, and she'll have someone watching her around the clock." He closed the doors.

Isaiah wanted to go with them to the hospital, but he needed to ensure Poppy was safe. He suspected the killer had used Mina's attack to separate them. The ambulance cut through the crowd and raced off.

Captain Hamill joined him, having just finished speaking to the police. The stress of the short trip had aged her, and dark bags under her eyes betrayed the nights she had lost.

"What happens now?" Isaiah asked, observing as the police sealed off access to the ship and the dock. The remaining guests were being escorted off the vessel and directed to join the others, who were already on the other side of the police tape at the end of the dock.

"The police are searching the ship. We've been ordered to anchor here until the investigation is complete. Since we were docked here when Mina was stabbed, the incident falls under local jurisdiction. With the evidence we handed over this morning, they don't want to be held responsible for any future incidents if we set sail again," Captain Hamill explained, clearly dissatisfied with the new development. "I'm relieved to get assistance with the investigation, but I don't like the idea of others rummaging through my ship. I want you to catch the person responsible before the police do, by any means necessary." She scanned the chaotic scene filled with angry guests, flashing lights, and sirens. "I think someone is trying to get your attention."

Isaiah saw Axel and Phoebe waving from behind the

tape while an officer stopped them from crossing. When he didn't see Poppy with them, his heart threatened to quit. He jogged over.

"They're with us," he said, and the officer backed off when Captain Hamill vouched for Isaiah. "Where's Poppy?"

Phoebe couldn't meet his eye, and Axel shook his head.

"We don't know," Phoebe said desperately. "A fan gave me a card to pass on, but she didn't seem right after reading it. She went to the bathroom, and when I checked on her, she was already gone."

"How long ago?" He'd been right; the killer had gone after Mina to separate them. He would never have left her alone if Mina had been with them.

"Twenty minutes? I'm so sorry – she was only gone less than five minutes before I went to check on her!"

Axel wrapped his arm around Phoebe's shoulder to comfort her.

*Hopefully, She had returned to the ship and has heard the police arrive.* But she might have seen Mina coming out on the stretcher, depending on how long it took her to get from the hotel to the beach. The killer had indeed timed their scheme perfectly; she had already been off the ship to deliver the note to Poppy while he was searching for Mina.

Isaiah swallowed his rage. This game of cat and mouse was growing tiresome.

## Chapter 24
# Engineering Execution
### Poppy

On the engineering level, the sirens outside were muted by the noisy thuds and thunders of the machinery around Poppy. Weaving her way through the maze of different machines, she saw the light in the security room was on, and she picked up a wrench to defend herself. She was willing to walk into a trap, but not without something to protect herself.

Carefully checking every corner as she made her way to the room, she was surprised that no guards had remained on board to ensure the room was protected. The surveillance screens were on, as though someone had just left. On the monitors, she caught sight of Mina on a stretcher being brought off the ship while the captain kept a hand on her abdomen. She tried to zoom in so she could see how badly Mina was injured but couldn't figure out the controls.

Then she noticed the gun and the earbud.

Given the note she had received, they were for her. *But why a gun?* Picking it up, she turned off the safety like Isaiah had shown her and put the earbud in her right ear.

"Hello?" she asked calmly.

"You got my gifts. I was worried Phoebe wouldn't give you my note. But you've been so easy to manipulate that I don't know why I'm surprised," the killer said.

Poppy glanced at the camera and saw Isaiah at the dock, standing with Captain Hamill and the police. Mina's attack was a distraction. Her friend had been targeted to get her on board alone.

"Now that you have me, why don't you come out, and we can end this now?" Poppy said. "I'm tired of your games, and sooner or later you'll have to face me."

"Why the rush? I'm still having fun," the killer laughed. Poppy recognised the laugh and the voice, but she needed to be sure. If she was going to call her out, she couldn't risk being wrong and looking like a fool. "Besides, you should be thanking me for all I've done for you. Without me, you'd probably be dead by now. Calliope, Joshua, even Patrice – they were all wrapped up in a plot to kill you."

"You want me to thank you for what? Protecting me? Are you meant to be my twisted guardian angel?"

"Protecting you?" That condescending laugh was starting to get under Poppy's skin. "You weren't theirs to kill. That right belongs to me, and I wouldn't let them get in my way."

"And what is it that I've done to you?"

"Poppy? What are you doing here?" Davide asked, standing in the doorway.

She froze when her eyes fell on the bloody serrated knife in his hand. He followed her gaze to the knife and sighed.

"I could ask you the same," Poppy said, trying to keep her voice steady. "Nice knife."

Davide stared at her like she was the mouse and he the cat.

"Put down the gun," he said calmly, wiping the blood from the knife on his trousers.

"You came to erase the footage. I'm guessing you don't want anyone to see you hurting Mina."

"Right on the money, but what are you doing here?" he said, pointing the knife in her direction.

"Now you know how it was so easy for me to get around the ship, mess with security footage, and use the ship like it was my own personal playground," the killer commented through the earbud. "Men really are so easy to manipulate. Not that I need to tell you that – you managed to convince a detective that you, a murderer, are worthy of protecting! Tell them you love them, fuck them, and suddenly they'll forget all their morals."

"I was told to come by your partner," Poppy said, trying to ignore the voice in her ear.

"Sophia sent you here? Then she must want me to finish the job," Davide said. "I have to say, I'm relieved; I really want all this to be over."

"Damn it, he spoiled the surprise," Sophia complained.

Poppy bit her lip to conceal her smile as Davide confirmed her suspicion. Sophia. Calliope had been murdered by her own niece. Why?

"Why are you doing this?" she asked Davide. "You don't know me or Mina. You've ruined your life for what?"

"No one knows I'm involved. No one suspects me, and there'll be no evidence once I fix the footage and toss this knife into the sea. I'll return to my life with the woman I love, and we'll finally have peace."

"You really shouldn't try stalling. I'd shoot Davide if I were you," Sophia sighed. "It's not like you haven't killed before. Would this be number four or five? It's hard to keep track."

Poppy chuckled in disbelief. Sophia was using her to tidy up the last loose end.

"You do realise I have a gun?" She waved it. "The woman you love so much gave it to me because with you out of the way, she's in the wind. She's killed anyone else in her way to get to me, and now she wants me to kill you."

"She would never turn against me," Davide snapped, stepping into the room.

Poppy tucked her hair behind her ear to expose the earbud. "See, I'm following her instructions."

Sophia laughed. "He won't believe you. He's blinded by love. He's killed for me, corrupted his soul for me. If he were to believe it was all for nothing, it would twist him up so badly that killing him would be a mercy."

"Put down the knife, and we'll walk out of here. The police are already searching the ship." Poppy pointed to the monitors. "You can tell them everything and save yourself." He had hurt Mina and maybe killed the others, or perhaps that had been Sophia. She suspected she'd never know who killed whom – not that it mattered now. All that mattered was stopping them from hurting anyone else.

"Do you think I'll turn against her to help you? We're here because of you, but that's her story to share," Davide said, taking a step forward.

Poppy backed up into the desk and raised the gun. "If Sophia wants me dead, then why go after Mina? She had no involvement in any of this."

Sophia answered first. "It's your fault for bringing her on board. She wasn't a part of my plan."

"Mina heard something she shouldn't have, and when I went to her room to silence her, you and Isaiah rudely interrupted," Davide said.

*Oh God, if we hadn't got back when we did, Mina would've been killed last night. Why didn't she get off the ship with us?*

"She said she would stay out of it, but then she had a change of heart and tried to use the gun you're holding against me this evening," Davide added, glancing at the monitors over her shoulders.

"The police are only getting closer," Sophia said. "I'll give you a choice. Shoot Davide, and I'll leave Isaiah alone. If you don't, then I won't just gut him. I'll ruin his reputation first. I know all about his friendship with Eckells and how forgiving he was when you confessed to your triple homicide. He'll be dead and his memory disgraced. Like Davide, you'll do anything for the person you love."

"What's she telling you?" Davide asked, suddenly looking unsure.

"To shoot you. I shoot you, and she'll spare Isaiah," Poppy said honestly.

"Shoot him, and we'll end this together," Sophia said, growing impatient. "Just the two of us. No one else will be hurt, and only one of us will walk away."

Poppy guessed her leniency in sparing Isaiah was prompted by the imminent arrival of the police. If Davide was taken into custody, her plan was over. Still, Poppy couldn't let Isaiah's life be ruined. Mina had nearly been killed. She had to put an end to this.

"I'm sorry, but you're only offering me death, and Sophia is offering a better deal," she said, tightening her grip on the gun.

Davide lunged at her in a desperate attempt to take her out. She fired at point-blank range. The sound was deafening as it echoed off the metal interior.

Davide froze, looking down at his chest. His knife struck her in the shoulder, and she howled in pain. He dropped to his knees, and it was only a matter of seconds before the light left his eyes.

Poppy gritted her teeth as she looked down at the knife

in her shoulder. She thought about removing it, but she was afraid of losing too much blood. She didn't drop her gun either, in case Sophia decided to appear from her hiding place and strike while she was injured.

"Thank you, Poppy! I knew we would make a great team," Sophia said, and the elation in her voice made Poppy sick. She had done her dirty work for her. "I'll see you soon."

Pain emanated down her arm and up her neck. She removed the earbud and tossed it in the bin under the desk. Stepping over Davide's body, she barely made it out of the room before flashlights blinded her.

"Put the gun down!" The orders came in a flurry of English and Italian. "Get on your knees!"

Poppy dropped to her knees and put down the gun.

"Put your hands up," an officer barked at her.

"I can't," she said, only raising one. "I've got a knife in my shoulder."

The officer held one arm behind her back and stood her up. She bit her lip to stop herself from crying out in pain, staring back at Davide's lifeless body as they walked her out of the engineering room. Paramedics were checking his pulse, but it was too late. They were wasting their time.

Given her injury, she didn't need an escort, but she was grateful not to be cuffed. The pain was bad enough.

"It was self-defence," she told them as they left the ship, though the officers were focused more on getting her outside than on listening to her excuses. She could feel the blood dripping down her arm to her hand. "Davide attacked Mina, and he would've killed me." She would follow Sophia's plan for now. She was going to end this on her own terms.

On the dock, she spotted Isaiah waiting with Captain

Hamill and felt a rush of relief. Adrenaline was the only thing stopping her from passing out.

Isaiah hurried towards them, but the officers got in his way. "She isn't a suspect. You need to release her," Isaiah yelled.

"She shot a man," the officer said bluntly. "We're taking her to the paramedics so she can be attended to. You can accompany her, sir, but we have questions for her and footage to review before determining whether it was self-defence."

"They're doing their job. Just come with me to get this fucking thing out of me," Poppy begged, not wanting to bleed to death because they were arguing. She looked for Sophia in the crowd, sure she would want to see her handiwork, but the sudden burst of agony as the officer helped her into the back of the ambulance made her forget everything else.

She sat on the stretcher while they examined the wound. In the breeze coming through the doors, she could feel how much she was sweating, the adrenaline working its way out of her system. Instinctively, she reached for Isaiah's hand, needing to feel grounded.

"Can you please remove it?" she asked the paramedic, whose nametag read 'Susana', as she hooked her up to a blood pressure monitor. The officers didn't leave the doors, making it clear she couldn't leave.

"We should really get you to a hospital. We need to X-ray the area," the paramedic said, looking to Isaiah to back her up.

"No hospitals. Please, I want it out. Just remove it and stitch me up," Poppy ordered, grateful that Isaiah didn't butt in or try to force her. She didn't want to lure Sophia to the hospital where Mina was.

The paramedics argued in Italian before conceding.

"It doesn't seem to be in too deep. We can try, but you need to sign a waiver," one of them said, filling a syringe. "Something for the pain."

The other paramedic handed Poppy a clipboard, and she scribbled her signature as they injected her shoulder. The sting wasn't nearly as painful as being stabbed. She doubted anything would be in the future.

Isaiah watched them like a hawk as they padded the area with gauze before removing the knife. Even with the painkillers, the pain blinded her, and she squeezed Isaiah's hand so tight she was sure she broke a bone or two.

"How's Mina?" she asked, trying to distract herself as they cleaned the wound and started on the sutures.

"She's in the hospital having surgery. We'll know more in a few hours," Isaiah said. "Don't you want to go and see her when she comes out?"

"No," Poppy said, a little too quickly, and Isaiah looked alarmed. "Sorry – the pain." Her reason was pathetic, but his brow relaxed as he accepted the excuse. "She'll need rest, and seeing me might stress her out. We'll go when she's out of danger and recovering."

An officer appeared asking for the evidence – the knife. He held out an evidence bag, and one paramedic handed it over while the other kept pressure on the wound and gave her something to help with the bleeding.

"Captain Hamill helped us examine tonight's surveillance footage, confirming that Davide was the one who attacked Mina and pulled the knife on Poppy. We'll still need to take your account, so you can't leave the country until we finish the investigation."

"We've given you some antibiotics and something for the pain, but you'll need to go to the hospital or see a doctor soon to make sure you don't develop an infection.

This is only a temporary fix," the paramedic cautioned, securing the bandage.

"I promise. Can I go?" Poppy was sure Sophia wasn't going to let her go far.

"Where are you going to be staying?" the officer asked. "We'll need to be able to find you."

"I don't know." Poppy looked to Isaiah.

"They can stay with us," Phoebe said, appearing with Axel.

Amid the pain, Poppy felt terrible at having ruined Phoebe's night. She had so much to celebrate, yet here she was, bailing them out at the scene of a murder.

"How did you get past the tape?" Isaiah asked as Axel hugged his friend.

"Told one of the officers we had important information. I found the waiter who gave me the note that I think sent Poppy here, but they were paid one hundred euro to pass it along by a woman wearing a hood, and they didn't get a look at her face, or a name. We tried to ask for cameras, but there weren't any in the staff smoking area where they were approached," Phoebe said, looking at the officer guiltily. "Sorry, I can't help we're their friends, and they'll be coming home with us if they're free to leave."

Poppy admired her fierce defence of those she cared for, feeling unworthy of such support. Tonight should have ended with a celebration, not them having to lie to an officer and risk going to jail themselves.

She was getting down from the ambulance with Isaiah and Axel's help when Captain Hamill confronted them. Poppy had been expecting this.

"Where did you get the gun?" the captain demanded, not caring who was around or who could hear. Poppy understood her grief, but she was putting her own life at risk by asking these questions. Sophia wouldn't accept another threat to her plan.

"It was in the surveillance room on the desk when I entered," she said. "It should be on camera."

"It is, but there's no footage of how it got there. It just magically appears. What happened with Davide? What were you talking about? Why did you have to shoot him? *Kill* him?"

"I'm sorry about your friend, but he was going to kill me. He wasn't in his right mind. I hope you'll see in time why I had to do what I did." Poppy tried to spell it out, not wanting the officers to understand her double meaning.

Captain Hamill wiped the tears from her eyes, studying Poppy closely. "I never should've trusted you – either of you. I knew it was going to get more of my people killed!"

The officers got between them, but Poppy knew the woman was angry and just needed to vent.

"I'm sorry he betrayed you," she said again as her own tears fell. The pain, the shock and whatever cocktail of drugs the paramedics had given her to keep her moving opened the floodgates. "But he attacked Mina and confessed to the others." She left out Sophia's involvement so it wouldn't start a manhunt. She knew she was Sophia's target and, unless prompted, wouldn't kill anyone else. "Davide came to delete the footage of what he did to Mina, and he would have killed me for trying to stop him."

"But why? He worked with me for five years. Why now?"

Poppy wanted to tell her the truth, that he'd been just a pawn in someone else's bigger game, and she would once it was over. If she survived to tell the story, she would learn what wrong she had done to Sophia to awaken such hatred. She despised Davide for hurting Mina and his part in this game, but he had got caught up in a wider web and thought he was helping and protecting someone he loved.

"I can't answer you that now," she admitted, and the betrayal in Captain Hamill's eyes stung her.

Recovering her composure, the captain left without another word to return to her waiting crew. The cool breeze off the coast caused Poppy's teeth to chatter – or the adrenaline was finally wearing off – and Isaiah wrapped his jacket around her shoulders.

"Don't take what she said to heart. She's in shock," Phoebe said softly.

But Poppy saw the doubt in Isaiah's eyes. He knew she was keeping secrets.

The paramedics and the officers finally gave the group the go-ahead to leave. Axel and Phoebe hailed a couple of taxis; Poppy figured the couple wanted to give them some space. Isaiah gave the address to the driver and helped her into the back seat. She winced as she bumped her shoulder against the hard leather seat. Isaiah was quick to help her settle against him so she didn't feel it too much when they went over the bumps and dips in the road.

"You promised me that you wouldn't leave Phoebe and Axel," he said sadly, holding her body against his. "I could've lost you. When I heard the gun go off and the officers refused to let me go to you, I thought my heart was going to stop."

Poppy's head waged war with her heart. All she wanted was to protect him, but all she seemed to do was cause him such pain and frustration. She couldn't tell him that she had killed a man so that he would be spared. She couldn't put that on him when it had been her choice. It had been her choice to take the lives of those who'd wronged her and others, and he had already put aside his duty to carry that secret.

"Are you going to say something? Please, Poppy, I need to understand," he said gently. "Do you not trust me? Is that why you went alone?" The hurt in his words crushed her already heavy heart.

"I got a note when we were at the party that said if I didn't go, I would find you in a pool of your own blood. I had already seen what happened to Joshua, and I couldn't bear the thought of your life being taken, of you being stolen from me. I've never had a chance to feel about someone how I feel about you. I can't even understand it. I trust you, but I don't trust you to protect yourself when it comes to me, whether it's your job or not, and I can't let you go," she told him, studying his face as though she was afraid she would forget. "You're safe now, and so is Mina. That's all that matters to me. I've never had people to love or fight for me, and now that I have it, I won't let it go. You can call me selfish, reckless, or stubborn, but I'm not giving up love now that I've found it." Her chest rose and fell sharply as she confessed her feelings, not wanting him to believe that she doubted him for even a second.

She silenced his anger by pressing her lips to his. Kissing him was like tasting heaven, like taking a deep breath after drowning. All thoughts of death and fear faded away.

"You did what you had to to survive," Isaiah said, holding her carefully so he wouldn't hurt her.

"I didn't do it to survive. It was a choice. You or him. I picked you," Poppy admitted.

"We don't need to talk about this now. You just need to rest," Isaiah murmured as the taxi pulled away from the curb. She didn't know if it was the crash of adrenaline or the cocktail of medications, but tucked under his arm, she sank into a deep and sudden sleep.

# Chapter 25
# Home Away from Home
## Isaiah

"How's Poppy doing? We have some extra pillows and blankets to make her more comfortable. There are also plenty of towels and anything else she might need in the bathroom," Phoebe said to Isaiah in the kitchen.

He'd carried Poppy to the spare room, and thankfully she hadn't woken when he'd left the room to talk with the others. Whatever the paramedics had given her had knocked her out. While she slept he had been tempted to redirect the taxi to the hospital, but he didn't want to cause her more distress, and she had been so adamant despite the severity of her injury and pain that he guessed she had a good reason.

"She's asleep, but I don't want to leave her too long in case she wakes up. Thank you for all you've done. I don't know what we would've done without you," Isaiah said, not wanting to burden them or bring up old traumas.

Phoebe opened the fridge and waved off his thanks. "No need to thank us. You're more than welcome – you've done so much for me, for us! It's the least we can do. There isn't much food in the fridge. We've been eating out mostly since the construction workers have been here, and we didn't want to be in the way, but I can pick up some food and necessities in the morning." She rattled on, eager to help, as she boiled the kettle and made them some tea. "I already texted the workers, and they're going to take a couple of days off, so you can stay for as long as you need. Axel called the hotel, and we've booked ourselves in to give you two some space."

"Are you *sure* you don't mind us staying? We're putting you out of your own home, and though I can't be sure, I have a feeling that the danger isn't over yet."

"You're staying here for as long as you need. I'm not taking no for an answer. Besides, it's not our first time in danger, and no one knows you're here. You'll have your own private pool and balcony. It can be your little holiday home while the police investigate." Phoebe smiled, sliding the mug towards him.

"Last time I say it, but thank you," Isaiah said, not wanting to be scolded again.

"Since the police are holding all your belongings, I left some clothes for you and Poppy on the chest of drawers outside the spare room," Phoebe said kindly.

"Right. I didn't even think about that," he admitted, tasting the extra sugar in his tea.

"For the shock – you could use the pick-me-up," Phoebe said, reading his expression. "She's going to be okay. She might never forget what's happened, but she'll learn to cope. It's in your nature to ask questions, to want to solve things, but just be patient with her, and she'll open up in her own time."

"I knew you two were going to be fast friends," Isaiah joked. "I wanted to ask… could you not tell anyone that we're here? The fewer people that know, the better." He wanted to err on the side of caution.

"My lips are sealed." Phoebe zipped her lips. "I've left the spare key in the kitchen in the porcelain duck by the door, and you already know the alarm code."

Her phone rang. From her tone, it was Axel.

"Okay, I'll be right there," she said before hanging up and putting her mug in the sink.

"Axel managed to get the event back under control. Some of the guests wandered down the beach to the scene, but most have returned, and they want us to check in and make sure everything is okay. I want to tip the staff something extra for all their work. He managed to get us a room, so there's nothing left to worry about. All you have to do is rest and look after Poppy."

Isaiah had been so distracted by what was happening with Poppy and the *Midas* that he'd forgotten about their event. She would never let on that it upset or bothered her that the chaos had detracted from the event. However, considering how hard they had worked, it would have been nice to have the night end without sirens and murder.

"We're only down the road, so call us if you need anything. Get some rest. You need to look after yourself too," Phoebe said, resting a reassuring hand on his arm before heading off.

Isaiah locked the door behind her and turned on the alarm system he had installed for them last year.

LYING beside Poppy to watch out for any signs of fever, Isaiah kept a hand on her as she slept in case he fell asleep, so he would be alerted when she woke up. He figured she would be in a lot of pain, and he didn't want her to experience that alone. Watching her chest rising and falling softly, he wished they had gone to the hospital to be safe.

He brushed a strand of hair from her cheek, and her eyes fluttered open.

"Mina!" Poppy bolted up, only to let out a howl of pain as she clutched her shoulder.

"Don't worry, Mina's fine. You're safe," Isaiah said, easing her back against the pillows.

She grimaced and positioned herself so she was leaning more on him than on her injured side.

"Take these," he said, handing her some painkillers that would help with the worst of it. She sighed in relief and took a glass of water from him. "How's your shoulder?" He had other questions, but he only cared about protecting her right now.

"It aches, but whatever they gave me still hasn't fully worn off. I'd say when it does, it won't be pretty. Where are Phoebe and Axel?" Poppy asked, taking in her surroundings. He had left the balcony doors open during the warm night so they could see the starry skies and coastline.

"They had to go back to the hotel, and they decided to stay the night so we could have some space," Isaiah told her, putting the glass of water on the bedside table.

"We should have stayed in the hotel. This is their home," Poppy said sadly.

"Phoebe is more than happy to help us, and she doesn't want you beating yourself up," Isaiah said, not wanting her to feel bad on top of every other emotion she was sure to be feeling. "Phoebe knows this is the safest place for us, so please don't think any more about it."

"We owe her a massive present when this is all over. This was meant to be her night," Poppy said.

"I'm sure she'll take you up on that, but right now, she

only cares that you're safe and healing." Isaiah kissed her hair, and she settled under his arm. He was sure she could hear his heartbeat. It sped up whenever she was close, but this time it was because he was nervous.

"You want to ask me what happened, what I didn't tell you before we got here?" Poppy asked, looking up at him.

"Davide wasn't the mastermind, was he?" Isaiah dared to ask.

"No."

He thought telling her what he had learnt would make it easier for her to open up. "You were talking to somcone before he arrived. I don't think the police paid attention to anything except what happened when you shot Davide, but I saw it on the security footage the captain sent me while you were sleeping. Who were you talking to?" He didn't want to sound like he was interrogating her. "I'm not accusing you of anything. I just need all the facts to protect you."

Why was she so reluctant to share? Had she been threatened? Did the killer have something on her? The footage had had no audio, and he desperately wanted to know who she was talking to.

Poppy took his hand and threaded her fingers between his own. "Have you ever been in love?"

The question surprised him. He hesitated, and she stared up at him, eyes wide with fear and hope. They had only known each other for less than a fortnight, but every day had felt like a decade. They had been through more together in a matter of days than most couples went through in a lifetime.

"Not until you," Isaiah confessed.

"You mean that?" she asked, sitting up so they could talk face to face. "Even after everything that's happened, everything I've told you?"

He noticed how she bit her lip to contain her smile, like she was afraid to be happy. He knew all her secrets, including some he should arrest her for, but instead, he loved her. It didn't feel possible.

Isaiah closed the gap between them and desperately kissed her concerns away. Not wanting to hurt her, he gently eased her towards him until she straddled him. The friction made her gasp against his mouth.

"I love you too." Her confession was barely a whisper against his lips.

Heat travelled down his spine as she ground herself against him in the most delicious rhythm. With only thin fabric separating them and her dress pushed up around her hips, his hard length started to throb with need. Her moans told him she couldn't take much more, either.

"You don't have to say it if you're not ready," he said, not wanting her to feel any pressure.

"You're the only person I've said that to and truly meant it." Poppy took his hand and placed it over her heart. "This is yours, and yours only."

Her words nearly stopped his heart, but when he went to kiss her, she pulled away, and fear twisted his gut.

"Did I hurt you?!"

"No, you didn't. But I need to know when you realized when it felt like—"

She didn't know how to ask the question, so he finished it.

"The first night, when you called me a hunky chunky detective, I knew I didn't stand a chance against you," he chuckled, holding her in his arms. "Why? Do you think what happened in the surveillance room will change how I feel about you? Because it won't." He rested his forehead against hers, practically hearing her thinking.

She removed herself from him but stayed close. He waited patiently, letting her take all the time she needed.

"Sophia. The woman I was talking to was Sophia," she told him at last. "She threatened to kill you, to ruin your career because of what you know about me, about what I've done. I knew I loved you when I didn't hesitate to pull the trigger. What I said in the taxi – I meant it when I said I wouldn't lose you. Davide was just another scapegoat. She wanted him to take the blame for Patrice, Joshua, Calliope, and even Mina. Davide was her escape plan, but I was the final piece of the puzzle."

"What's next?" Isaiah asked, digesting this. He had a dozen more questions but forced himself to remain quiet and listen.

"Me. It's only me and Sophia left. She'll find me when the time is right. I don't know why or what I've done to fuel such hatred. I don't know when she'll approach, but I don't doubt it'll be soon. She's as tired of this game as I am, but I also think she'll wait until I'm home. There's too much heat on us here and too many eyes on the investigation. She doesn't want to get caught, and her self-preservation should protect us for a little while," Poppy said. "Patrice and Joshua's deaths were merely to prevent her from being named and caught. She wants to protect her own life as much as she wants to take mine. That plays in our favour."

"You want to use yourself as bait." Isaiah read between the lines, wondering why she was hesitating to share this or look at him. She had shot Davide to protect him, and now she was going to end it herself. If she was right, time was on their side. "Once we're home, I'll use every resource I have to find her. She won't get away with this. Tomorrow, I'll talk to Captain Hamill and the police. She won't be able to leave the country."

"We've got no evidence against her. As far as everyone living knows, she's just another guest on the ship with an alibi for two of the deaths on board. If you go after her, she'll kill you and disappear. But if we continue to live as normal, go home, and let her think that I'm going along with her plan, she'll come after me – and I'll be ready. We'll be ready. If you tell the police and Captain Hamill, we'll be back in the dark."

He made to argue, but her lips slammed against him, silencing him. He could taste her desperation, how much she needed him to believe in her, that this was what she needed. If Sophia knew what Poppy had done, going to the police was mutually assured destruction. She would end up in a cell right next to Sophia's.

"Trust me?" she asked, holding his face in her hands.

He took a breath. "I trust you."

## Chapter 26
# Right The Ship
### Poppy

Poppy would have much preferred for Isaiah to stay in bed with her, but Captain Hamill called him early the next morning to help the local police go through events on the ship. He didn't want to leave her, but they both understood they needed to cooperate. Given what had happened with Davide, she understood that the captain wasn't ready to face her yet. She was scheduled to go to the police station this afternoon when he returned anyway, so they had no reason to cross paths until the captain was ready.

After a careful shower, Poppy found the first aid kit in Phoebe's kitchen and cleaned her shoulder as best she could. She hadn't developed a fever and the wound wasn't red or inflamed, so she wasn't too worried about an infection. An oversized T-shirt and a pair of Phoebe's shorts were a struggle to get on by herself, but better than staying in last night's dress. The pain when she tried to use her right arm was the worst of her concerns, so she tried to keep it tucked closely to her side.

When she found breakfast and a strawberry milkshake

prepared for her in the fridge, she wished Isaiah was home so she could thank him properly. Hopefully it wouldn't be long before he returned from the *Midas*. Even though her deal with Sophia had secured Isaiah and Mina's safety for now, Poppy worried Sophia would go back on her word, and she hated him being away. With her injured shoulder, she couldn't protect herself or anyone else without him.

Outside in the sun, she sat on the cushioned lounger and ate breakfast by the pool while waiting for Phoebe to come by. Isaiah had mentioned she would stop by and keep her company while he was gone. If it hadn't been for the murderer on the loose, she would've felt like she was on holiday. She couldn't thank Phoebe enough for all her help. For the first time in her life, Poppy found herself surrounded by good people instead of being miserable and lonely. But she also understood how it felt to have people to lose, and it stirred a new fear in her she didn't know existed.

"Phoebe, I'm down here!" she called out as she heard the sliding door open, easing herself up slowly. "I've got watermelon and chocolate muffins to spare."

She turned, and saw Sophia walking down the steps to the patio.

"Thanks, but I already ate. The breakfast at the hotel was phenomenal, though I was disappointed when I saw Phoebe and not you in the breakfast room," she drawled.

"How'd you get in here?" Poppy was sure that Isaiah had mentioned setting the alarm before leaving. Sophia didn't seem to have any weapons, but then again, she couldn't be sure what she had in her purse.

"You should tell your friend that her construction workers must remember to lock the windows and side doors when they leave. I didn't even have to break a sweat to get in here." With her sundress, oversized sunglasses, and chunky sandals, Sophia looked like a movie star, not a woman on a murder spree.

"Did you hurt Phoebe?" Poppy asked, dread coursing through her.

"Don't worry, Phoebe's unharmed. I overheard her talking with her boyfriend, and she was kindly going to the market to pick you up a few things," Sophia said, sitting on the lounger beside Poppy's. About five feet were between them, but it still felt too close for Poppy. Was she just here for a friendly chat? "You really have a talent for making people like you – going out of their way to help you. If only they knew that you were like me. Ruthless, merciless, a killer." She spoke like it was something to be proud of.

"We are nothing alike." Poppy didn't kill because she wanted to, because she enjoyed it.

"Let's not lie to each other. I thought after last night that we could at least be honest with each other," Sophia said, removing her glasses and placing them on the table beside her breakfast.

"I've nothing to hide. You already know all my secrets." Poppy glanced at the knife she'd used to butter her toast, which she could use as a weapon, but Sophia was ignoring it. Was she so sure that Poppy wouldn't attack her first? She would have, if she didn't have questions that needed answering.

"Good. How's the shoulder? Looks painful." Sophia winced. "You should've shot Davide when I told you to. Now you'll have a nasty scar on your perfect porcelain skin."

"Let's not waste time on small talk. Phoebe is meant to come by, and I don't want her interrupting what you have planned for me," Poppy said bluntly.

Sophia grimaced as she refused to play along.

"Being Calliope's niece, you must despise me because

of the things my aunt did to yours, but you killed Calliope. I just want to know – why?" Poppy leaned forward, trying to get closer in case she needed to grab the knife. With her shoulder, she wasn't all that fast on her feet. "You could've gone to the police about what you knew about me and ruined my life in an instant. I hardly think I'm worth some lengthy and arduous plan."

Sophia looked taken aback, studying her as though she was trying to figure out whether Poppy was lying. "You really don't know who I am? What you've done?"

She reached into her bag, and Poppy flinched, but she only pulled out a folded piece of paper.

"Read it." Sophia held it out to her, and Poppy hesitated until Sophia dropped it on the table between them. Poppy only picked up the papers when Sophia backed away, in case she was only using the papers to distract her. She scanned the legal document.

"Out loud," Sophia snapped.

"*Refusal of Parental Rights.*" The rest was legal jargon she didn't see much point in reading; her eyes drifted to the signature at the end. "Signed by… Martha Roe. M-my aunt is your birth mum?" she stammered.

The date of birth told her that Sophia, her biological cousin, had been born four years before Martha had taken Poppy in. The symbol at the top of the document was from the orphanage she'd been taken from. It all made sense now – why her aunt had donated to the orphanage for so many years. Had it been hush money to keep the orphanage quiet because Martha gave up one child just to adopt another to appear as the saviour of her orphaned niece in the headlines? She'd never known anything about it, never known her aunt had given up a child. In a way, it made sense and confirmed a lifelong suspicion – that Poppy was a PR stunt to carry off Martha's angelic image.

Anyone could have a child, but adopting and raising an orphan, giving them a charmed life, was front-page news. Could her aunt really have been so twisted?

Or maybe Martha had known she could never love or treat a child how they deserved and simply used Poppy as a replacement. In her eyes, Sophia had made a lucky escape – but she doubted her cousin felt that way. Her murderous nature made sense now too. Sociopathy ran in Martha's blood.

"And the penny drops," Sophia said smugly. "The woman who raised you, gave you everything, and made you who you are, gave me up and then died before I had a chance to know her. You took her from me."

Poppy's blood ran cold. "If there was ever a reason for revenge, that's a good one."

"I'm relieved you aren't going to try and deny it." Sophia remained unnervingly calm.

"That would only waste time." Poppy shrugged. "Can I ask how you ended up with Calliope before we get to the avenging part? My curiosity tends to get the better of me." She wanted to know, and she needed to stall for Isaiah to return. She could only hope that he would return before Phoebe.

"I went searching for my mother, but I found Calliope first. She was my mother's emergency contact when she gave birth to me. I didn't know about their strenuous relationship. Still, Calliope took me in and promised to introduce me to Martha to help mediate the situation."

"I don't think Calliope would've been the right choice in that situation," Poppy said.

"No. In fact, she threatened Martha. Told her that she'd go to the press and reveal how the golden mother of Hollywood gave up her own child. I didn't learn this until later, when I went to Martha's house. I found her address in Calliope's things and couldn't wait any longer. It was you who answered the door. You thought I was a fan. You were even kind enough to give me a signed album. I wanted to tell you who I was, but you closed the door on me."

Poppy couldn't even place the interaction.

"Closing the door on you was probably a mercy. My aunt would've called the police on you for trespassing," she said, wanting Sophia to know what Martha was like. "I understand your desire to want to know her, that you want to avenge a woman who might've been your mother by blood. I don't think this will change your plans, but believe me when I tell you that she didn't have a loving bone in her body. I'm afraid that if you knew her, truly knew her, you wouldn't have wasted so much time and energy avenging her. If you think that I stole your mother from you, whether because she raised me or because I killed her, I'm afraid you're wrong. Martha had no interest in being a mother, not to me or anyone. Consider yourself lucky that she gave you up. You said you were raised by a loving family. You should have stayed with them."

"My family might've loved me, but something was always missing. A hole in my heart that could never be filled. The day I finally met Martha, that hole started to heal."

"What did Martha want from you? What did she ask of you? To keep your existence a secret, to hide in the shadows, probably for your own benefit until the time was right?" Poppy watched as Sophia's calm composure started to fracture. She had hit a nerve.

"I'm afraid you've given yourself away. Martha told me how, when she told you about me and about the adoption, you wanted me to be kept a secret. You feared I'd ruin your tour and steal the spotlight from you. She promised me that once the tour was over, she would reveal my identity, but in the meantime, I had to stay with Calliope and play along."

"I knew nothing. Martha used me as an excuse to hide her true nature." Poppy shook her head. "I wouldn't have cared. I would've been happy to learn I had a cousin. *She* wanted you to stay hidden. She didn't want her image tainted, because she wanted you to stay with Calliope and use any information you discovered living with Calliope against her."

"You only know all that because she told you. You aren't going to turn me against my mother by twisting what happened," Sophia argued.

"No – it's because she raised me. I know how she loved to twist and manipulate the truth until you don't even recognise right and wrong anymore," Poppy said. "The version of herself that Martha showed you was nothing but fiction. She was an award-winning actress who tricked you into hiding and feeding her secrets about others. You can kill me, but you deserve to know the truth about her."

To her surprise, Sophia only sighed. "Maybe you're right. My mum might have manipulated me and used me, but that's the only side I'll ever know of her, because *you* killed her. You stole her from me. I can't confront her, argue with her, or ask her why she didn't love me or why she gave me up but took you in – because you killed her! I was there that night. I saw you at the top of the stairs. I'd had a fight with Calliope because I knew of her involvement in the plans to kill my mum, to kill you, and I was coming over to warn the both of you. She gave me the access code to the back gate so I wouldn't be seen, but when I went to the side of the house, I saw you standing over her body. I saw the blood."

Poppy listened, understanding what she had taken from

her. She couldn't blame Sophia for not being able to realise what it had taken Poppy years to. It didn't matter what Poppy told her or the horror stories she could share; Sophia couldn't grasp what she had experienced, because her desire to know her mum outweighed all other reasoning or explanations.

"I understand why you hate me. I can't bring her back. I wish I had known about you, and I'm sorry that you had to witness her death in the way you did, but that's all I'm sorry for," Poppy stated.

"You're sorry you took her from me, but not about killing her? She made you what you are now," Sophia snapped. "You would've been nothing without her."

"I was just a living doll for her to play with, to manipulate. A chess piece to move around a board she controlled and designed. I know what it's like to lose a mother; I know the pain you're feeling, but she never would've been what you imagined," Poppy argued. "I never wanted fame. Is that what this is about? Do you think I stole your life in the spotlight? You were her daughter, and you think I replaced you? You've made a terrible mistake. You had the chance at a great life, free of her tight grip."

"She gave you the chance to be someone!" Sophia cried.

"She didn't give me a chance at anything; it was beaten into me, whether I liked it or not. I'm sorry she gave you up, but that was her choice. I wish she had kept you and you had taken my place, because you deserved the life I never wanted. Maybe since you shared the same dreams, she wouldn't have been so cruel or controlling – but she gave you up. That was her choice. A choice she made years before I landed on her doorstep. You can blame me for her death, but not for the life she forced upon me."

"You call my mother cruel, manipulative, and controlling, but don't forget that I know what you did. I know about the dance teacher, the maid, and your old driver. You're hardly innocent," Sophia scoffed. "You've taken as many lives as I have, so don't act like you have the moral high ground. When Mum told me you didn't want anything to do with me, I followed you. Turns out we both have a killer instinct."

"I had my reasons – ones I don't have to share with you."

"And yet *I'm* the monster for saving you. Duggery had planned to kill both you and my mother. At first I wanted to protect you, but then you killed my mother, and I couldn't let them get to you first. I started with Duggery – best to start with the head of the monster – but sadly, Joshua walked in when I was slitting his throat." Sophia shrugged it off like such a gruesome act was normal.

Hearing that Duggery was dead was a shock. Poppy wished she were sad, but she wasn't. That probably gave them another thing in common. She didn't admit it, instead letting Sophia continue her story. Sophia clearly derived pleasure from her brutal acts.

"Joshua freaked, and I gave him a choice: help me or die. He had already agreed to kill you once, so I didn't think it was much of a choice. Still, Joshua panicked and backed out like a coward. I didn't expect he'd have the balls to bribe Patrice and tell Calliope what I was up to. Patrice should've known better than to record their conversation; Calliope didn't mind when I took her out. However, she was upset when I left the body in your tub. I didn't think she would be so upset, and despite her using me to blackmail Martha, I didn't want her dead. I didn't expect her to be the one to attack me. I didn't even have a weapon on me, and the old bird had some fight left in her. The night was ruined – I'd hoped we would run into each other at the opera. I thought my dress was a nice little easter egg, but after fighting with Calliope, it got blood on it so I couldn't wear it." Sophia rubbed her scalp, and Poppy recalled the hair fibres Isaiah had found in Calliope's fist. "I had already given Joshua a chance, and like they say, fool me once, blah blah. So he had to die."

"How did you get the dress? That was one of Martha's most prized possessions. I doubt she gave it to you," Poppy said. Davide must have told her about the colour damaging the camera's ability to identify her. Using her dress, Martha had helped Sophia with her plot from beyond the grave.

Sophia chuckled, taken aback. "That's what you want to ask after all I've told you?"

"Does it matter? They're already dead. You killed them because they got in your way and left a trail to you, and you couldn't have that." Poppy didn't want her to have the satisfaction of getting to tell her story, to feel like she was some god who had outsmarted them all. She was just as cold-hearted and twisted as Martha.

"You're right, I couldn't leave any loose ends. However, you're wrong about the dress. Perhaps you didn't know Martha as well as you thought. She gave it to me the first day we met. She told me that she'd worn it when she won her first award, but that I was more important than any prize or fame. It was her promise to me to make up for the time we lost."

Sophia's smile nearly killed Poppy. She really believed every word Martha had told her.

"And you promised her in return never to reveal who you were and never let Calliope do the same," Poppy said, understanding Martha's motives better than anyone.

"You really have to ruin everything with your negativity."

"It's how I was raised," Poppy said, but her tongue felt heavy.

Sophia glared at her. "With you dead, Martha will have the daughter she needs to continue her legacy. A legacy I will commit to upholding once I reveal my identity to the world. You resented who she was, but I'll make sure she never dies."

She was right. Poppy had killed Martha, but her memory would live on forever. Vilified or sanctified, depending on who told her story.

"I think we've had enough stalling. I know you're waiting, hoping Isaiah will return and play the white knight. Still, I'm afraid all that's left is for you to die." Sophia stood like she was bored by their conversation. "But you should know – I've been stalling too."

"You're not going to lay a hand on me," Poppy said, picking up the knife. To her confusion, the sudden movement made her woozy, and the knife clattered against the tiles as her hand refused to grasp it. Poppy stared at her numb hand, then looked at the tray of food.

"I don't have to. I hope you enjoyed the strawberry milkshake. It looked delicious when Isaiah was so kind as to make it before he left. It was so easy to slip in a little something extra special. I won't need these anymore." Sophia tossed the empty bottle of pills onto Poppy's lap.

She read her aunt's name on the bottle. *That explains why she didn't have a weapon.* Poppy had already drunk it. She forced herself to stand, to put distance between them, but her legs trembled as she backed away towards the pool.

"Poetic, isn't it?" Sophia said, following her. "I thought you should go out the same way as my mum. An accident, a tragedy. You'll be found in the pool, having sadly drowned after consuming too many pills. With that nasty shoulder wound and all you've been through, it would make sense if you took a few too many painkillers."

"They'll… find out… what you did," Poppy rasped, each word heavy and laboured. She collapsed by the edge of the pool and shook her head, trying to get her vision to focus, trying to stay conscious. Specks plagued her vision, and when she tried to get away from the water's edge, her limbs, which were as heavy as stone, refused to cooperate.

"I wouldn't be so sure; this isn't the first murder I've got away with." Sophia crouched down beside her. "I also have to back out of our deal. I'm afraid Mina and Isaiah will have to die too. Given their unwavering loyalty, I can't trust them not to leave your death alone. If you're dead and I'm in prison, then this really would have all been for naught, and I can't let that happen."

Poppy attempted to swing at her, but Sophia easily dodged her.

"I wouldn't waste your energy. You're going to need it." She tenderly tucked a strand of hair behind Poppy's ear, looking at her like a helpless, injured bird. Then she shoved her harshly.

Poppy crashed into the water and sank into darkness.

# Chapter 27
# Drowning Sorrows
## Isaiah

Isaiah was opening the small gate to the villa when he heard a bell chime behind him.

"I thought you'd be gone a couple more hours," Phoebe said, pulling up beside him on her bike. A tote bag filled with groceries was tucked into her bike basket.

"The police want me to bring Poppy to the station this afternoon. I told them everything and they've collected all the evidence, so there wasn't much else I could help them with," he said, taking the groceries from the basket and carrying them up for her. He'd left out what he knew about Sophia. Though he hated impeding their investigation, he didn't want to break Poppy's trust.

"Pity you're back so soon. I was looking forward to gossiping about you with Poppy," Phoebe joked as they walked down the side passage so she could lock up her bike. Chaining it to the wall, she paused. "Did you leave the side gate open when you left?"

"No, I used the front door," Isaiah said, not liking the look on Phoebe's face. He knew when she was worried. "Maybe it was the workers?"

"No, I checked it last night before Axel and I left, or at least I thought I did," Phoebe said, walking toward the door and pushing it open. "Poppy could've gone for a walk."

"I doubt it – not with her shoulder causing her so much pain." Isaiah pulled her gently behind him and handed her the groceries, which she put back in her basket before following him.

"Stay here and call the police. Tell them you have an intruder." He drew his gun.

Phoebe pulled out her phone immediately and started dialling, but before he could go anywhere, they both heard a loud splash.

"Poppy!" Isaiah shouted, bolting into the garden just in time to see Poppy sink beneath the clear water. He dropped his gun and dived into the pool without thinking, wrestling her back to the surface. Above the water, he prayed for her to open her eyes, but she was out cold.

Fear coiled around his heart, threatening to squeeze the life from him. He couldn't lose her now, not when they had come so far.

"Please, Poppy, open your eyes for me," he pleaded, wading through the water to the edge.

He was about to lift her out when they were covered by a shadow.

"Let her go," Sophia ordered, and Isaiah stilled in the water. She must have hidden in the hedges when she heard him approaching.

He stared up at Sophia, pointing his own gun at him. How could he have been so careless? He should have left his weapon with Phoebe, just in case.

"Sophia, you don't want to do this," he said, trying to buy time until the police arrived; if she heard the sirens, she might run off. From the blood soaking through Poppy's shirt, her wound had opened up.

"I really do, and I'm glad you're both here," Sophia said, smiling smugly. "I might as well do you now and save myself the time later."

"I told the police about you," he lied. "They're already looking for you. You'll never get out of the country without being arrested."

Behind Sophia, Phoebe approached slowly with a brick in her hand.

"You have nothing on me. Even if I'm arrested, there's no evidence other than your meaningless accusations. Now, let her go. Or I'll shoot the both of you."

"You didn't plan on killing Calliope, and you were sloppy. They have hair fibres that will lead them to you, and she scratched her killer. How much do you want to bet that they find your skin cells under her nails?" Even if she killed them, she wasn't going to get away with murder.

"I was her guest on board; it wouldn't be a stretch to find my hair or DNA on her." Sophia shrugged. Your delaying tactics aren't going to work. You're both going to die today."

"I don't think so," Isaiah argued.

Sophia glared at him, aiming the gun, her anger making her less aware of her surroundings.

"I don't think so either," Phoebe said, bringing the brick down on her head.

Sophia went down like a sack of potatoes, bleeding from a nasty gash on the back of her head. Phoebe dropped the brick and looked like she was going to be sick.

"Help me," Isaiah said urgently, getting Poppy to the ledge.

Phoebe snapped out of her trance and helped him ease

Poppy onto the side. "She's breathing," she told him, resting Poppy on her side so she coughed up some water. Isaiah took some deep breaths as he scrambled out of the pool and got to Poppy's side.

With Poppy safe, Phoebe grabbed Isaiah's gun and pointed it at Sophia.

"Poppy?" Isaiah called, resting her on his lap. Her eyelids fluttered, but it seemed like she couldn't focus on him. There was no blood around her head, so she hadn't hit her head.

"These were on the sun lounger," Phoebe said, her hand shaking as she handed him a bottle of pills in Martha Roe's name. It was empty. "This must be how she got her into the water. She drugged her first."

"The sedatives are keeping her unconscious," Isaiah said, listening to Poppy's shallow breathing until the ambulance arrived in case she stopped breathing. The sirens were music to his ears, until he tried to move her. Blood pooled beneath her as her stab wound opened. Isaiah gritted his teeth to contain his rage at Sophia, putting pressure against the wound.

"Go to the front and direct the paramedics. Show them the bottle of pills, but don't talk to the police unless I'm with you," he ordered.

"Okay, I'm going," Phoebe said, handing him the gun and rushing out of the side gate.

Poppy heaved awake. He rolled her onto her side again as she threw up her stomach contents. Hopefully, some of the pills hadn't been absorbed yet. Her breathing was short and rough as she stared up at him.

Sophia grumbled as she regained consciousness, but he doubted she had the strength to do harm. If Sophia didn't get help soon, she wouldn't last long.

"I knew you'd come," Poppy rasped, struggling to open her eyes.

"Of course. I'm here and not going anywhere." He held her close, trying to keep pressure on her shoulder so she didn't lose too much blood. "You're going to be fine; help is almost here."

A fierce cry startled them both. Blood pooling down her face, Sophia charged at them with a knife.

Everything became a blur. Isaiah threw himself in front of Poppy, knowing with a cold certainty that this was it. He was going to die.

Two gunshots rang out, and he stopped breathing for a second – then realised it was Poppy holding the gun. He stared at Sophia, who had been shot twice in the chest. She stood over them, frozen, before falling limply onto the grass. Her eyes stared up at the sky as life left her.

Poppy dropped the gun and passed out in his arms.

He didn't have time to process anything before two paramedics followed Phoebe into the garden and crouched beside them. Isaiah reluctantly handed her over to them so they could work. In a blur, Poppy was loaded onto a stretcher, and Isaiah asked Phoebe to go with her while he checked Sophia's pulse. She was gone, and Poppy's secret was safe. She wouldn't have to spend her life looking over her shoulder.

He wiped the gun clean and quickly kicked the brick Phoebe had used to knock Sophia out into the pool to wash away any prints. He didn't want her to have to go back to court after what she had been through; he would tell them that he'd struck Sophia before getting into the pool.

Another set of paramedics arrived, along with the police, and Isaiah stayed with Sophia's body to make sure they got the right story. The police took his statement while the paramedics loaded Sophia in the next ambulance. Thankfully, the officer didn't keep him long and agreed to escort him to the hospital. He didn't want Poppy to wake again and find he wasn't with her.

# Chapter 28
# Vacation's Over
## Poppy

### *Two Weeks Later*

After all they had been through, Poppy had never expected them to make it home to Ireland without further complications. She'd half-expected their flight to be delayed, the airport to go on strike, or a natural disaster to prevent her from leaving. The last thing she'd anticipated was boarding their flight on time without a paparazzi ready to interrogate them about the *Midas* incident, a harrowing experience that had left them all scarred.

Yet all that had occurred on the *Midas* and afterwards had been swiftly dealt with, and the case closed with Sophia's demise. The guests and owner of the ship were not keen on a lengthy investigation that could damage their reputation, and with no killer to charge, the incident could be kept out of the media. Poppy felt that enough in her life had been covered up, but she didn't want Mina, Isaiah, or Phoebe smeared across the papers. One day it would probably come out and someone would go snooping, but as she lay in the Irish hospital, today wasn't the day.

"How are you feeling?" Isaiah asked, bringing her the strawberry milkshake she'd requested because having to fast for surgery had sucked. Sophia hadn't ruined them for her completely.

"Groggy, but pleasantly numb," Poppy said, not even attempting to move her right arm until the physio came by. She might have survived Sophia's attempt to drown her, but her shoulder had suffered significant trauma. Once the hospital in Italy had given her the all-clear to travel, she'd been ordered to return home and have surgery to repair the damage. Despite the physical and emotional toll, Poppy was determined to heal and move forward.

"You did great, and the surgeon doesn't think you'll need another. With physio and time, you should heal up nicely," Isaiah said, kissing her forehead. "The nurse should be back soon to check on you."

He was always so careful not to hurt her. When they had flown home to Dublin, she hadn't thought he would survive constantly checking on her and Mina. Mina liked being obsessed over less than she did, and when Eckells had threatened to send a private plane for them, she'd threatened to quit. It hadn't stopped him. He'd even been waiting for them at the airport, so Poppy had finally got to put a stern face to the name. She'd thought he'd be furious about the chaos she had brought down on his ship, but to her surprise, all he cared about was their well-being.

"I love my nurse," she answered Isaiah, still fuzzy from the anaesthetic.

"Should I be jealous of her?" he teased.

"Maybe – she has the good painkillers," Poppy said, sipping her shake slowly. She was so hungry, she'd take a bite out of Isaiah soon. The cold shake helped soothe her dry throat for now.

"Can't argue with you there," Isaiah said, sitting in the armchair beside her.

"How's Mina?" Poppy asked, disappointed she wasn't with him but understanding that Mina needed all the rest she could get. Mina had probably texted, but Poppy's phone was still in the cupboard with her clothes, and she didn't have the strength yet to get out of bed and check it. They could FaceTime when she got home; video calls had become a must during their recovery. They had even binge-watched a couple of series to help with their boredom. Two people who usually lived with packed schedules didn't do well on bed rest.

"She's going stir-crazy at home. Eckells insisted she move into his penthouse above the club, since she has a long recovery ahead of her and refused to stay in the hospital," Isaiah said. Poppy was sure the next time she saw the duo that they would have either killed each other or got married.

"At least we can book physio appointments together. Friends who recover from attempted murder stay together!"

"You wouldn't be talking about me, would you?" Mina asked coming through the door with her purple, bejewelled walking stick.

"Only when it's behind your back! You didn't have to come. I'll be home tomorrow," Poppy said, as Eckells followed close behind and helped Mina sit at the end of Poppy's bed.

"You'd come if it was me. Besides, coming here was the only way he'd let me out of the house," Mina said, talking about Eckells as though he wasn't in the room.

"Doc said that unless it's for physio, you should be resting. Don't blame me for following their post-op instructions," Eckells said, looking at Mina like this wasn't the first time they had discussed it. "I'm just looking out for my employee. The last time I let you out of my sight, you nearly ended up dead."

Poppy glanced at Isaiah and tried to conceal her smile. They knew he cared about her far more than any boss they had ever known. If Poppy had met Eckells out and about, she would have been intimidated by him. Yet with Mina he was utterly smitten, starkly contrasting to the ruthless businessman she had heard about.

"Are you going to hold this over me forever? I think I learned my lesson," Mina groaned, gesturing to her legs.

"No, but until you've recovered, I'm going to make sure you get the help you need, whether you like it or not." Eckells was probably the only person who could make looking after someone sound like a threat.

"Don't be too hard on him. He's only trying to help." Poppy winked at Mina, and she rolled her eyes. Eckells almost smiled, though it looked like the gesture might cause him pain.

"You're looking rough," he said briskly, ever the charmer.

"Thanks. Hospital gowns and hair nets aren't exactly flattering," Poppy said, looking at her gown and compression socks.

"I was talking about your boyfriend." Eckells smirked, jabbing at Isaiah.

Poppy had noted how exhausted Isaiah looked too. His captain at work hadn't been all that thrilled about his involvement in the case in Italy. Still, thankfully, he hadn't been fired – only suspended for disobeying orders. His partner Michael had come by to tell him he was lucky to only receive a slap on the wrist. Since Duggery had been found in his office, and Sophia was seen leaving his office on the cameras across the street, Captain Roberts had admitted that he was right to investigate the murders. As Sophia had followed Poppy to every scene without taking as much caution as she should, she'd ended up taking the blame for Poppy's crimes.

Sophia's potential imprisonment had she lived, had forced Poppy to ask herself whether she deserved to suffer the same fate. They had both killed, and both believed they were justified in their actions. Unlike Sophia, though, Poppy knew she would never kill again now that she and those she cared for were safe. Even if she felt like justice had been done, she still felt the weight of the lives she had taken, the chain of events she had triggered, and she accepted that she would carry the consequences for the rest of her life.

"Is the security necessary?" she asked, looking at the door where two bodyguards were waiting.

"Better to be safe than sorry. I wanted you to have peace of mind while you're recovering," Eckells said, looking at Isaiah as though they had already discussed the matter.

"Don't bother trying to reason with him. You can't," Mina said, glancing at Eckells, who winked at her.

"I love the walking stick. The jewels make it pop," Poppy said, liking the new modifications. Davide had damaged the ball and socket joint in her right hip.

"Did it myself. I had to do something, since I'm under house arrest," Mina said, folding the walking stick to fit in her tote bag.

"Only Mina would consider a penthouse suite a jail cell," Eckells grumbled, putting his hand in his pockets.

"It's more the warden who likes to hover." Mina smiled. Eckells rolled his eyes.

"Do you two want the room? We can give you some privacy if you want to continue flirting," Isaiah put in. Mina blushed, while Eckells suddenly found the heart monitor fascinating.

"How's the shoulder?" Mina asked innocently.

"How's your leg?" Poppy countered, and they both erupted into laughter. Poppy groaned as the movement jarred her shoulder.

Isaiah and Eckells looked at the pair like they had lost their minds.

A nurse came in and looked at the crowd around Poppy's bed. "Plenty of visitors, I see. Don't worry, everyone. She is in great hands and should be out of here soon. How's the pain?" the nurse asked as Isaiah gave her space to work.

"About a five," Poppy said, and Mina held her good hand.

"Let's help you with that," the nurse said, adjusting her pain meds. Relief washed over her body, making her sleepy. "Time to leave, everyone; she needs to get her rest."

The last thing Poppy wanted was to be alone. "Can't they stay a little longer?" she pleaded, and the nurse caved with a heavy sigh.

"Ten more minutes."

Poppy would leave some gifts for the nurses when she left.

"I'll come by tomorrow when you're home," Mina promised, squeezing her hand reassuringly. Poppy despised all that Mina had been through because of their friendship, but she wouldn't have changed anything, because it had brought a true friend into her life. Two friends, considering Phoebe hadn't stopped checking in since they left Italy. She owed Phoebe her life; without her interference, Sophia would have killed them both.

"We'll see how you are after physio. You're always wrecked after and shouldn't be pushing your luck," Eckells said, like a real mother hen.

"Told you, a warden." Mina took out her walking stick and smacked Eckells gently in the shin. He grumbled and rubbed it. Then he clenched his jaw and, before she could protest, scooped Mina into his arms and off Poppy's bed.

"Put me down!" Mina insisted, but Eckells ignored her.

"See you tomorrow, Poppy," he called over his shoulder as he carried her out of the room. They could be heard arguing all the way down the hall.

"Who's going to tell them about their feelings for each other?" Poppy yawned, enjoying their theatrics.

"They'll figure it out eventually," Isaiah chuckled.

"You don't have to leave, right?"

He shook his head, and she moved over so he could lie beside her.

"Just rest; I'm going to be right here beside you," Isaiah said, brushing her hair behind her ear as she started to doze off. "The more you sleep, the sooner we can get you home."

"Home sounds pretty great," Poppy yawned, settling into his arms as he held her. Isaiah pressed his lips to hers.

Without anything left to fear, a new future waited for her – for them. Finally safe, Poppy drifted to sleep in his arms, a home away from home.

# Acknowledgements

Thank you for reading Poppy and Isaiah's story! I really hope you loved your time aboard the Midas. Poppy's story was the perfect way to round out Autumn and Phoebe's dynamic duo. These women have been through so much, and they'll always have a special place in my heart. Poppy and Isaiah's story is the most murderous book I've written, and I loved every second.

**Readers!** I'll never get tired of thanking you. Thank you for sticking with me and for your never-ending support and encouragement. This is my fifth year publishing, and I couldn't be doing what I love without you! Every share, comment, review, fabulous video, or photo helps me more than you could ever know. I'll never take you for granted.

A massive thank you to Emma, @emmas.edit my dearest editor. As always, she helped me work out the final kinks. She truly has the magic editing touch. Writing wouldn't be as fun without our chaotic process (or your roasting).

To Pru, who has the patience of a saint! She created the gorgeous cover for TSS almost a year before the book was even written. Thank you for giving my book such a stunning face.

A special thank you to another Emma, @emmasbook-page, who helped prep the book for editing. You helped me spot the little hiccups that tried to slip through.

To my mumsy-poodle, who is always the first to read my stories, thank you for always being in my corner and never doubting me.

And a big thank you to my fabulous sister-in-law, who helped me bring my characters to life! Seeing them illustrated is a dream come true.

# Did you pre-order The Situation Ship?

Scan the QR code below to get your bonus chapter!

Thank you so much for pre-ordering Poppy and Isaiah's story.

# Join The Mailing List

Sign Up To Be The First To Hear About:

- Advanced Release Copies
- Cover Reveals
- Teasers & More

# Ms Perfectly Fine

One house, two strangers, and a dark secret.
What could go wrong?

Autumn Adler, a famous concert pianist, is making her solo comeback to the stage after a tragic accident, and she can't afford any distractions. Of all the things that could go wrong, she never expected her landlord to rent out the ground floor of her home to Elijah Wells – a game designer in the midst of building his own company. Autumn loves her townhouse, and she refuses to give it up. However, Elijah is equally stubborn. As the days pass, Autumn's efforts to make him leave only further his desire to win her over. It seems as though neither can win this battle of wills.

Yet as Autumn's showcase approaches, a seemingly innocent gift turns into something far more alarming. Can the two call a truce and figure out what's going on?

# Not Another Rockstar

Who Knew Falling in Love Could Be So Bloody Dangerous!

After the video of her rockstar fiancé's tragic car crash is released, Phoebe Fletcher is hit with false accusations. Thrust into the relentless media spotlight, the budding artist becomes the focus of obsessive fans, putting both her life and aspirations in jeopardy.

Phoebe seeks refuge with her ex's band, the Brothers of Anarchy, where she forms a bond with the brooding drummer, Axel Adler. She knows fans will tear her apart if she moves on too fast, but Axel's wavering care and encouragement sparks a fiery connection between them.

In the midst of fame, betrayal, and illicit love, Phoebe and Axel must navigate a web of lies and treachery, or risk losing all they hold dear.

# About the Author

Kate Callaghan released her debut YA dark fantasy trilogy, *Crowned A Traitor: A Hellish Fairytale* in 2020. She loves dark tales, villains and happily-ever-afters—something you will find in all of her books. Chatting with readers and getting to share many different stories is her favourite part of being an indie author. Currently she lives in Dublin. She loves dramas with subtitles (to silence the characters), coffee, and reading too many mysteries and romances. If missing, please check your local coffee shop. You will find her with her computer and an iced beverage.

Follow the links below if you want to know to learn more about future stories! Signed copies are also available on the author's website.

www.callaghanwriter.com

www.ingramcontent.com/pod-product-compliance
Lightning Source LLC
Chambersburg PA
CBHW030333310726
48979CB00001B/13
* 9 7 8 1 9 1 6 6 8 4 2 0 1 *